Mercury

Hope Larson

atheneum books for young readers
new york london toronto sydney

ATHENEUM BOOKS FOR YOUNG READERS

An imprint of Simon & Schuster Children's Publishing Division

1230 Avenue of the Americas, New York, New York 10020

ATHENEUM BOOKS FOR YOUNG READERS is a registered trademark of Simon & Schuster, Inc.

For information about special discounts for bulk purchases, please contact Simon & Schuster Special Sales at 1-866-506-1949 or business@simonandschuster.com.

The Simon & Schuster Speakers Bureau can bring authors to your live event. For more information or to book an event, contact the Simon & Schuster Speakers Bureau at 1-866-248-3049 or visit our website at www.simonspeakers.com.

Also available in a hardcover edition.

Book design by Hope Larson and Sonia Chaghatzbanian

The text for this book is set in Times New Larson.

Manufactured in the United States of America

First Edition

10 9 8 7 6 5 4 3 2 1

Library of Congress Control Number: 2009903638

ISBN 978-1-4169-3588-9 (pbk)

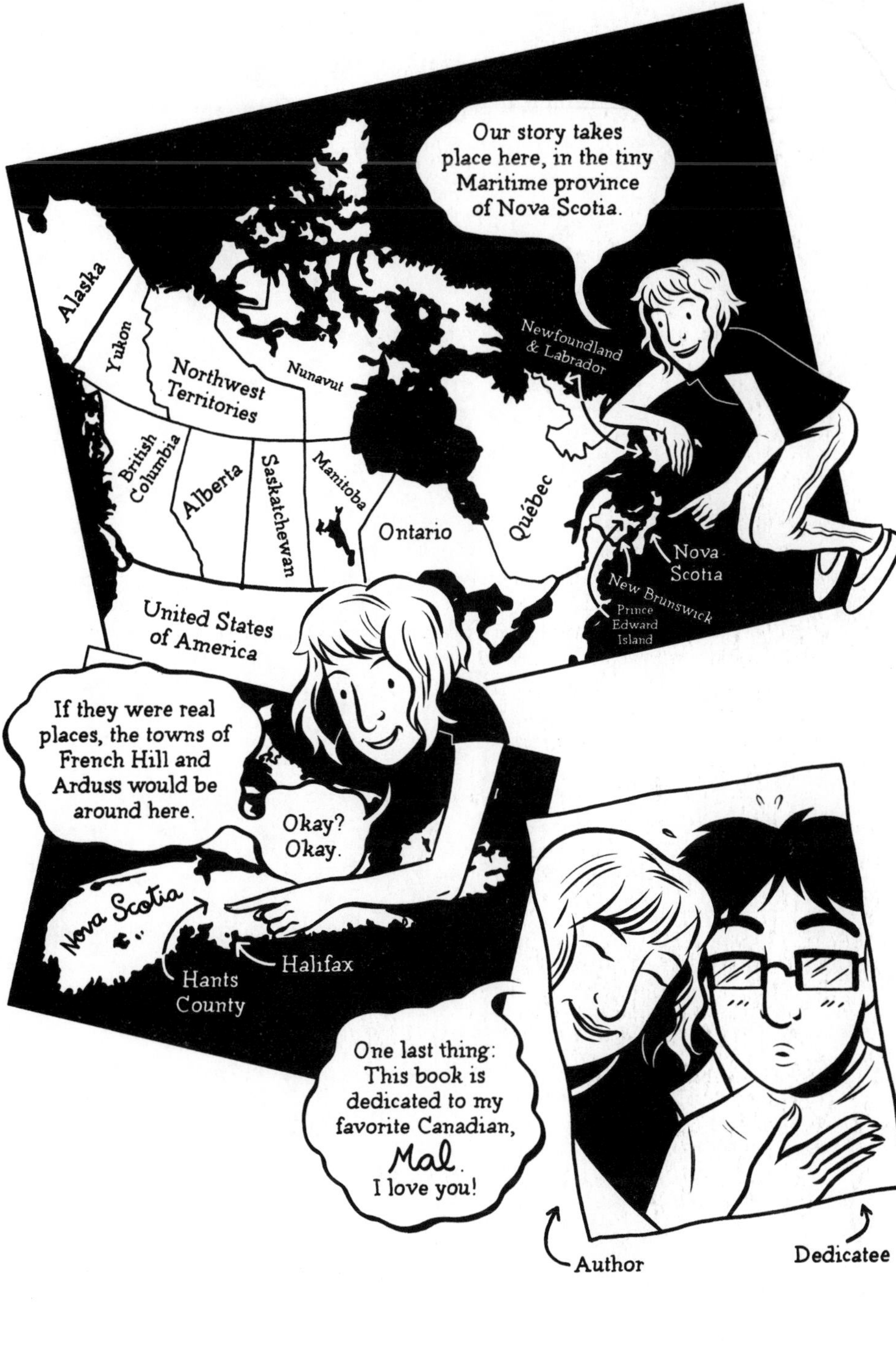
Our story takes place here, in the tiny Maritime province of Nova Scotia.
Alaska
Yukon
Northwest Territories
Nunavut
Newfoundland & Labrador
British Columbia
Alberta
Saskatchewan
Manitoba
Ontario
Québec
Nova Scotia
New Brunswick
Prince Edward Island
United States of America
If they were real places, the towns of French Hill and Arduss would be around here.
Okay? Okay.
Nova Scotia
Hants County
Halifax
One last thing: This book is dedicated to my favorite Canadian, Mal. I love you!
Author
Dedicatee

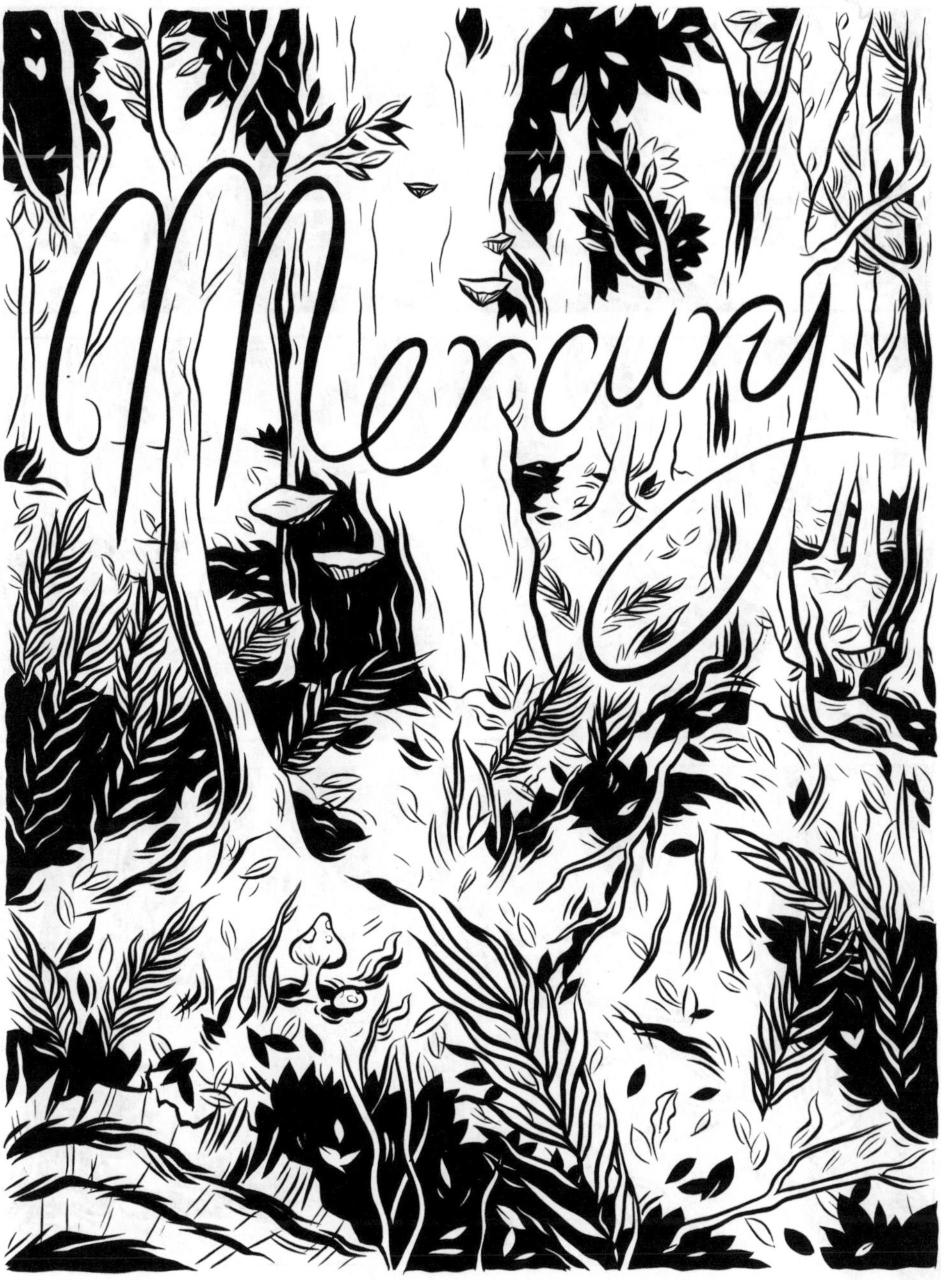
Mercury

1400

1435

1680

2

1735

1755

1778

1812

3

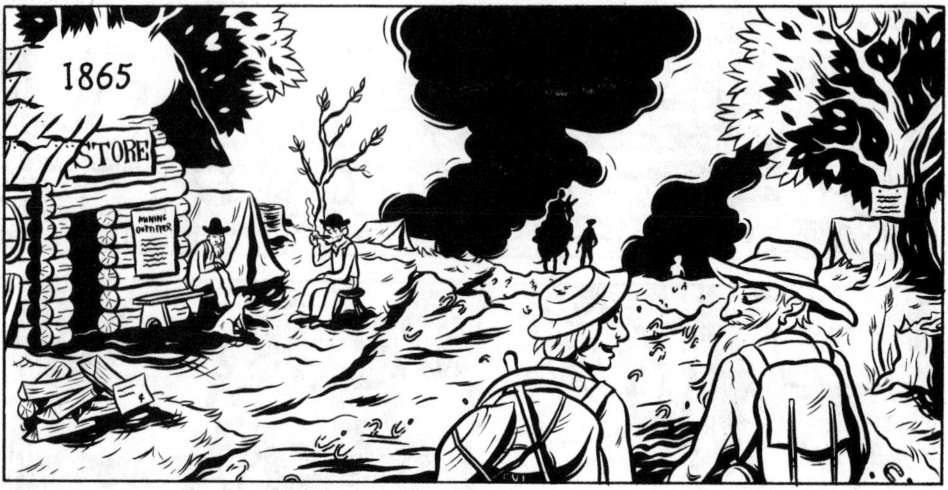
1865
STORE
MINING OUTFITTER

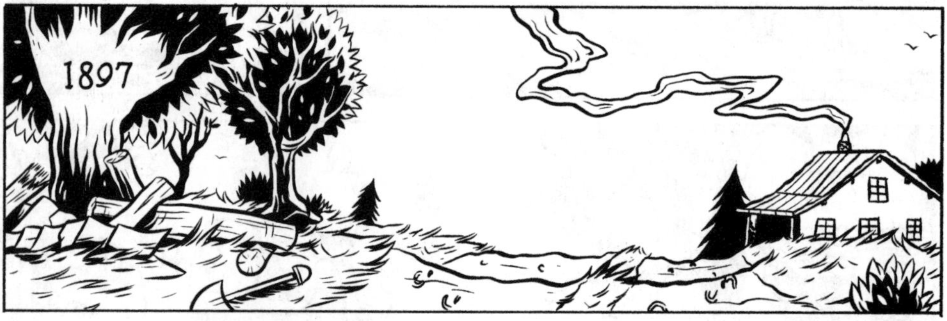
1897

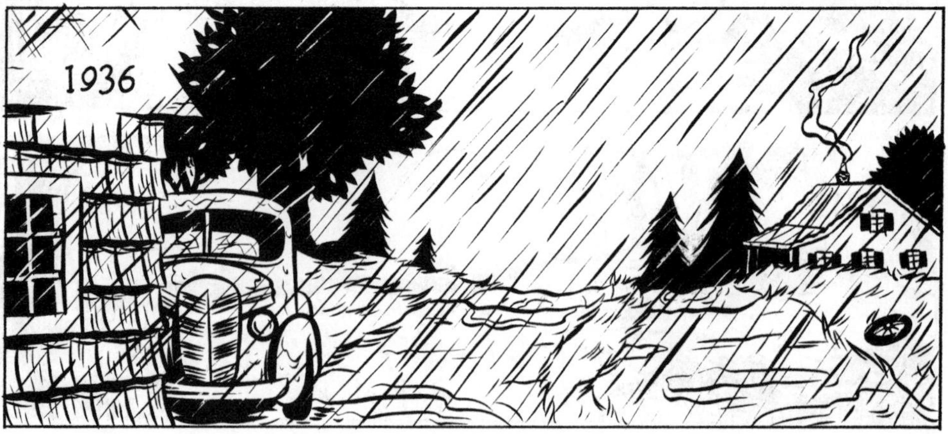
1936

1974
PARKING
GROCERY
1982
PARKING
2009
August 31, 5:15 PM
French Hill, Nova Scotia, Canada

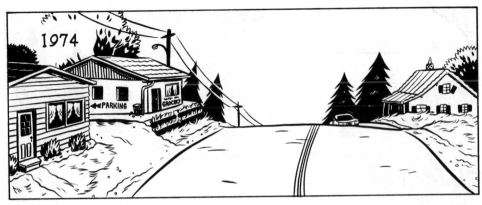

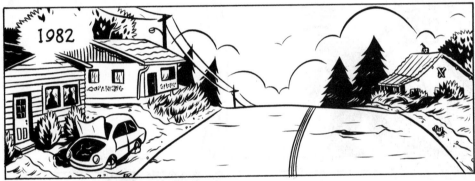

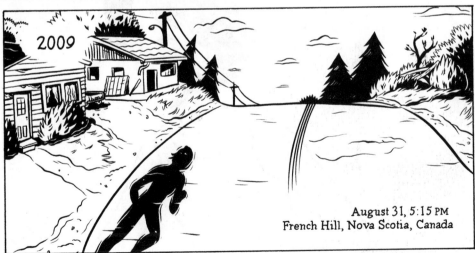

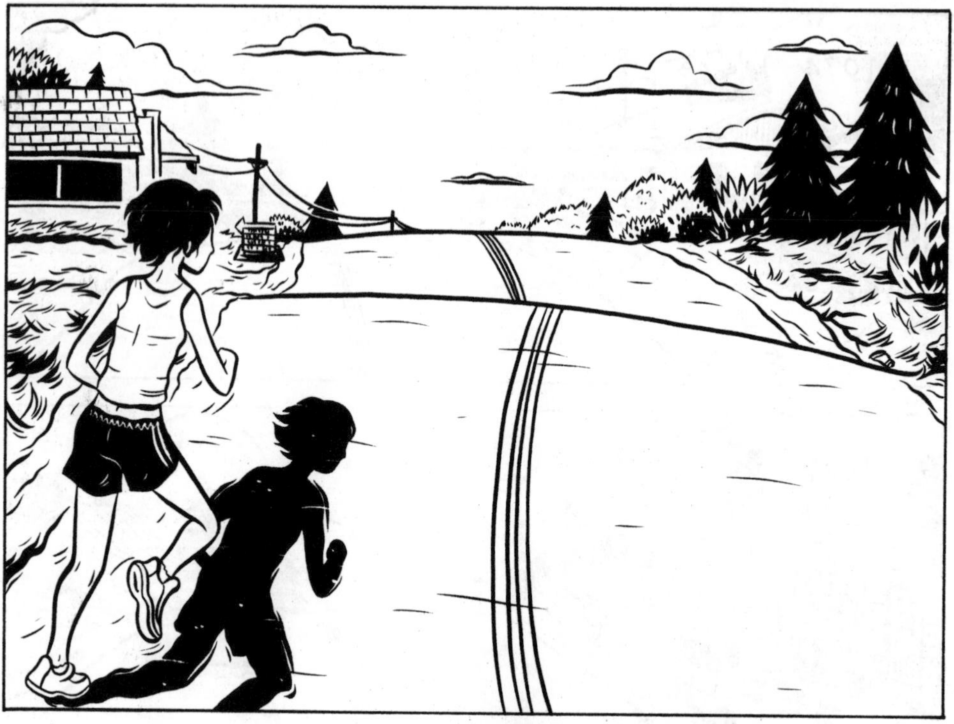

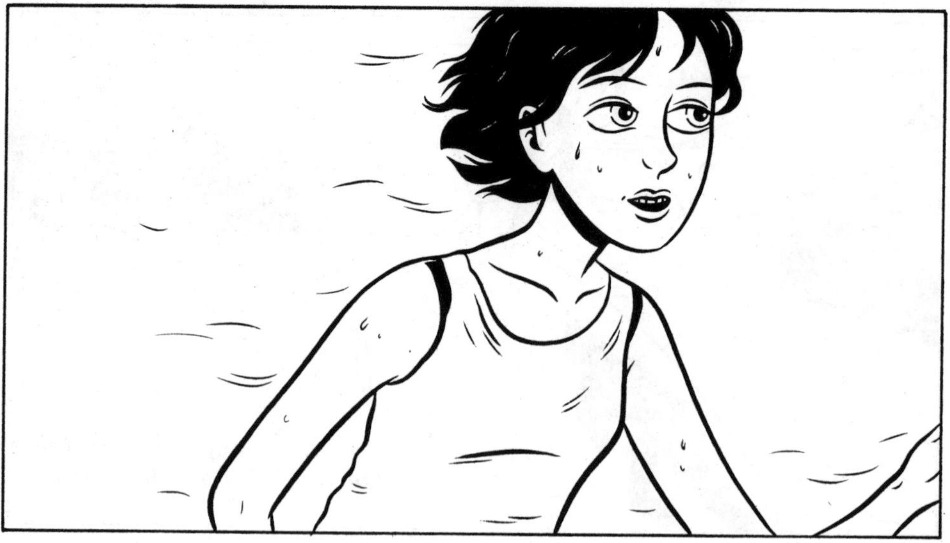

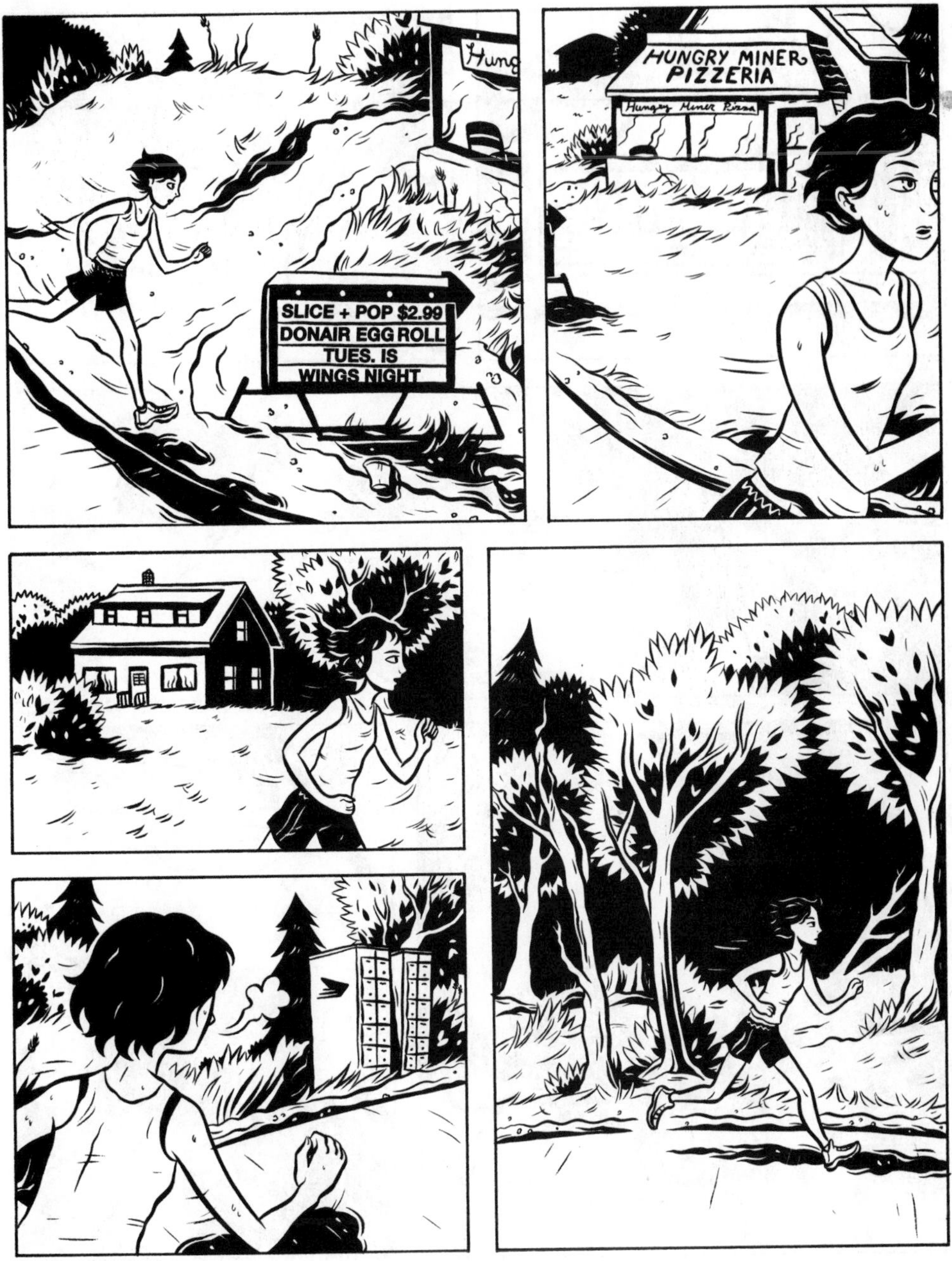
SLICE + POP $2.99
DONAIR EGG ROLL
TUES. IS
WINGS NIGHT
HUNGRY MINER PIZZERIA
Hungry Miner Pizza

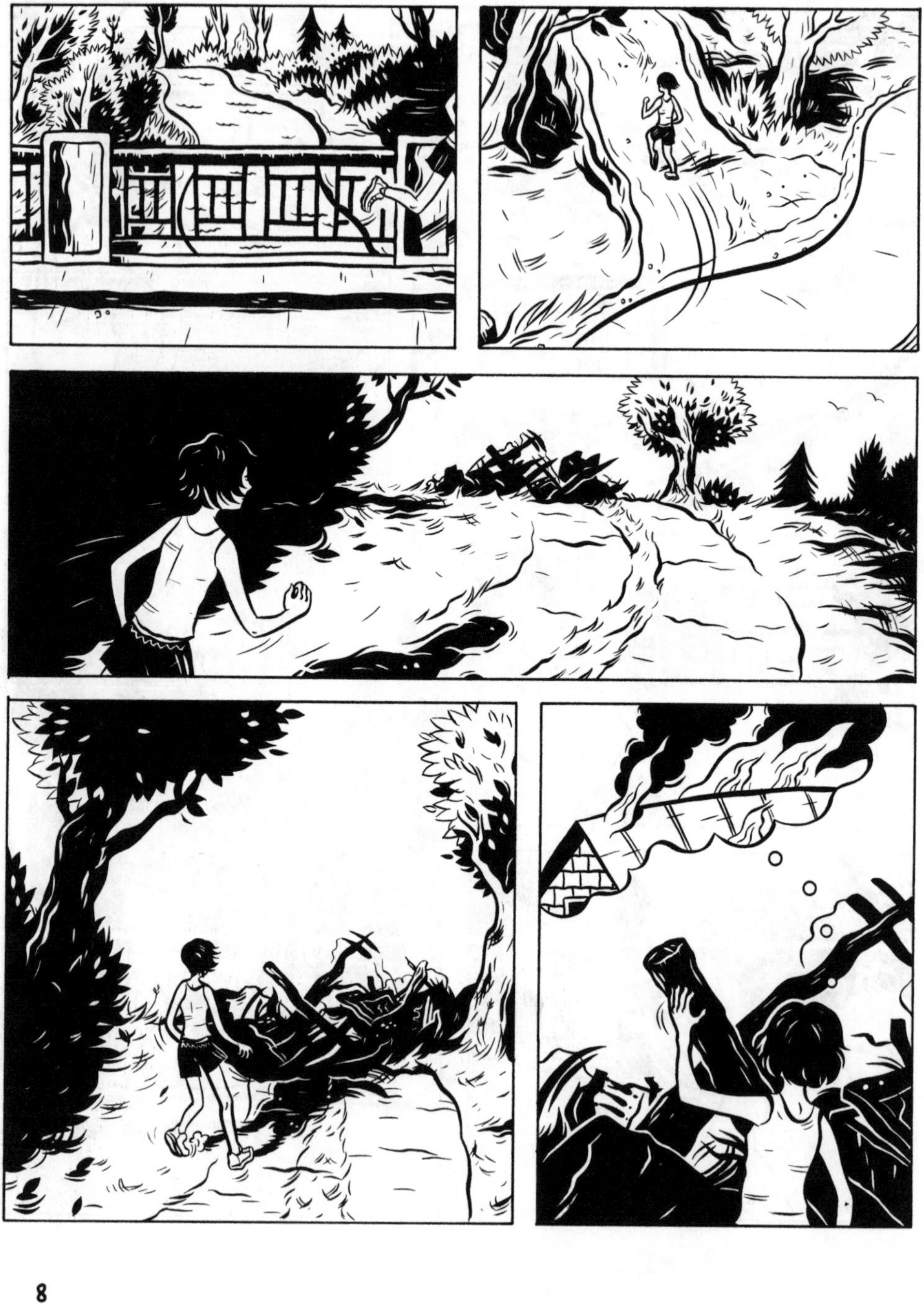

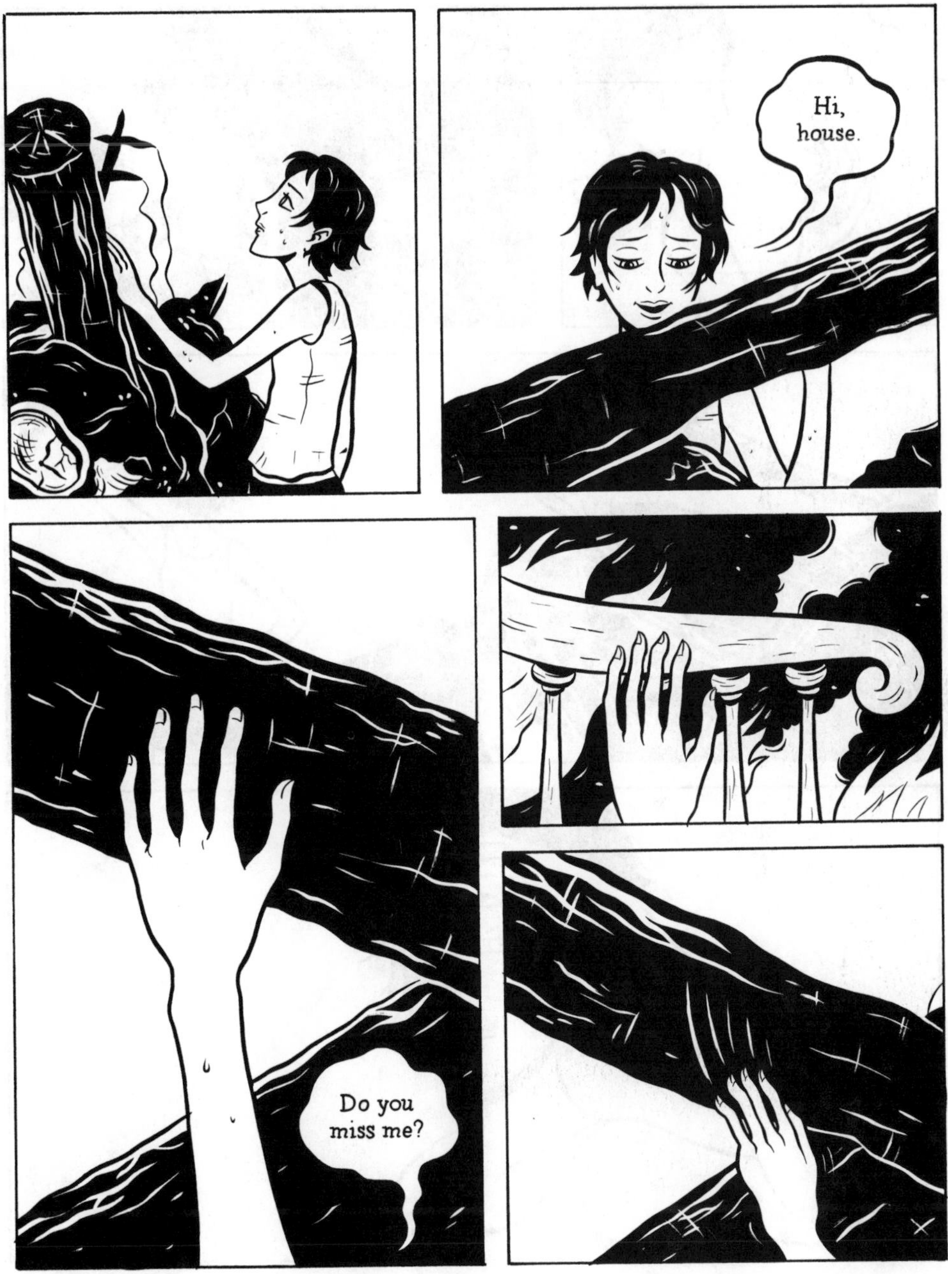
Hi, house.
Do you miss me?

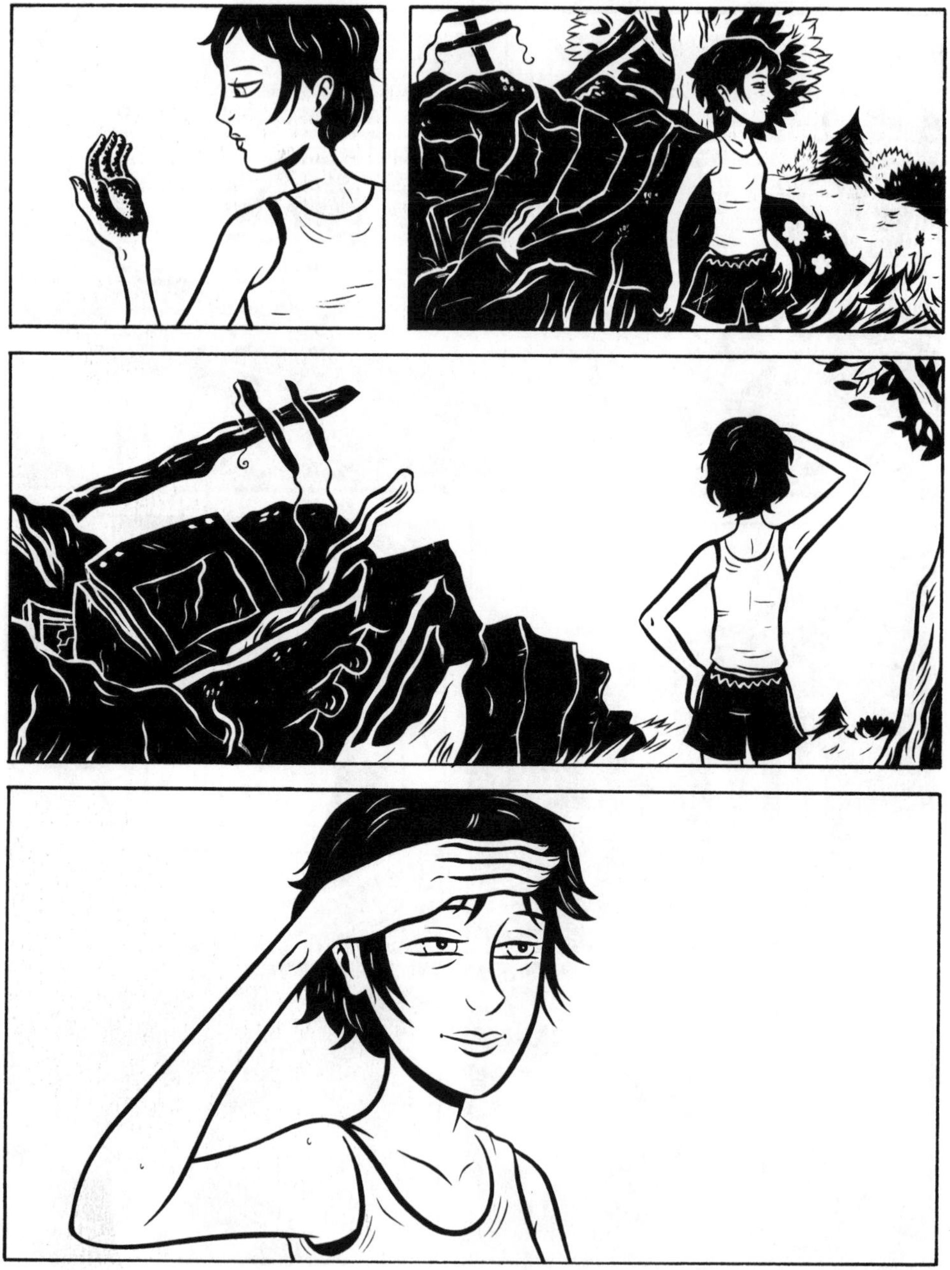

Hello, river.
kiss!

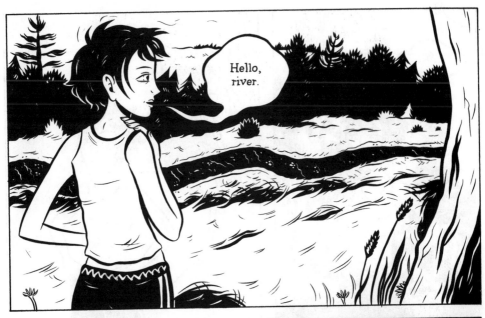

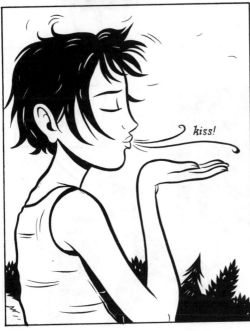

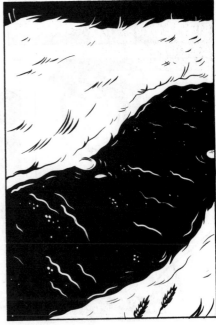

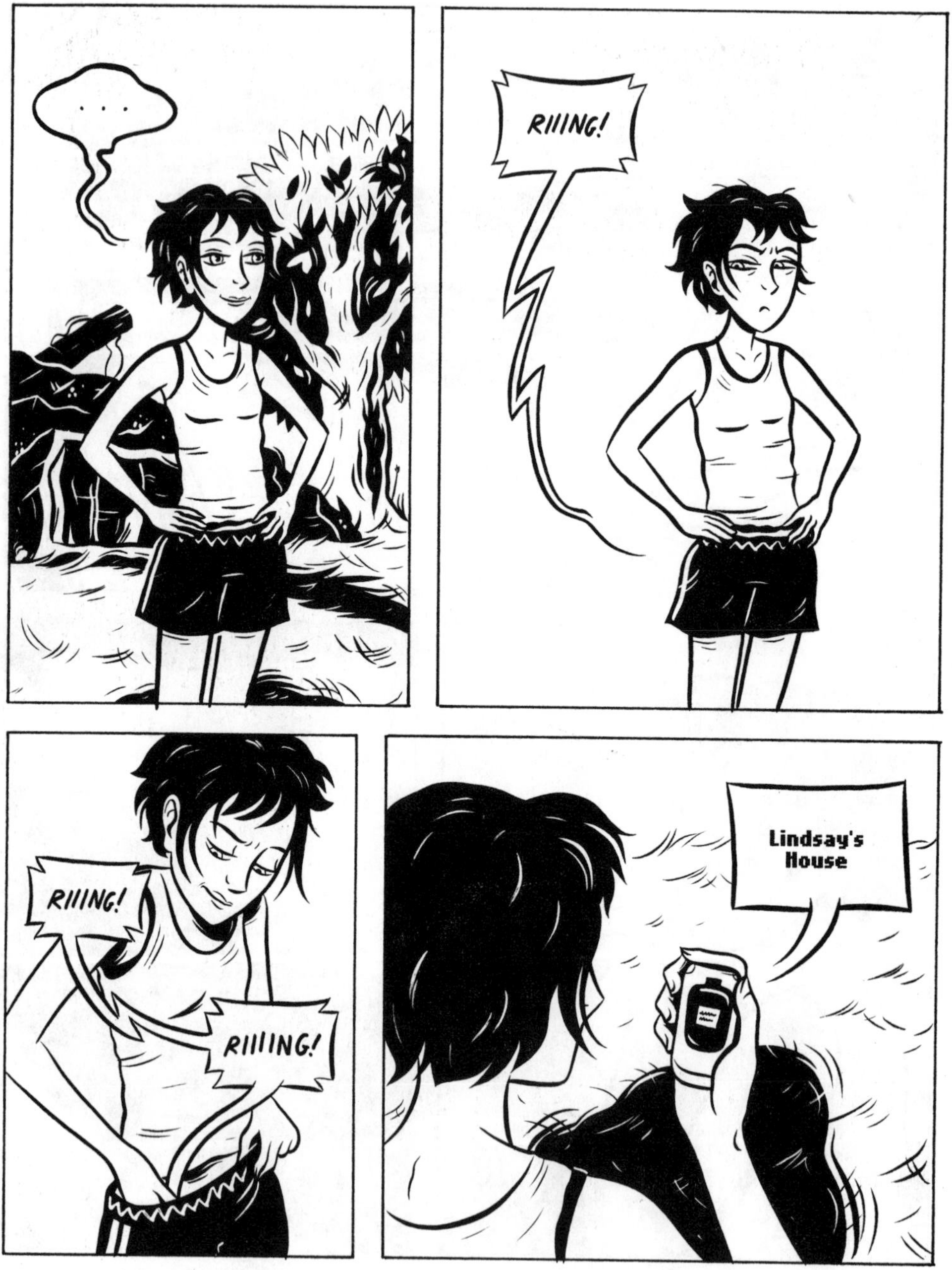
. . .
RIIING!
RIIING!
RIIIING!
Lindsay's House

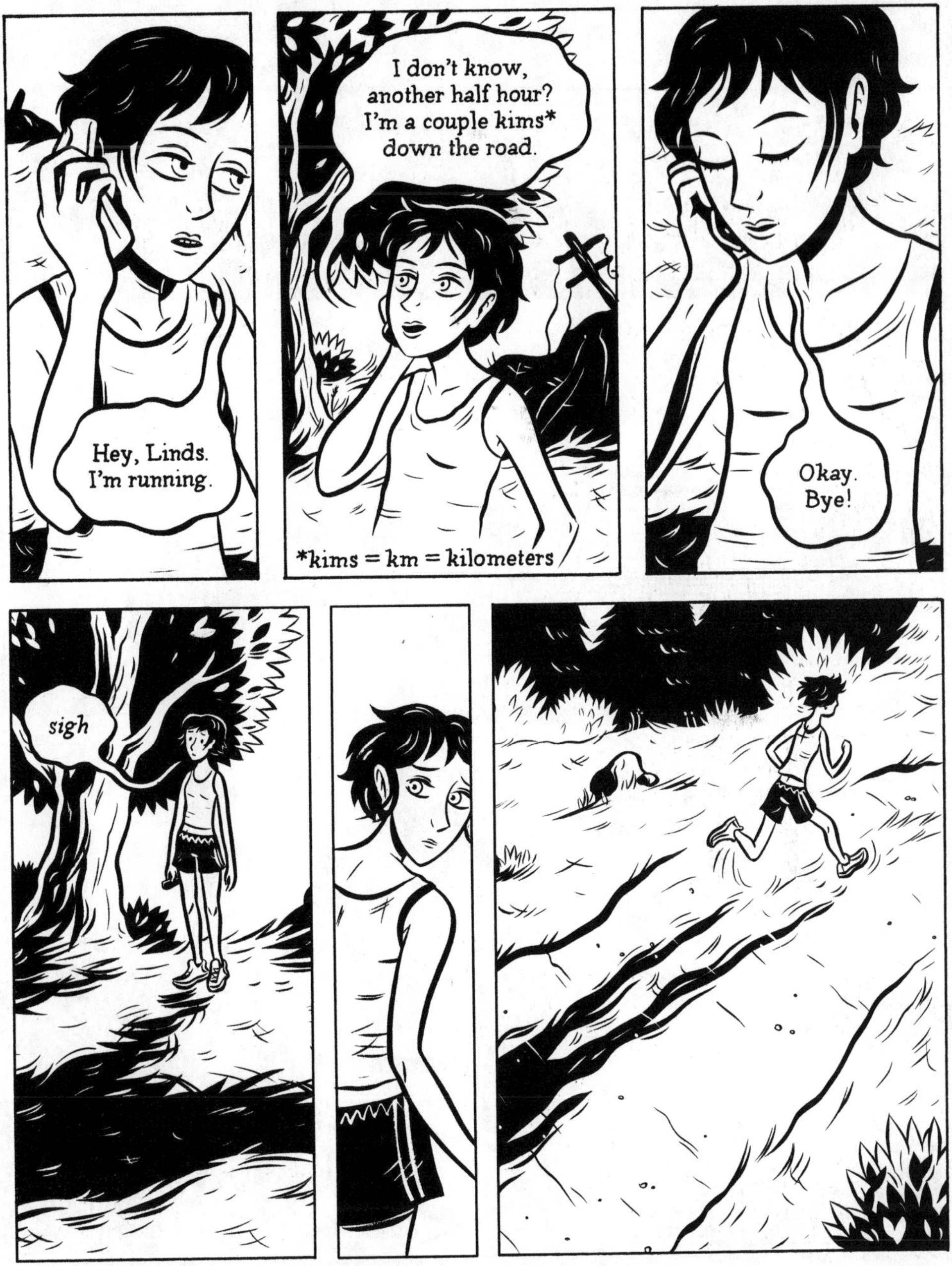
Hey, Linds.
I'm running.
I don't know, another half hour? I'm a couple kims* down the road.
*kims = km = kilometers
Okay. Bye!
sigh

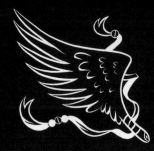

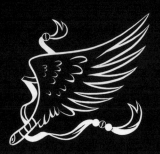

1859

August 31, 2:38 PM
French Hill, Nova Scotia
(Pre-Confederation)

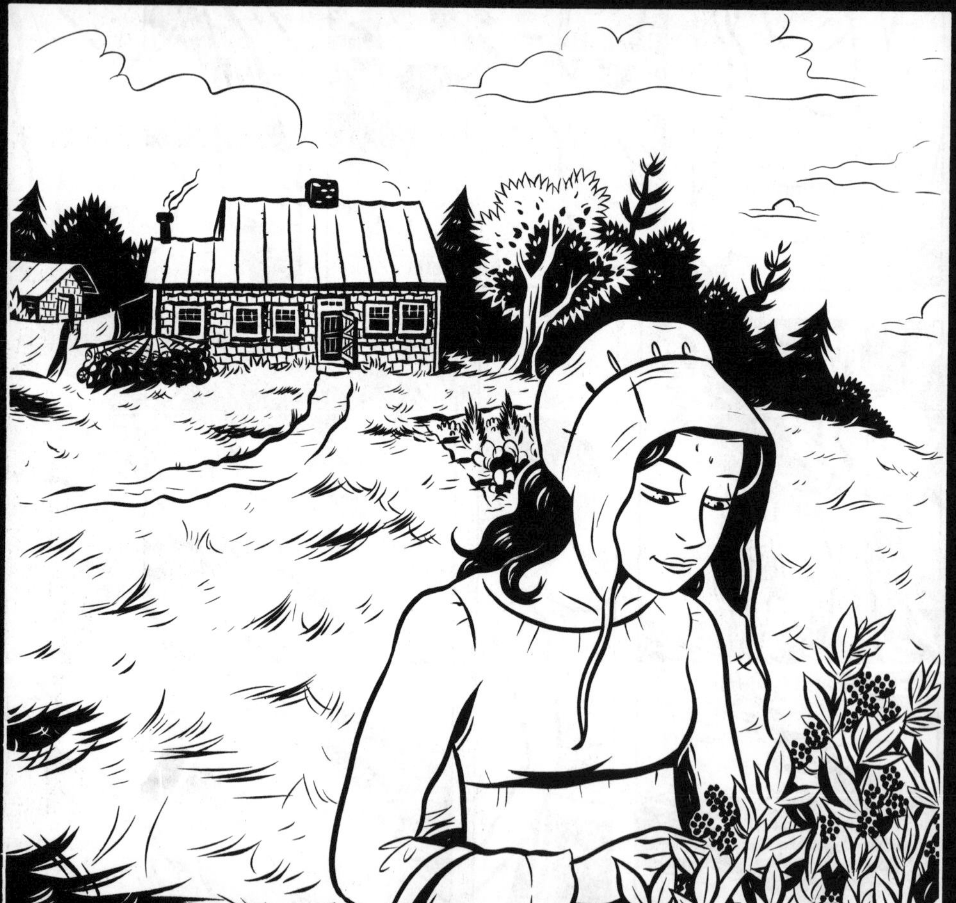

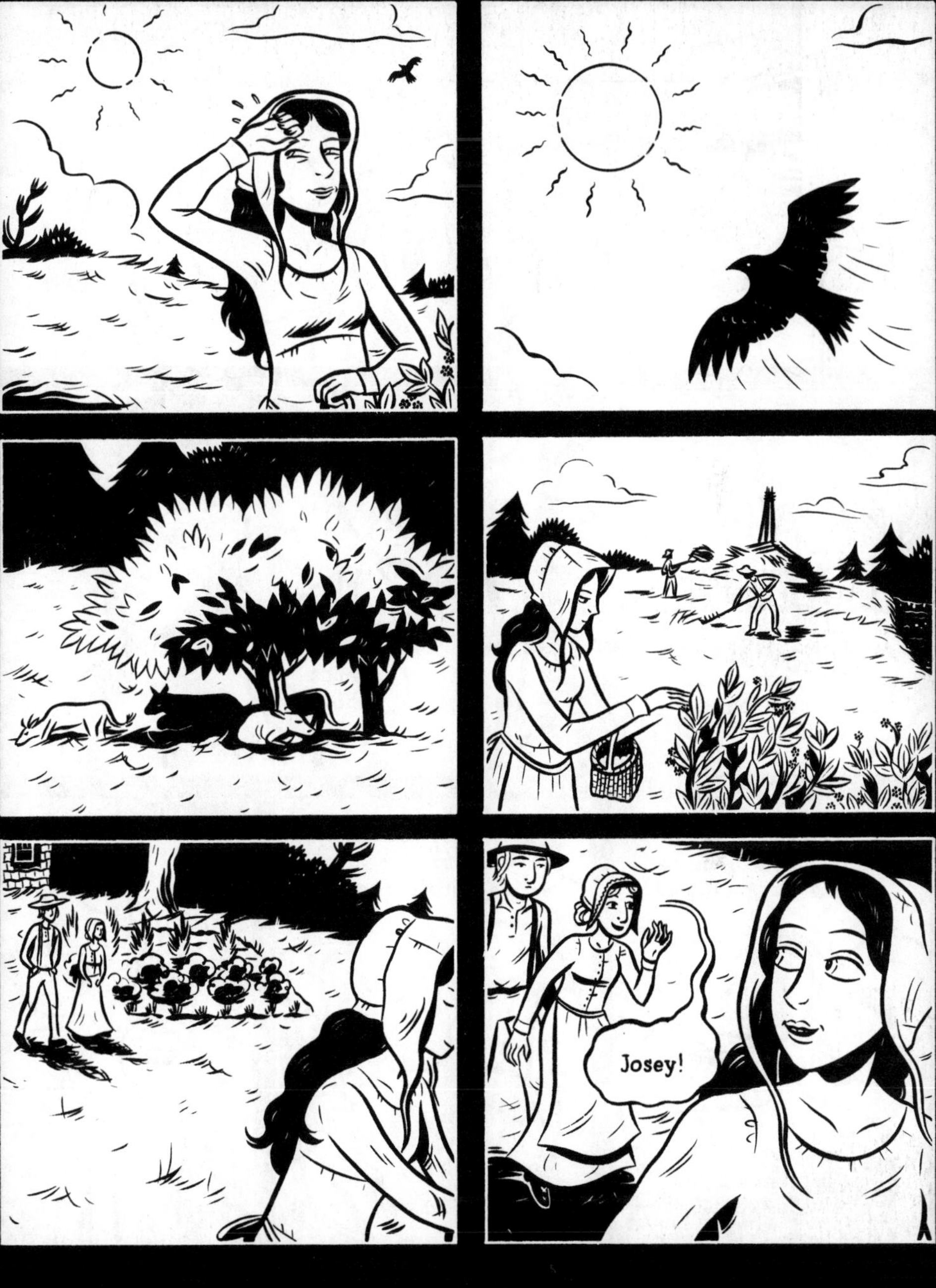
Josey!

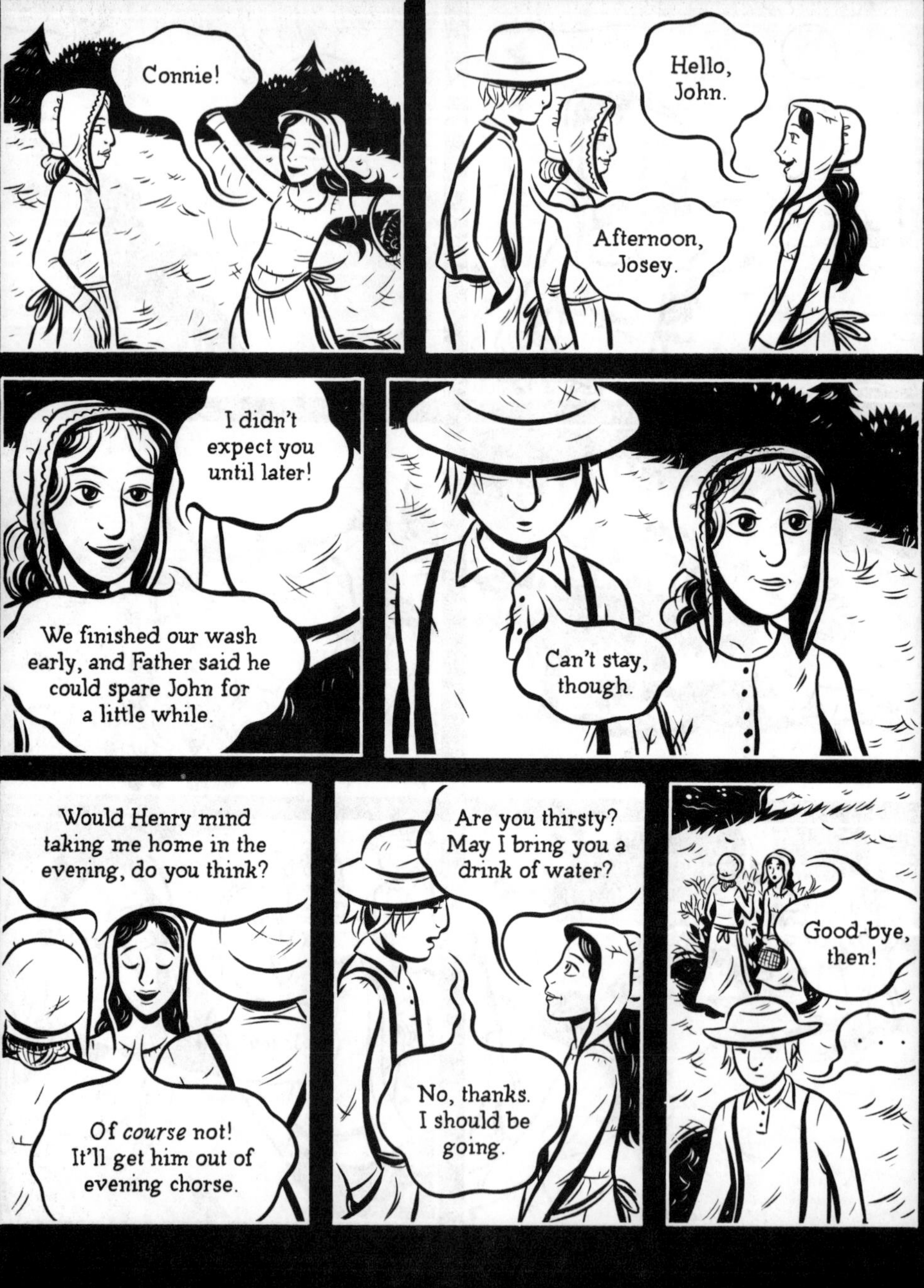
Connie!
Hello, John.
Afternoon, Josey.
I didn't expect you until later!
We finished our wash early, and Father said he could spare John for a little while.
Can't stay, though.
Would Henry mind taking me home in the evening, do you think?
Of *course* not! It'll get him out of evening chorse.
Are you thirsty? May I bring you a drink of water?
No, thanks. I should be going.
Good-bye, then!
. . .

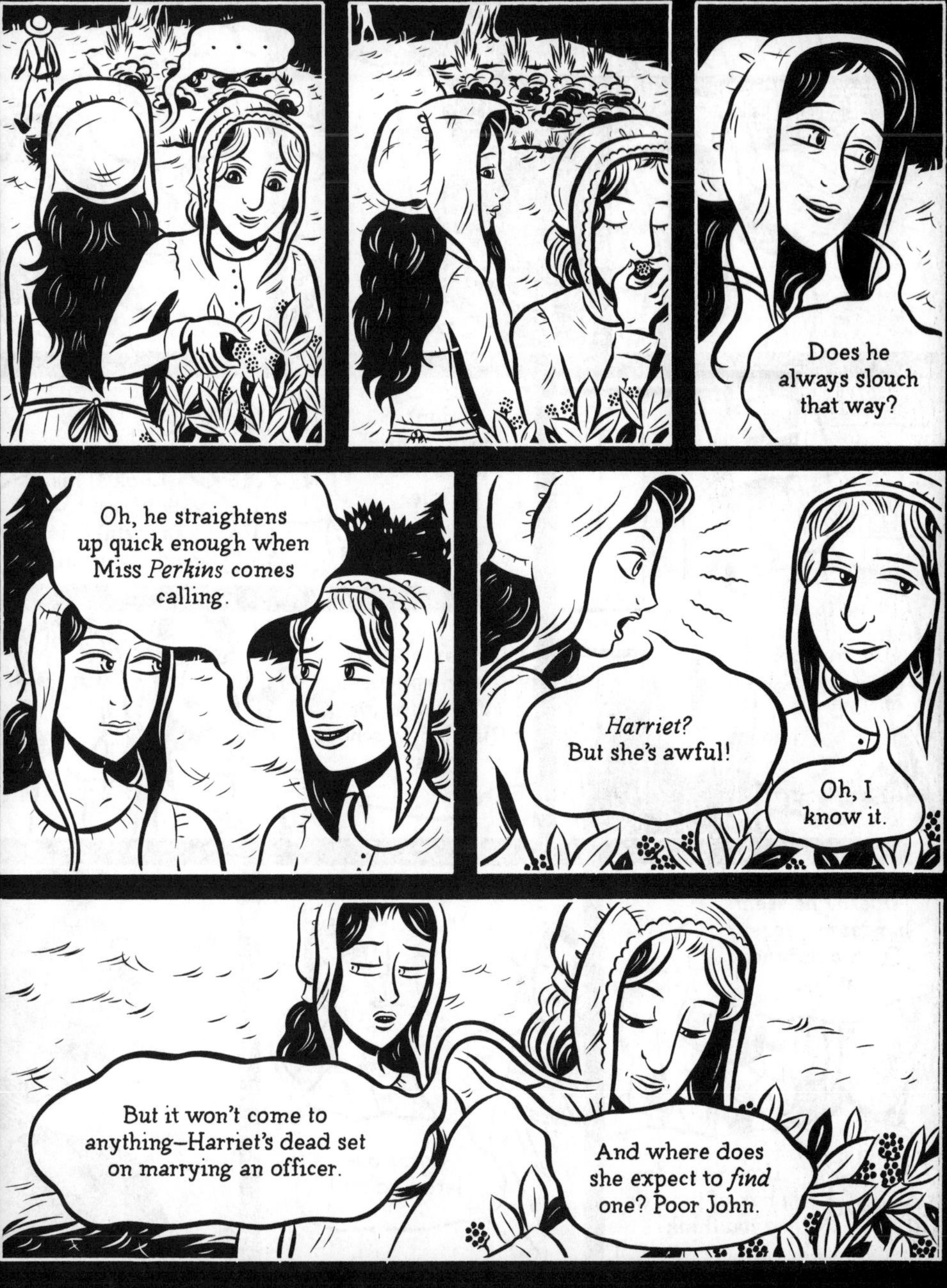
Does he always slouch that way?
Oh, he straightens up quick enough when Miss *Perkins* comes calling.
Harriet? But she's awful!
Oh, I know it.
But it won't come to anything—Harriet's dead set on marrying an officer.
And where does she expect to *find* one? Poor John.

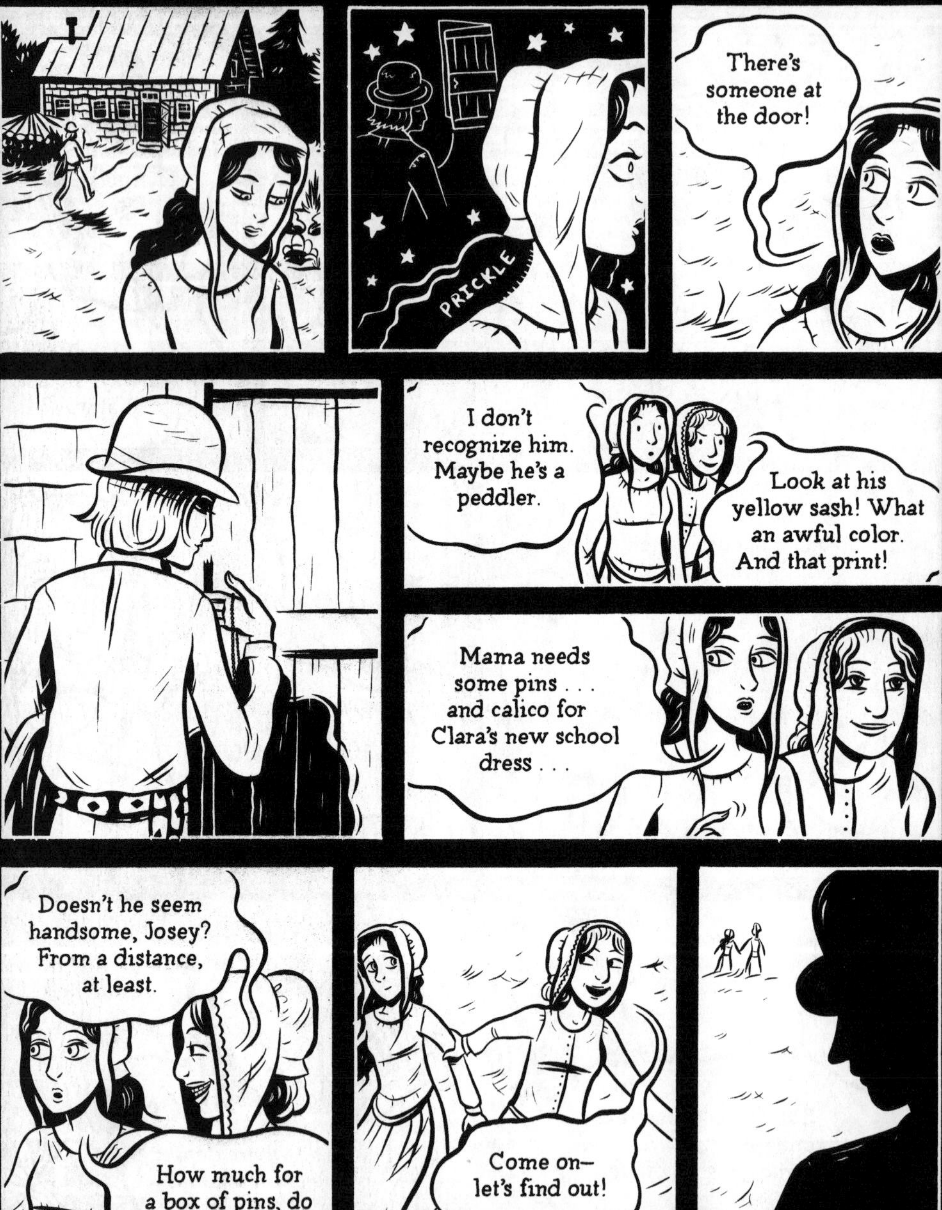
PRICKLE
There's someone at the door!
I don't recognize him. Maybe he's a peddler.
Look at his yellow sash! What an awful color. And that print!
Mama needs some pins . . . and calico for Clara's new school dress . . .
Doesn't he seem handsome, Josey? From a distance, at least.
How much for a box of pins, do you think?
Come on— let's find out!

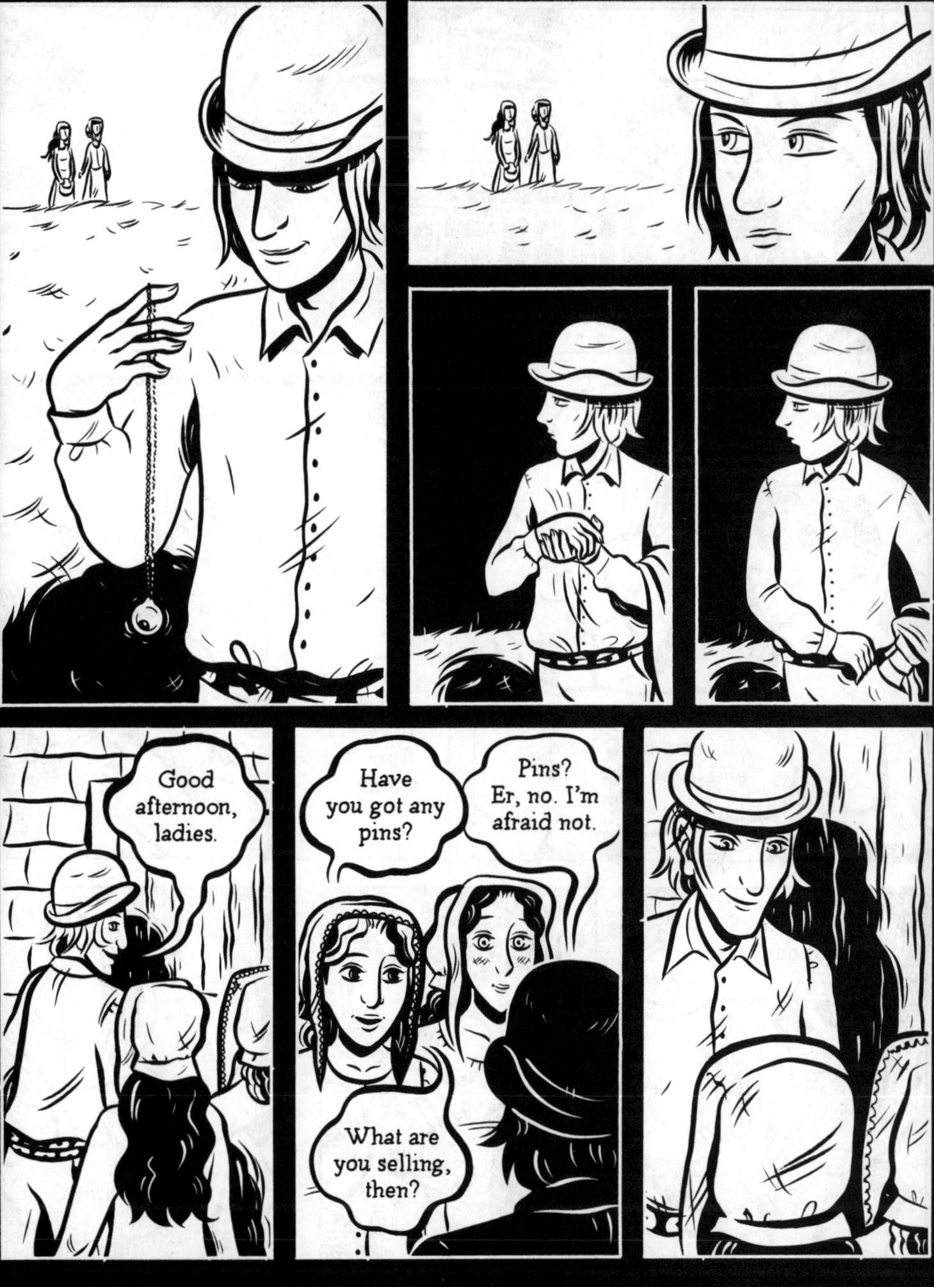
Good afternoon, ladies.
Have you got any pins?
Pins? Er, no. I'm afraid not.
What are you selling, then?

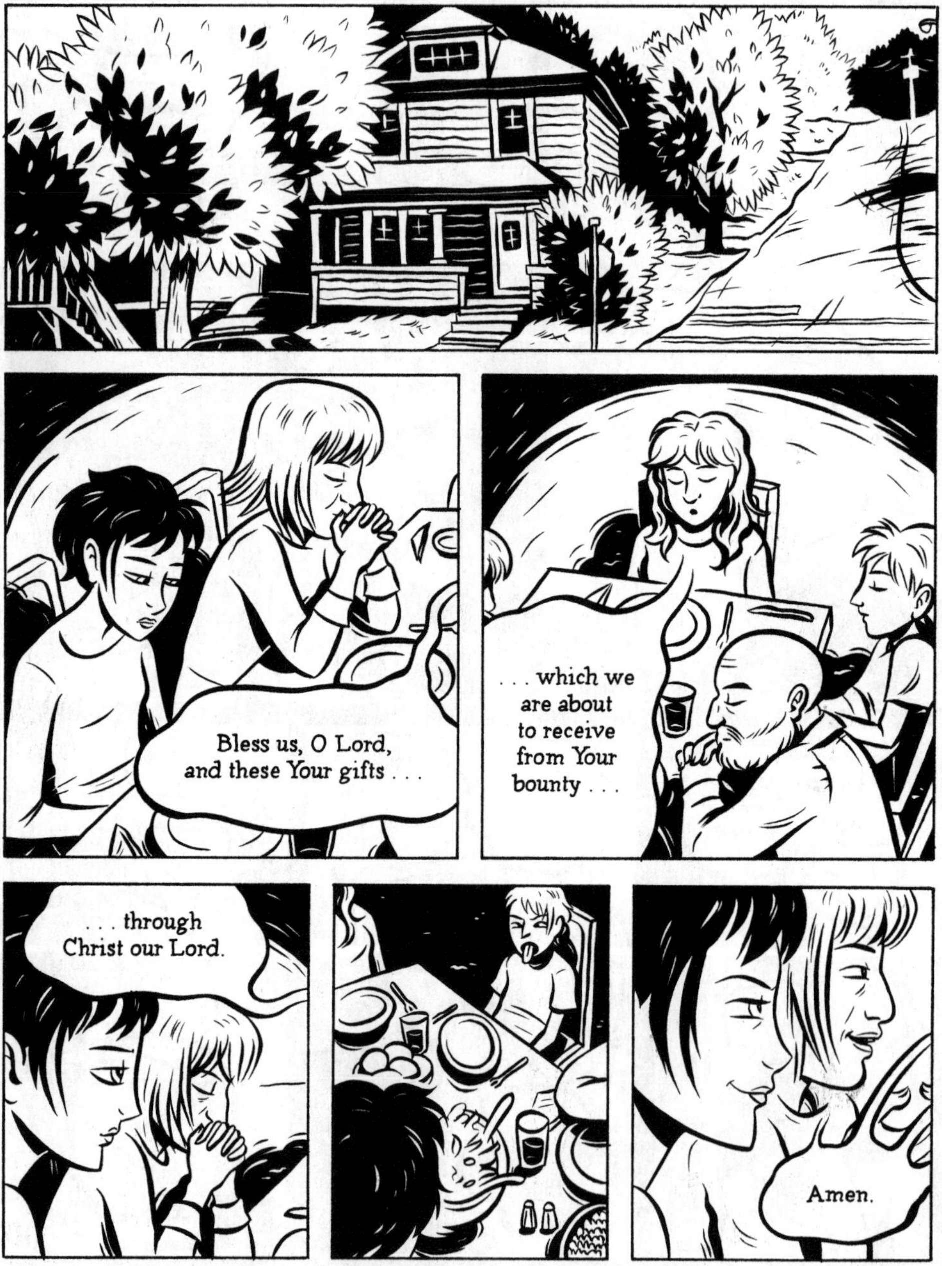
Bless us, O Lord,
and these Your gifts . . .
. . . which we are about to receive from Your bounty . . .
. . . through Christ our Lord.
Amen.

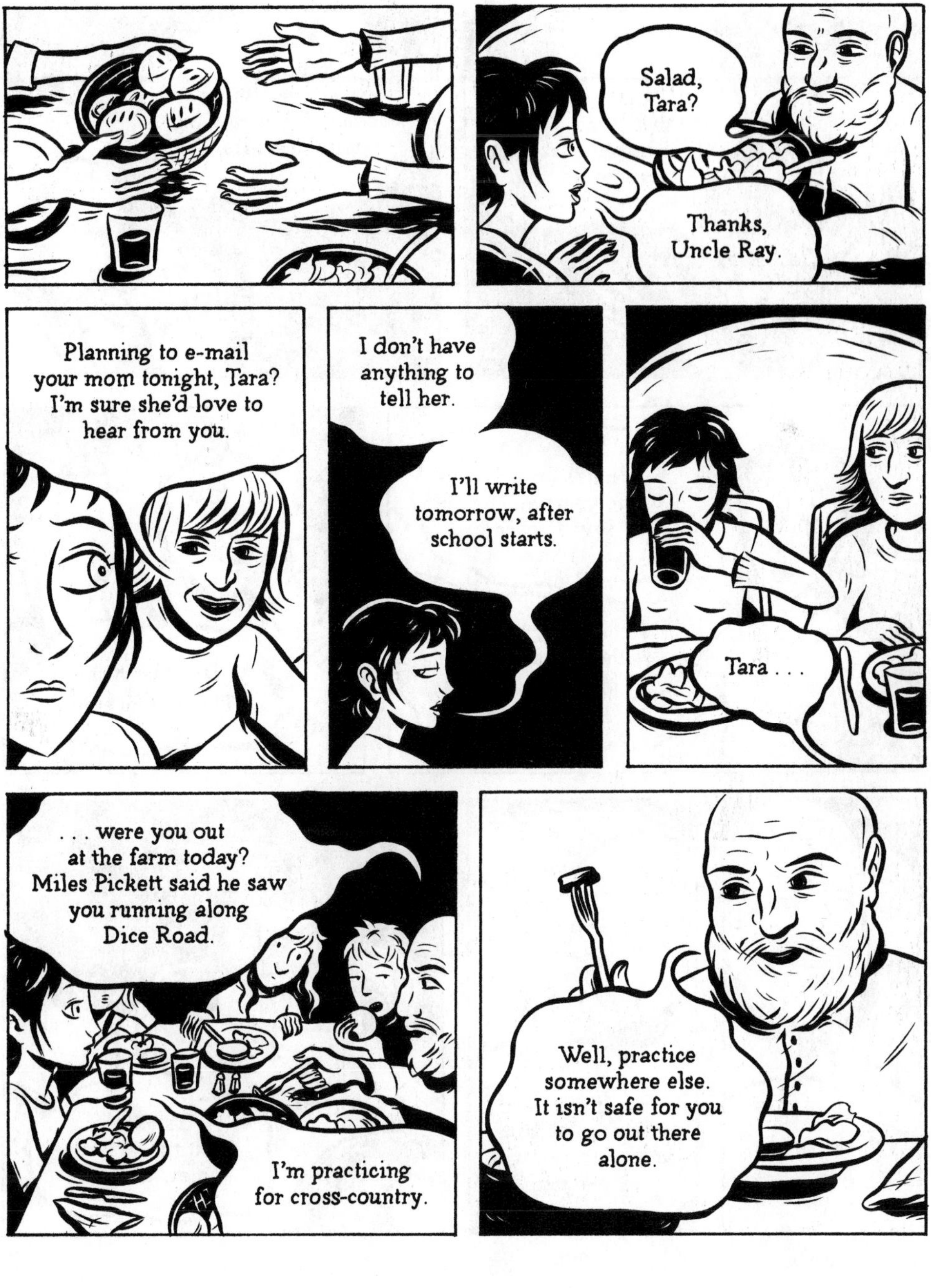
Salad, Tara?
Thanks, Uncle Ray.
Planning to e-mail your mom tonight, Tara? I'm sure she'd love to hear from you.
I don't have anything to tell her.
I'll write tomorrow, after school starts.
Tara . . .
. . . were you out at the farm today? Miles Pickett said he saw you running along Dice Road.
I'm practicing for cross-country.
Well, practice somewhere else. It isn't safe for you to go out there alone.

Ray, it's perfectly safe. We know everyone out there, and Tara has her phone in case she gets into trouble.

With the house gone, those woods will be crawling with poachers.

What?! I lived there two years and never saw a poacher!

Not to mention the perverts cruising around in their pickup trucks. . . .

Don't be such an alarmist, Dad.

I'm a *realist*, honey.

Tara, if you need a ride to the farm, your aunt or I will drive you.

It's okay. Next time I'll run somewhere else.

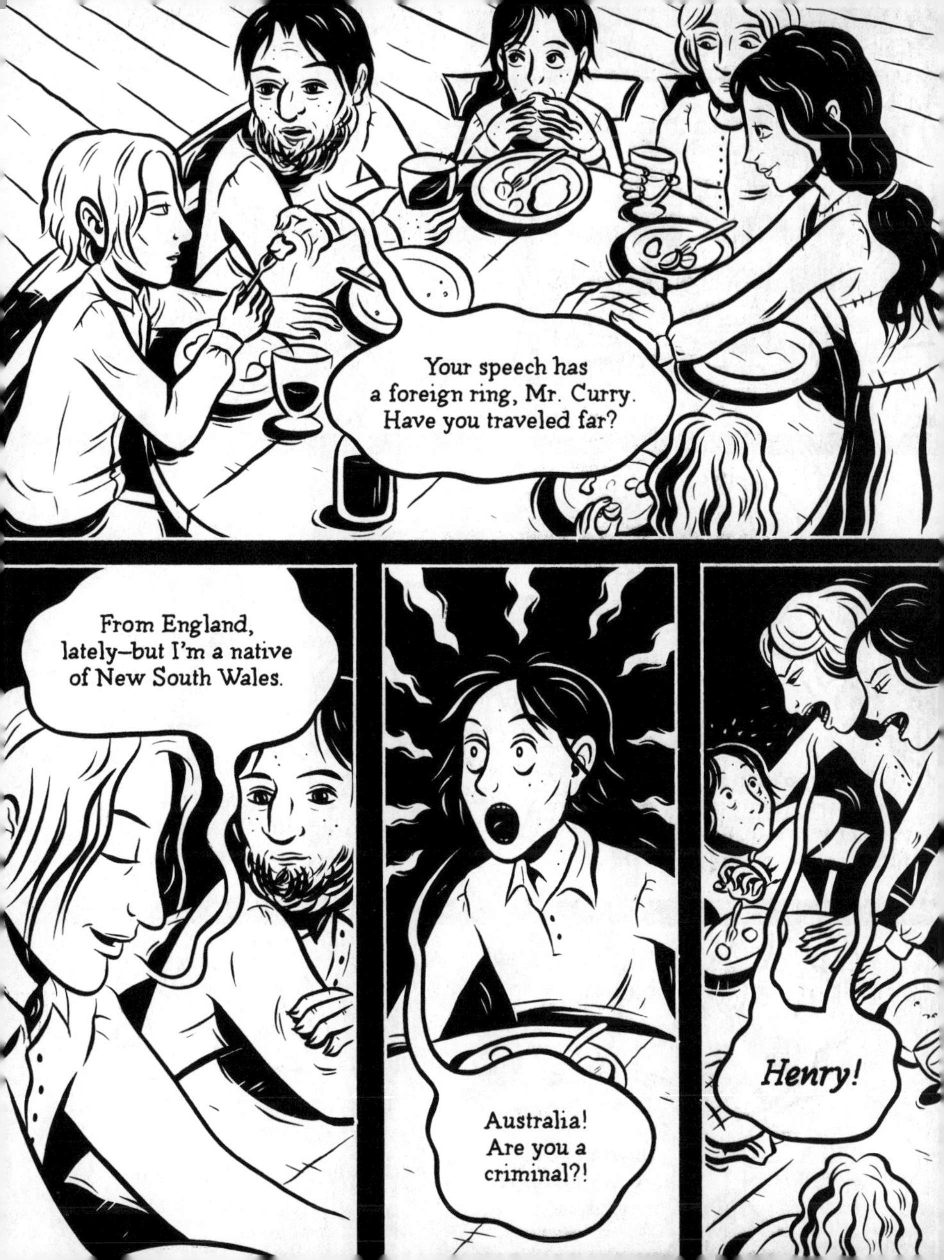
Your speech has a foreign ring, Mr. Curry. Have you traveled far?
From England, lately—but I'm a native of New South Wales.
Australia! Are you a criminal?!
Henry!

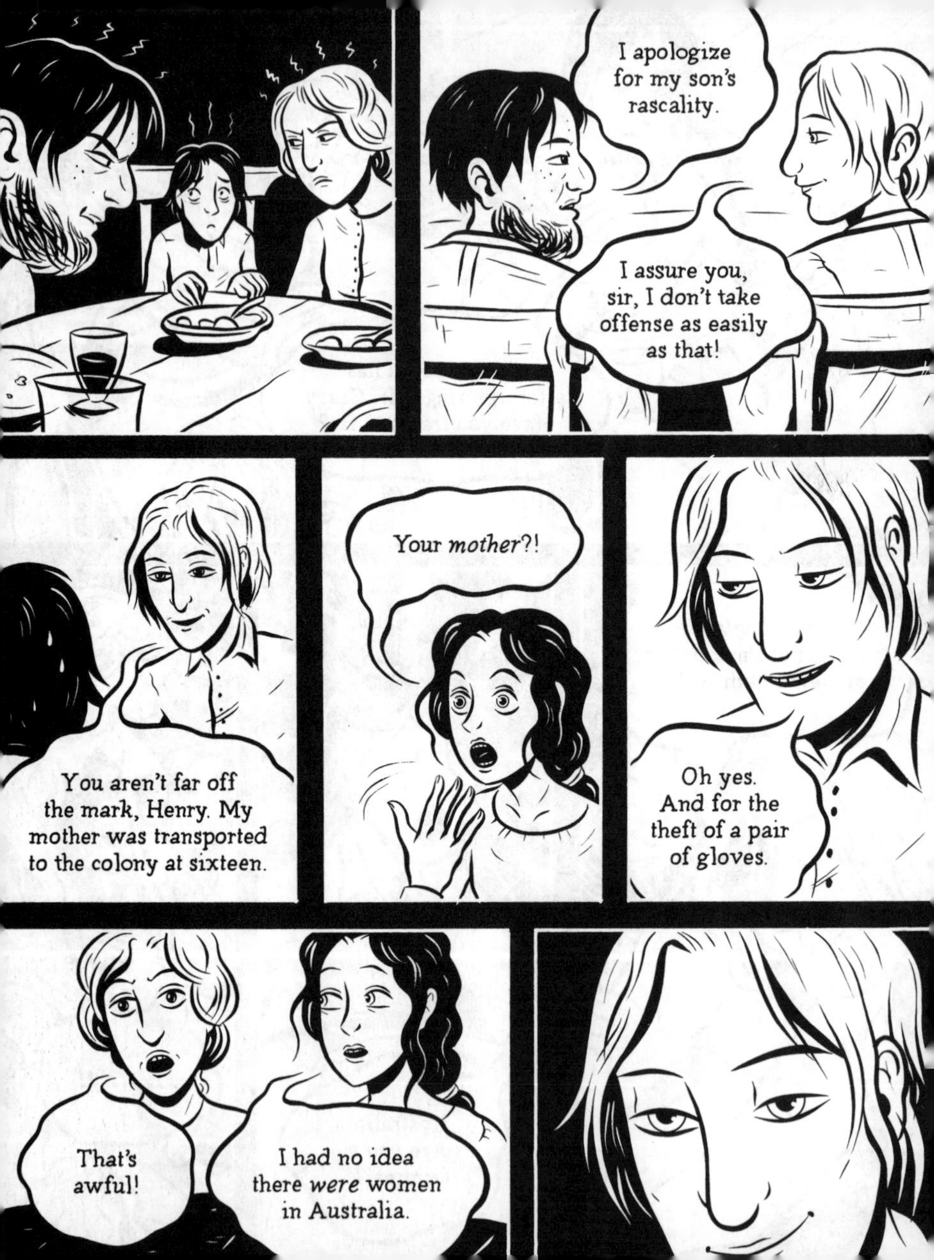
I apologize for my son's rascality.
I assure you, sir, I don't take offense as easily as that!
You aren't far off the mark, Henry. My mother was transported to the colony at sixteen.
Your *mother*?!
Oh yes. And for the theft of a pair of gloves.
That's awful!
I had no idea there *were* women in Australia.

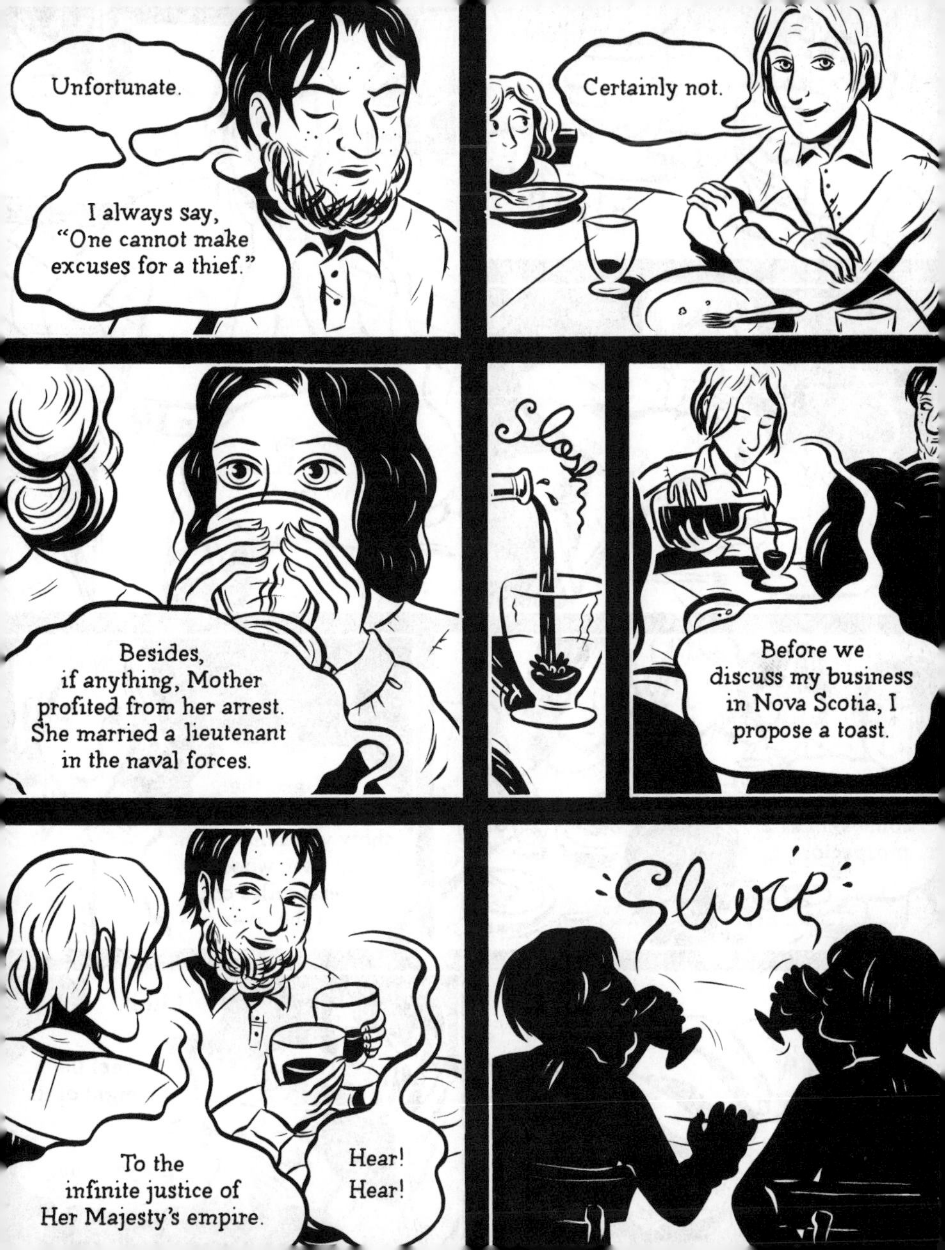

Unfortunate.
I always say, "One cannot make excuses for a thief."
Certainly not.
Besides, if anything, Mother profited from her arrest. She married a lieutenant in the naval forces.
Slosh
Before we discuss my business in Nova Scotia, I propose a toast.
To the infinite justice of Her Majesty's empire.
Hear! Hear!
Slurp

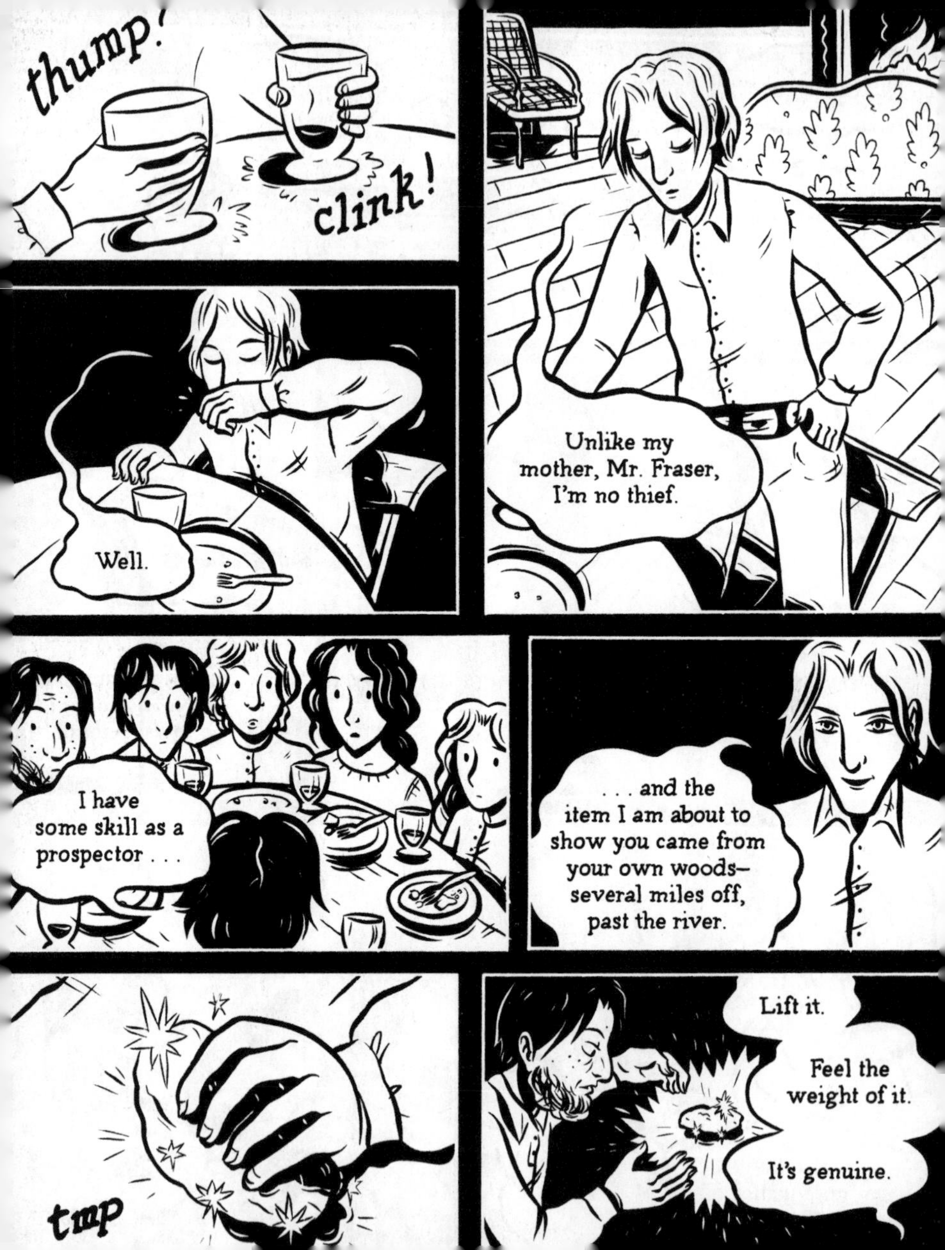
thump!
clink!
Well.
Unlike my mother, Mr. Fraser, I'm no thief.
I have some skill as a prospector . . .
. . . and the item I am about to show you came from your own woods— several miles off, past the river.
tmp
Lift it.
Feel the weight of it.
It's genuine.

Gold.

What were you asking me before?

The price of a box of pins?

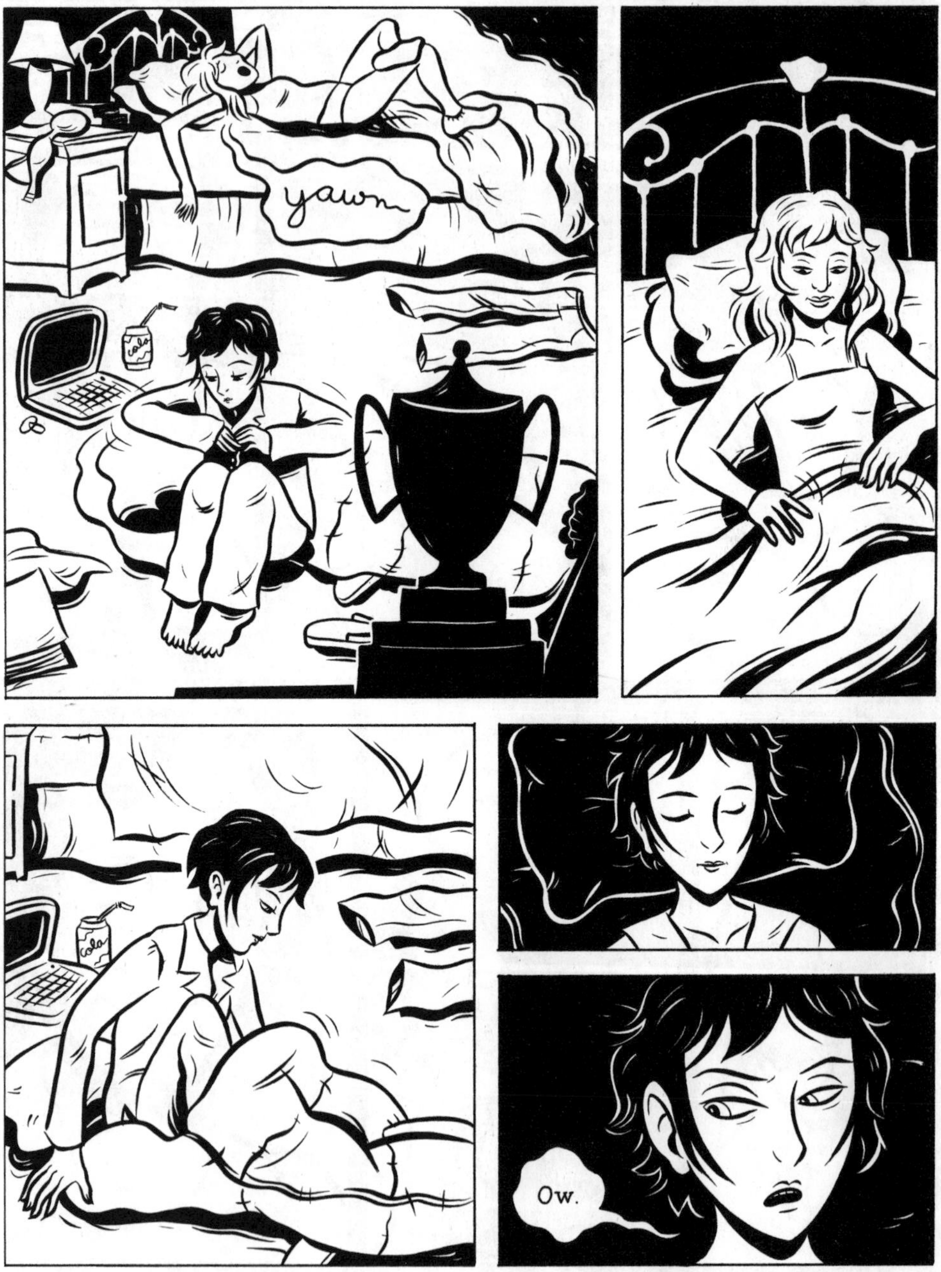
yawn
cola
cola
Ow.

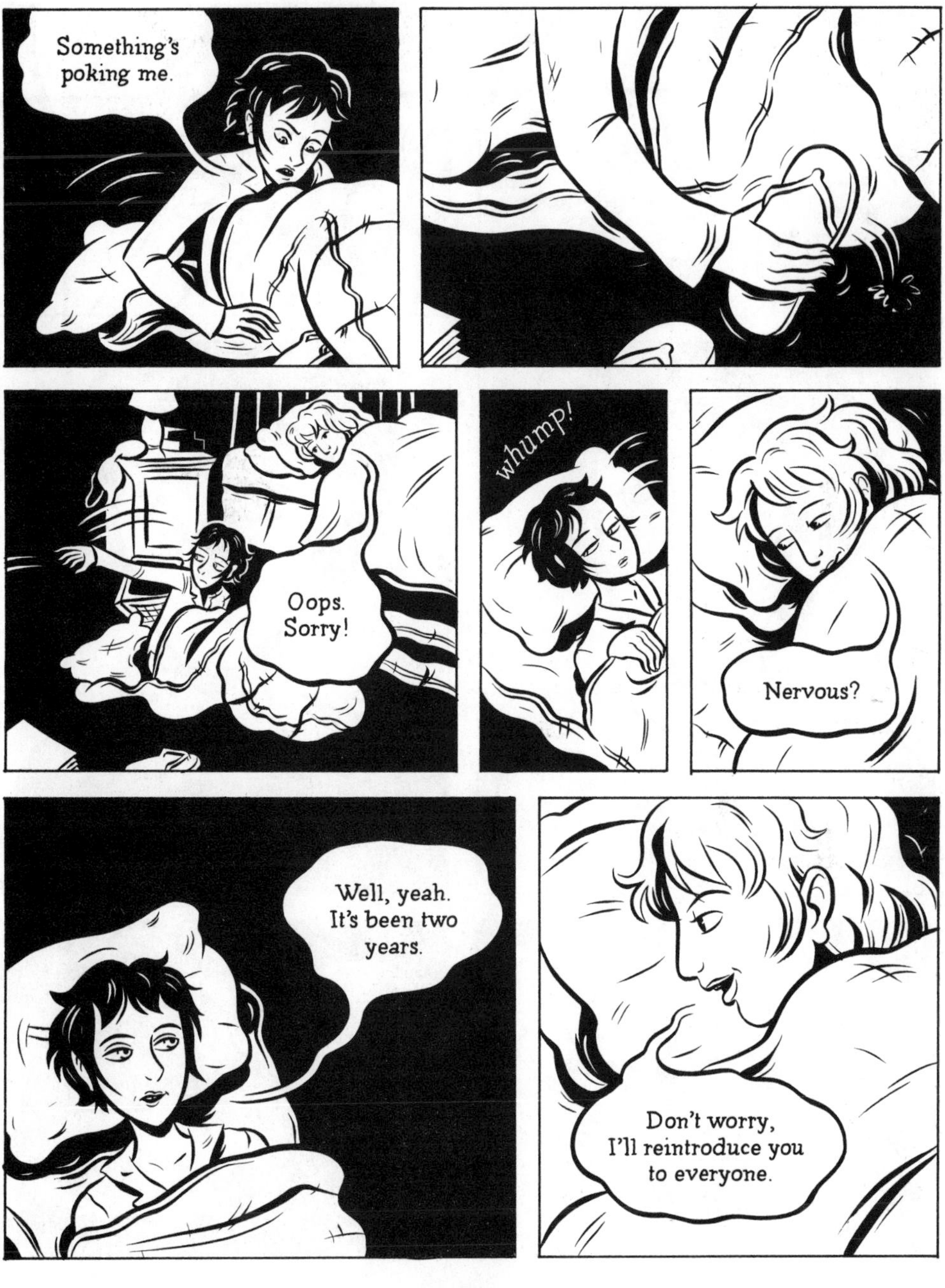
Something's poking me.
Oops. Sorry!
whump!
Nervous?
Well, yeah. It's been two years.
Don't worry, I'll reintroduce you to everyone.

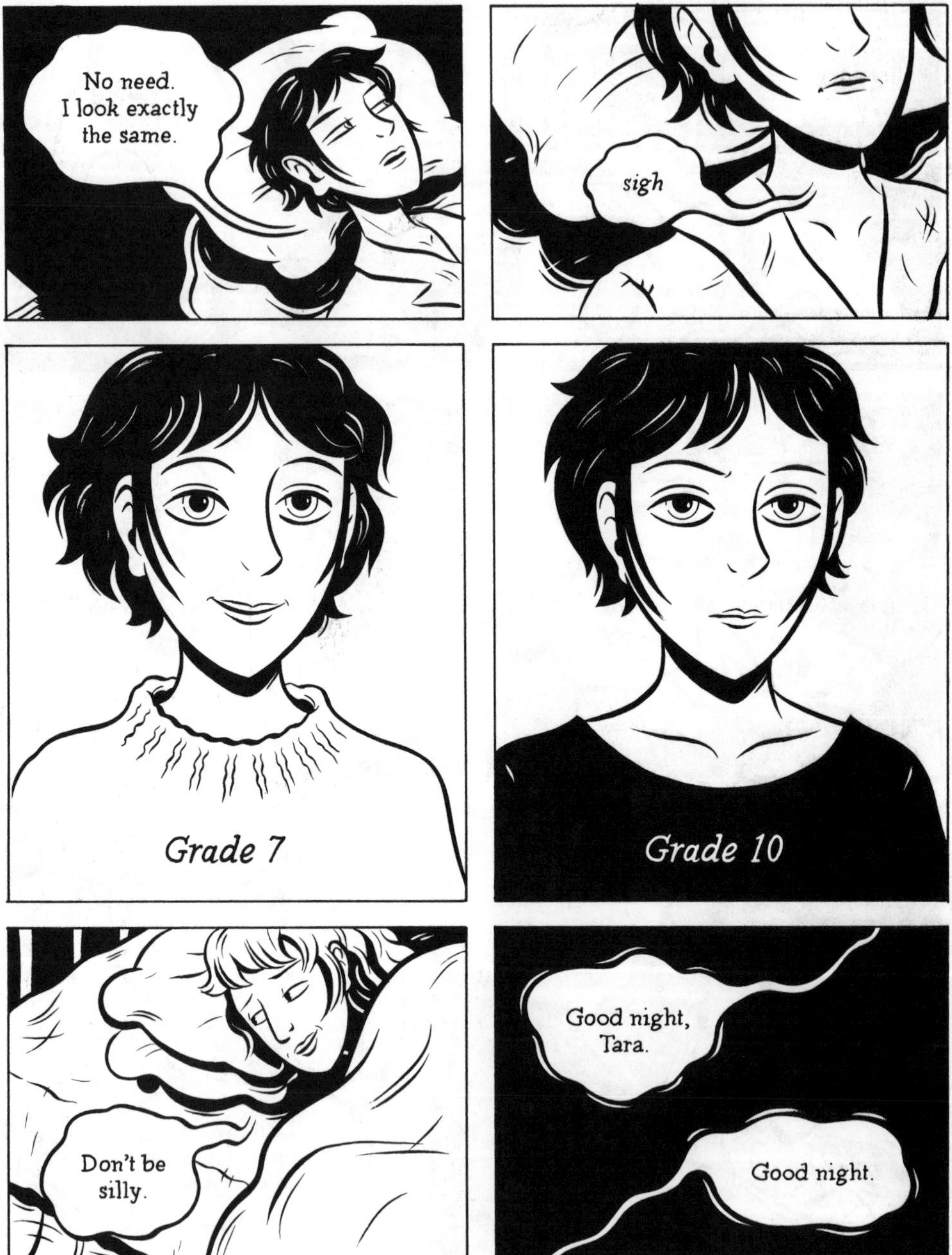
No need. I look exactly the same.
sigh
Grade 7
Grade 10
Don't be silly.
Good night, Tara.
Good night.

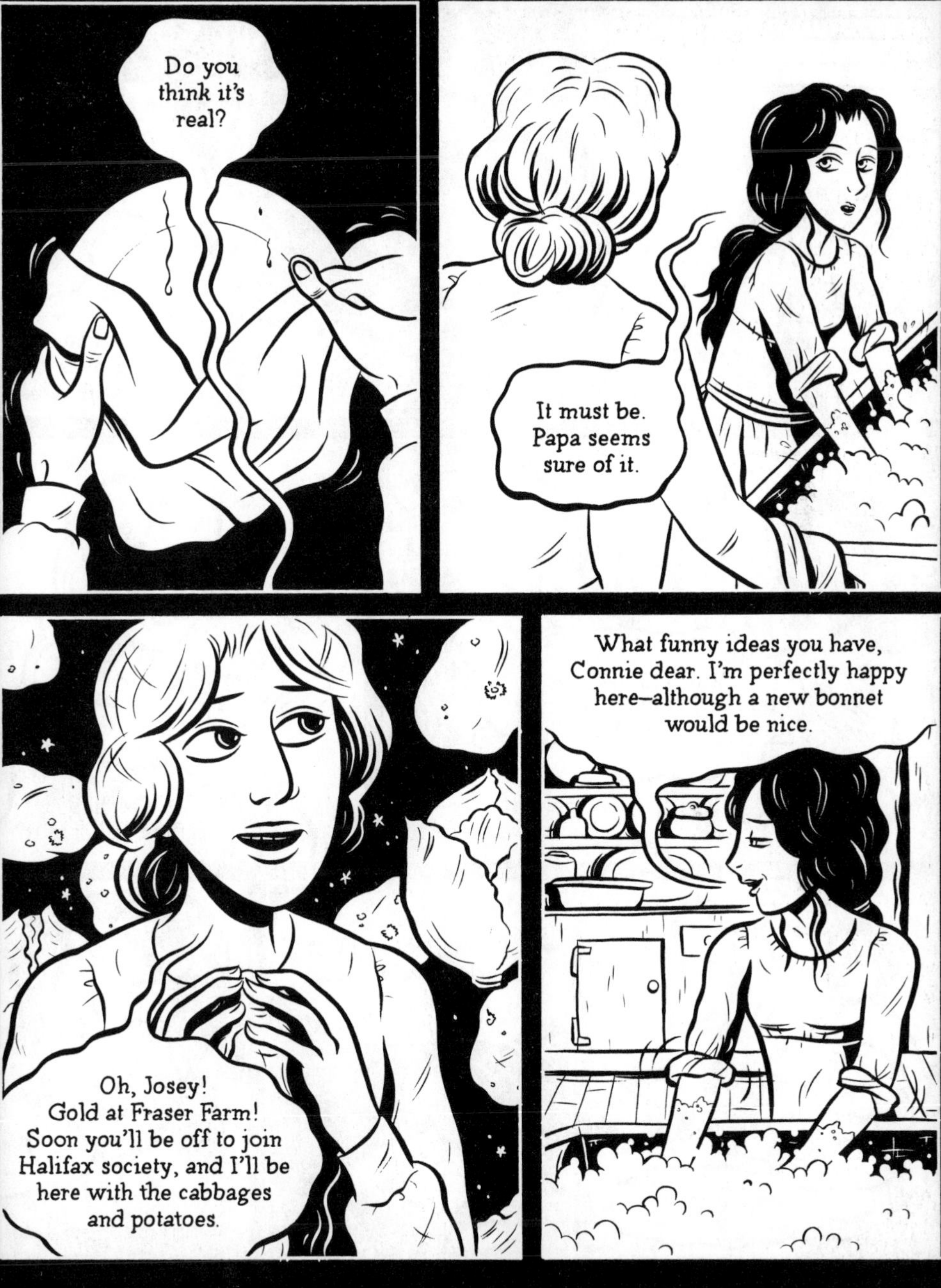

Do you think it's real?
It must be. Papa seems sure of it.
Oh, Josey! Gold at Fraser Farm! Soon you'll be off to join Halifax society, and I'll be here with the cabbages and potatoes.
What funny ideas you have, Connie dear. I'm perfectly happy here–although a new bonnet would be nice.

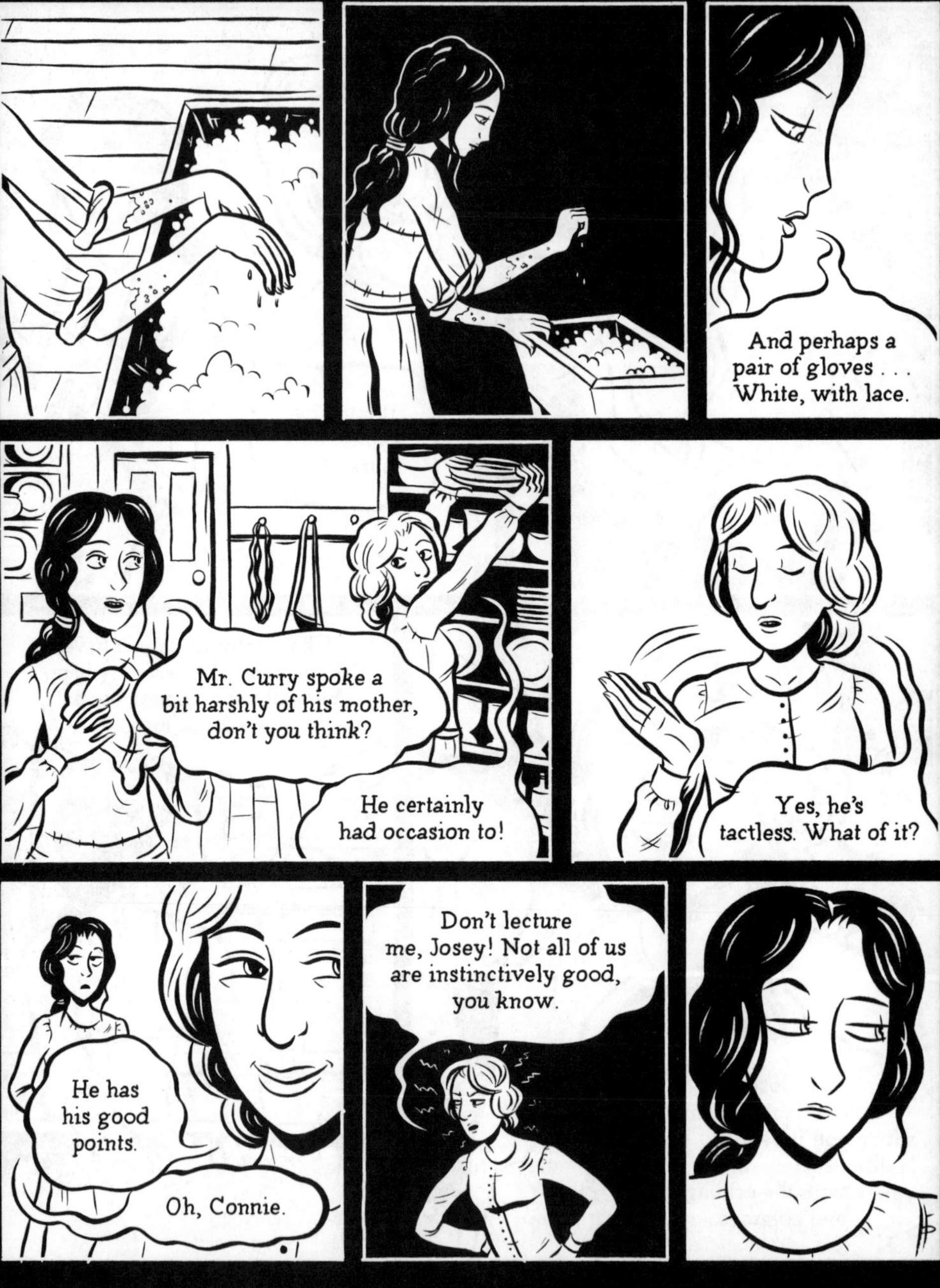
And perhaps a pair of gloves . . . White, with lace.
Mr. Curry spoke a bit harshly of his mother, don't you think?
He certainly had occasion to!
Yes, he's tactless. What of it?
He has his good points.
Oh, Connie.
Don't lecture me, Josey! Not all of us are instinctively good, you know.

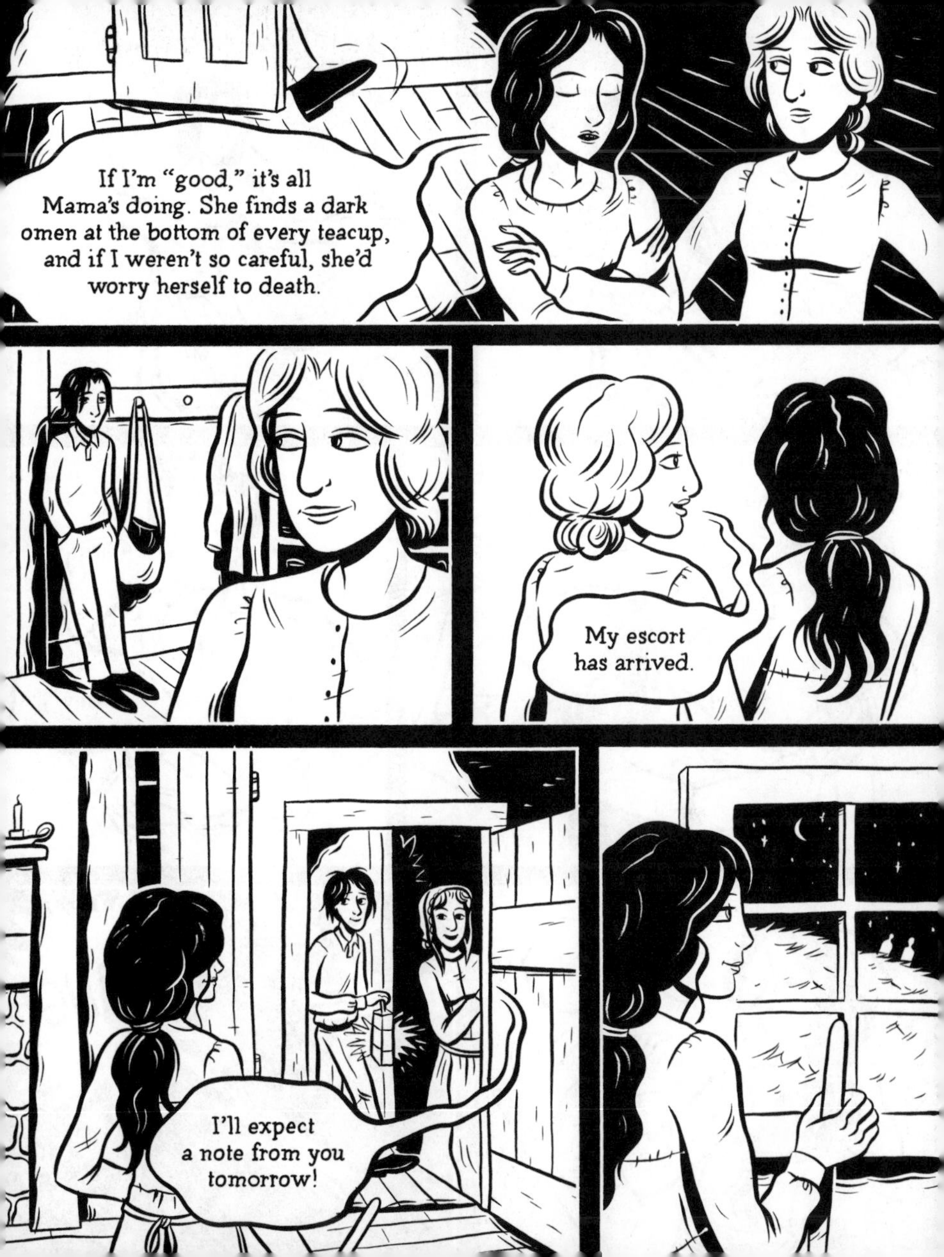
If I'm "good," it's all Mama's doing. She finds a dark omen at the bottom of every teacup, and if I weren't so careful, she'd worry herself to death.
My escort has arrived.
I'll expect a note from you tomorrow!

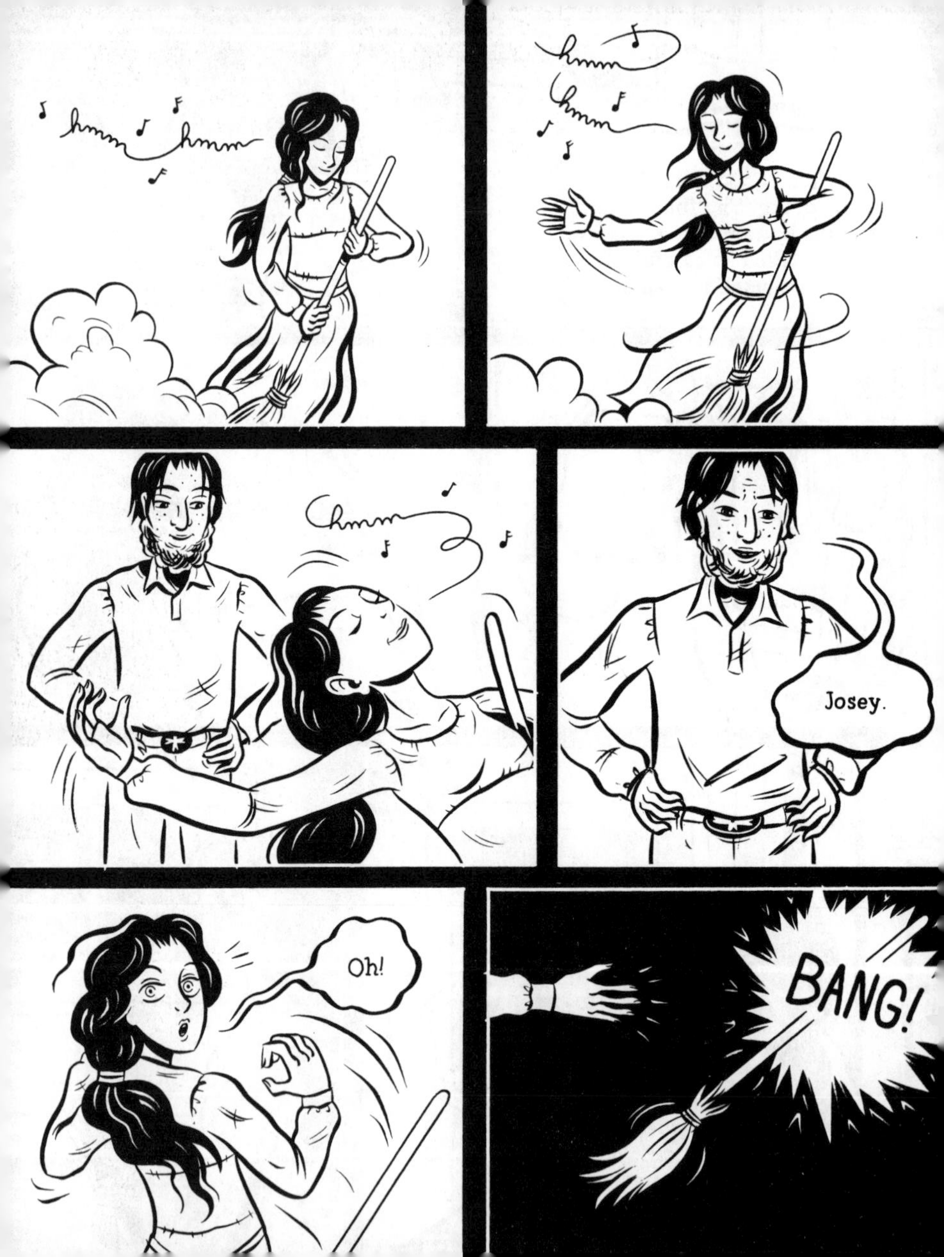
hmm hmm
hmm hmm
hmm
Josey.
Oh!
BANG!

You startled me, Papa!

In the morning I'll be going with Mr. Curry to verify his claim.

But Mama's coming home tomorrow! She'll be angry, and—

Josephine . . .

sigh

We'll be home by dark. She can berate me then.

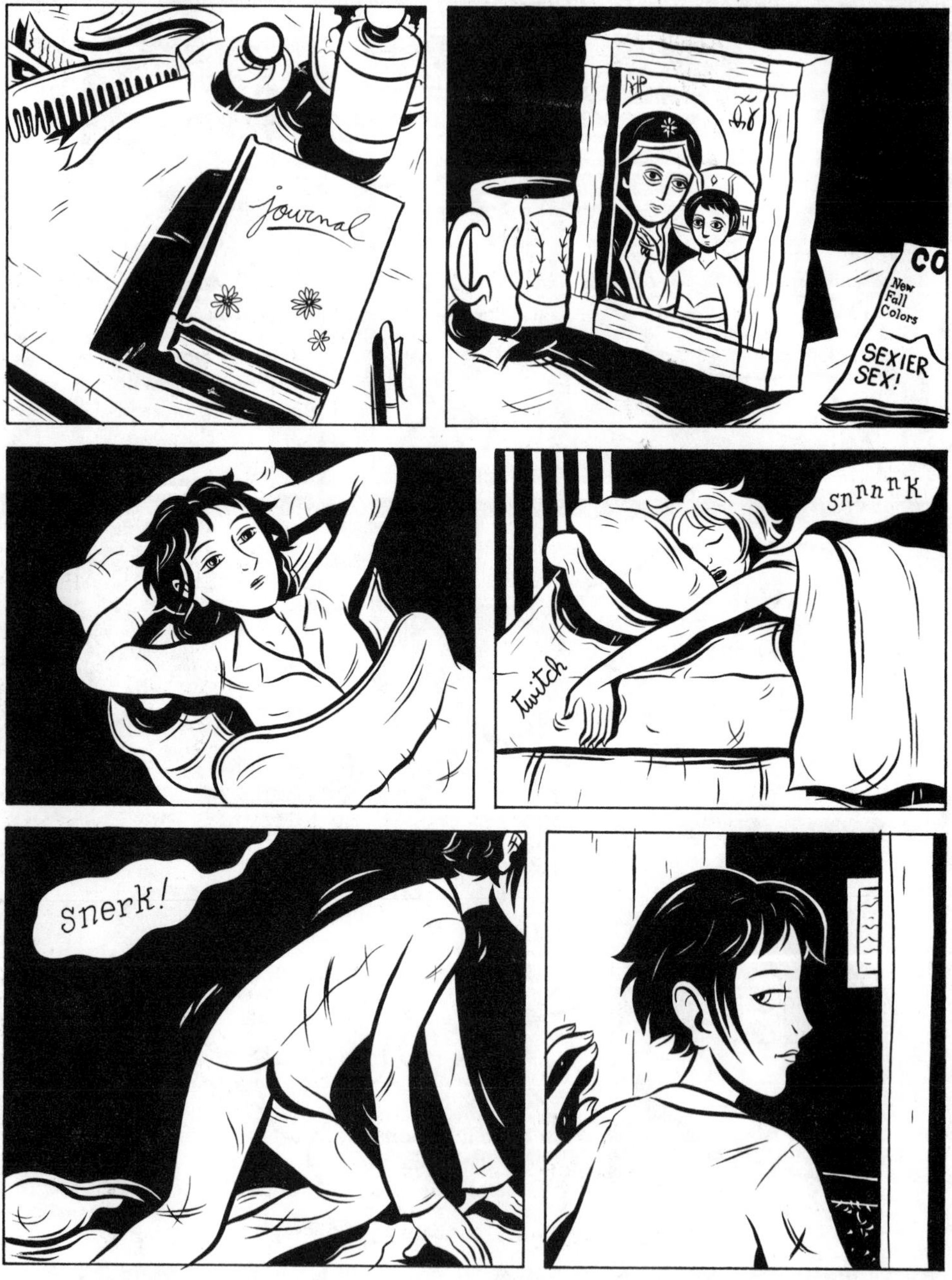
journal
CO
New Fall Colors
SEXIER SEX!
snnnnK
twitch
snerk!

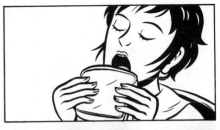

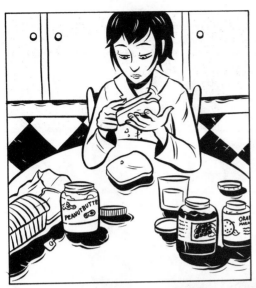

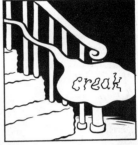

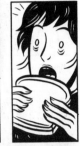

PEANUTBUTTE
ORA
MARM
creak
I thought I heard a little mouse down here.
KIES
Sorry, did I wake you?
. . .
PEANUTB
Oh, no. I was reading.

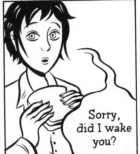

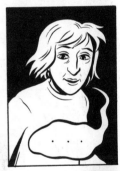

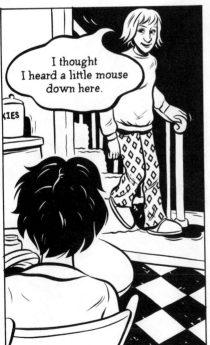

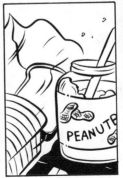

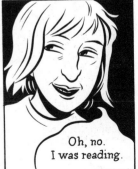

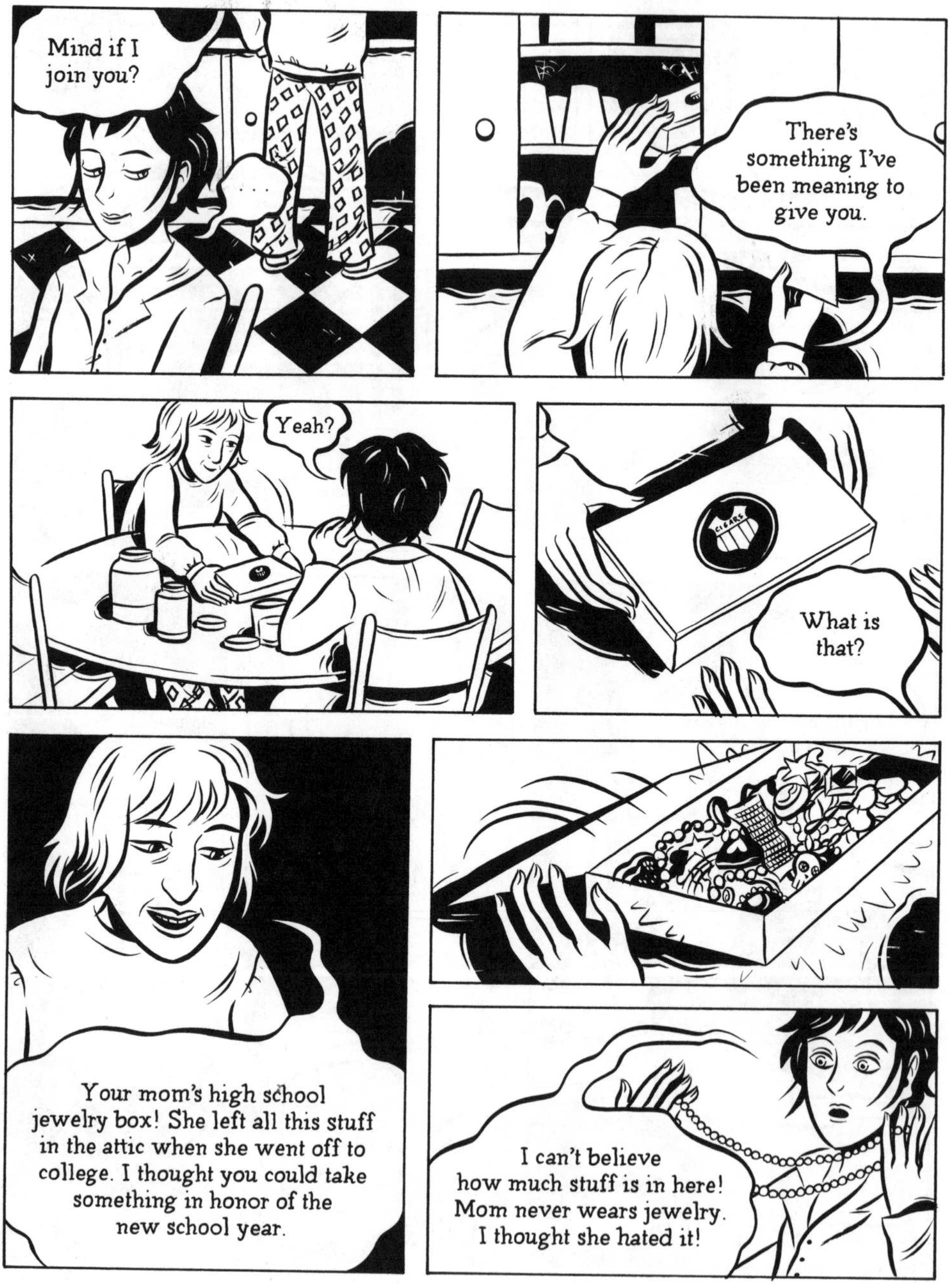
Mind if I join you?
. . .
There's something I've been meaning to give you.
Yeah?
CIGARS
What is that?
Your mom's high school jewelry box! She left all this stuff in the attic when she went off to college. I thought you could take something in honor of the new school year.
I can't believe how much stuff is in here! Mom never wears jewelry. I thought she hated it!

Ha, ha! No.

Just wedding rings.

Hey, *Dad* was the one who'd leave his ring at home and go bar hopping.

So I've heard.

Let's forget I said anything.

I imagine the oil sands* don't provide Kat with many opportunities to dress up. We should send her to the spa for Christmas, remind her she's still female.

Maybe the two of you could go together, hm?

*The Athabasca Oil Sands, an oil-rich region in northern Alberta.

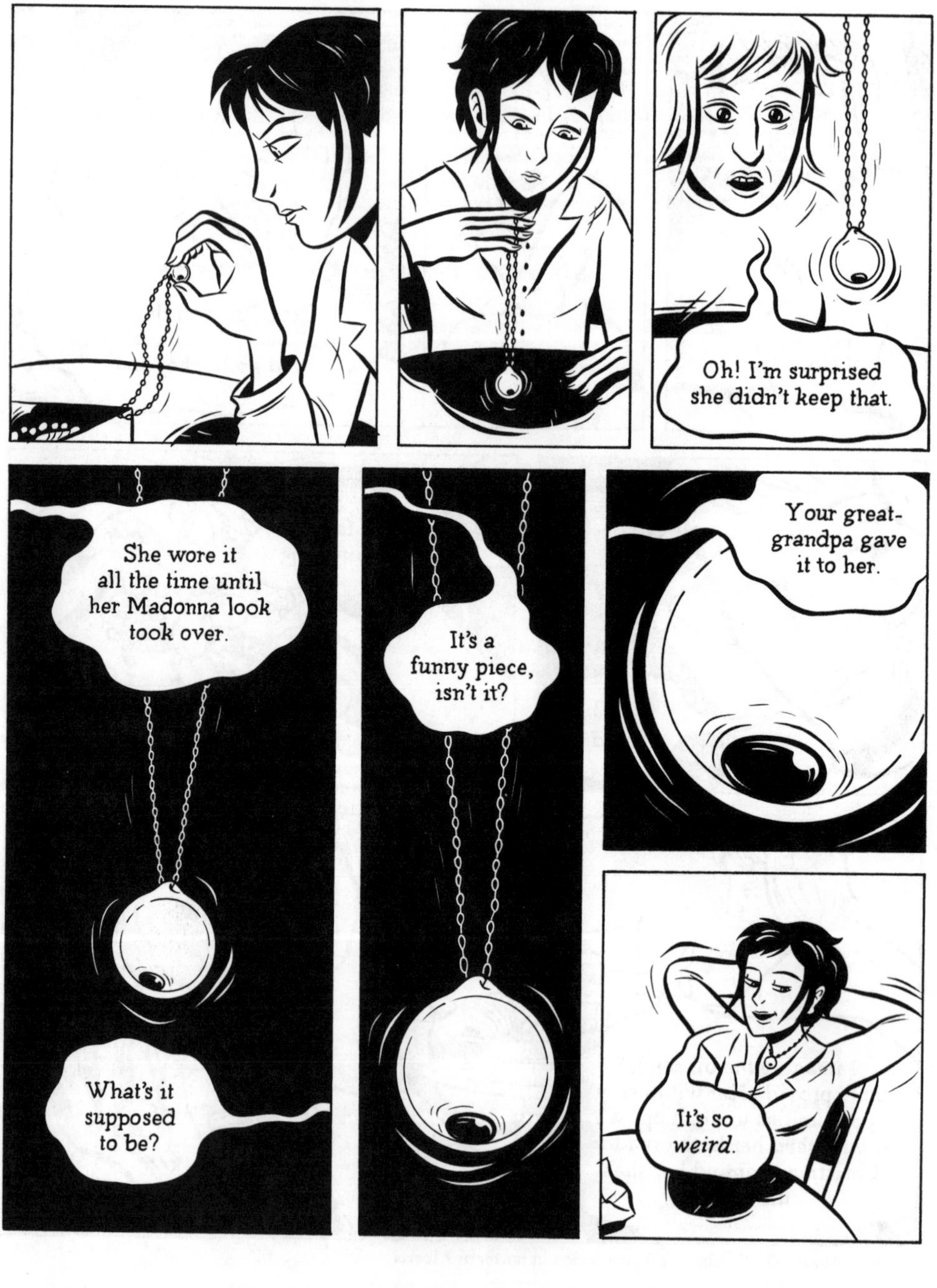
Oh! I'm surprised she didn't keep that.
She wore it all the time until her Madonna look took over.
What's it supposed to be?
It's a funny piece, isn't it?
Your great-grandpa gave it to her.
It's so *weird*.

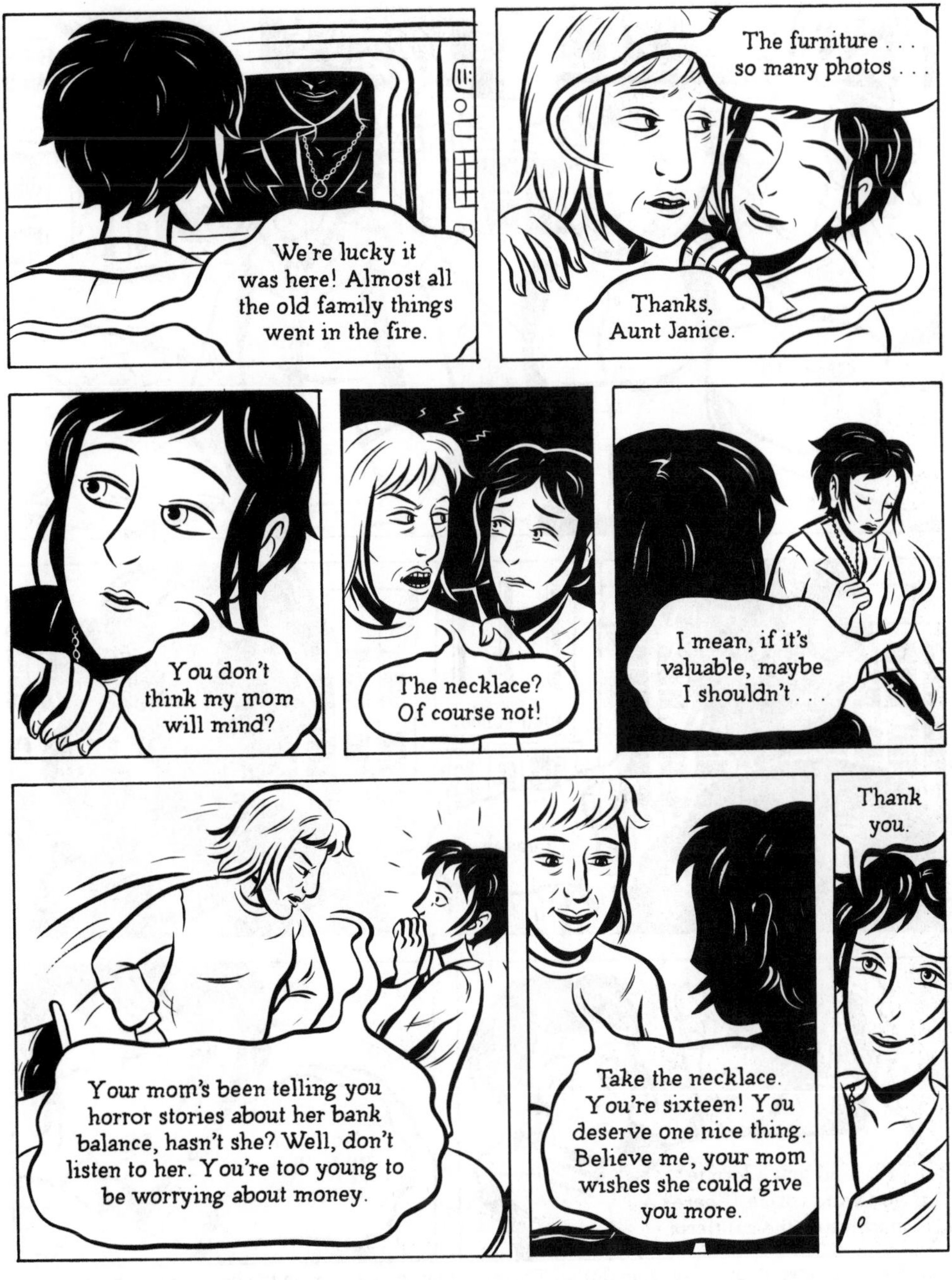
We're lucky it was here! Almost all the old family things went in the fire.
The furniture . . . so many photos . . .
Thanks, Aunt Janice.
You don't think my mom will mind?
The necklace? Of course not!
I mean, if it's valuable, maybe I shouldn't . . .
Your mom's been telling you horror stories about her bank balance, hasn't she? Well, don't listen to her. You're too young to be worrying about money.
Take the necklace. You're sixteen! You deserve one nice thing. Believe me, your mom wishes she could give you more.
Thank you.

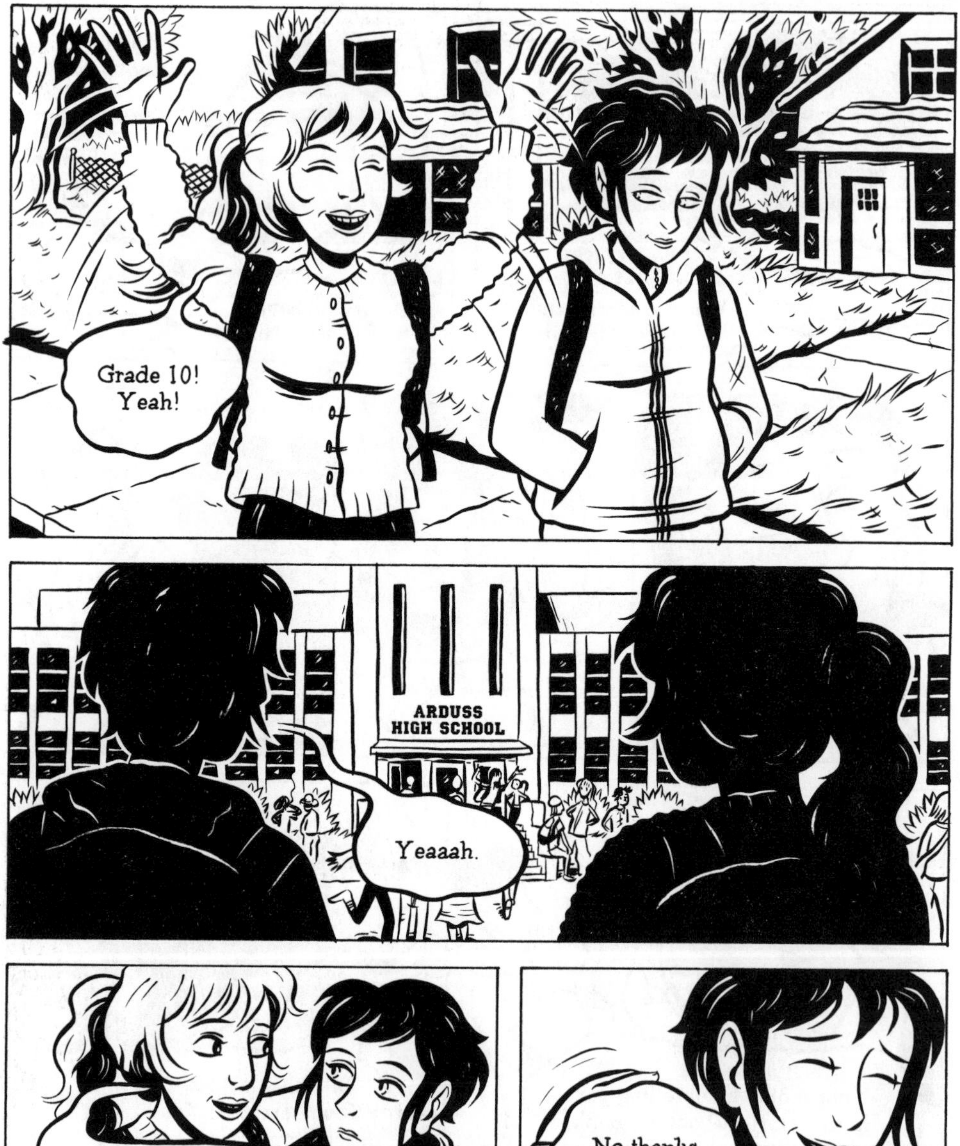
Grade 10!
Yeah!
ARDUSS
HIGH SCHOOL
Yeaaah.
I'll lend you a loonie*
if you want coffee. There's a
machine in the cafeteria.
No thanks.
I'll be fine in
a minute.

*loonie: A coin worth one Canadian dollar. There's a picture of a loon on the back, hence the name.

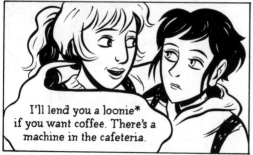

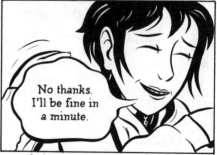

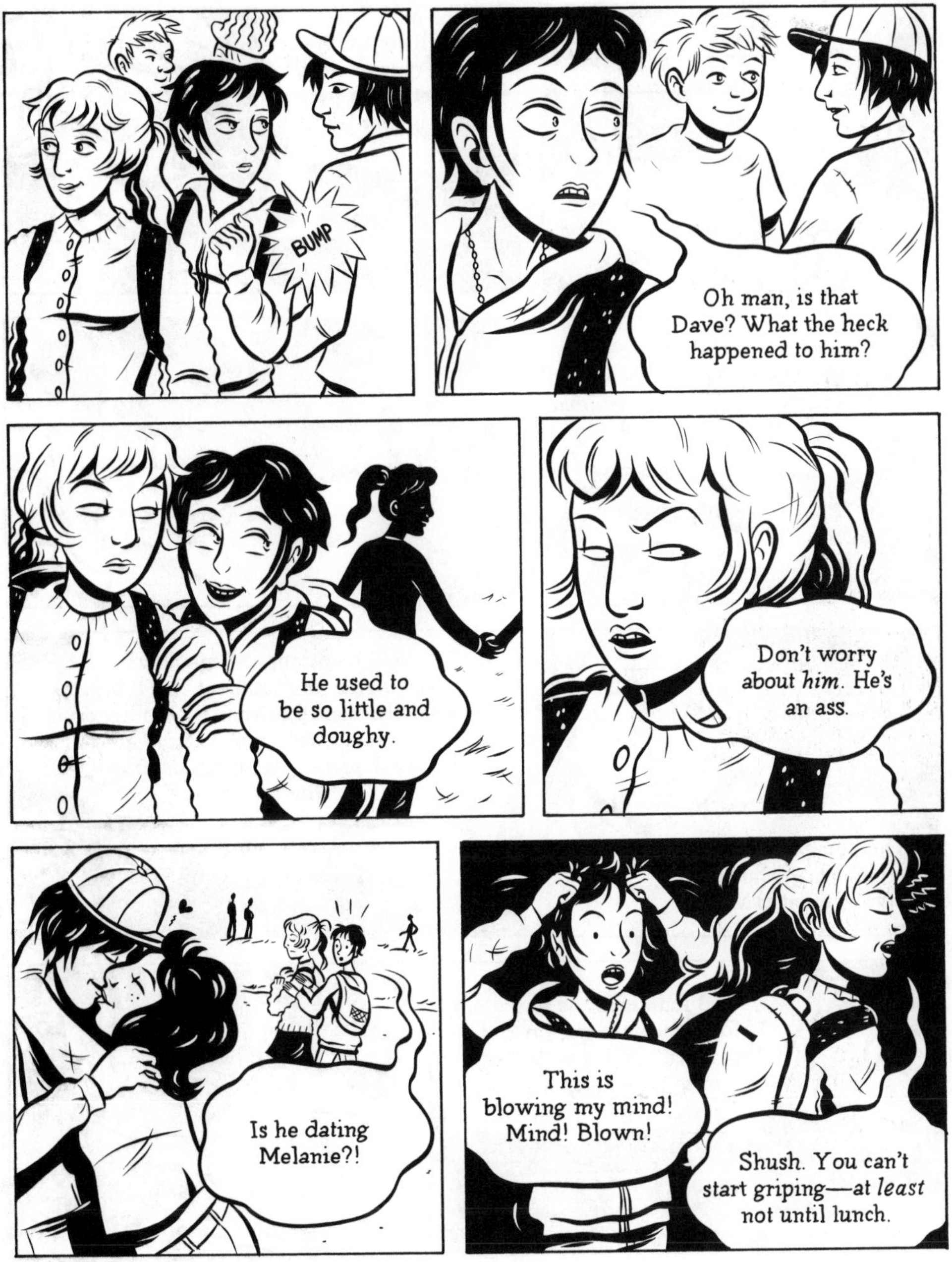
BUMP
Oh man, is that Dave? What the heck happened to him?
He used to be so little and doughy.
Don't worry about *him*. He's an ass.
Is he dating Melanie?!
This is blowing my mind! Mind! Blown!
Shush. You can't start griping—at *least* not until lunch.

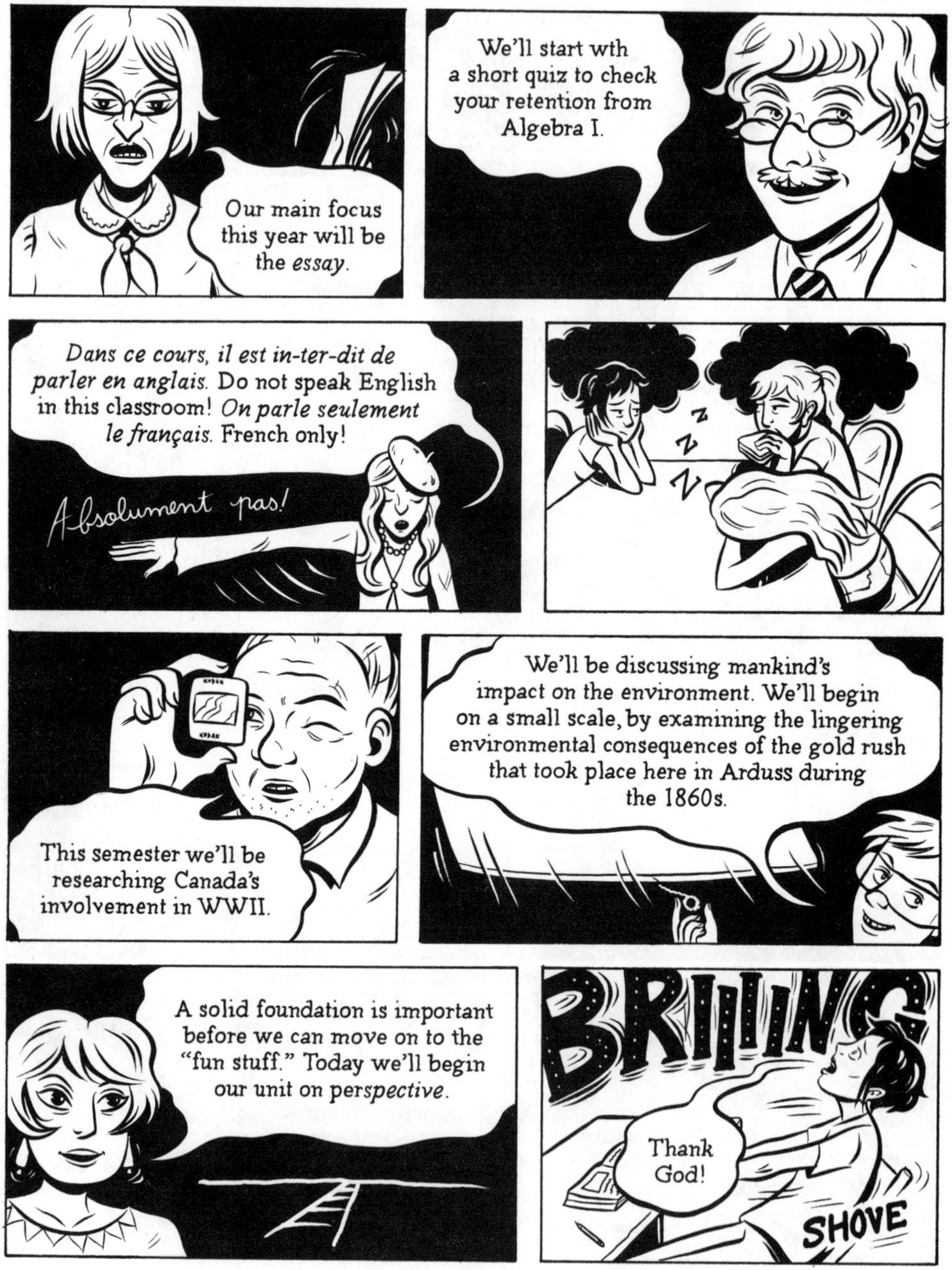

Our main focus this year will be the *essay*.
We'll start wth a short quiz to check your retention from Algebra I.
Dans ce cours, il est in-ter-dit de parler en anglais. Do not speak English in this classroom! *On parle seulement le français.* French only!
Absolument pas!
Z Z Z
This semester we'll be researching Canada's involvement in WWII.
We'll be discussing mankind's impact on the environment. We'll begin on a small scale, by examining the lingering environmental consequences of the gold rush that took place here in Arduss during the 1860s.
A solid foundation is important before we can move on to the "fun stuff." Today we'll begin our unit on per*spective*.
BRIIING
Thank God!
SHOVE

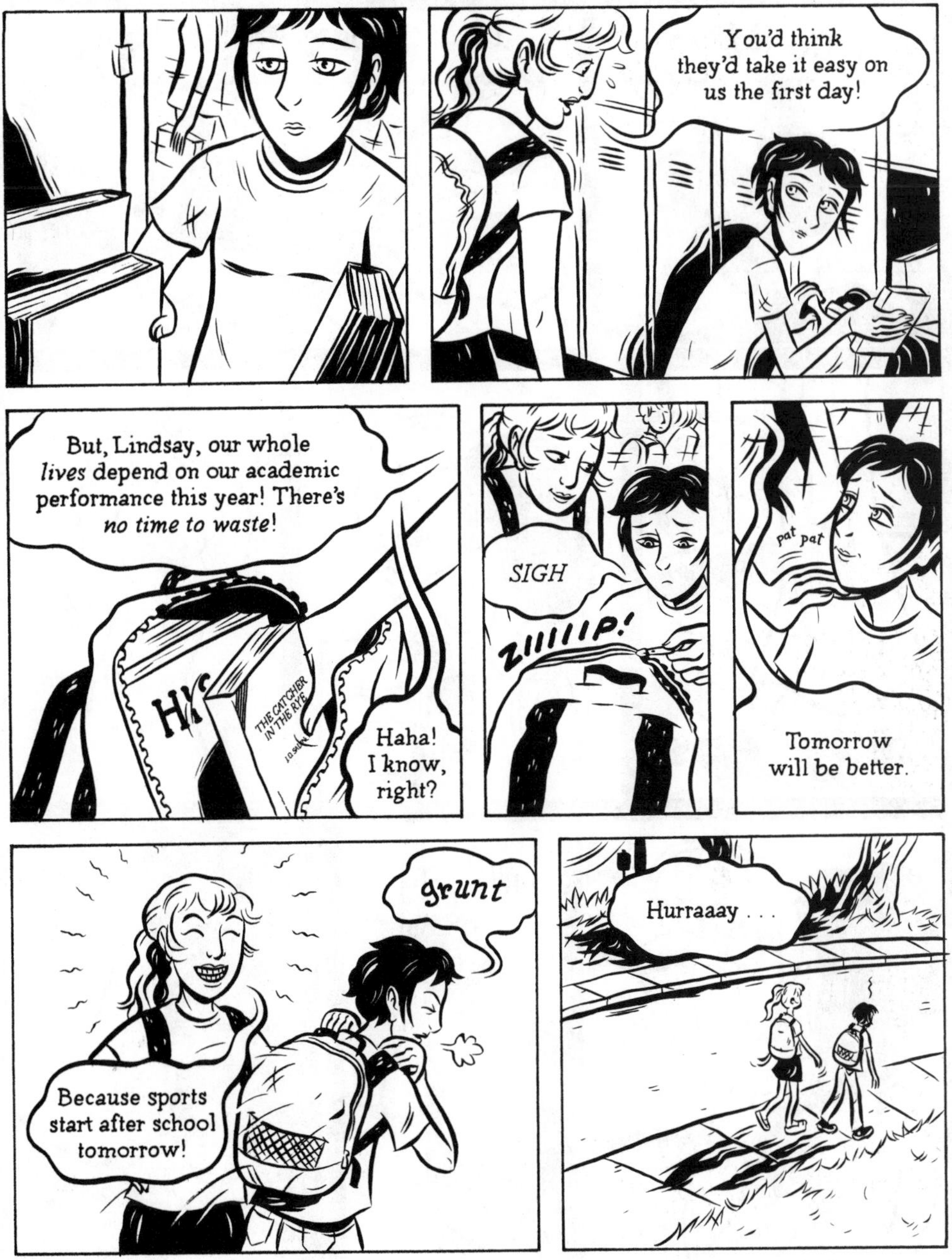

You'd think they'd take it easy on us the first day!
But, Lindsay, our whole *lives* depend on our academic performance this year! There's *no time to waste*!
THE CATCHER IN THE RYE
Haha! I know, right?
SIGH
ZIIIIIP!
pat pat
Tomorrow will be better.
grunt
Because sports start after school tomorrow!
Hurraaay . . .

CO CO Ri CO!
yawn
SHUT!
Z
creeeee

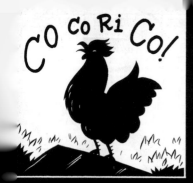

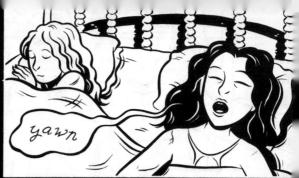

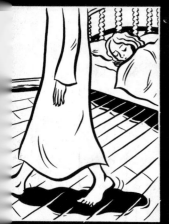

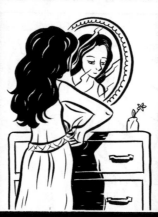

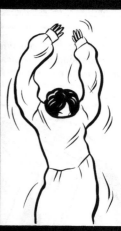

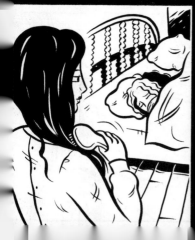

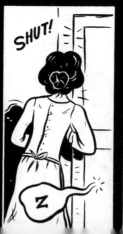

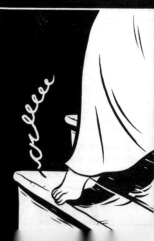

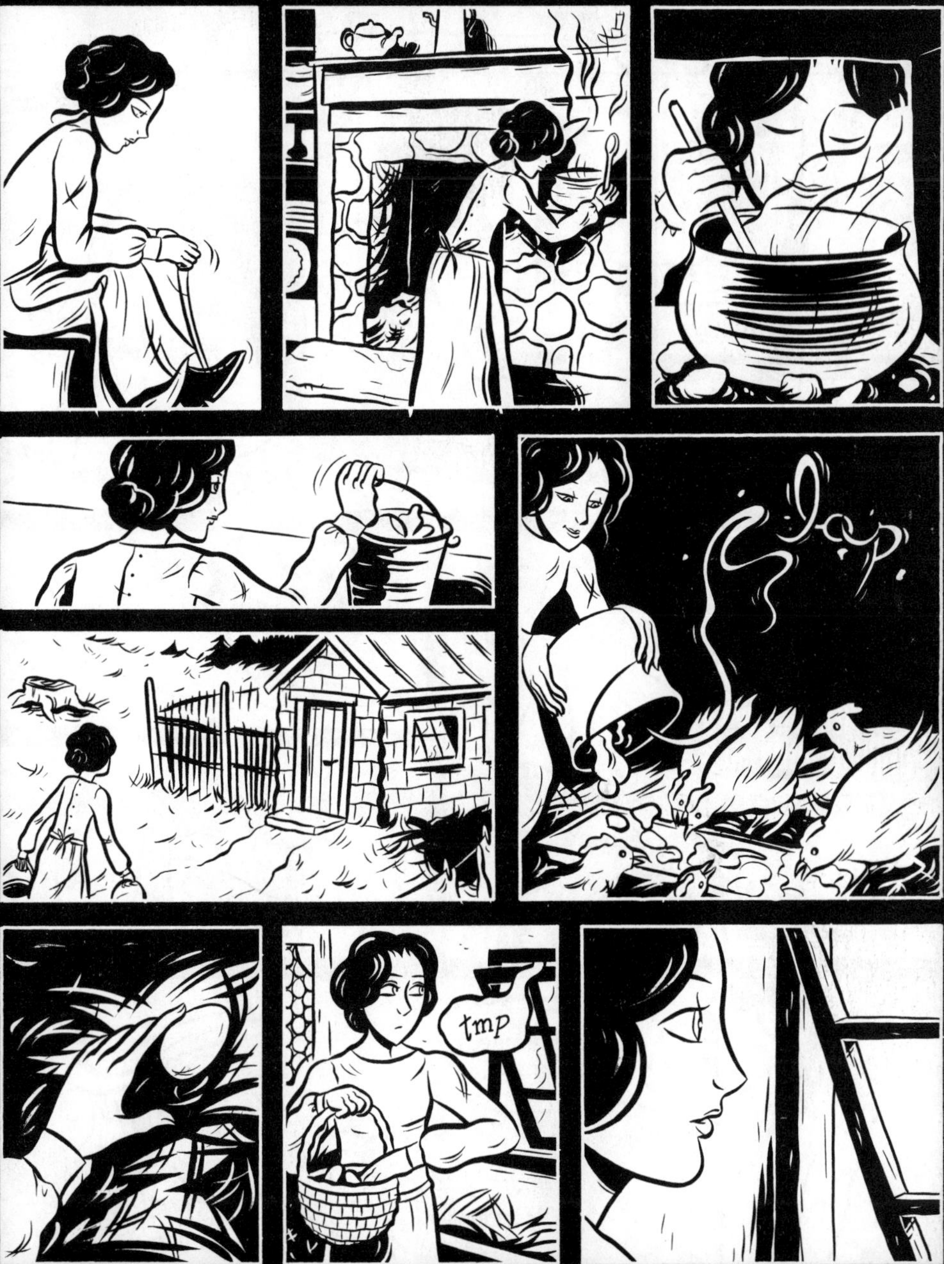
slap
tmp

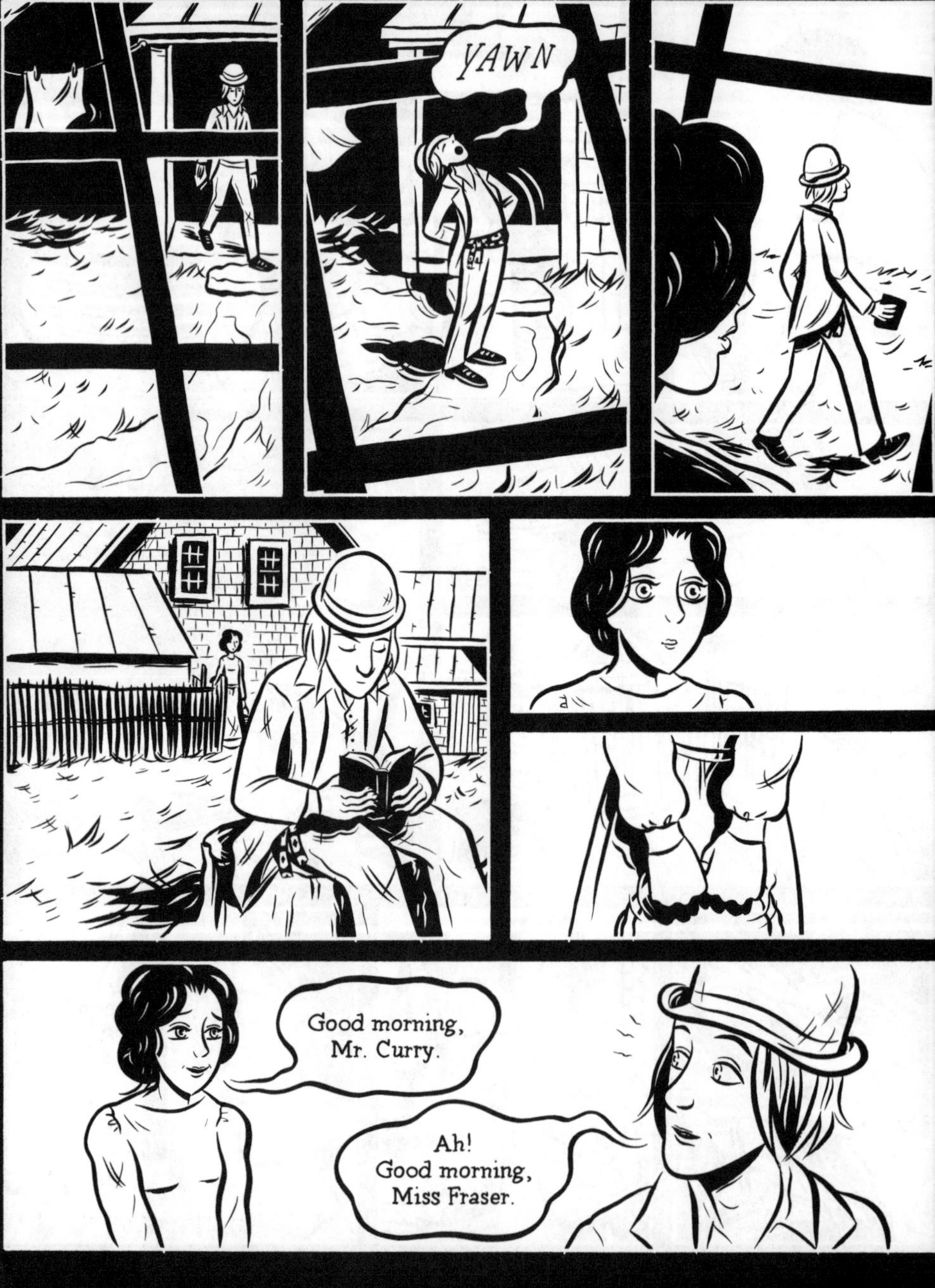
YAWN
Good morning, Mr. Curry.
Ah! Good morning, Miss Fraser.

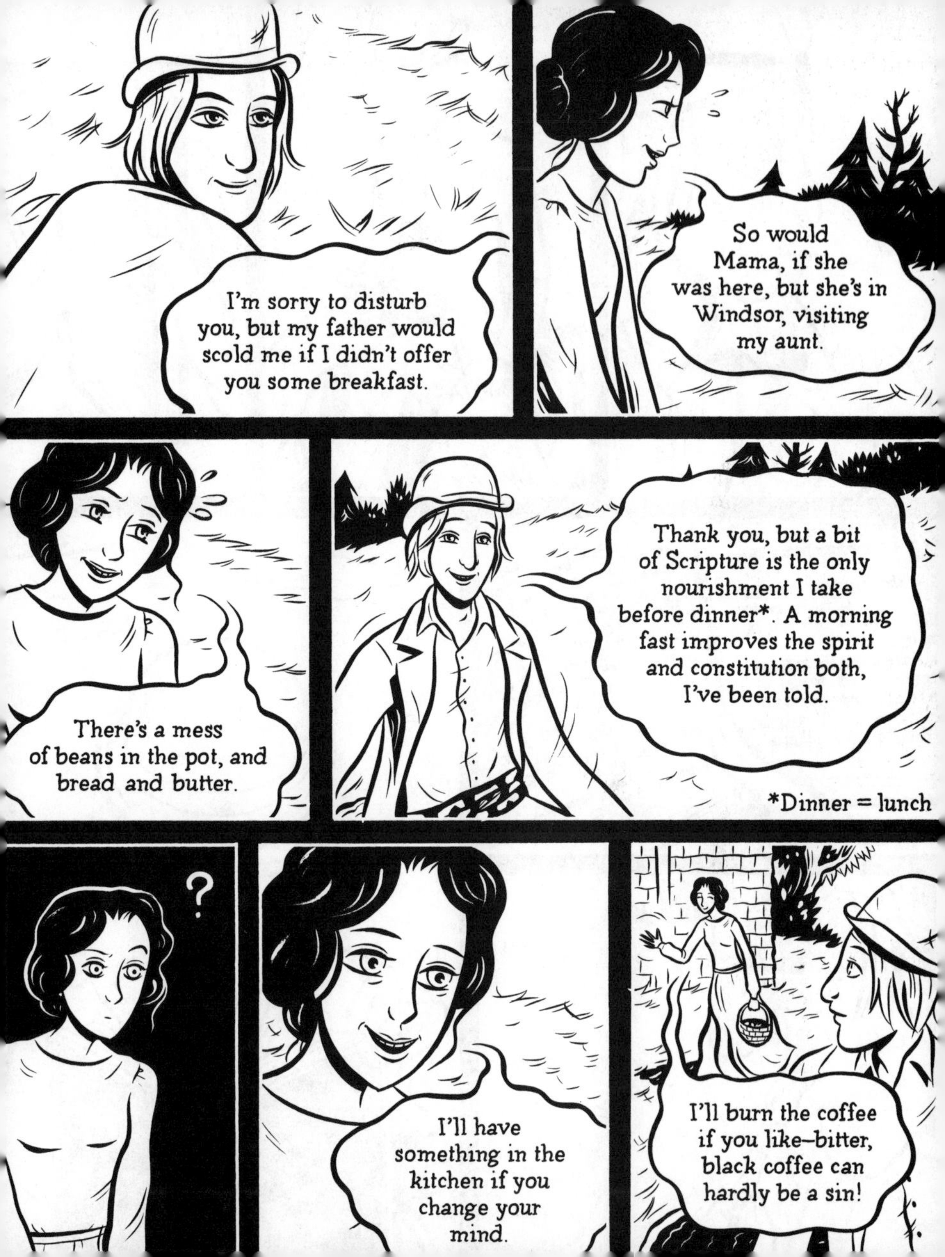
I'm sorry to disturb you, but my father would scold me if I didn't offer you some breakfast.
So would Mama, if she was here, but she's in Windsor, visiting my aunt.
There's a mess of beans in the pot, and bread and butter.
Thank you, but a bit of Scripture is the only nourishment I take before dinner*. A morning fast improves the spirit and constitution both, I've been told.
*Dinner = lunch
?
I'll have something in the kitchen if you change your mind.
I'll burn the coffee if you like–bitter, black coffee can hardly be a sin!

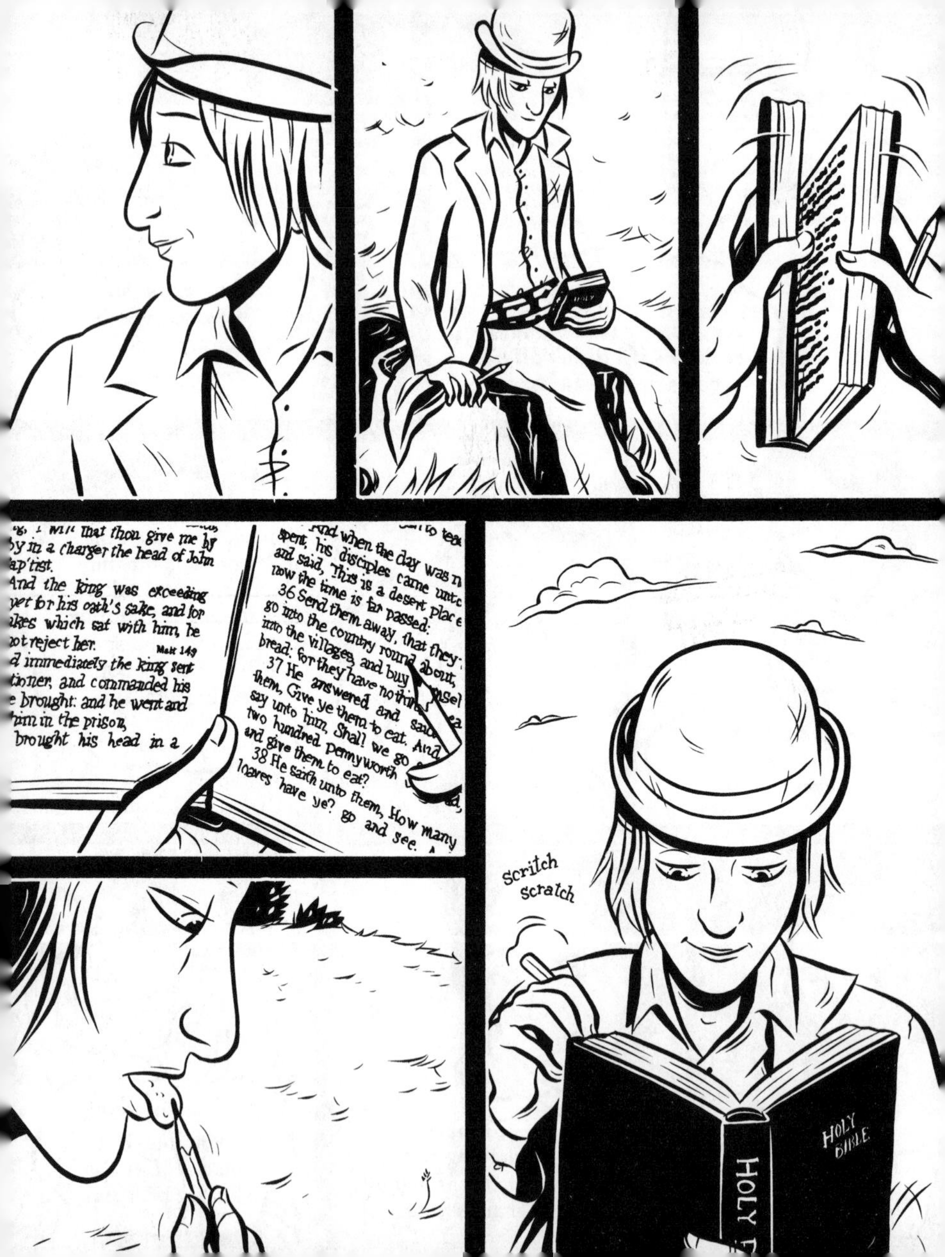

HOLY
that thou give me by
by in a charger the head of John
ap'tist.
And the king was exceeding
yet for his oath's sake, and for
akes which sat with him, he
ot reject her.
Matt 14:9
d immediately the king sent
tioner, and commanded his
e brought: and he went and
him in the prison,
brought his head in a
And when the day was
spent, his disciples came unto
and said, This is a desert place
now the time is far passed:
36 Send them away, that they
go into the country round about,
into the villages, and buy
bread: for they have nothing
37 He answered and said
them, Give ye them to eat. And
say unto him, Shall we go
two hundred pennyworth
and give them to eat?
38 He saith unto them, How many
loaves have ye? go and see.
Scritch
scratch
HOLY BIBLE
HOLY

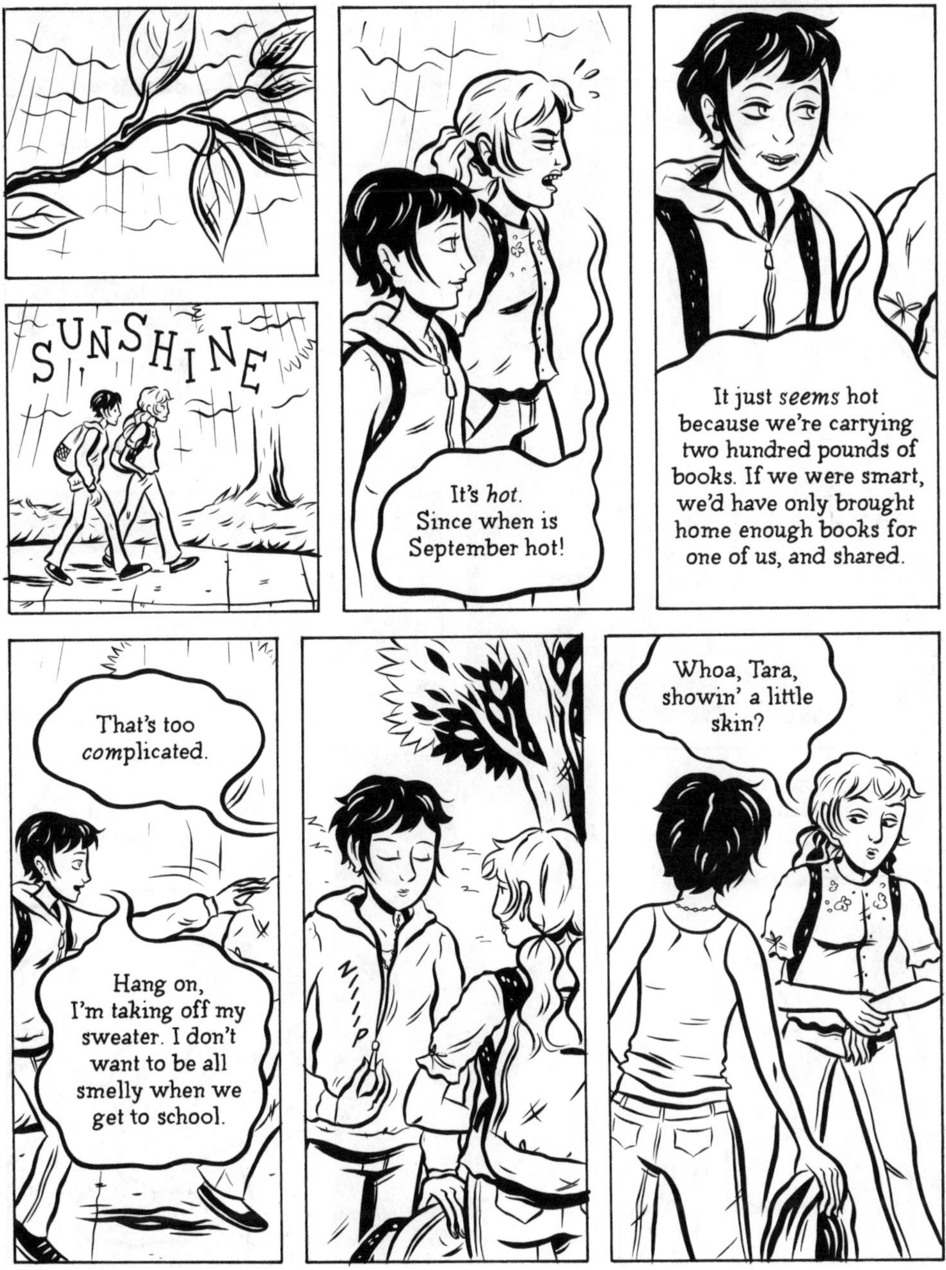
SUNSHINE
It's *hot*. Since when is September hot!
It just *seems* hot because we're carrying two hundred pounds of books. If we were smart, we'd have only brought home enough books for one of us, and shared.
That's too *com*plicated.
Hang on, I'm taking off my sweater. I don't want to be all smelly when we get to school.
ZIIIP
Whoa, Tara, showin' a little skin?

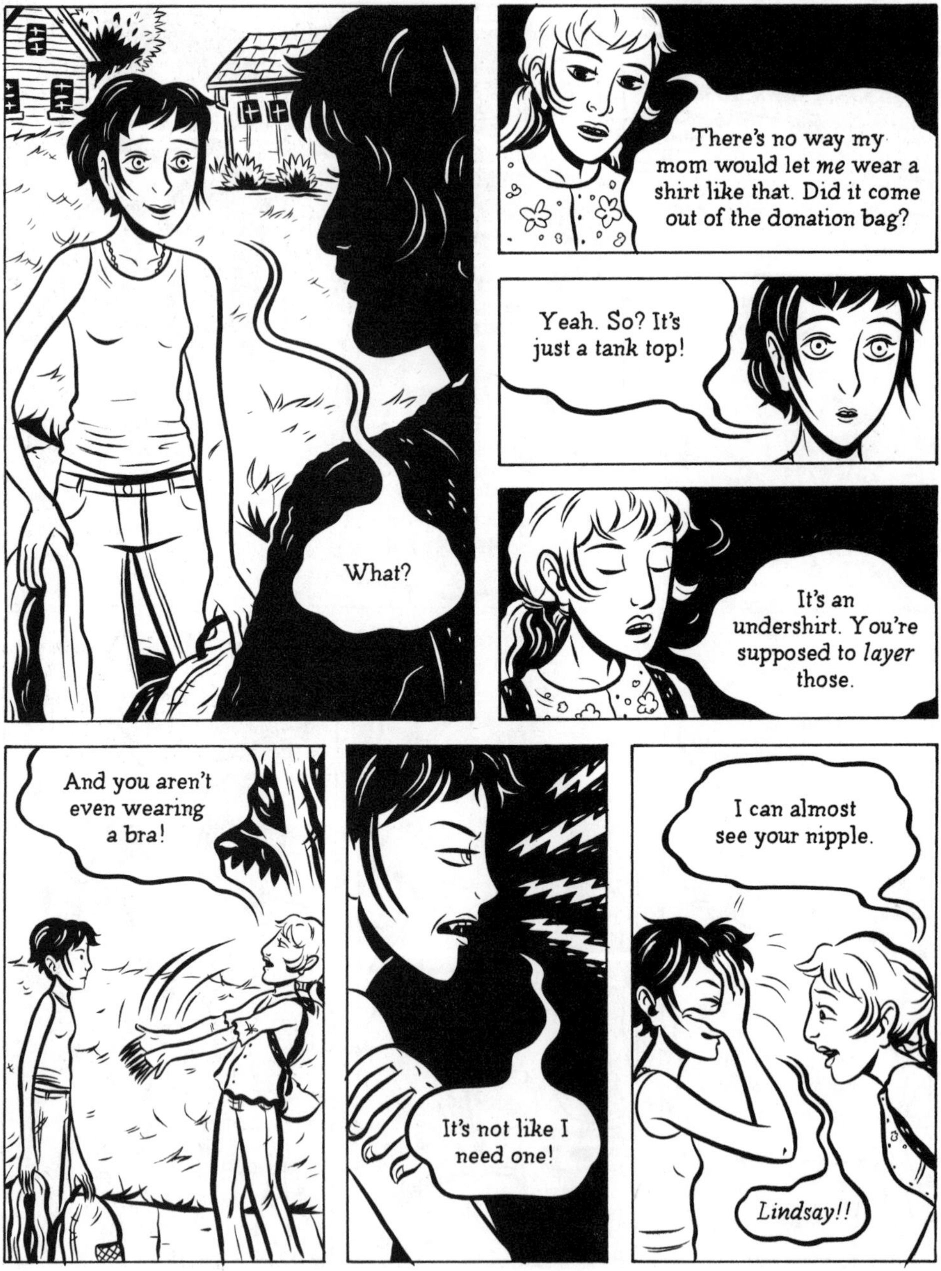
What?
There's no way my mom would let *me* wear a shirt like that. Did it come out of the donation bag?
Yeah. So? It's just a tank top!
It's an undershirt. You're supposed to *layer* those.
And you aren't even wearing a bra!
It's not like I need one!
I can almost see your nipple.
Lindsay!!

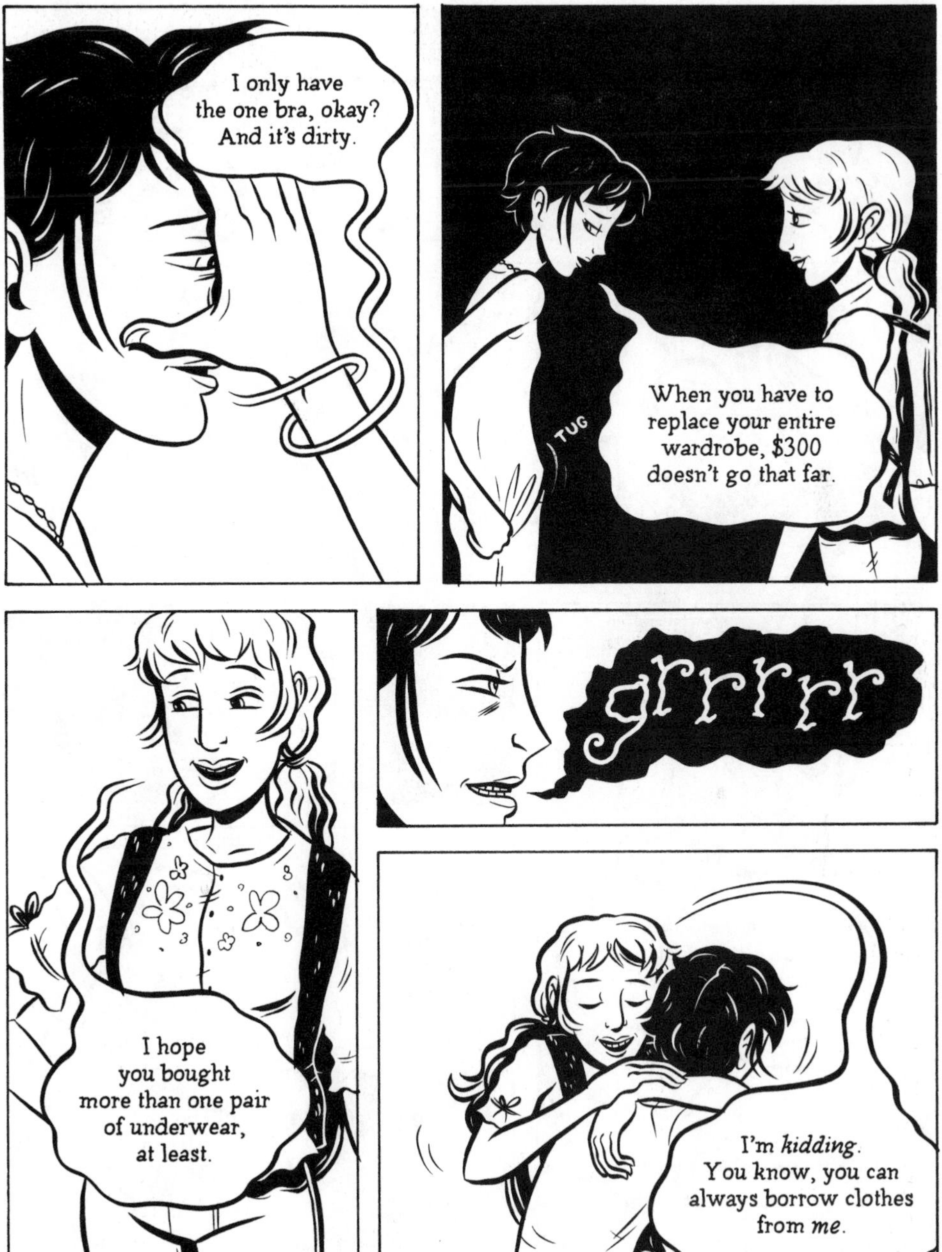
I only have the one bra, okay? And it's dirty.
TUG
When you have to replace your entire wardrobe, $300 doesn't go that far.
I hope you bought more than one pair of underwear, at least.
grrrrr
I'm *kidding*. You know, you can always borrow clothes from *me*.

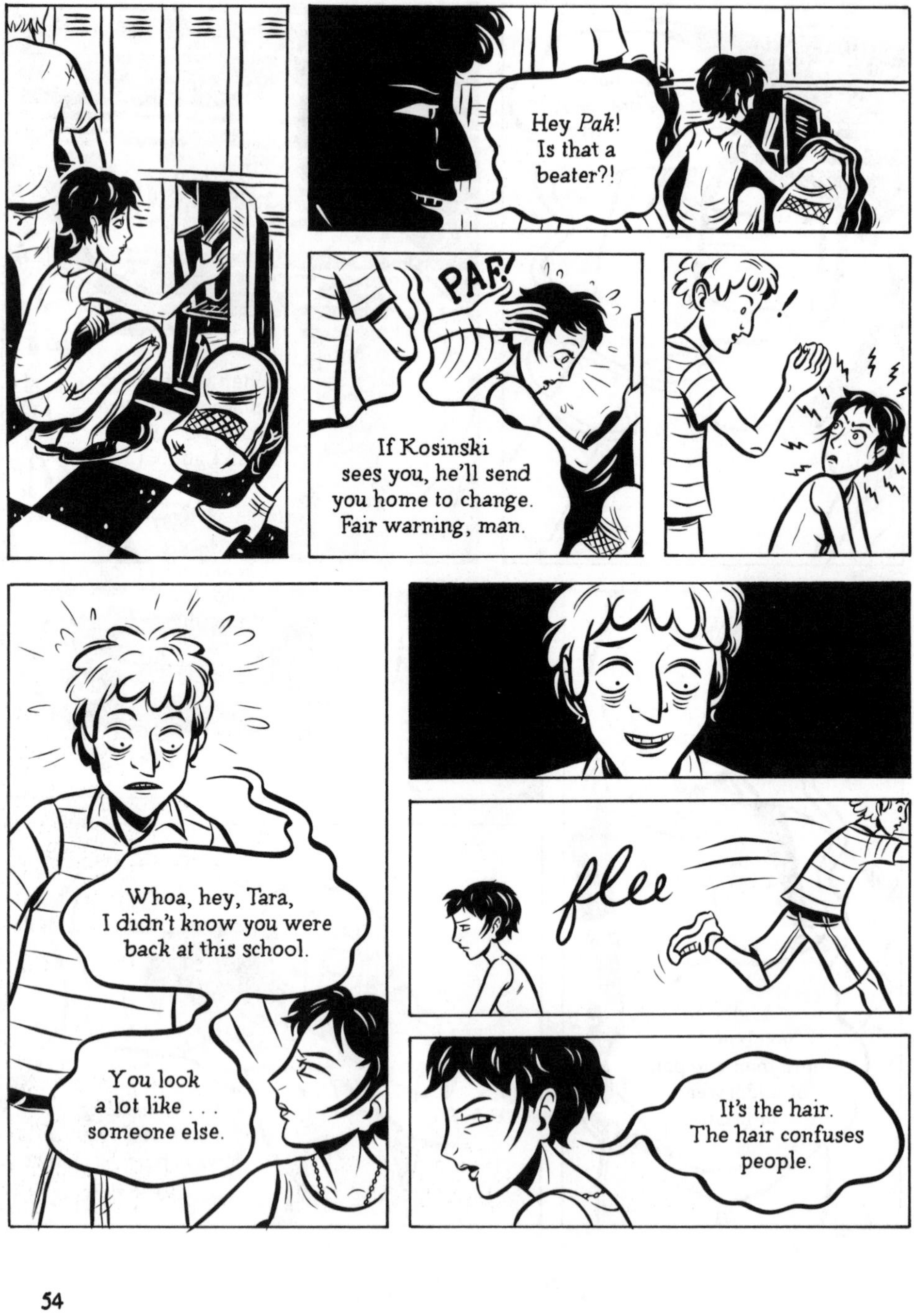
Hey *Pak*! Is that a beater?!
PAF!
If Kosinski sees you, he'll send you home to change. Fair warning, man.
!
Whoa, hey, Tara, I didn't know you were back at this school.
You look a lot like . . . someone else.
flee
It's the hair. The hair confuses people.

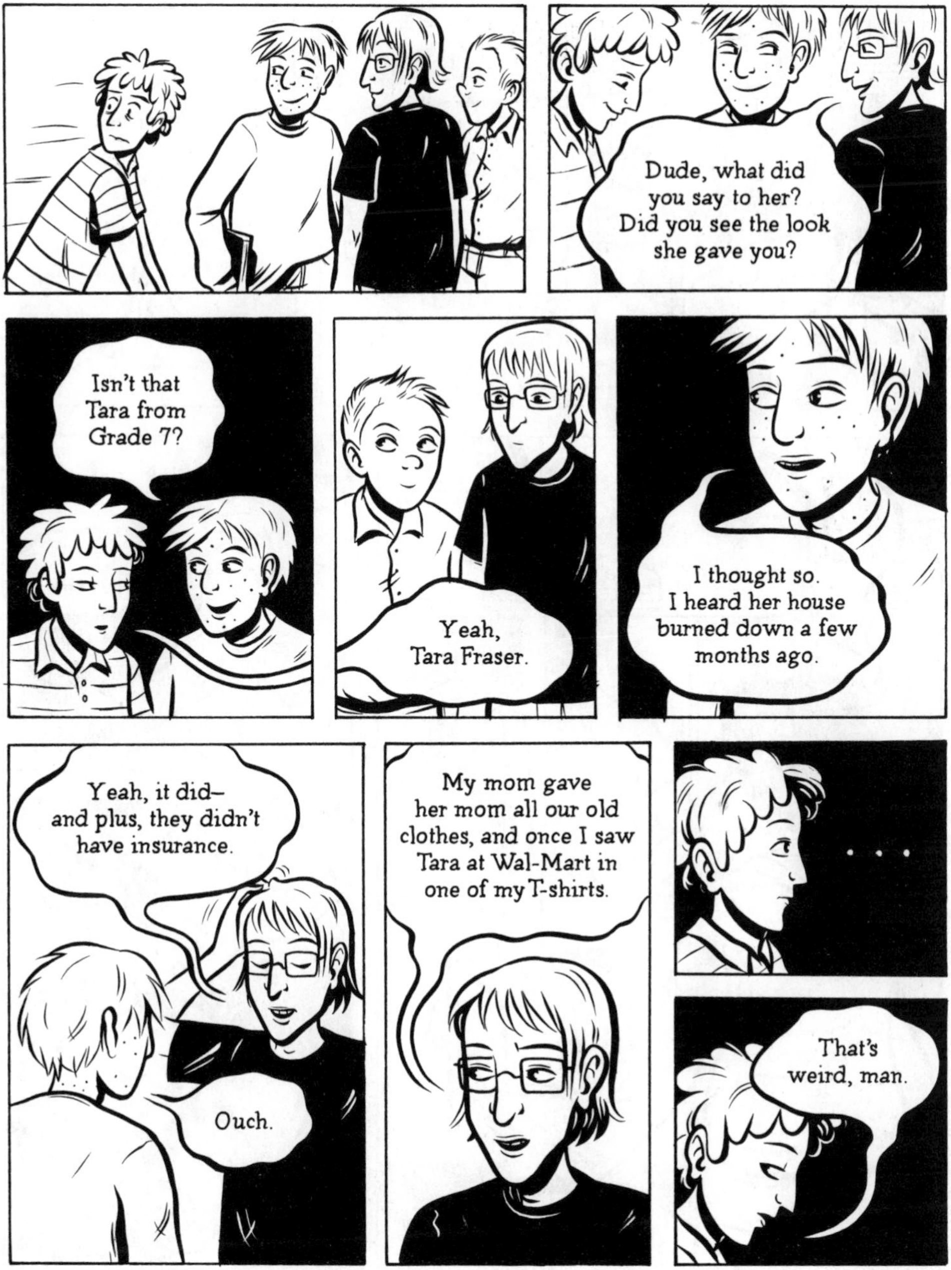
Dude, what did you say to her? Did you see the look she gave you?
Isn't that Tara from Grade 7?
Yeah, Tara Fraser.
I thought so. I heard her house burned down a few months ago.
Yeah, it did– and plus, they didn't have insurance.
Ouch.
My mom gave her mom all our old clothes, and once I saw Tara at Wal-Mart in one of my T-shirts.
. . .
That's weird, man.

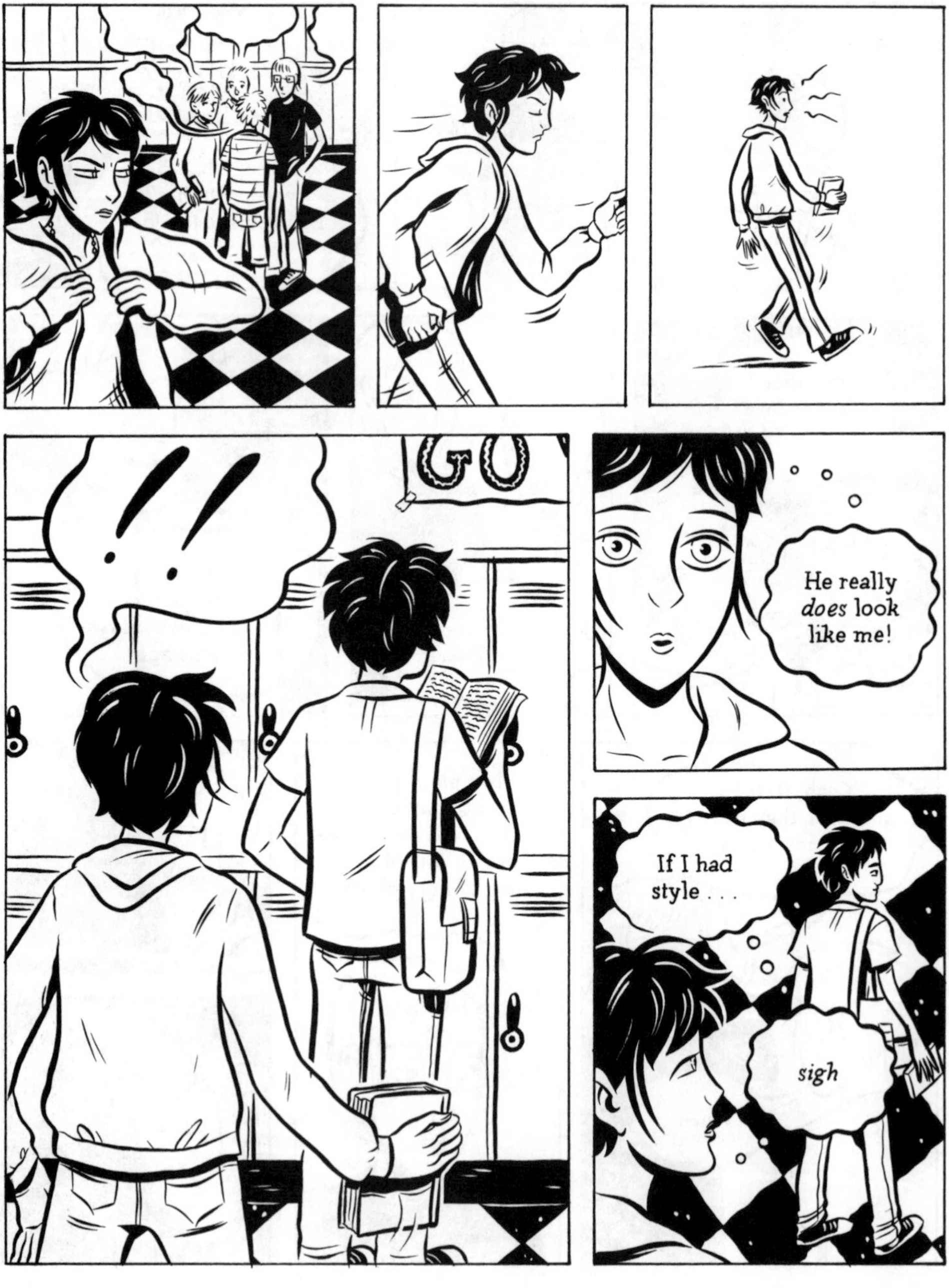
!!
He really *does* look like me!
If I had style . . .
sigh

What?
THUNK!
STUPID

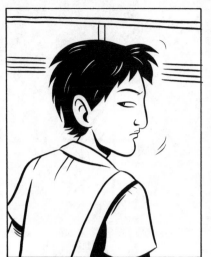

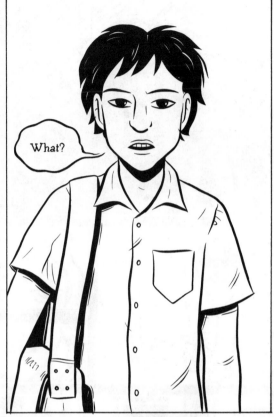

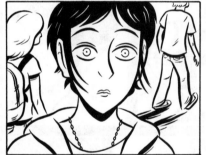

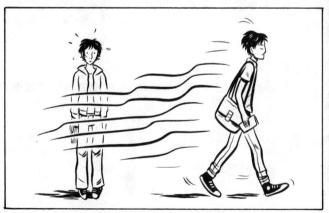

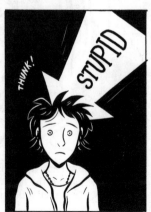

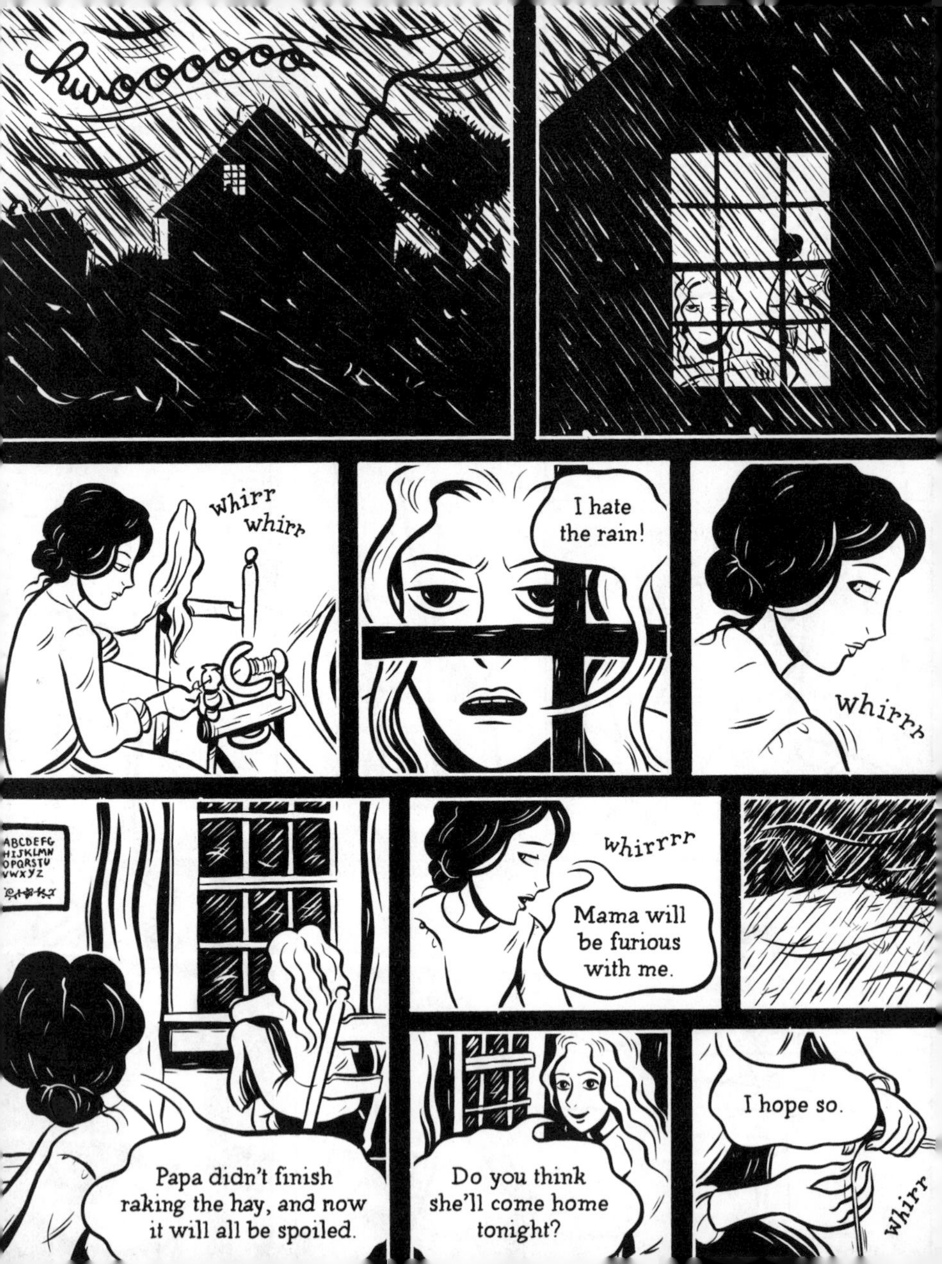
hwooooooo
whirr whirr
I hate the rain!
whirrr
Papa didn't finish raking the hay, and now it will all be spoiled.
whirrrr
Mama will be furious with me.
Do you think she'll come home tonight?
I hope so.
whirr

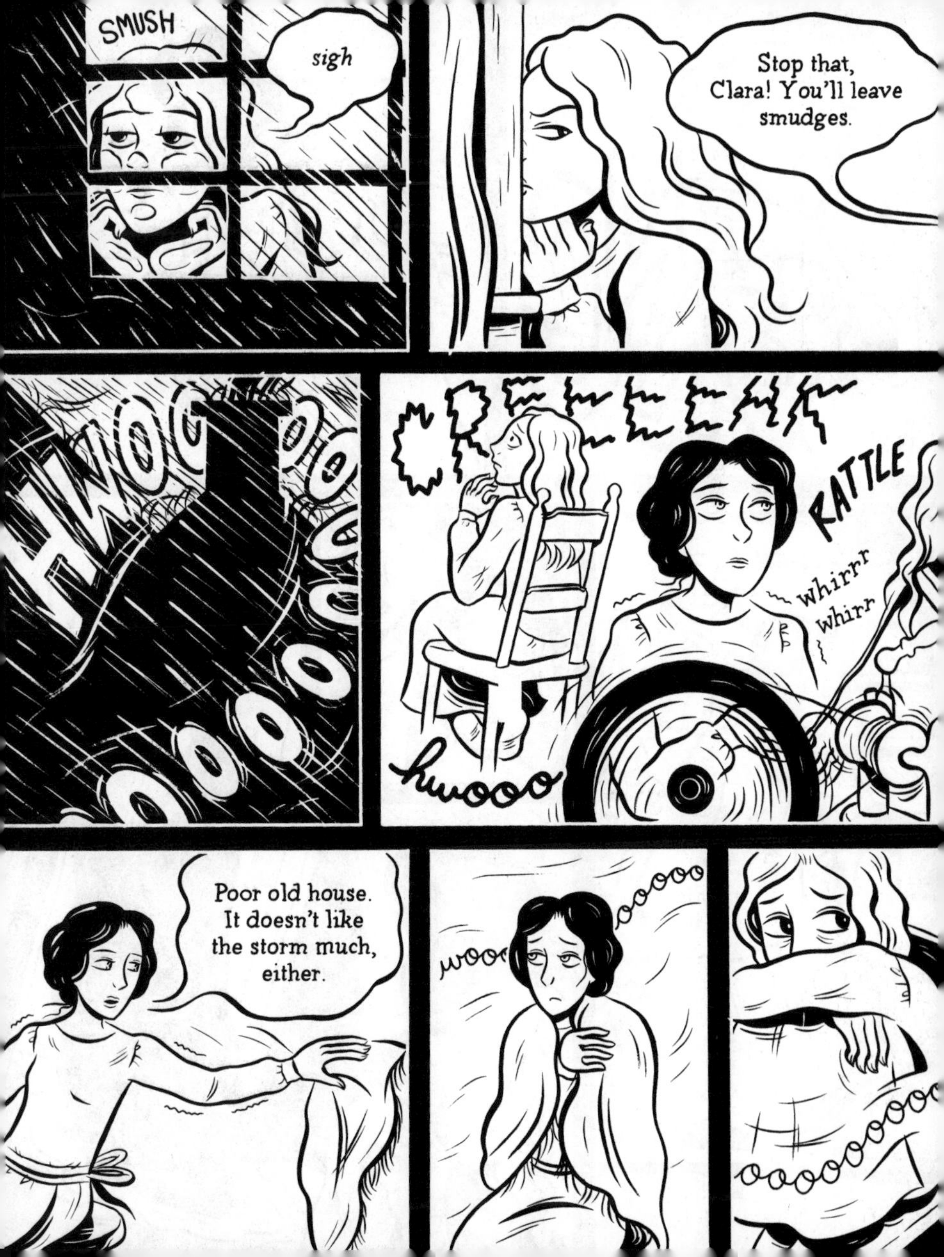
SMUSH
sigh
Stop that, Clara! You'll leave smudges.
HWOOOOOOOOO
CREEEAK
RATTLE
whirrr whirrr
hwooo
Poor old house. It doesn't like the storm much, either.
ooooo
woo
oooooooooo

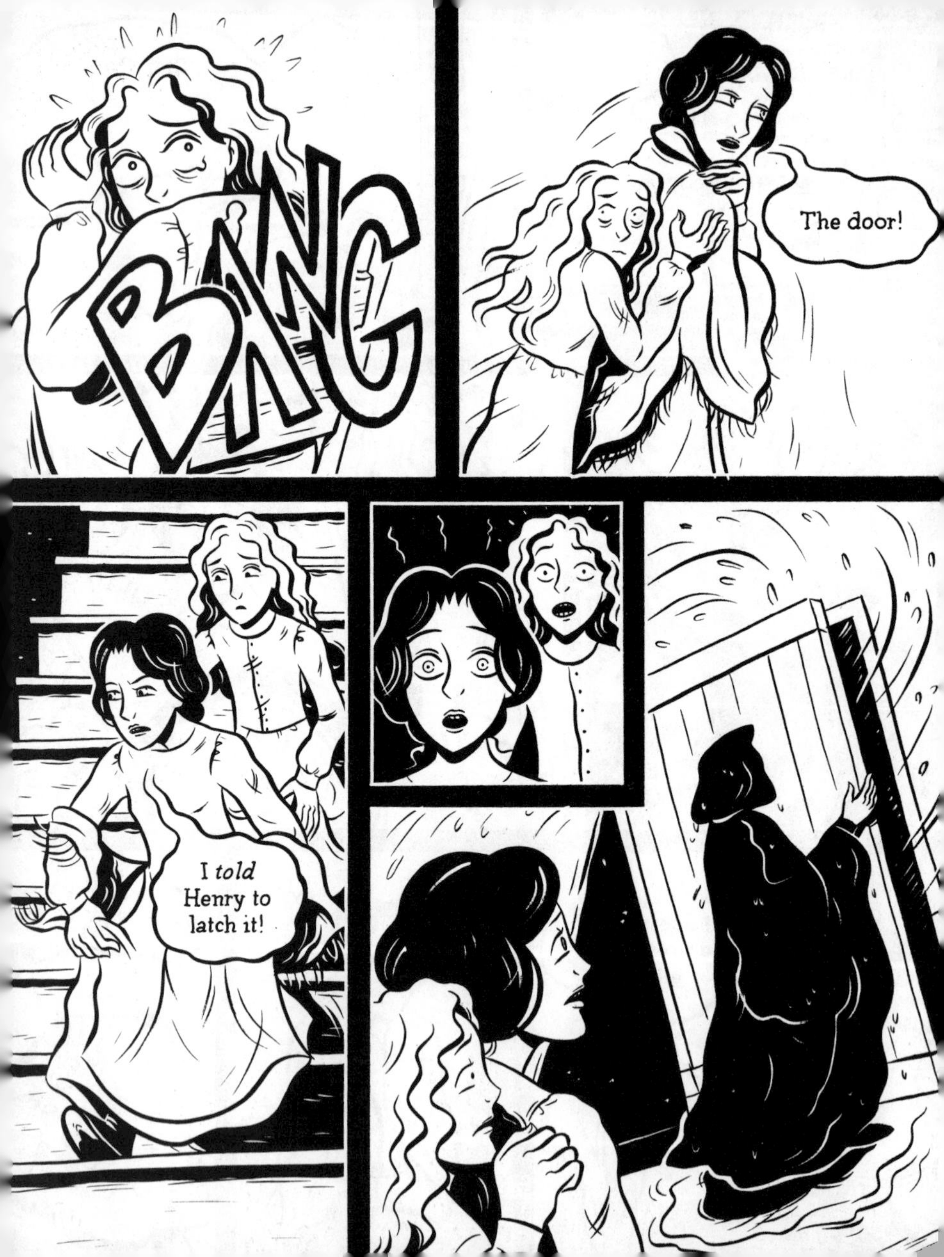
BANG
The door!
I *told* Henry to latch it!

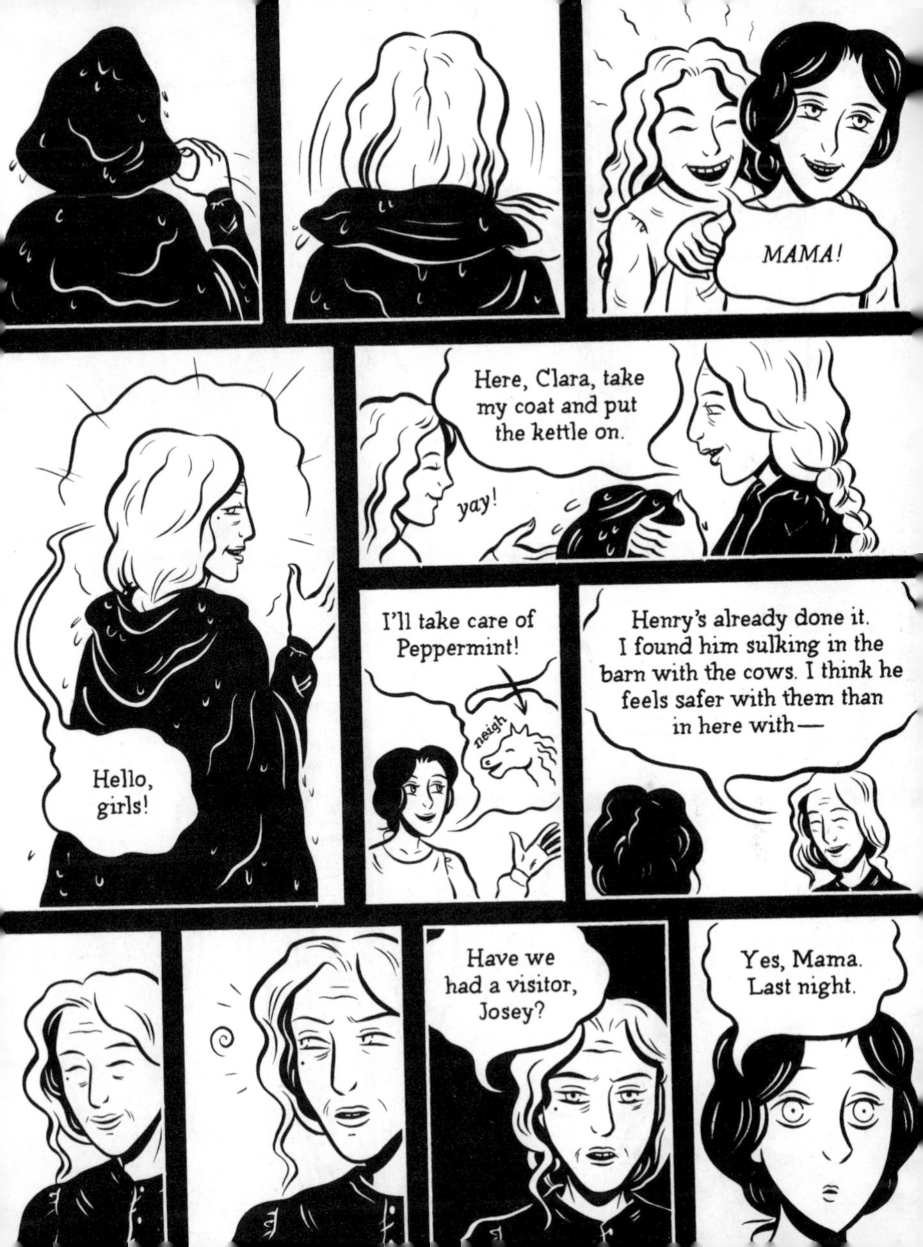
MAMA!
Hello, girls!
Here, Clara, take my coat and put the kettle on.
yay!
I'll take care of Peppermint!
neigh
Henry's already done it. I found him sulking in the barn with the cows. I think he feels safer with them than in here with—
Have we had a visitor, Josey?
Yes, Mama. Last night.

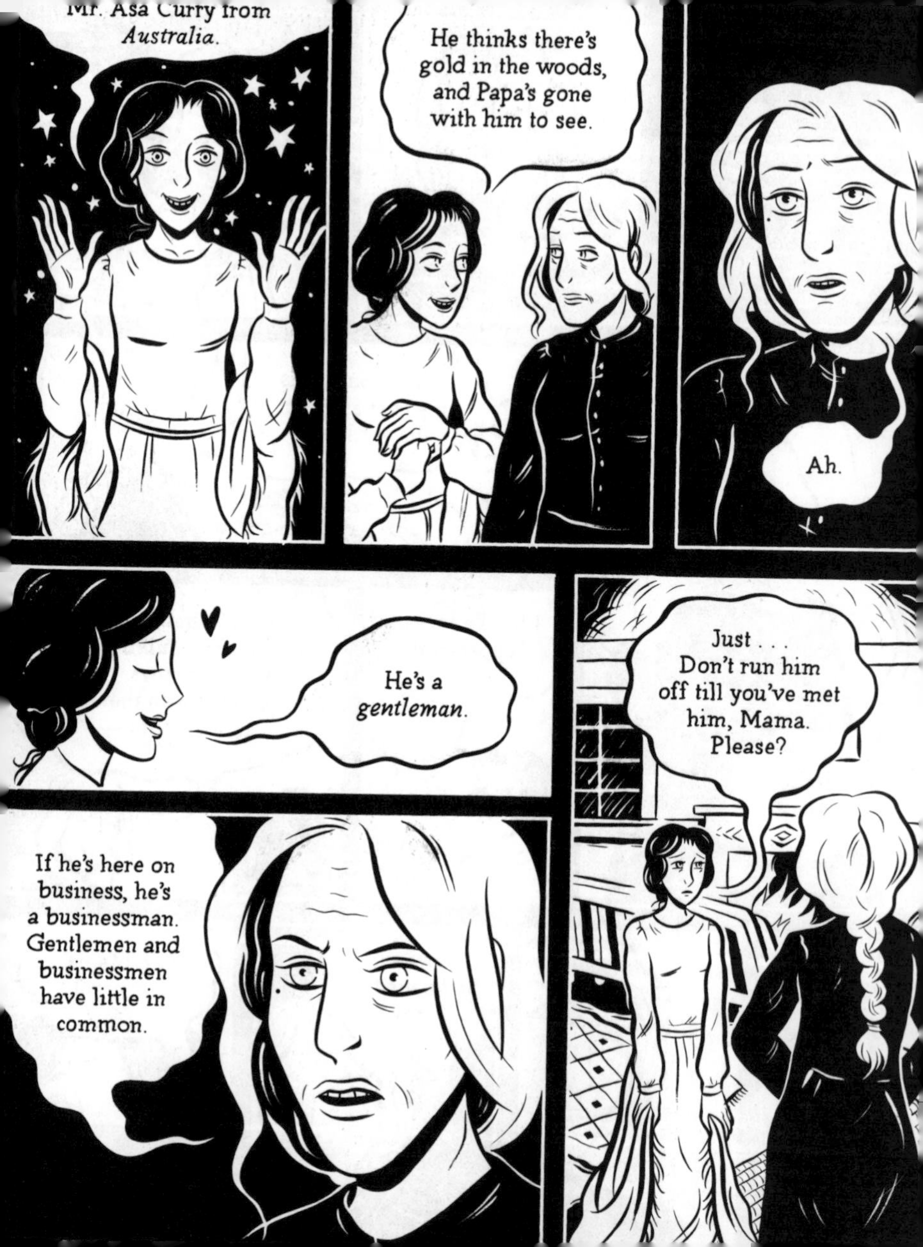

Mr. Asa Curry from *Australia*.
He thinks there's gold in the woods, and Papa's gone with him to see.
Ah.
He's a *gentleman*.
Just . . . Don't run him off till you've met him, Mama. Please?
If he's here on business, he's a businessman. Gentlemen and businessmen have little in common.

I like him very much. Connie met him, and she likes him too.

Connie was raised by brothers, Josephine. She's accustomed to a rougher sort of company.

Ah. I see your father has left the hay to spoil again.

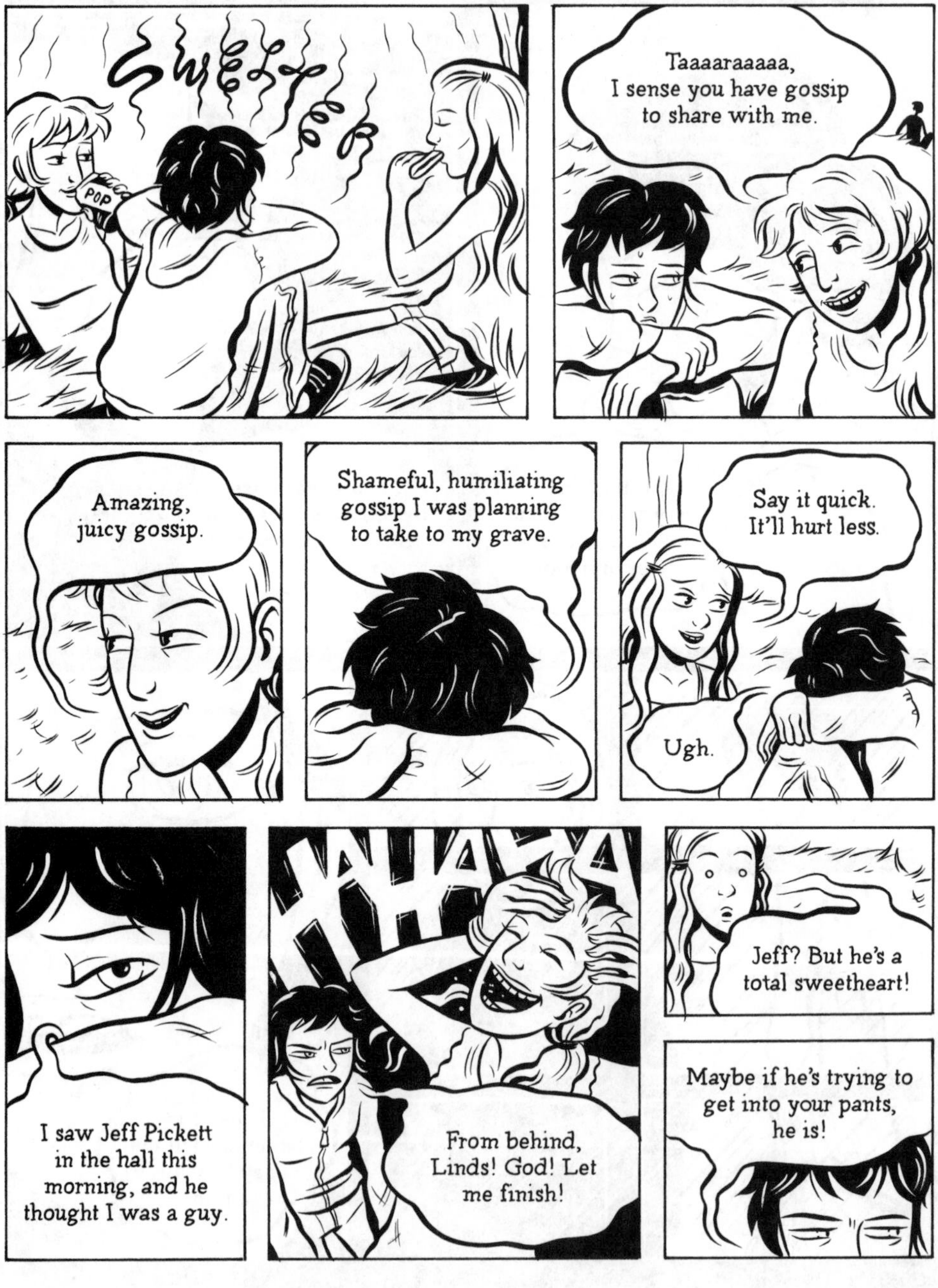
SWELTER
POP
Taaaaraaaaa,
I sense you have gossip
to share with me.
Amazing,
juicy gossip.
Shameful, humiliating
gossip I was planning
to take to my grave.
Say it quick.
It'll hurt less.
Ugh.
I saw Jeff Pickett
in the hall this
morning, and he
thought I was a guy.
HAHA
From behind,
Linds! God! Let
me finish!
Jeff? But he's a
total sweetheart!
Maybe if he's trying to
get into your pants,
he is!

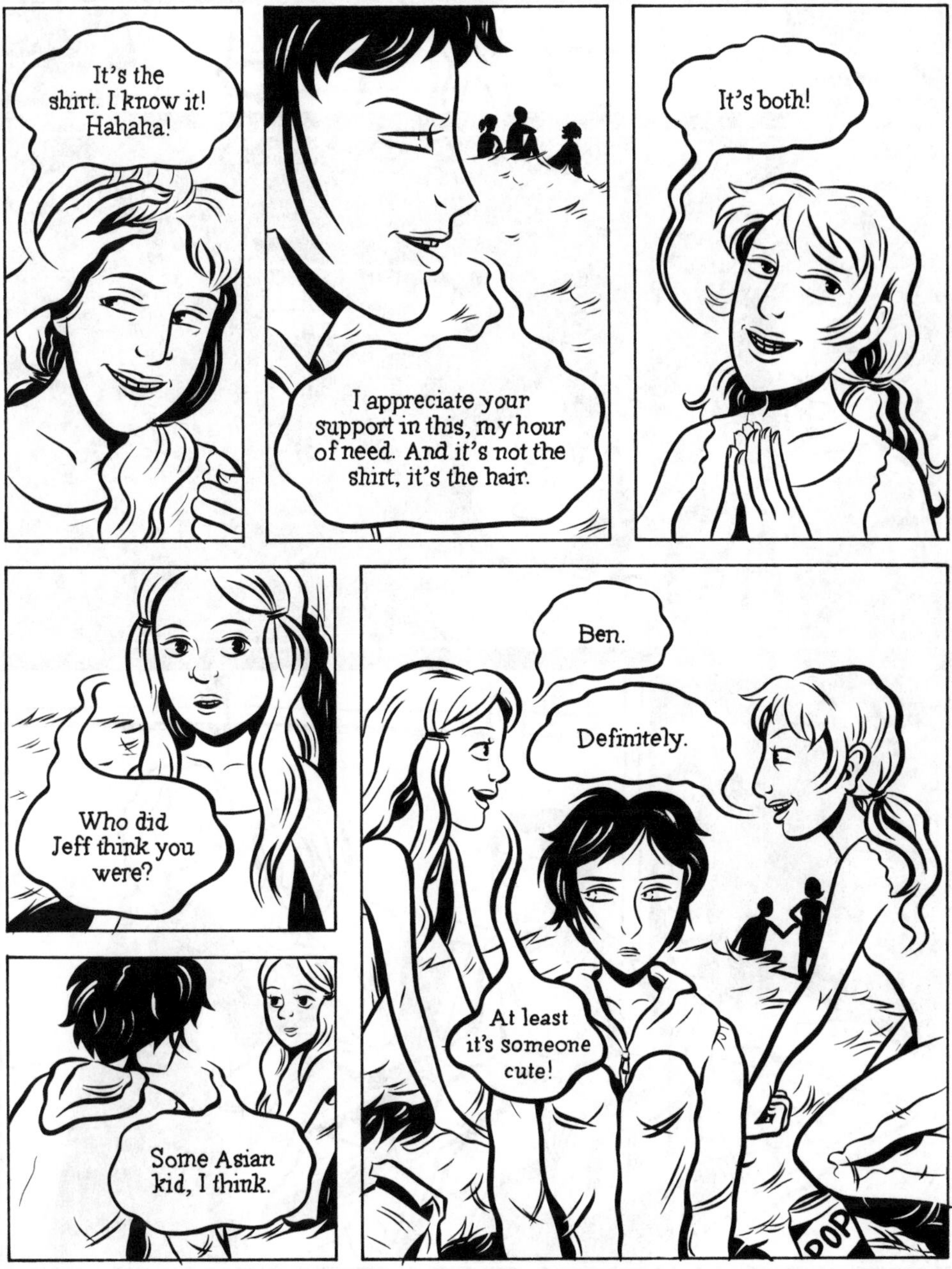
It's the shirt. I know it! Hahaha!
I appreciate your support in this, my hour of need. And it's not the shirt, it's the hair.
It's both!
Who did Jeff think you were?
Some Asian kid, I think.
Ben.
Definitely.
At least it's someone cute!
POP

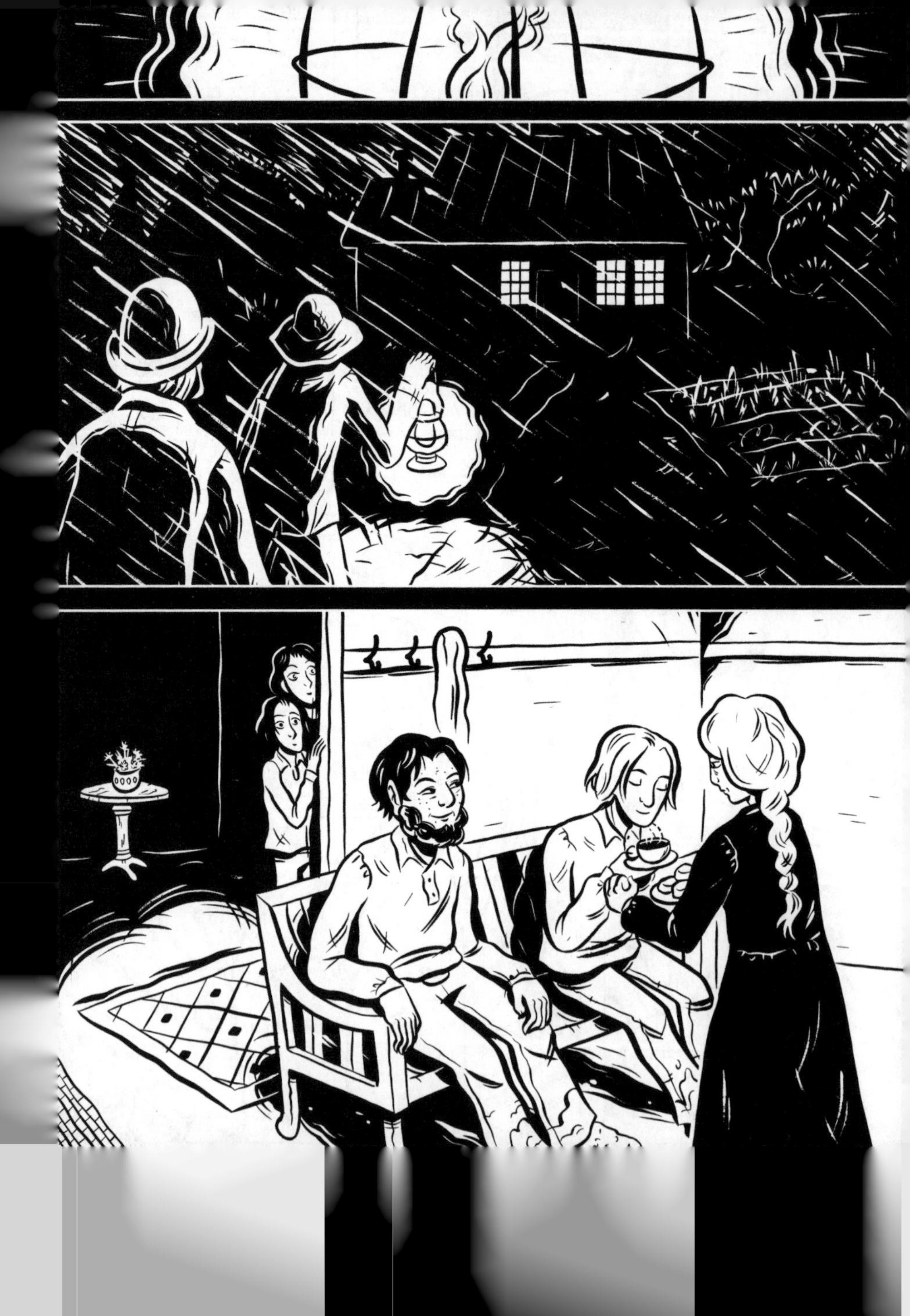

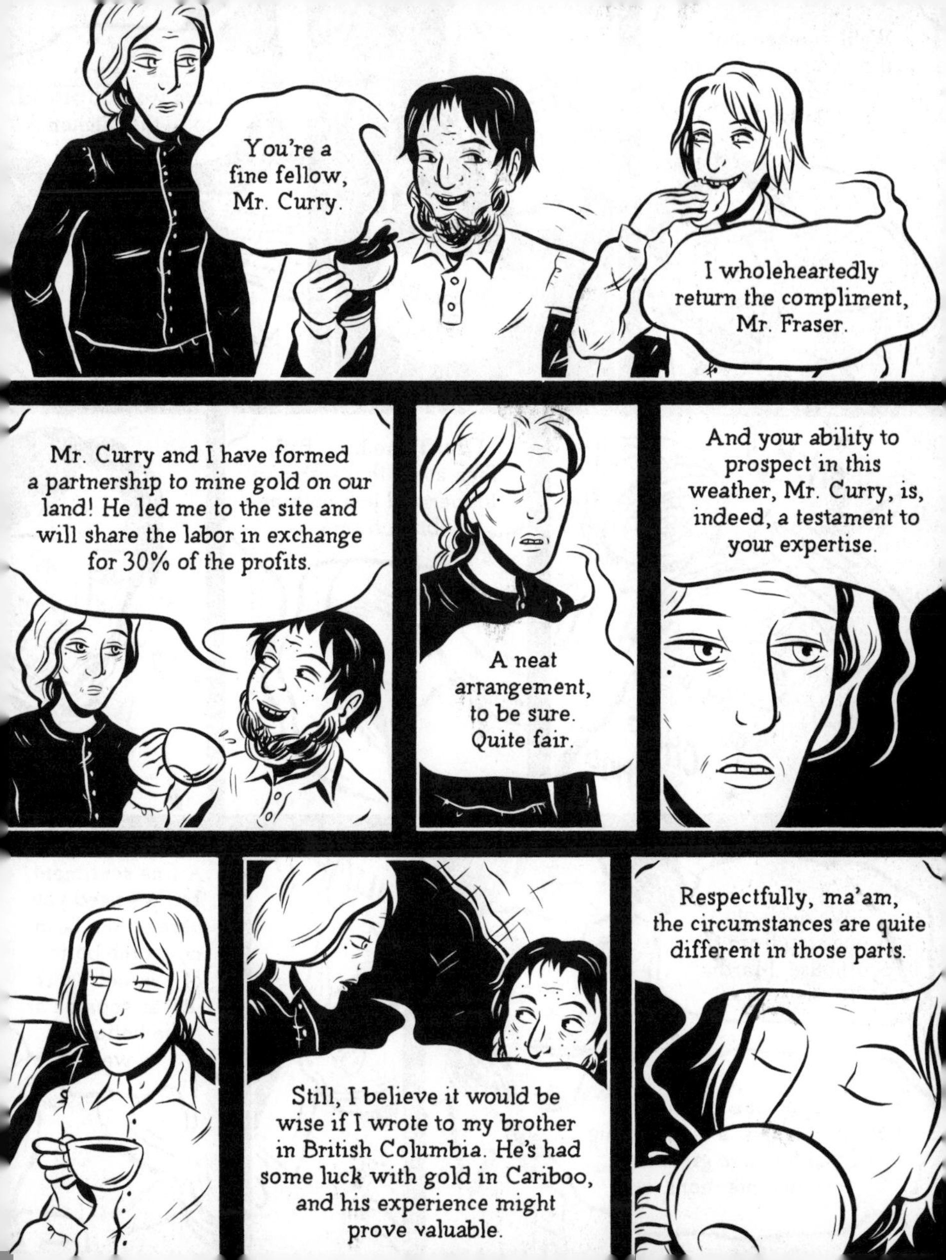
You're a fine fellow, Mr. Curry.
I wholeheartedly return the compliment, Mr. Fraser.
Mr. Curry and I have formed a partnership to mine gold on our land! He led me to the site and will share the labor in exchange for 30% of the profits.
A neat arrangement, to be sure. Quite fair.
And your ability to prospect in this weather, Mr. Curry, is, indeed, a testament to your expertise.
Still, I believe it would be wise if I wrote to my brother in British Columbia. He's had some luck with gold in Cariboo, and his experience might prove valuable.
Respectfully, ma'am, the circumstances are quite different in those parts.

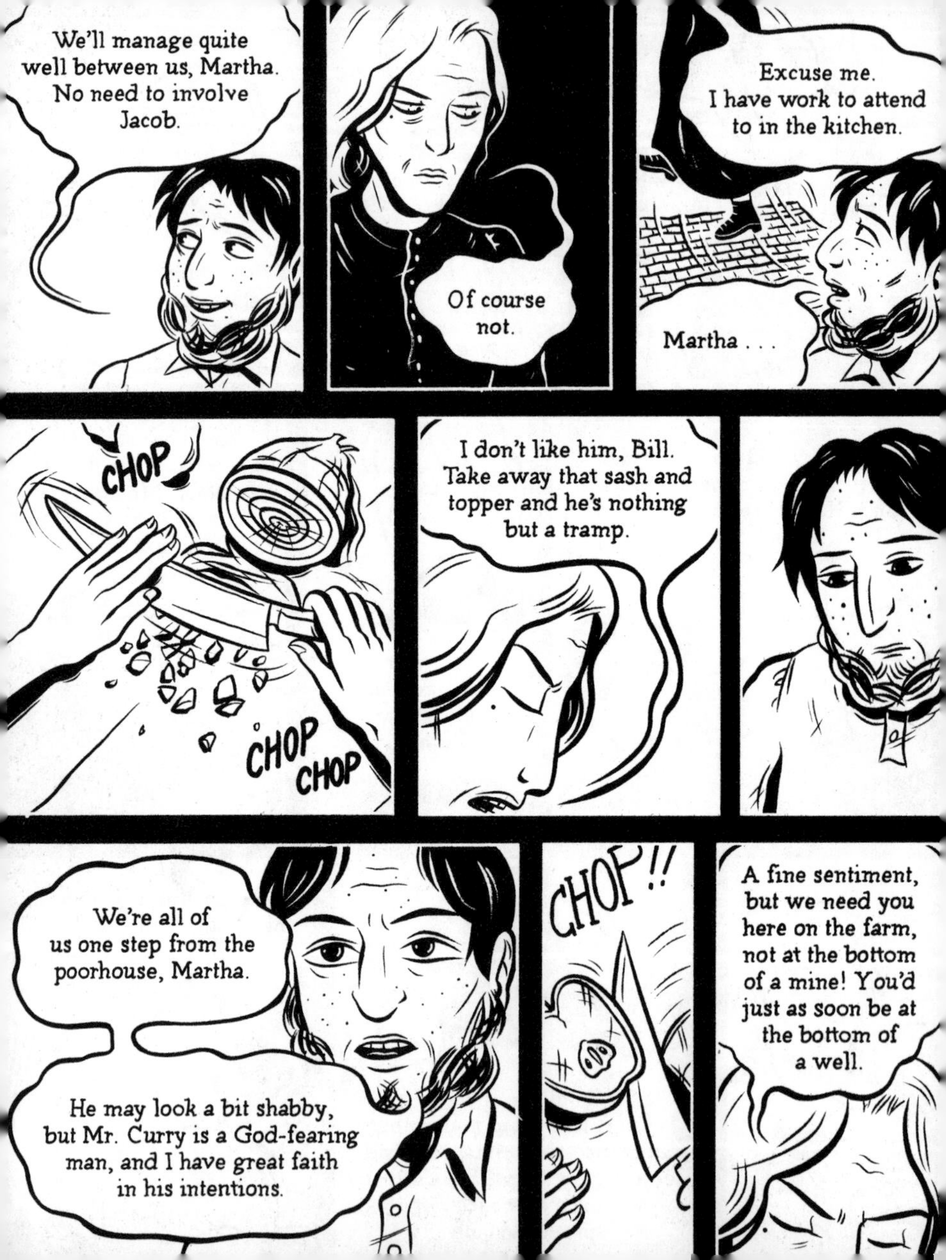
We'll manage quite well between us, Martha. No need to involve Jacob.
Of course not.
Excuse me. I have work to attend to in the kitchen.
Martha . . .
CHOP
CHOP
CHOP
I don't like him, Bill. Take away that sash and topper and he's nothing but a tramp.
We're all of us one step from the poorhouse, Martha.
He may look a bit shabby, but Mr. Curry is a God-fearing man, and I have great faith in his intentions.
CHOP!!
A fine sentiment, but we need you here on the farm, not at the bottom of a mine! You'd just as soon be at the bottom of a well.

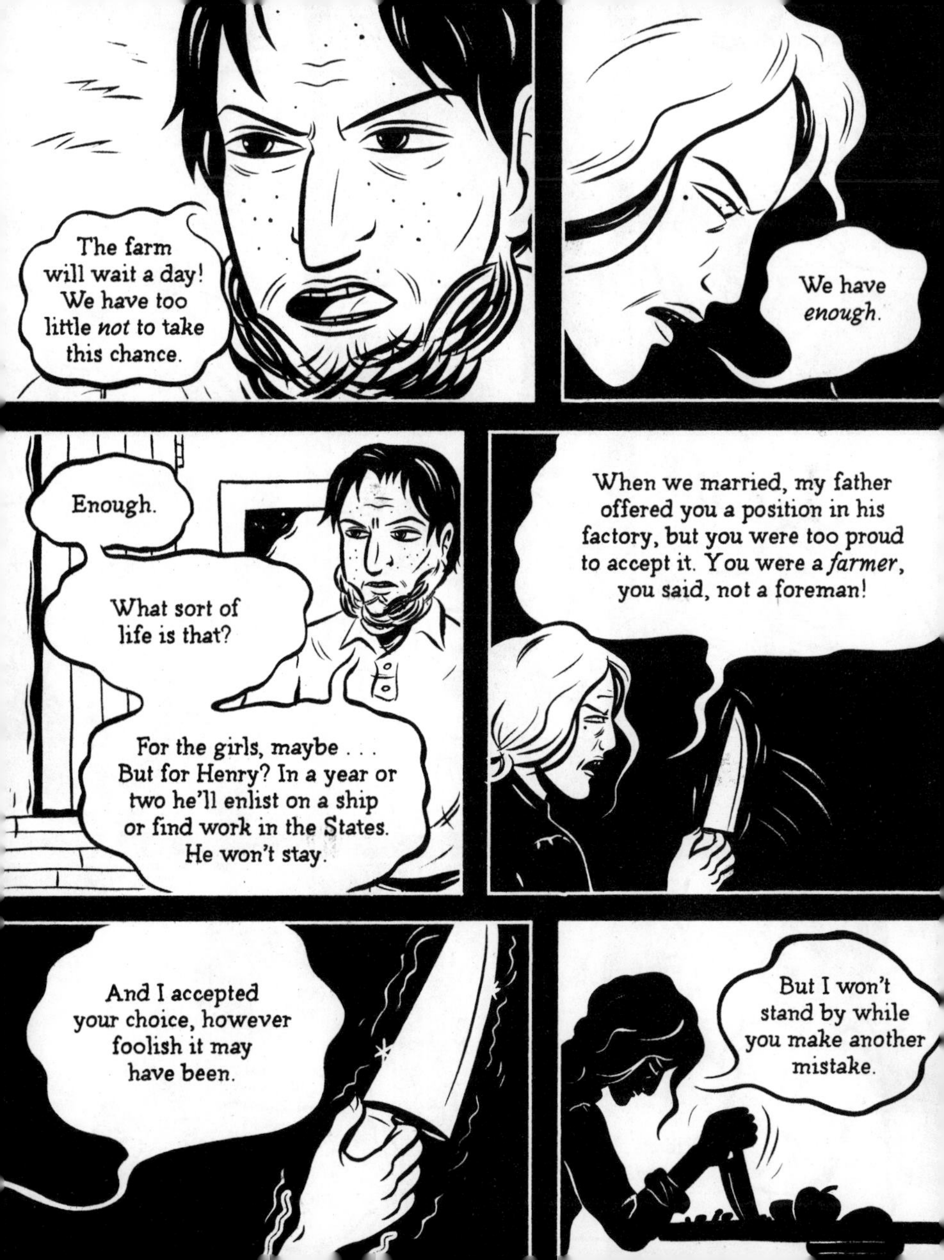

The farm will wait a day! We have too little *not* to take this chance.
We have *enough*.
Enough.
What sort of life is that?
For the girls, maybe . . . But for Henry? In a year or two he'll enlist on a ship or find work in the States. He won't stay.
When we married, my father offered you a position in his factory, but you were too proud to accept it. You were a *farmer*, you said, not a foreman!
And I accepted your choice, however foolish it may have been.
But I won't stand by while you make another mistake.

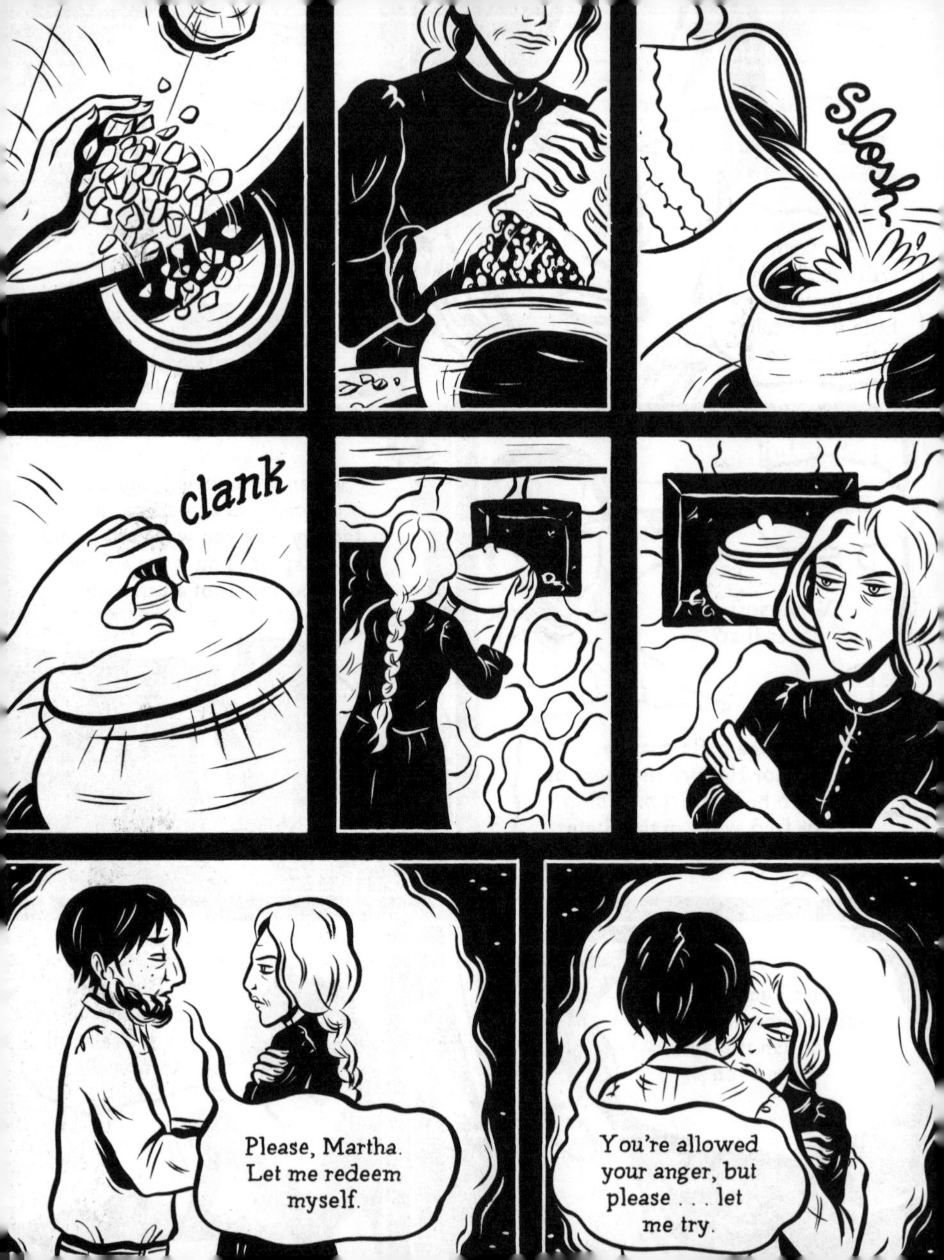
Slosh
clank
Please, Martha. Let me redeem myself.
You're allowed your anger, but please . . . let me try.

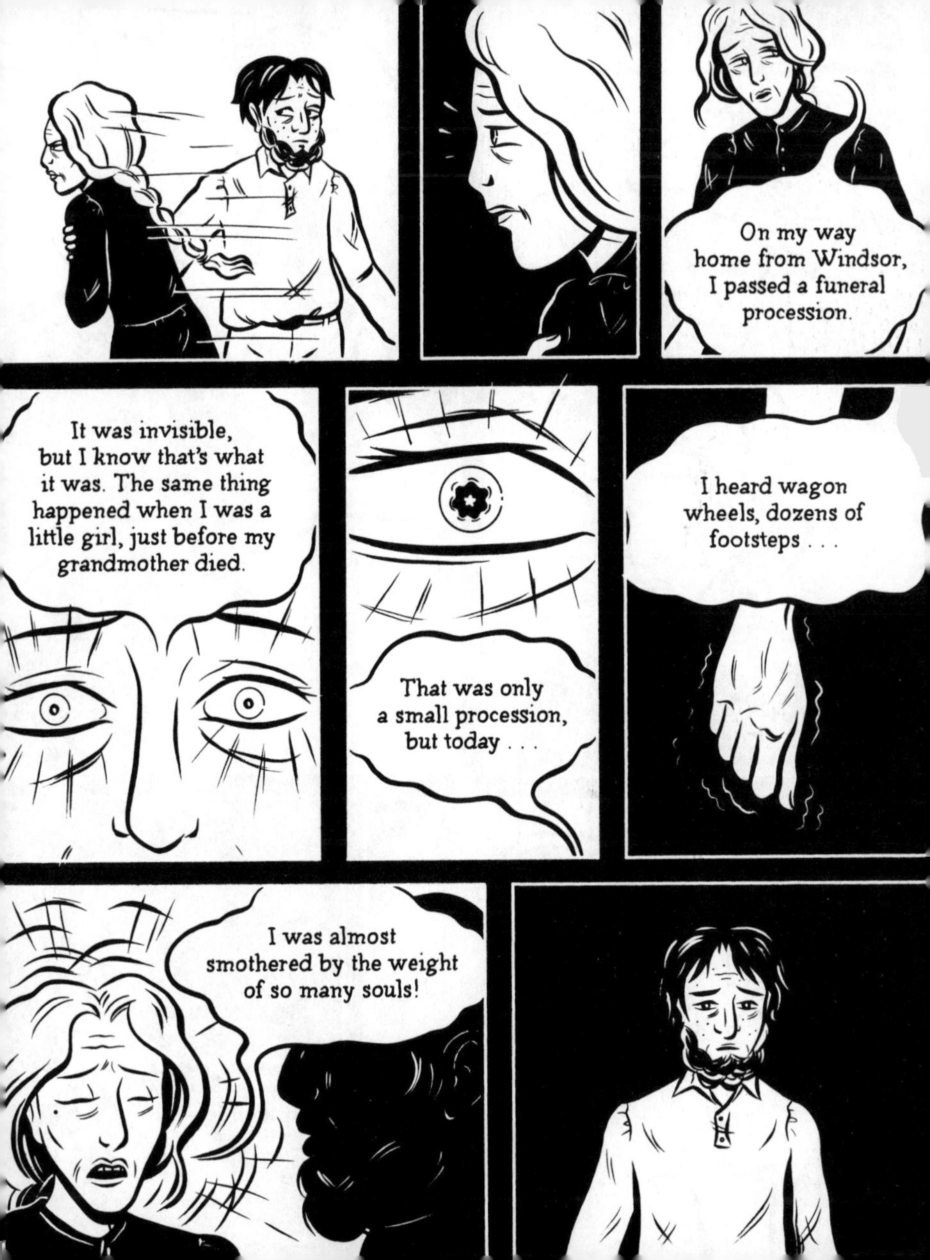
On my way home from Windsor, I passed a funeral procession.
It was invisible, but I know that's what it was. The same thing happened when I was a little girl, just before my grandmother died.
That was only a small procession, but today . . .
I heard wagon wheels, dozens of footsteps . . .
I was almost smothered by the weight of so many souls!

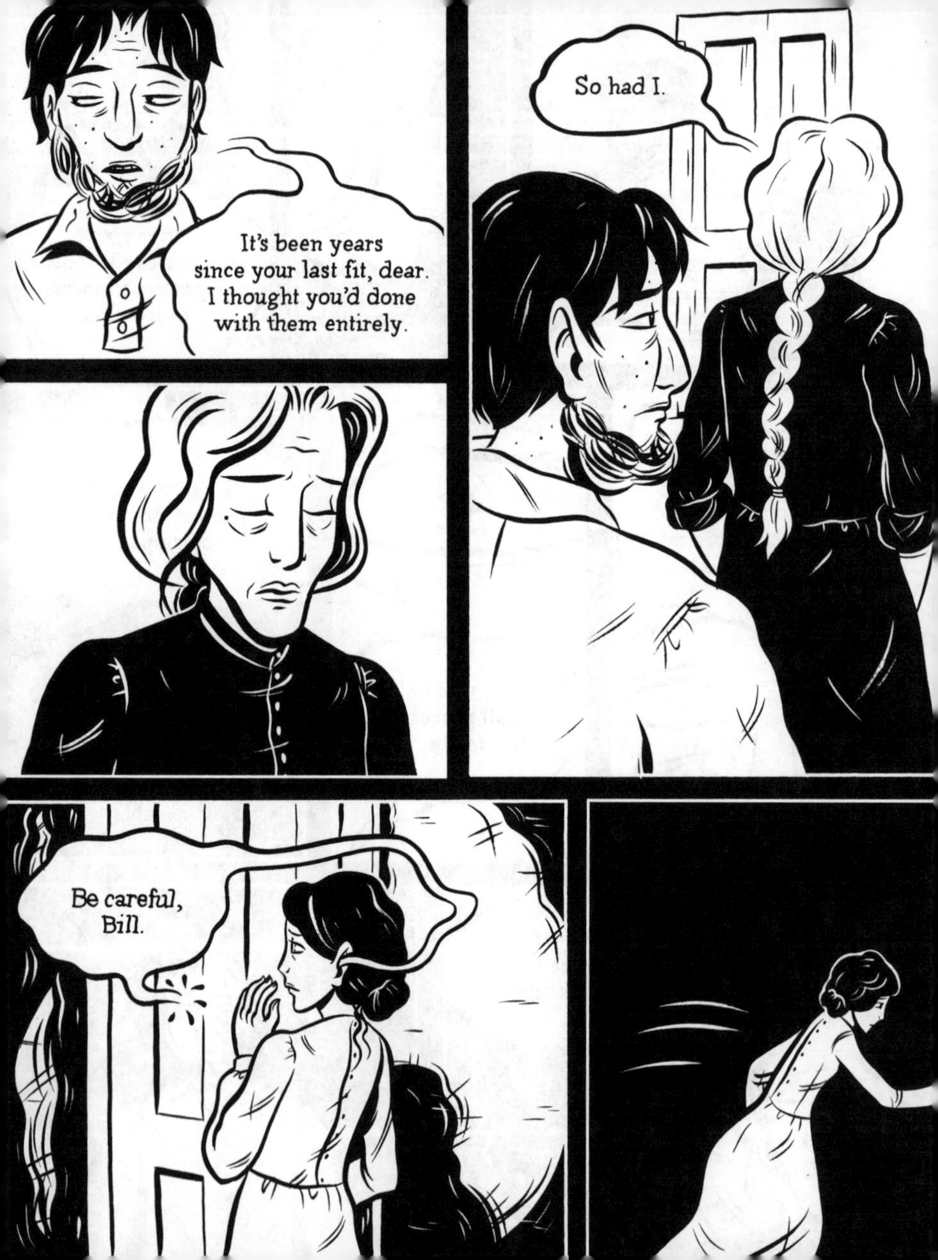
It's been years since your last fit, dear. I thought you'd done with them entirely.
So had I.
Be careful, Bill.

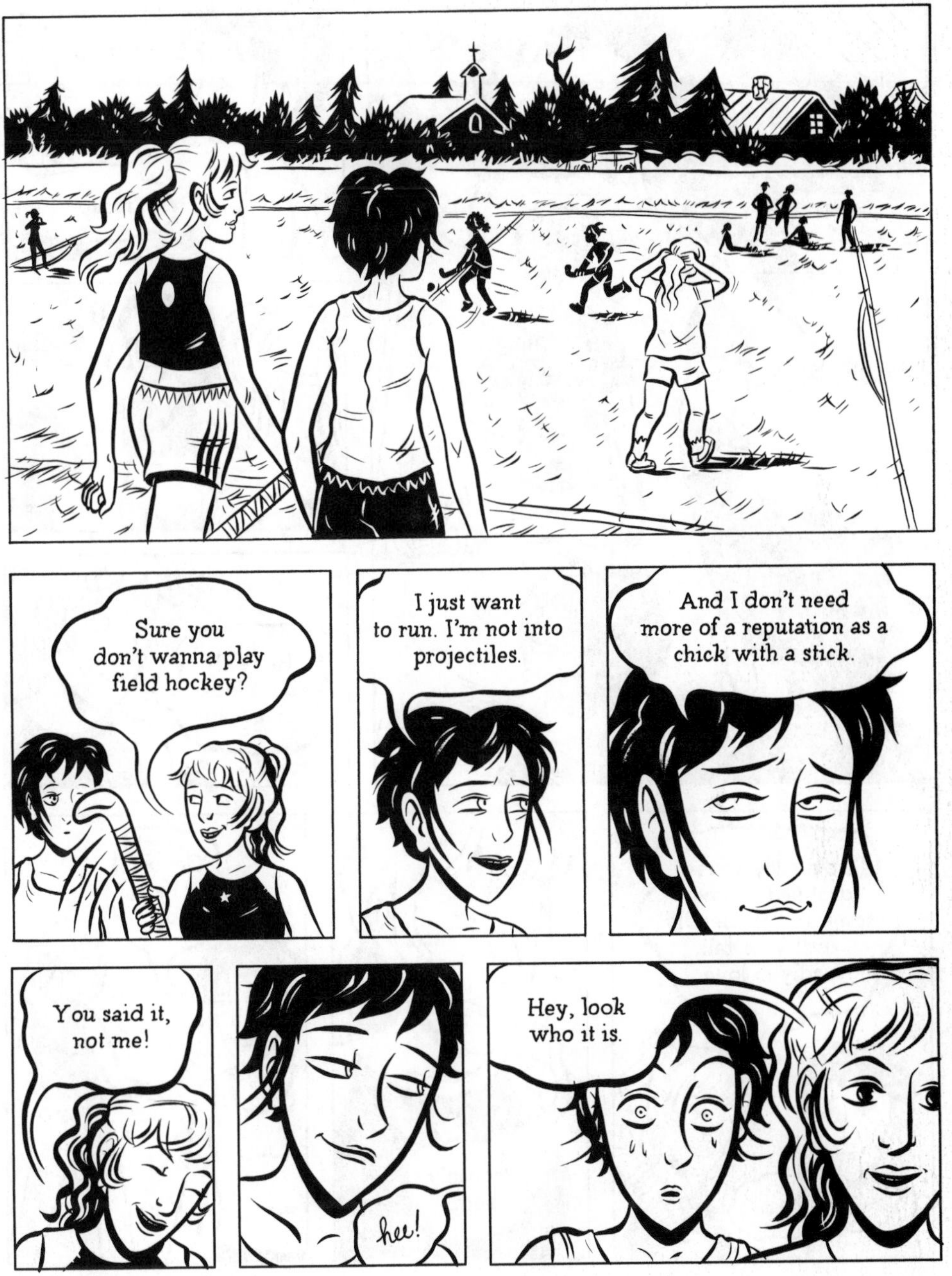
Sure you don't wanna play field hockey?
I just want to run. I'm not into projectiles.
And I don't need more of a reputation as a chick with a stick.
You said it, not me!
hee!
Hey, look who it is.

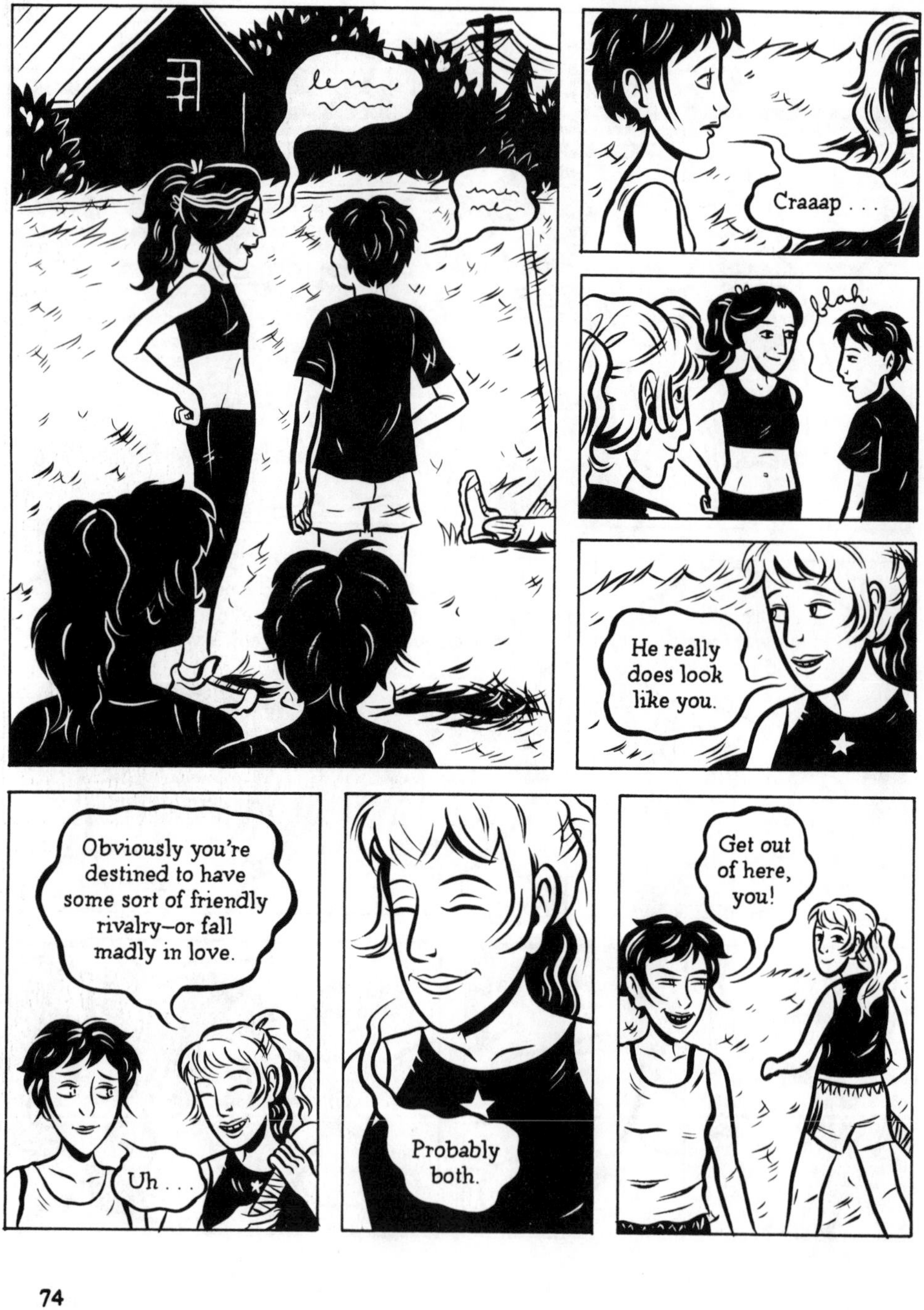
Craaap . . .
blah
He really does look like you.
Obviously you're destined to have some sort of friendly rivalry—or fall madly in love.
Uh . . .
Probably both.
Get out of here, you!

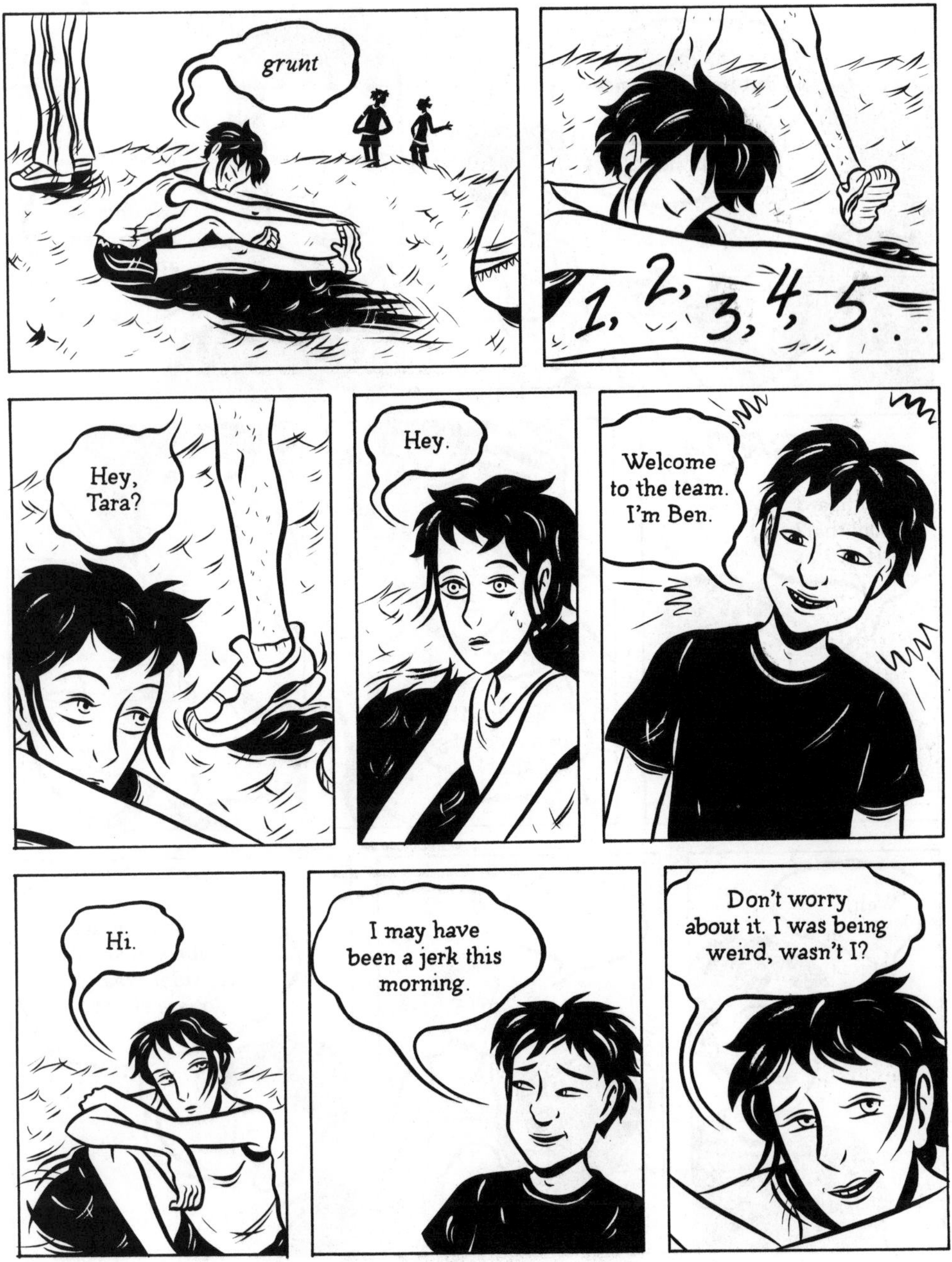
grunt
1, 2, 3, 4, 5...
Hey, Tara?
Hey.
Welcome to the team. I'm Ben.
Hi.
I may have been a jerk this morning.
Don't worry about it. I was being weird, wasn't I?

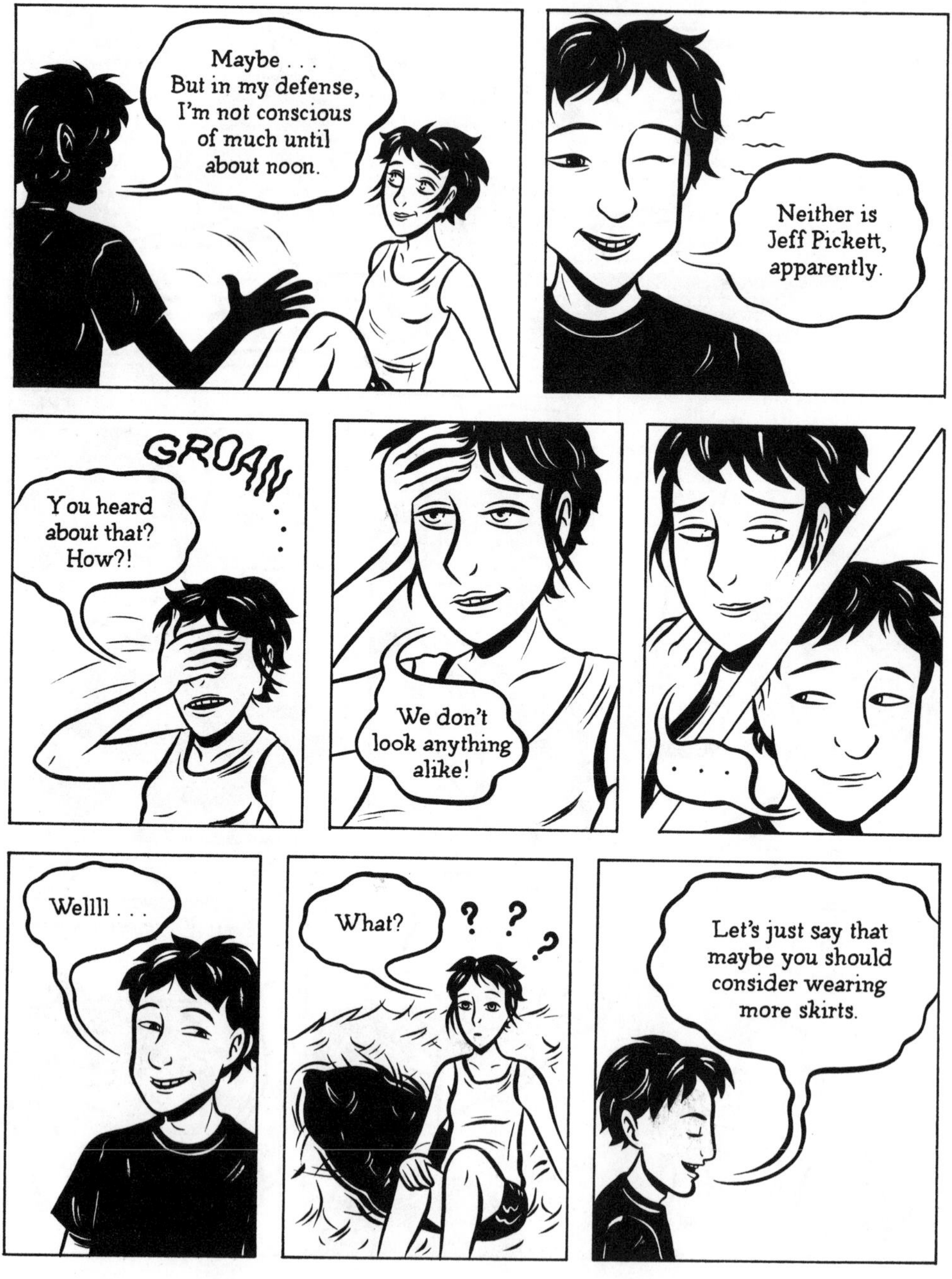

Maybe . . . But in my defense, I'm not conscious of much until about noon.
Neither is Jeff Pickett, apparently.
GROAN . . .
You heard about that? How?!
We don't look anything alike!
. . .
Wellll . . .
What?
? ? ?
Let's just say that maybe you should consider wearing more skirts.

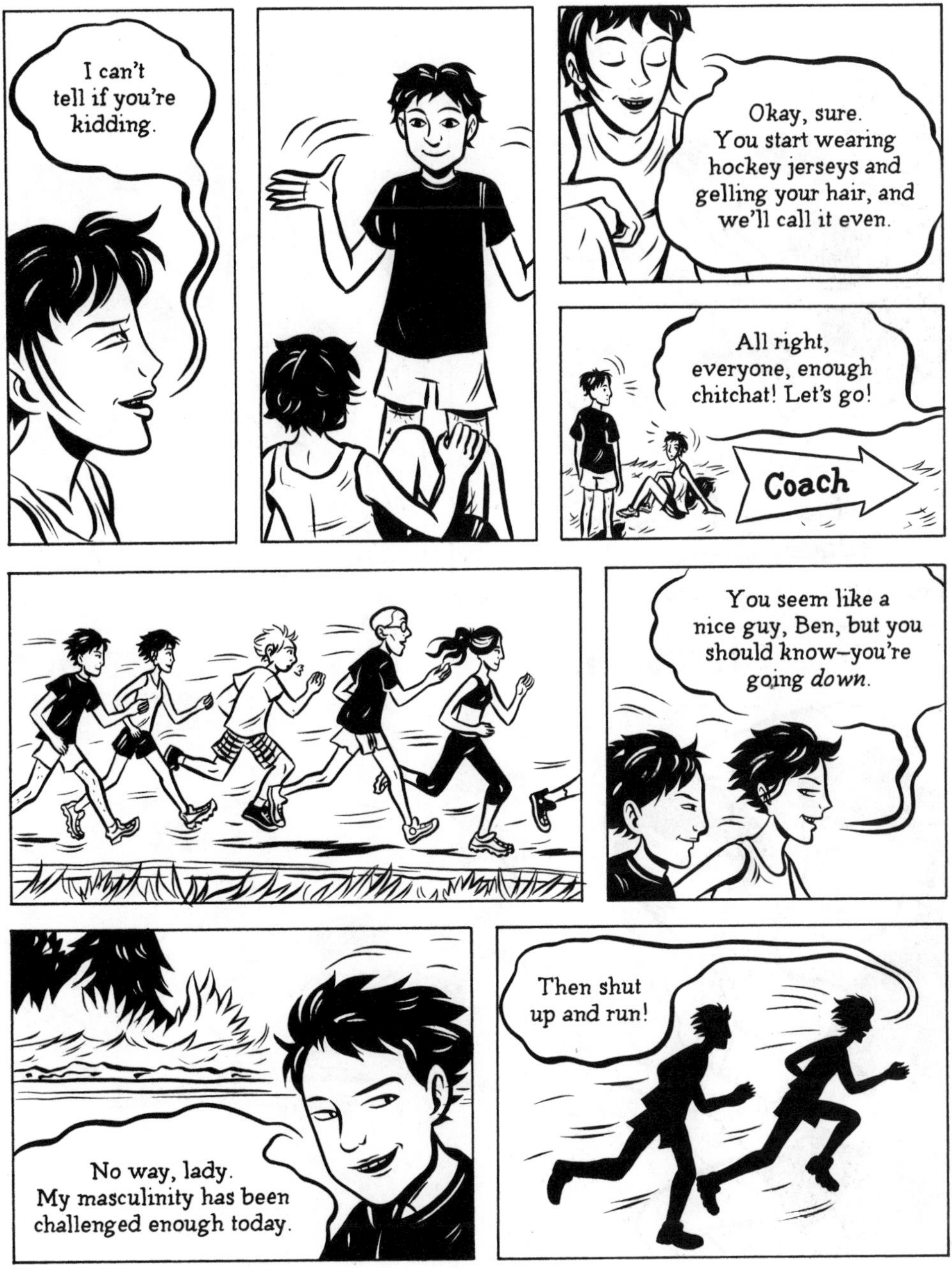
I can't tell if you're kidding.
Okay, sure. You start wearing hockey jerseys and gelling your hair, and we'll call it even.
All right, everyone, enough chitchat! Let's go!
Coach
You seem like a nice guy, Ben, but you should know—you're going *down*.
No way, lady. My masculinity has been challenged enough today.
Then shut up and run!

0.351 km

1.038 km

1.706 km

2.452 km
(almost finished)

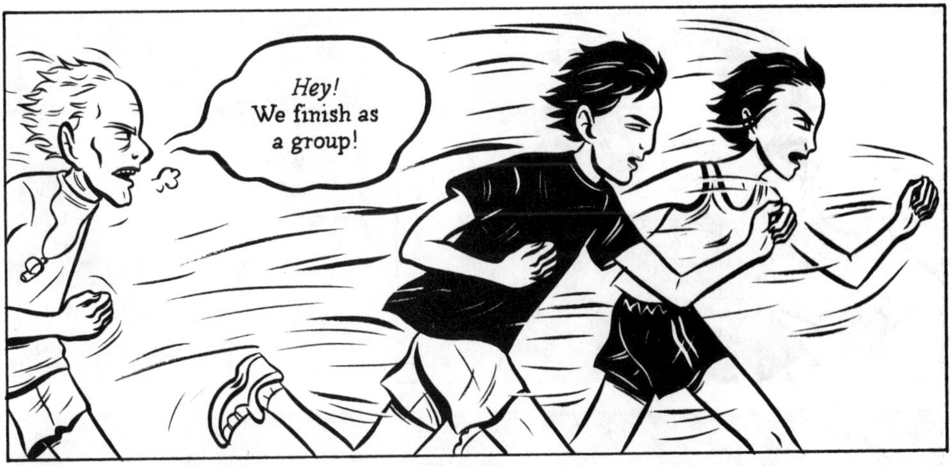
Hey! We finish as a group!

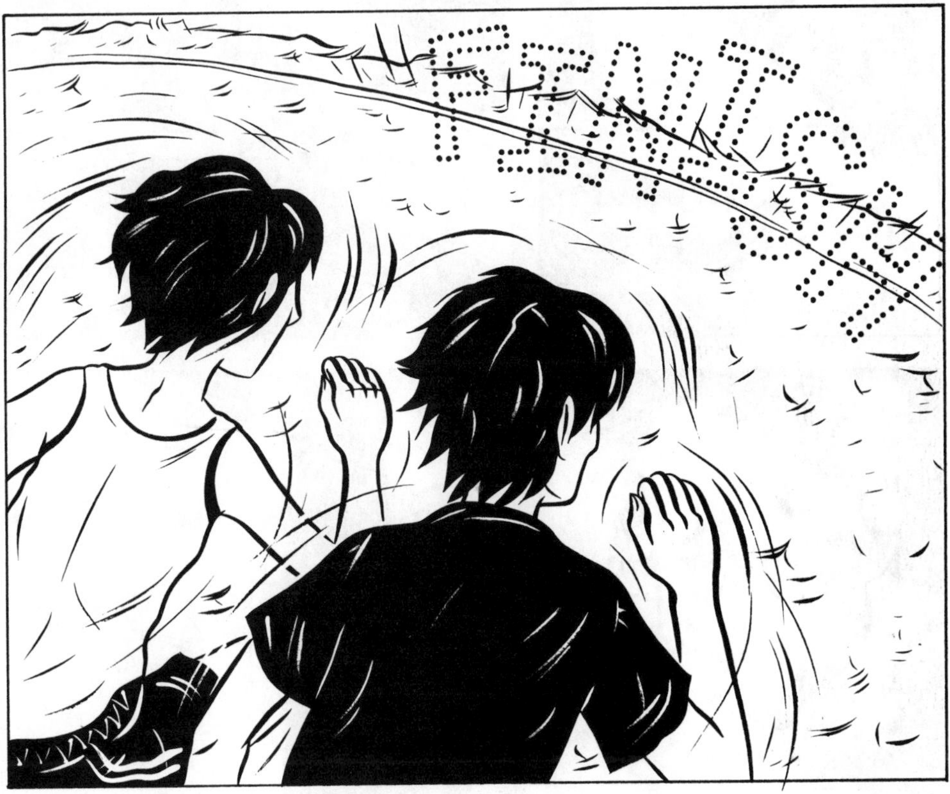
FINISH

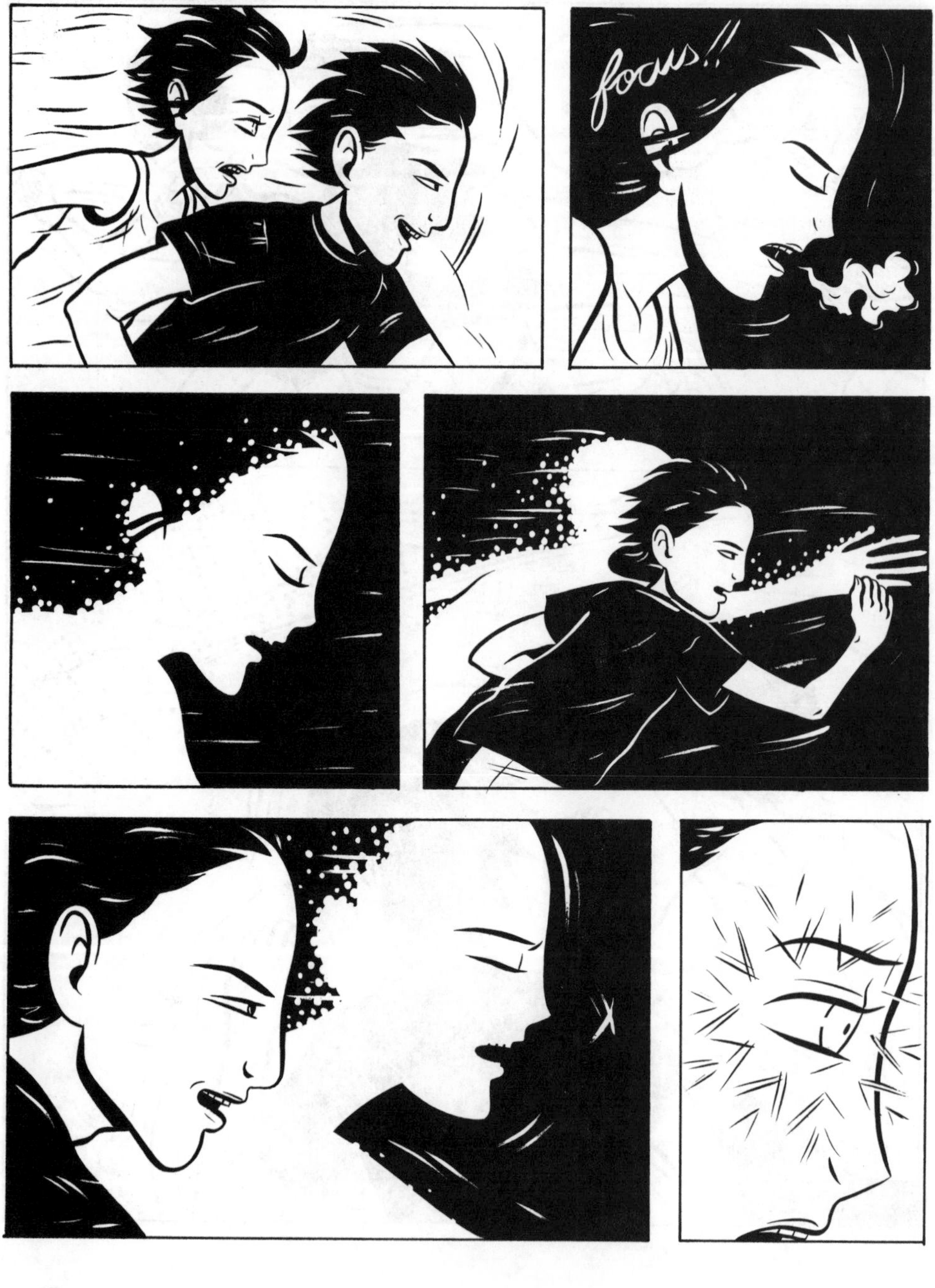
focus!!

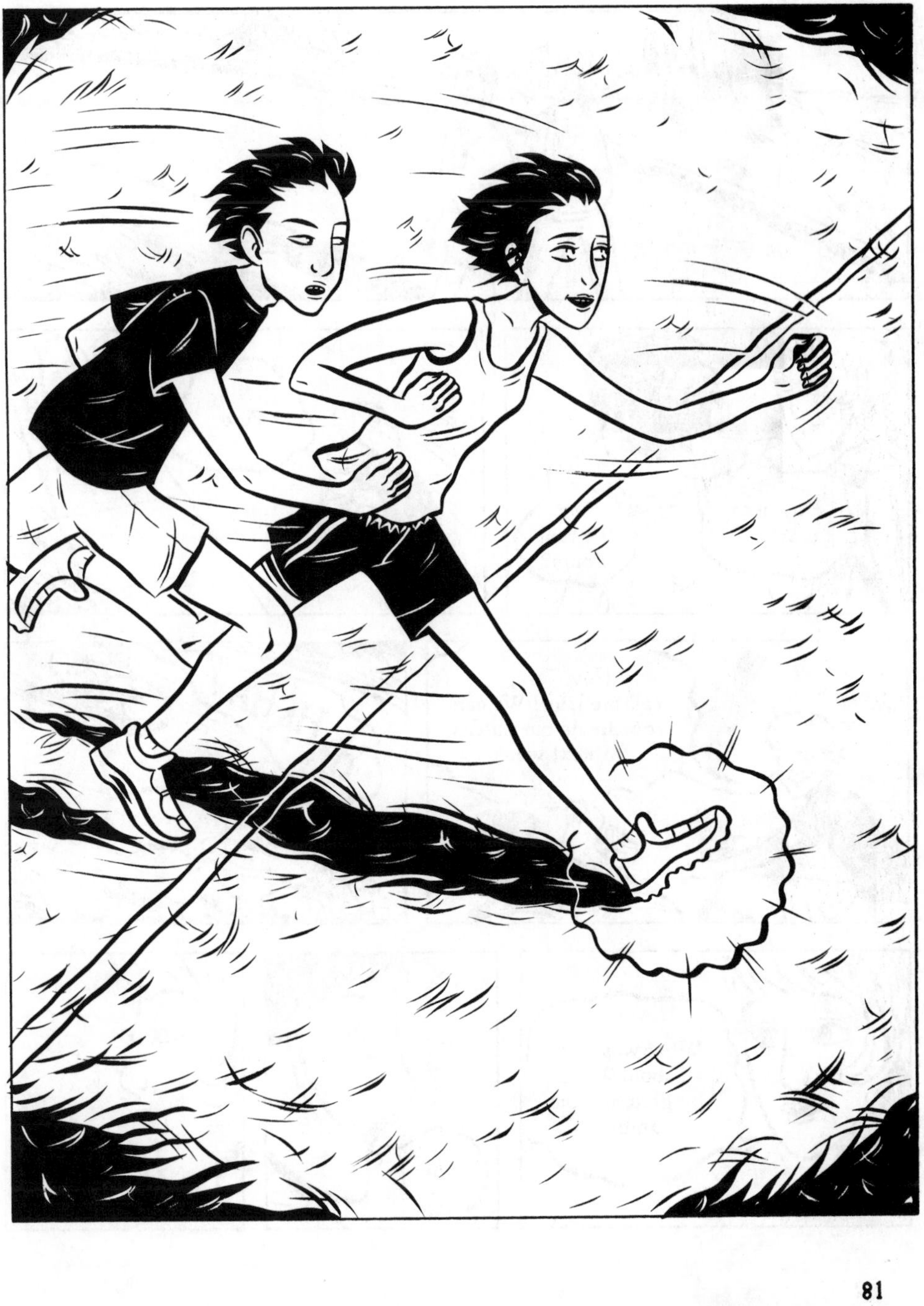

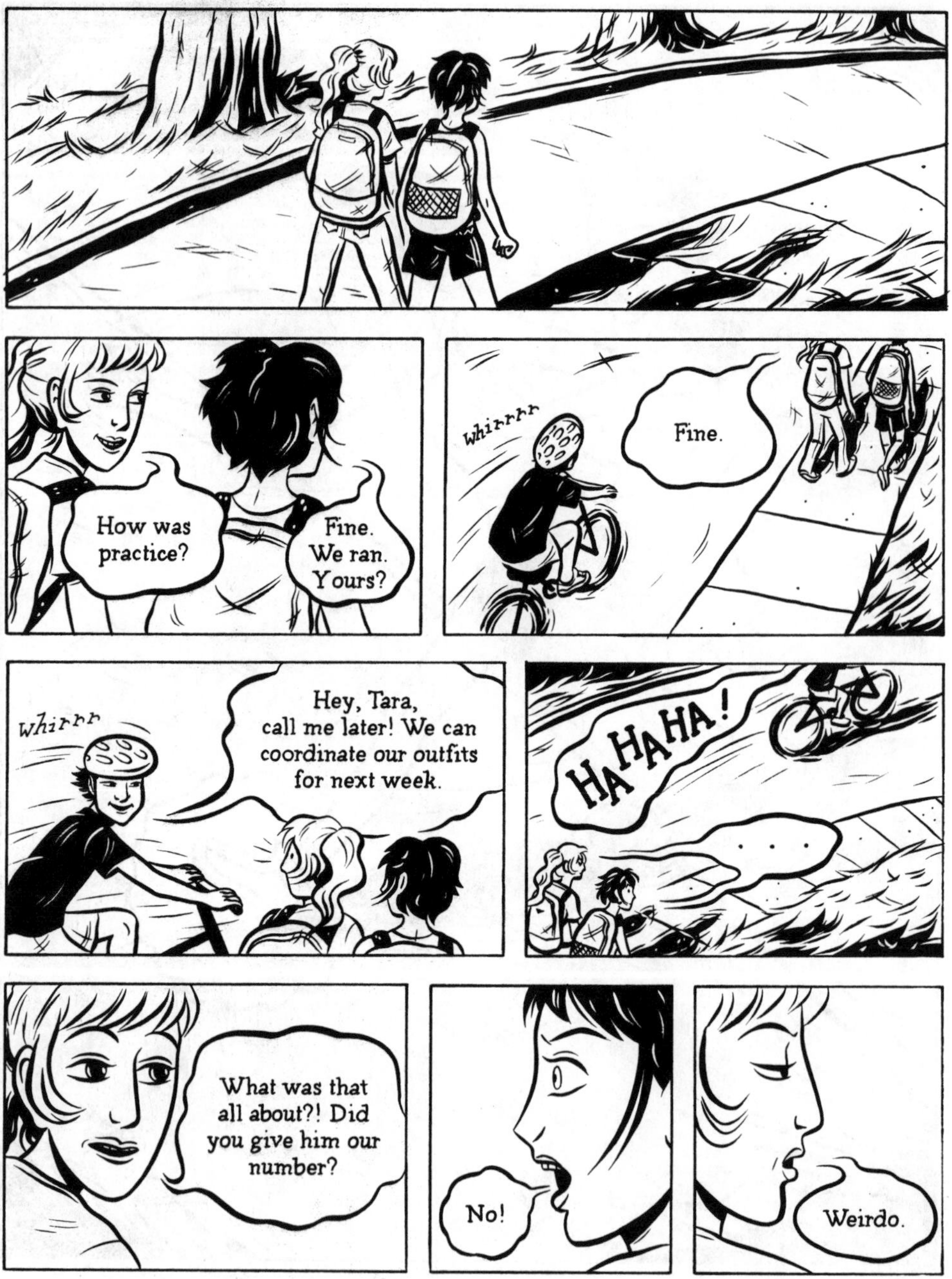
How was practice?
Fine. We ran. Yours?
whirrrr
Fine.
whirrr
Hey, Tara, call me later! We can coordinate our outfits for next week.
HAHAHA!
. . .
What was that all about?! Did you give him our number?
No!
Weirdo.

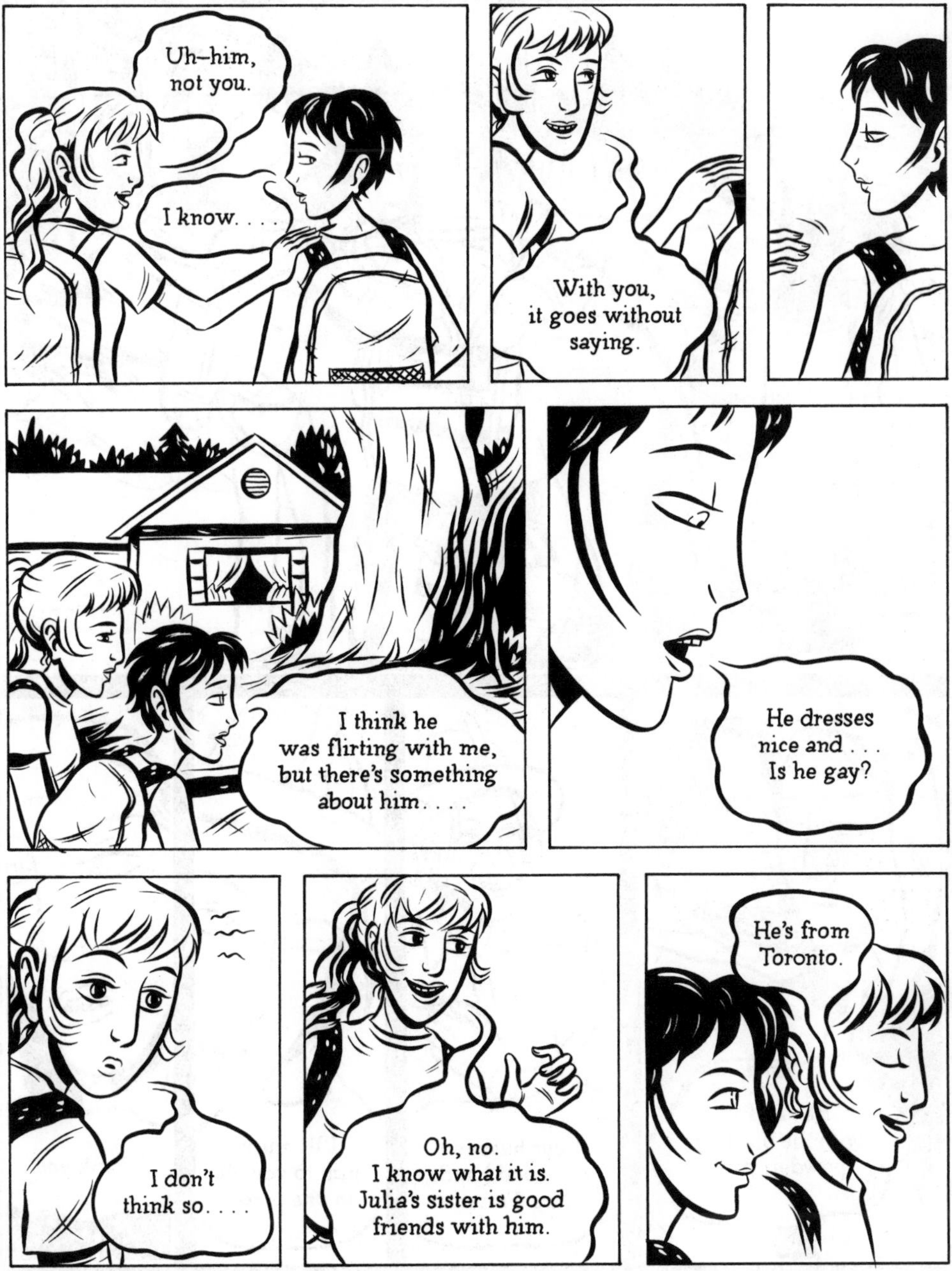
Uh—him, not you.
I know. . . .
With you, it goes without saying.
I think he was flirting with me, but there's something about him. . . .
He dresses nice and . . . Is he gay?
I don't think so. . . .
Oh, no. I know what it is. Julia's sister is good friends with him.
He's from Toronto.

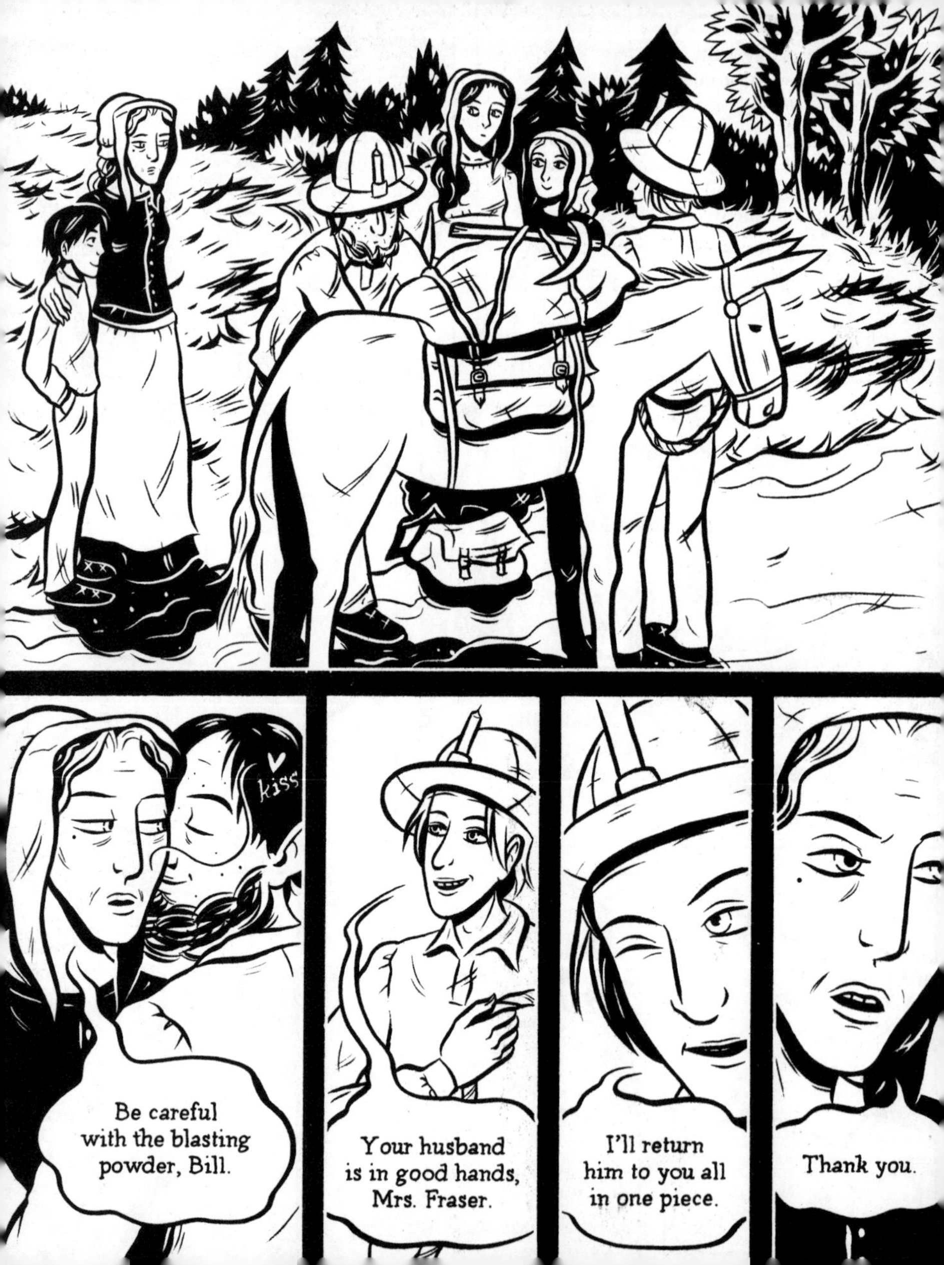
kiss
Be careful with the blasting powder, Bill.
Your husband is in good hands, Mrs. Fraser.
I'll return him to you all in one piece.
Thank you.

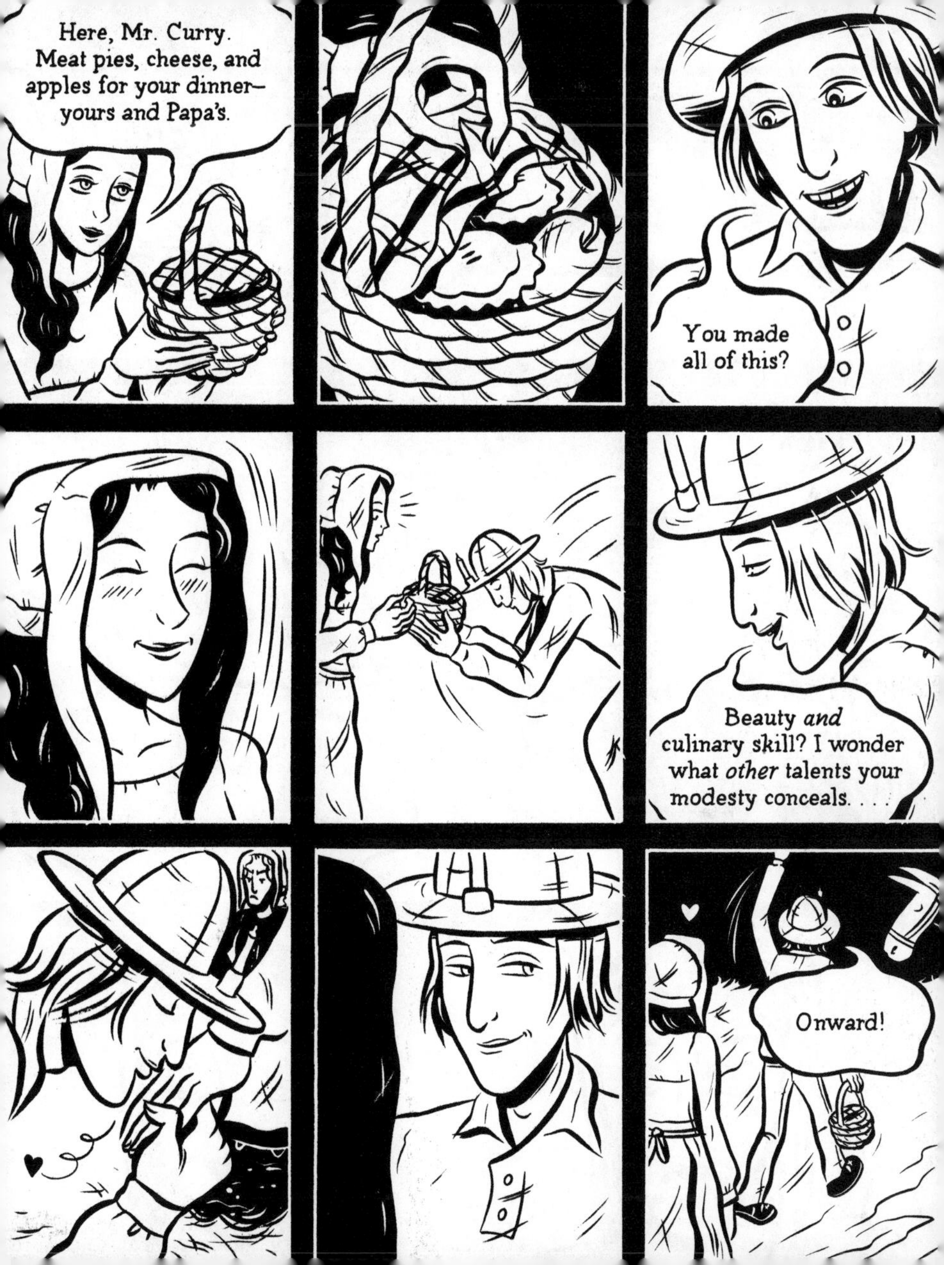
Here, Mr. Curry. Meat pies, cheese, and apples for your dinner—yours and Papa's.
You made all of this?
Beauty *and* culinary skill? I wonder what *other* talents your modesty conceals. . . .
Onward!

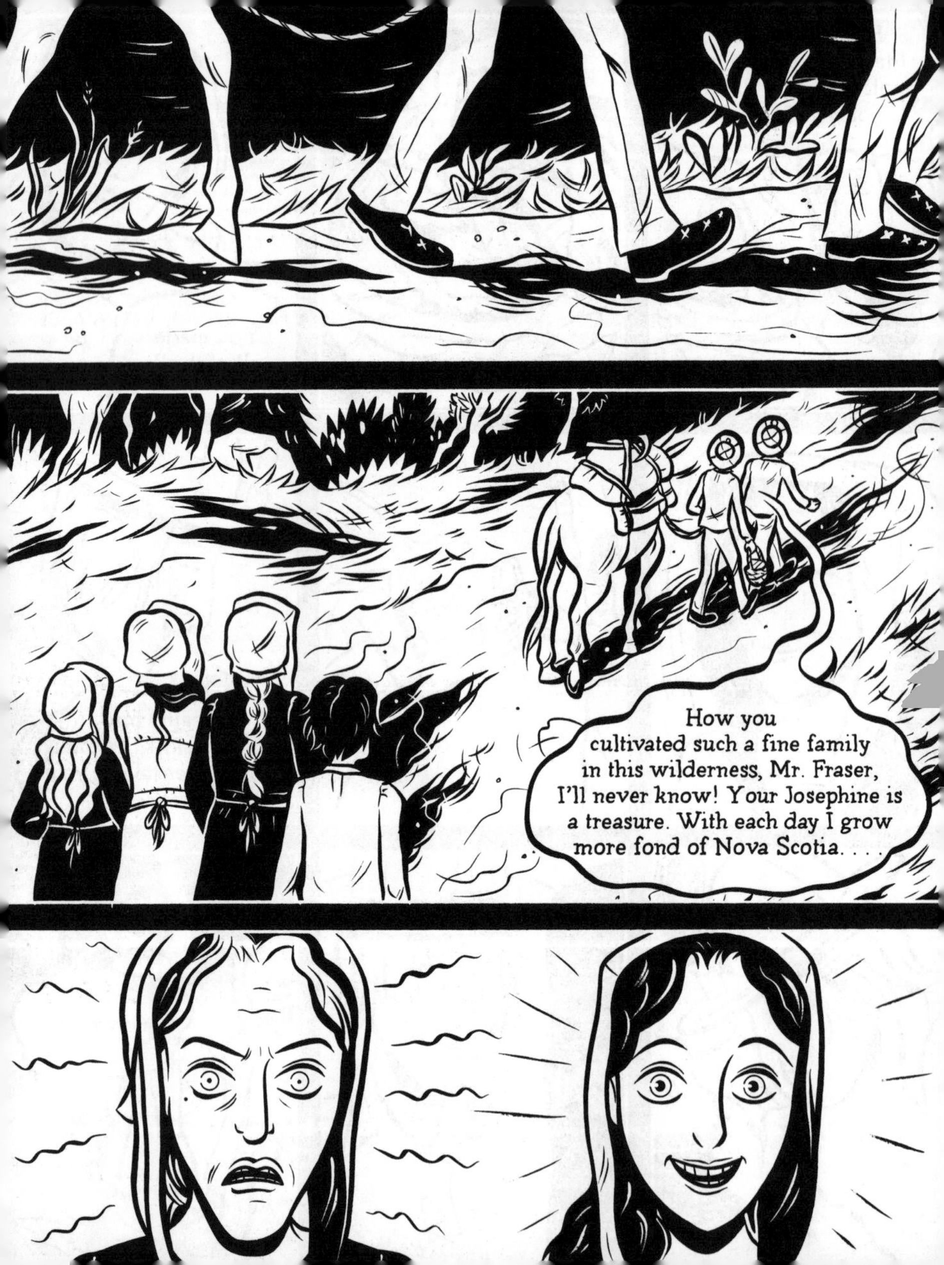
How you cultivated such a fine family in this wilderness, Mr. Fraser, I'll never know! Your Josephine is a treasure. With each day I grow more fond of Nova Scotia. . . .

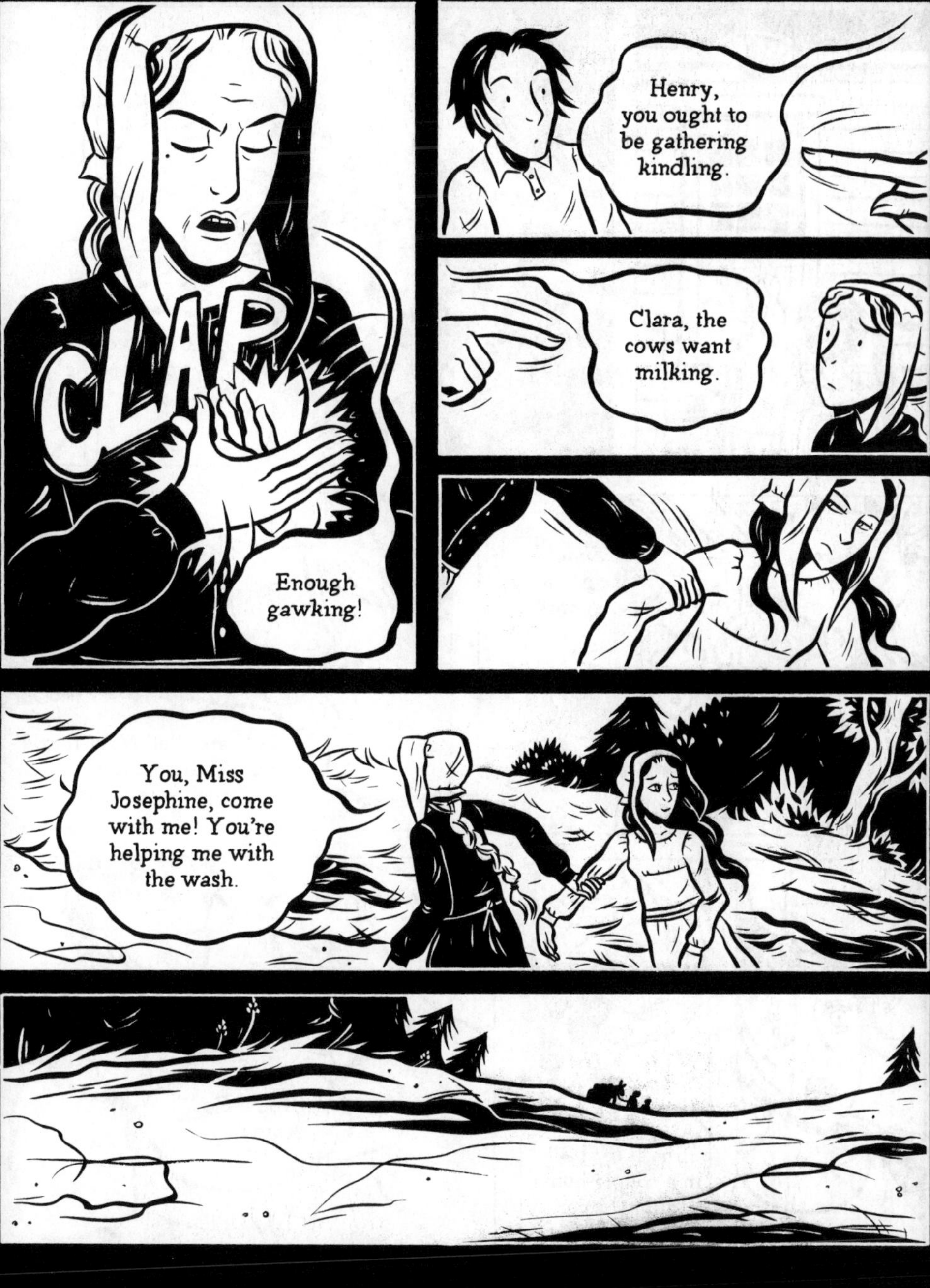
CLAP
Enough gawking!
Henry, you ought to be gathering kindling.
Clara, the cows want milking.
You, Miss Josephine, come with me! You're helping me with the wash.

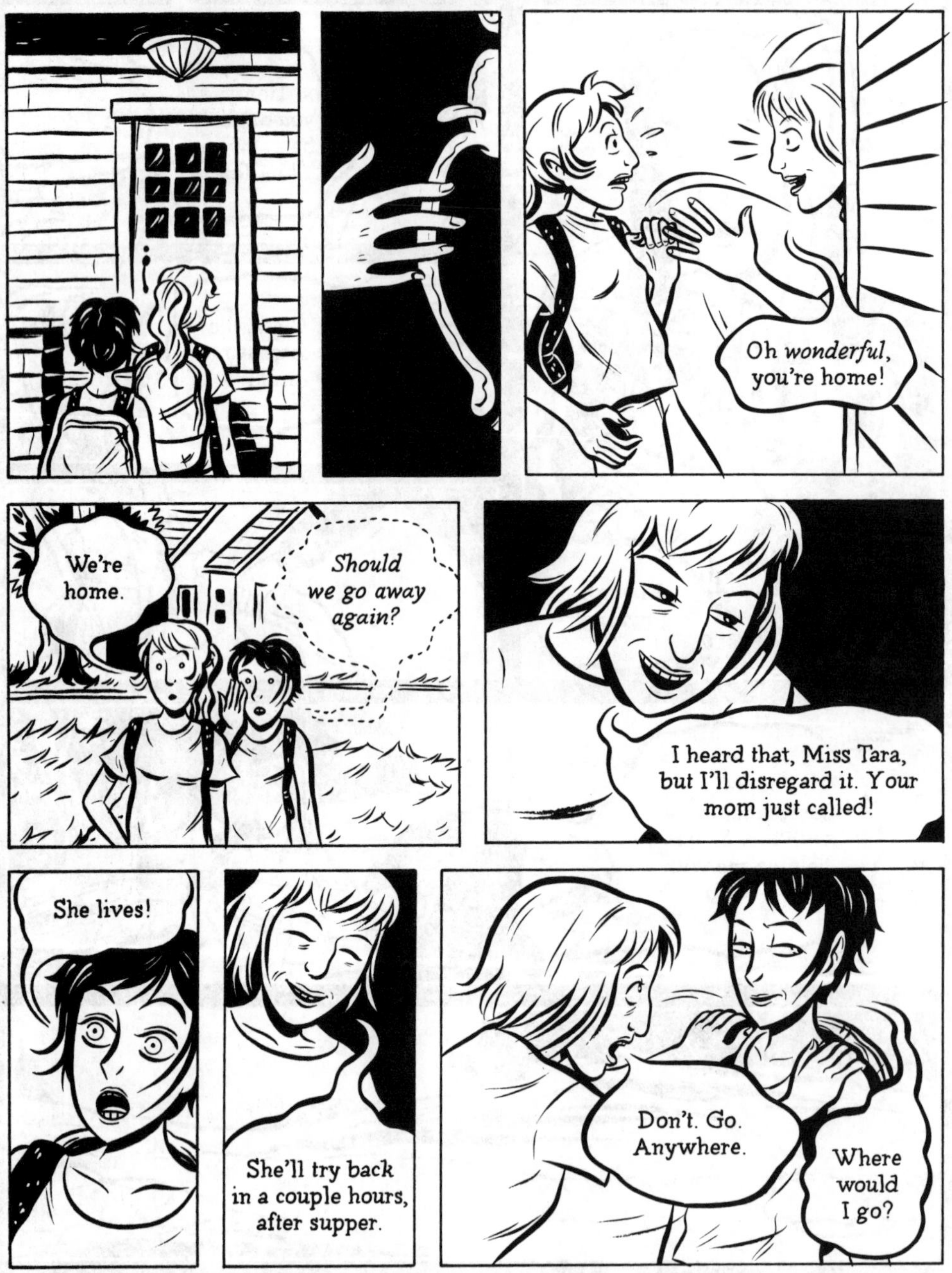
Oh *wonderful*, you're home!
We're home.
Should we go away again?
I heard that, Miss Tara, but I'll disregard it. Your mom just called!
She lives!
She'll try back in a couple hours, after supper.
Don't. Go. Anywhere.
Where would I go?

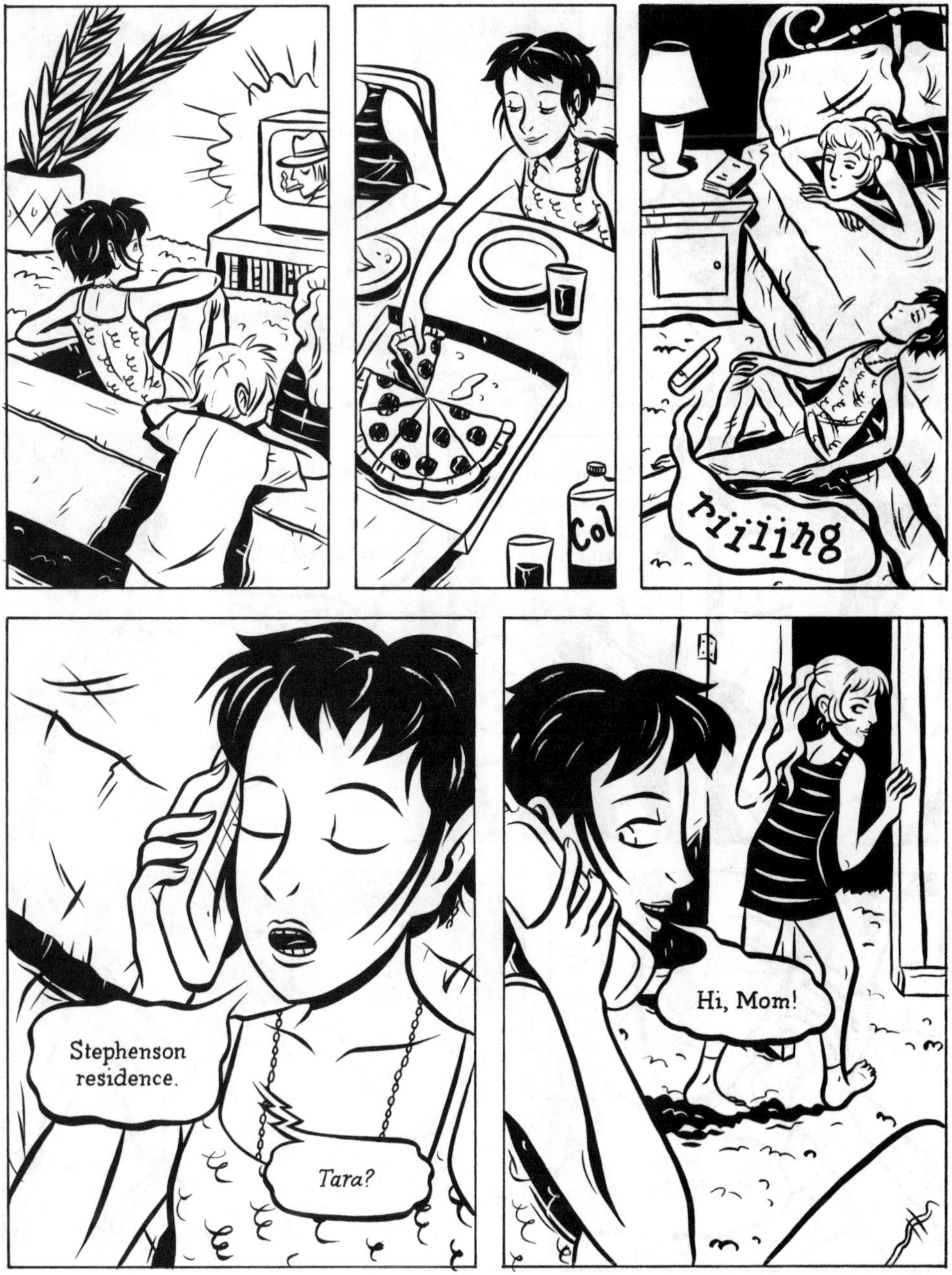
riiiing
Stephenson residence.
Tara?
Hi, Mom!

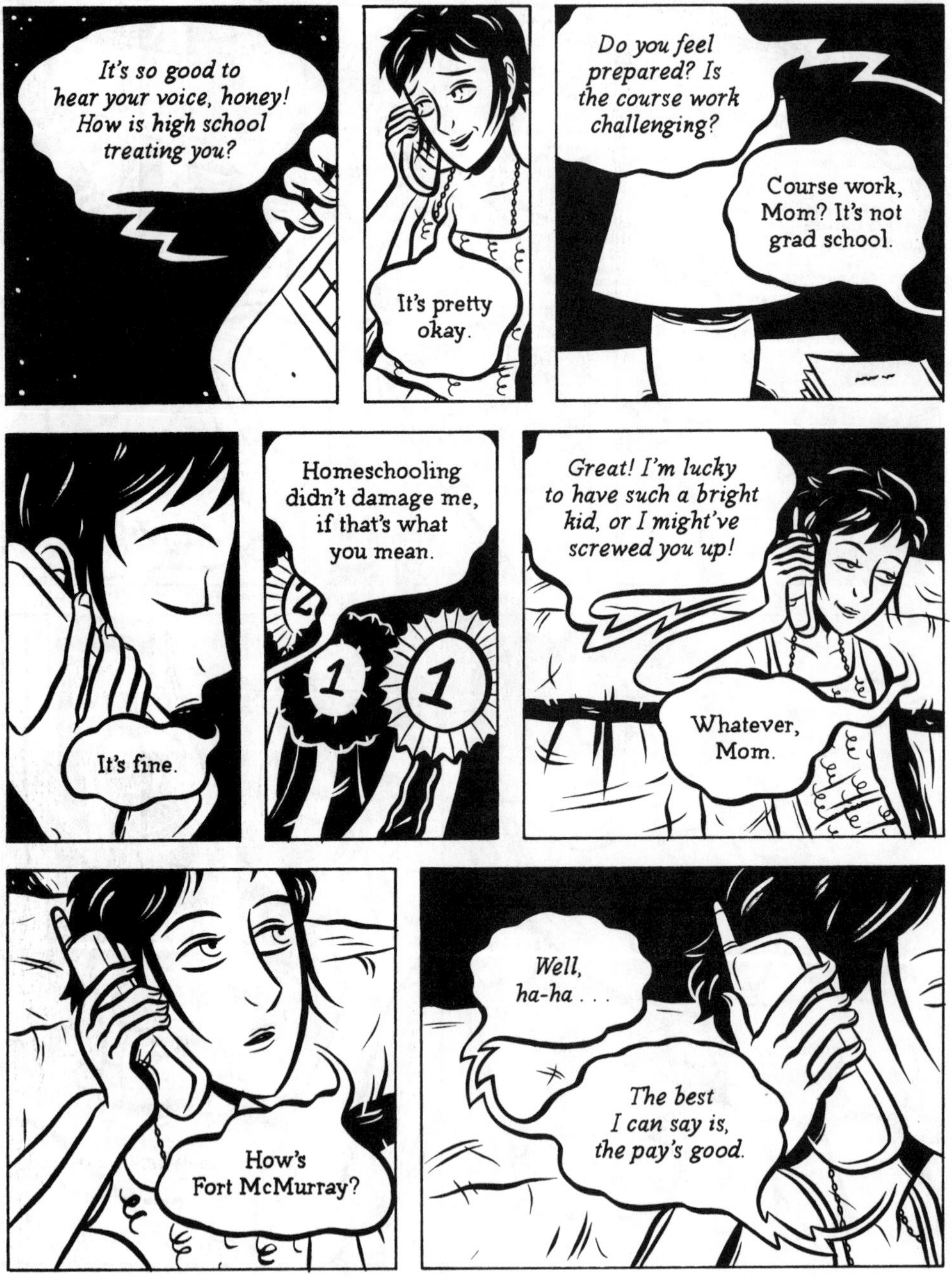
It's so good to hear your voice, honey! How is high school treating you?
It's pretty okay.
Do you feel prepared? Is the course work challenging?
Course work, Mom? It's not grad school.
It's fine.
Homeschooling didn't damage me, if that's what you mean.
1
1
Great! I'm lucky to have such a bright kid, or I might've screwed you up!
Whatever, Mom.
How's Fort McMurray?
Well, ha-ha . . .
The best I can say is, the pay's good.

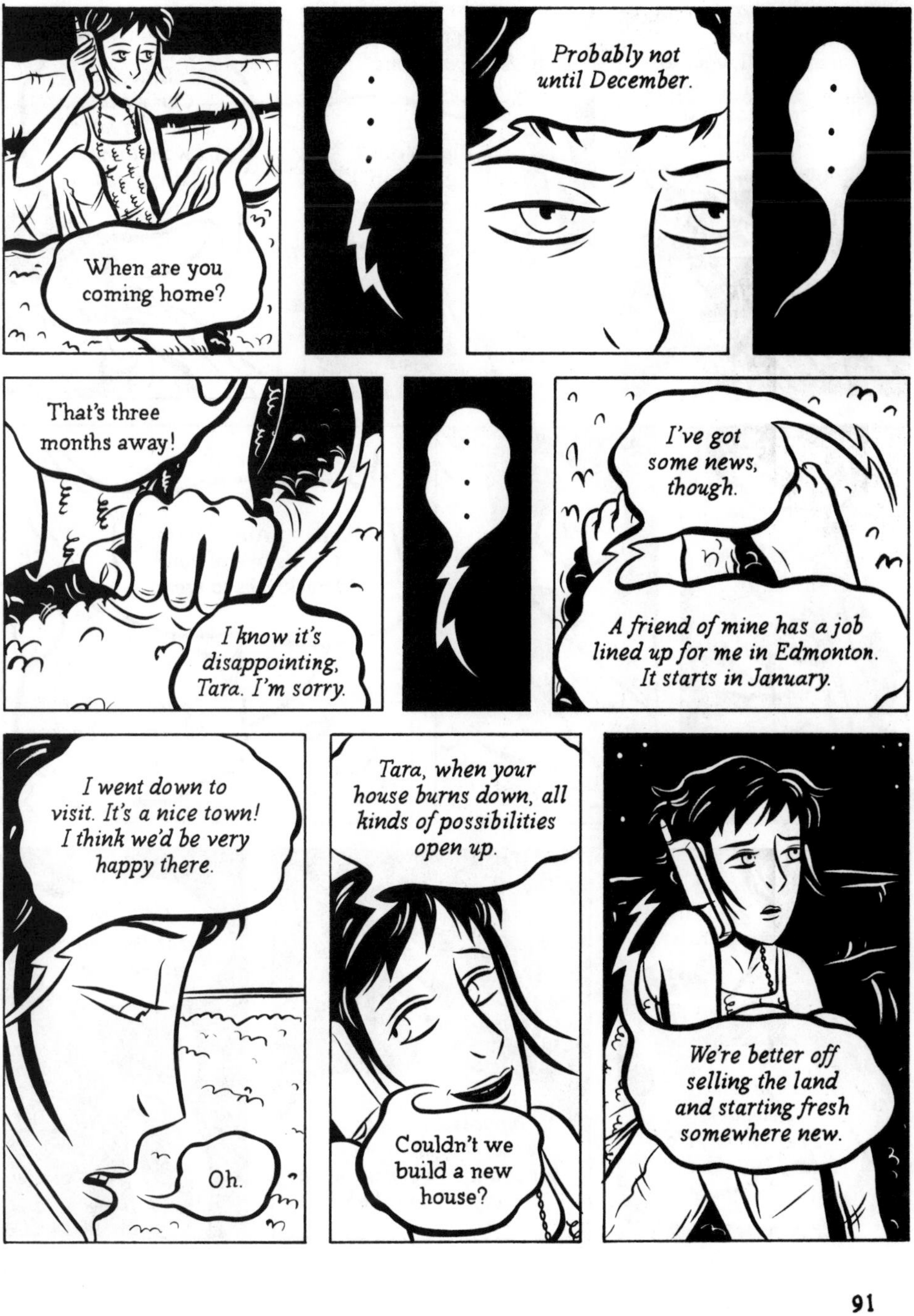
When are you coming home?
...
Probably not until December.
...
That's three months away!
I know it's disappointing, Tara. I'm sorry.
...
I've got some news, though.
A friend of mine has a job lined up for me in Edmonton. It starts in January.
I went down to visit. It's a nice town! I think we'd be very happy there.
Oh.
Tara, when your house burns down, all kinds of possibilities open up.
Couldn't we build a new house?
We're better off selling the land and starting fresh somewhere new.

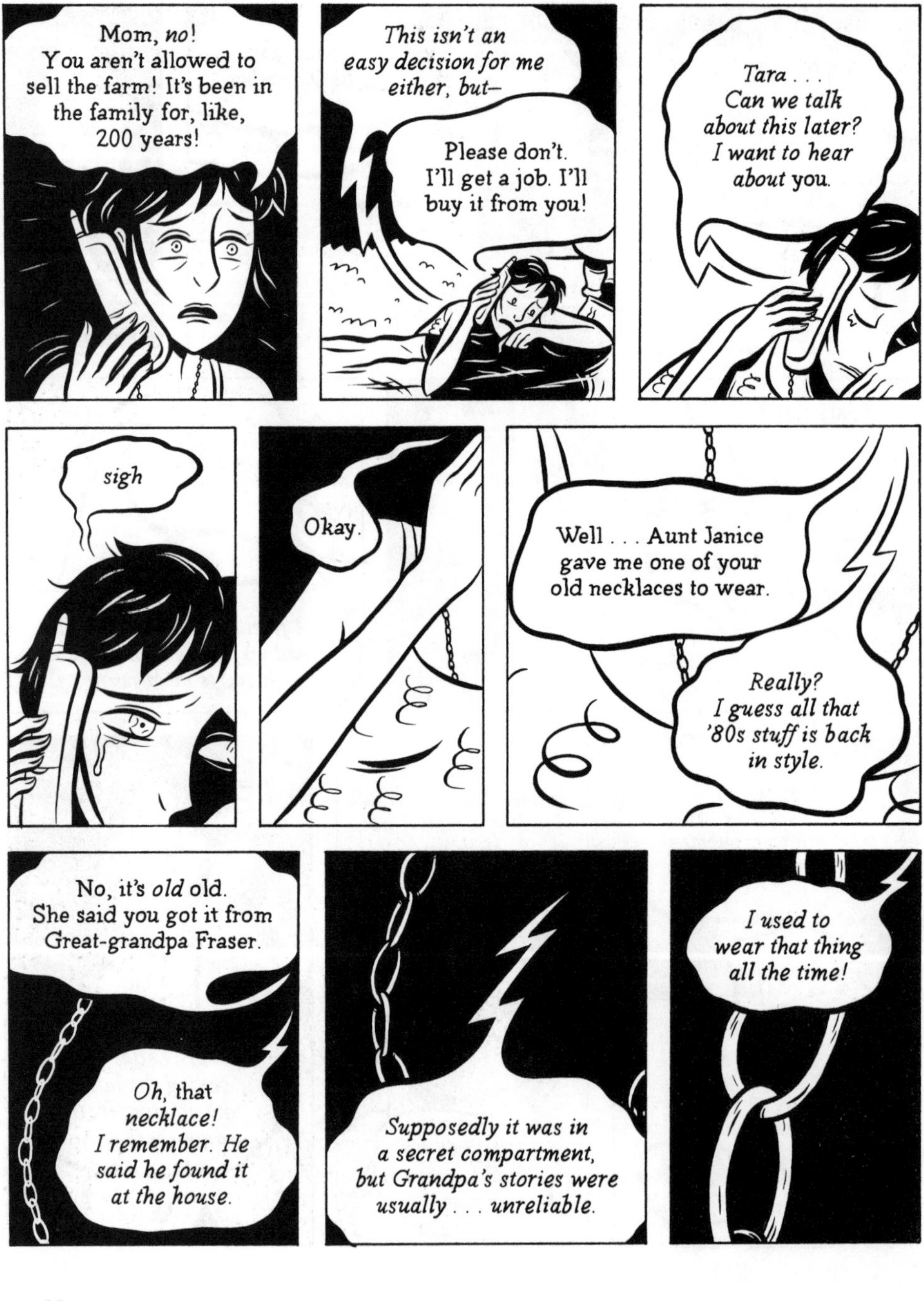
Mom, *no*! You aren't allowed to sell the farm! It's been in the family for, like, 200 years!
This isn't an easy decision for me either, but–
Please don't. I'll get a job. I'll buy it from you!
Tara . . . Can we talk about this later? I want to hear about you.
sigh
Okay.
Well . . . Aunt Janice gave me one of your old necklaces to wear.
Really? I guess all that '80s stuff is back in style.
No, it's *old* old. She said you got it from Great-grandpa Fraser.
Oh, that *necklace! I remember. He said he found it at the house.*
Supposedly it was in a secret compartment, but Grandpa's stories were usually . . . unreliable.
I used to wear that thing all the time!

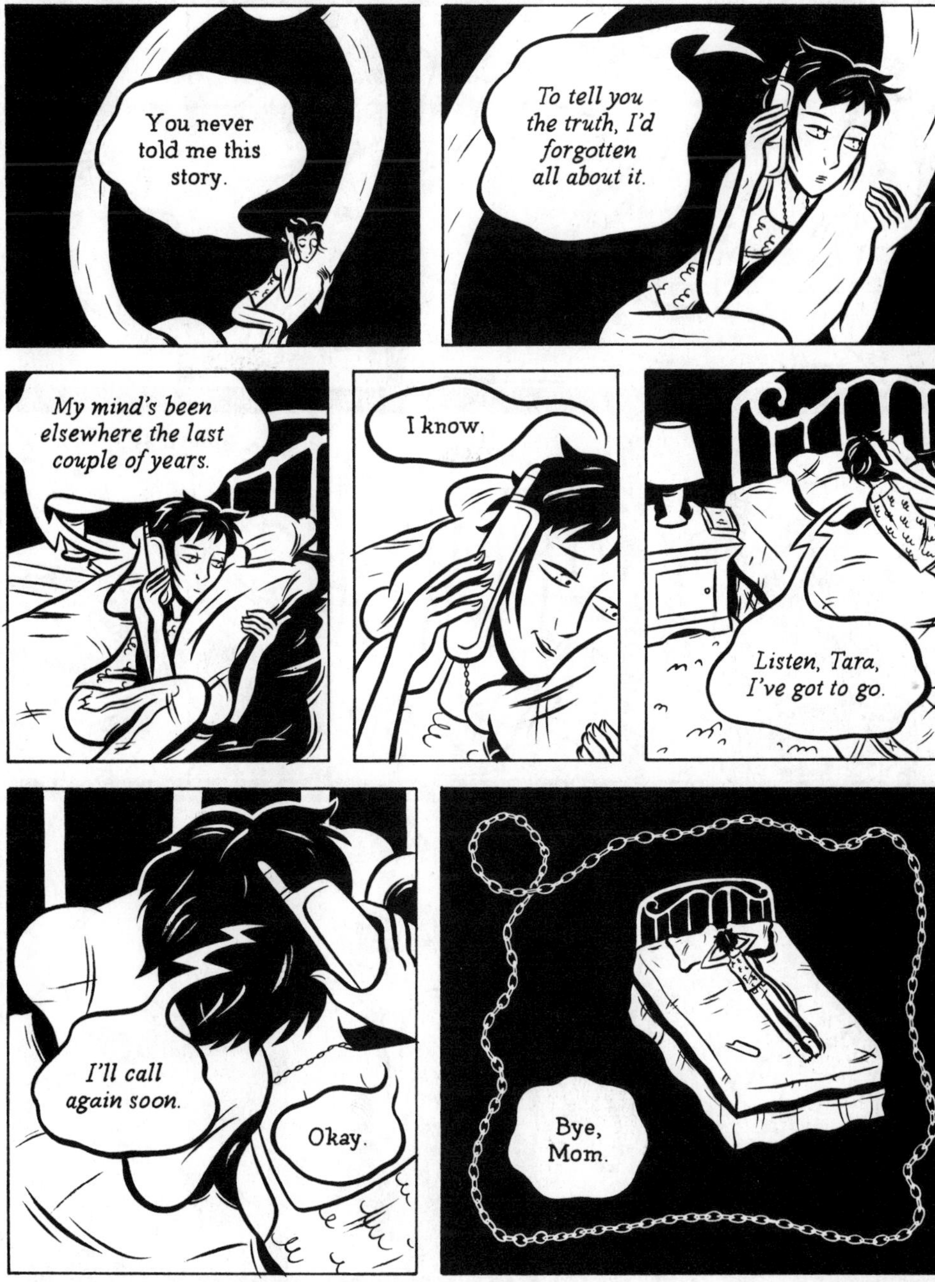
You never told me this story.
To tell you the truth, I'd forgotten all about it.
My mind's been elsewhere the last couple of years.
I know.
Listen, Tara, I've got to go.
I'll call again soon.
Okay.
Bye, Mom.

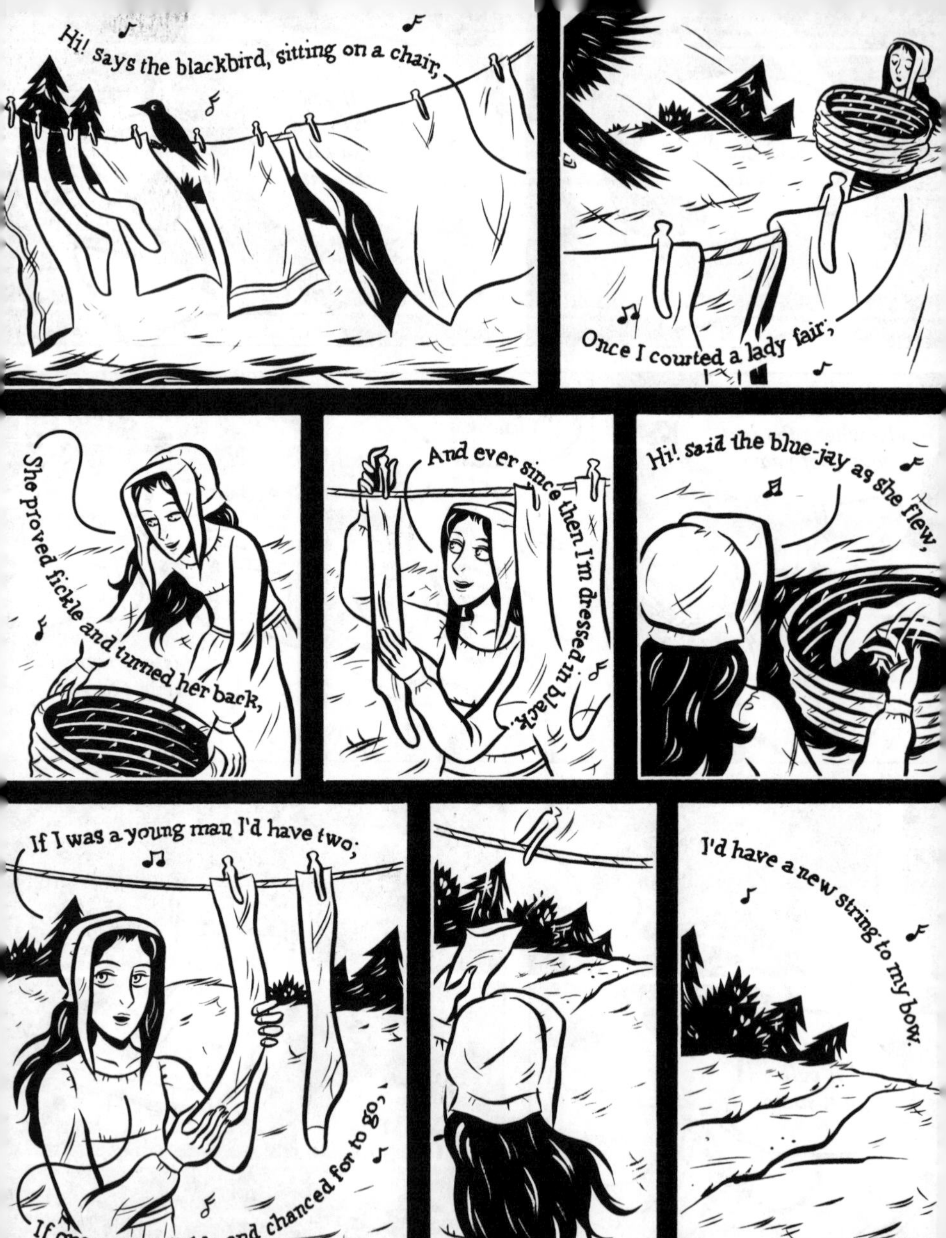
Hi! says the blackbird, sitting on a chair,
Once I courted a lady fair;
She proved fickle and turned her back,
And ever since then I'm dressed in black.
Hi! said the blue-jay as she flew,
If I was a young man I'd have two;
If one proved fickle and chanced for to go,
I'd have a new string to my bow.

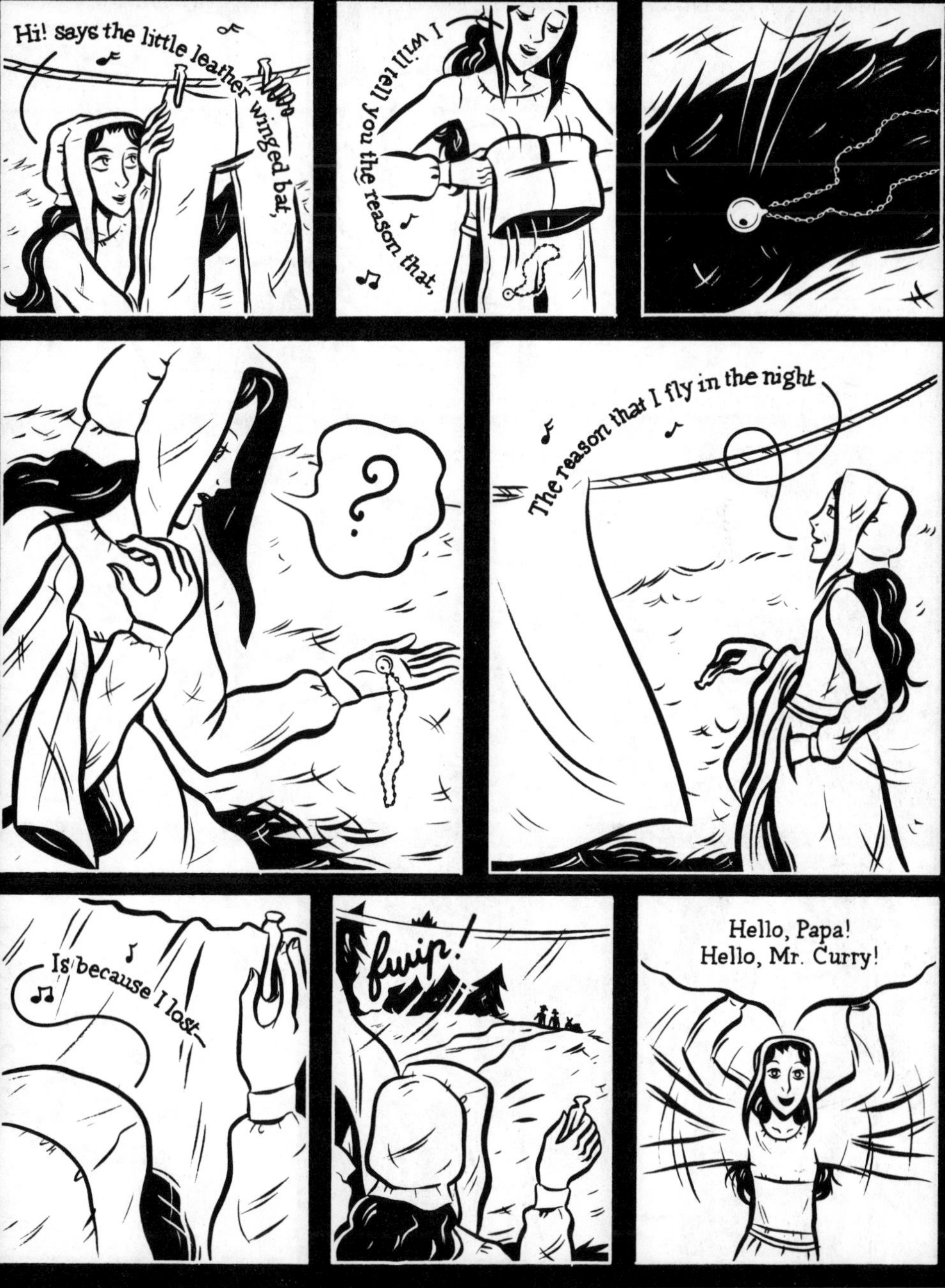
Hi! says the little leather winged bat,
I will tell you the reason that,
?
The reason that I fly in the night
Is because I lost
fwip!
Hello, Papa!
Hello, Mr. Curry!

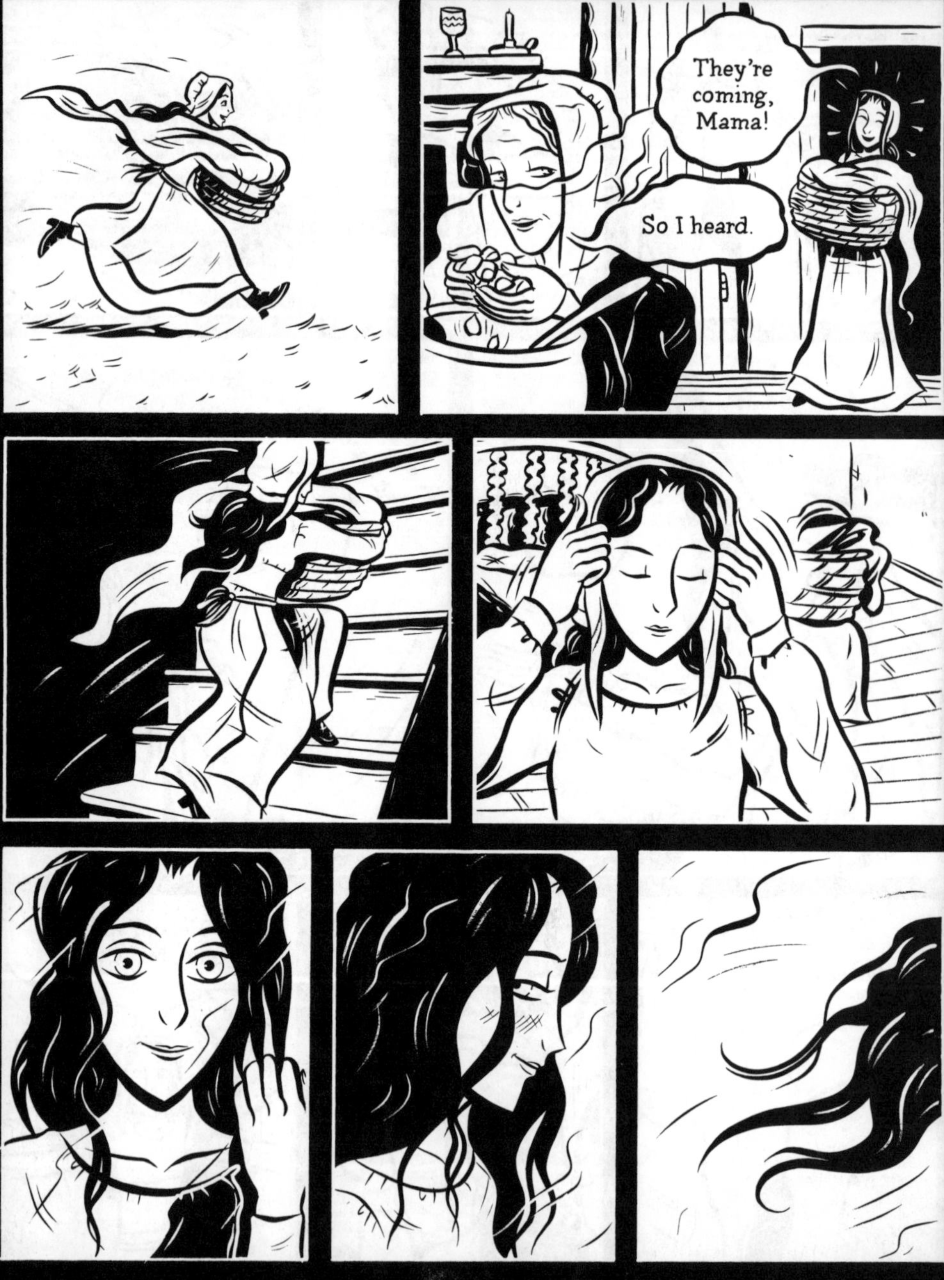
They're coming, Mama!
So I heard.

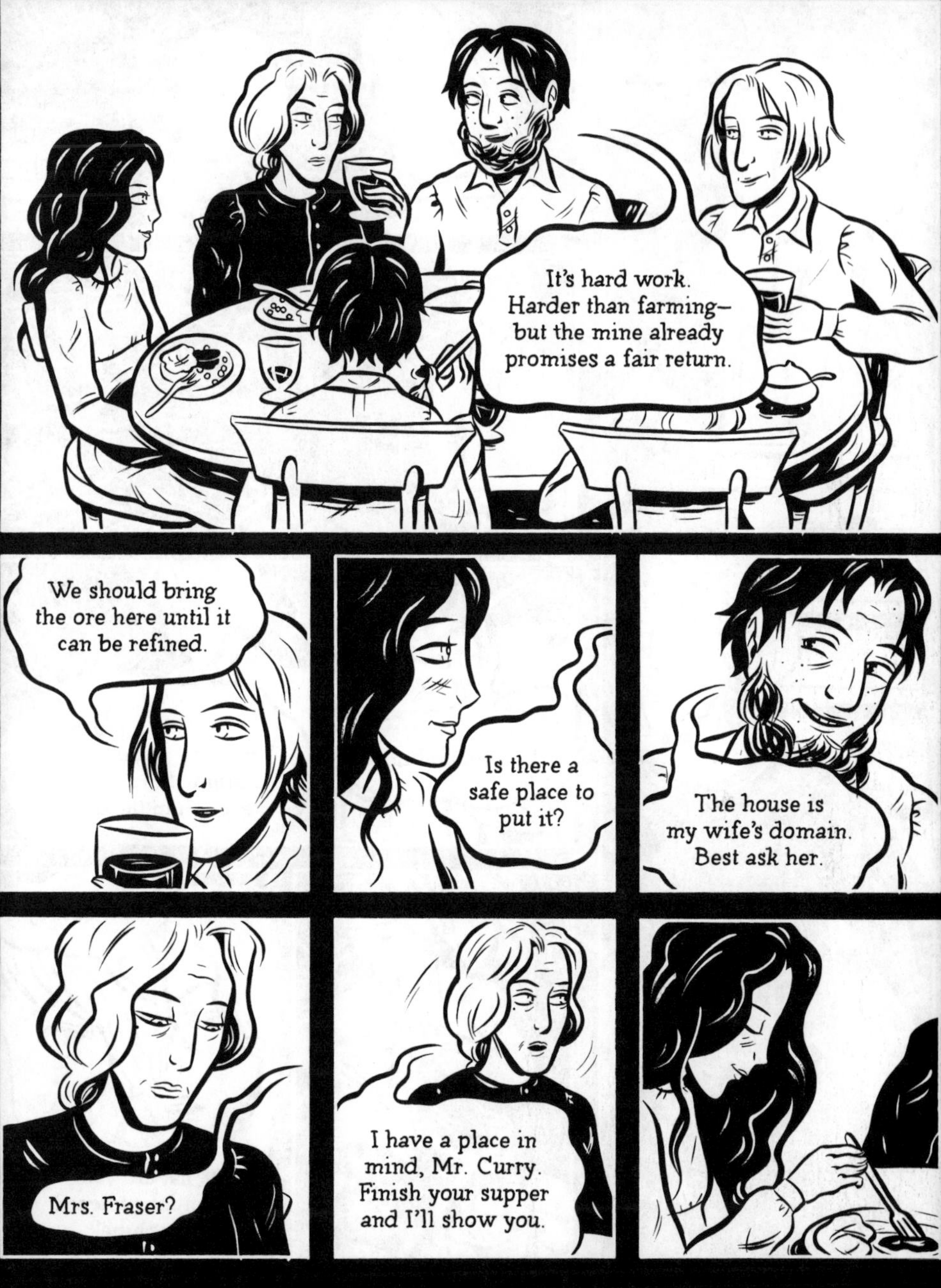
It's hard work. Harder than farming– but the mine already promises a fair return.
We should bring the ore here until it can be refined.
Is there a safe place to put it?
The house is my wife's domain. Best ask her.
Mrs. Fraser?
I have a place in mind, Mr. Curry. Finish your supper and I'll show you.

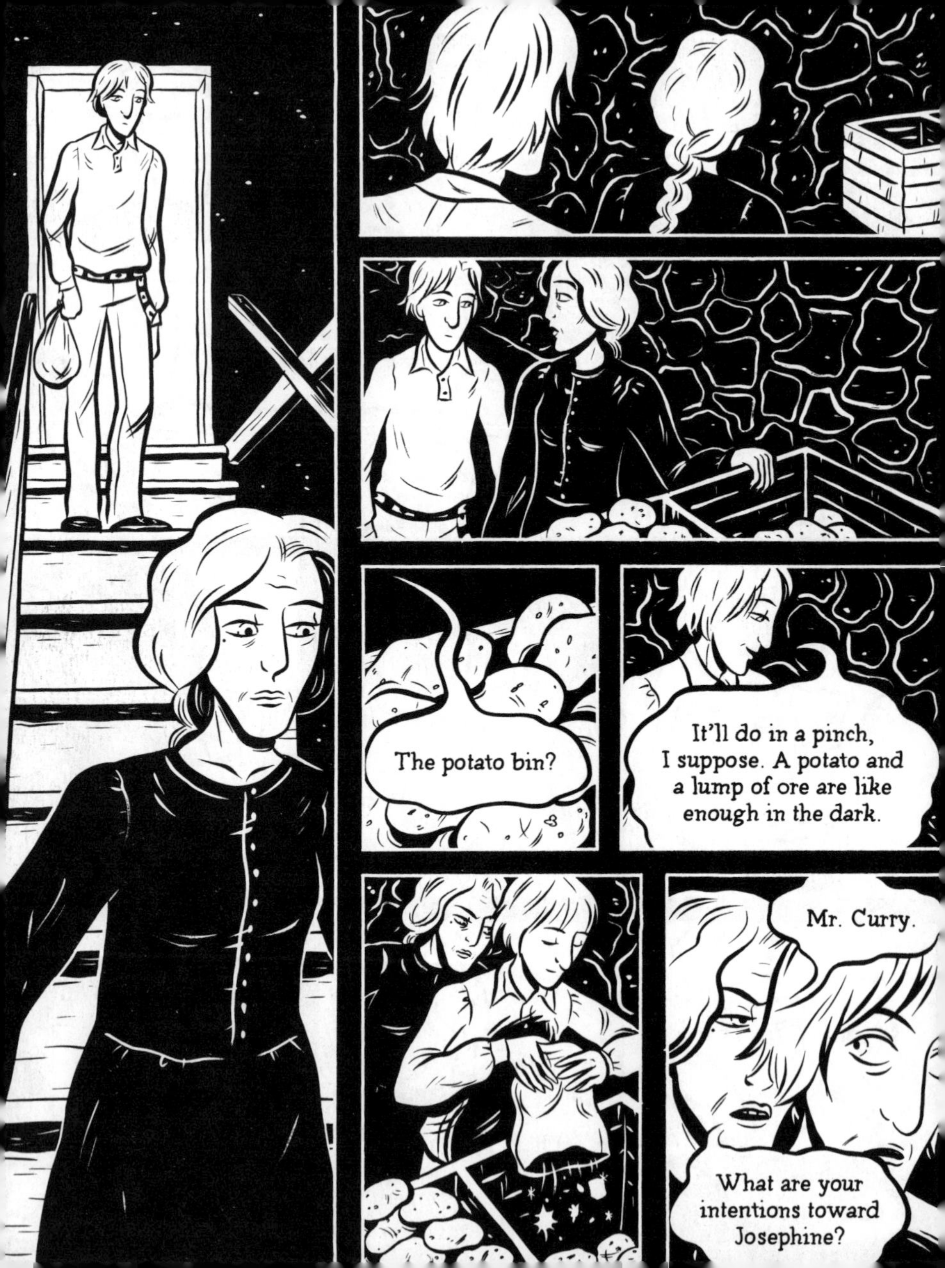
The potato bin?
It'll do in a pinch, I suppose. A potato and a lump of ore are like enough in the dark.
Mr. Curry.
What are your intentions toward Josephine?

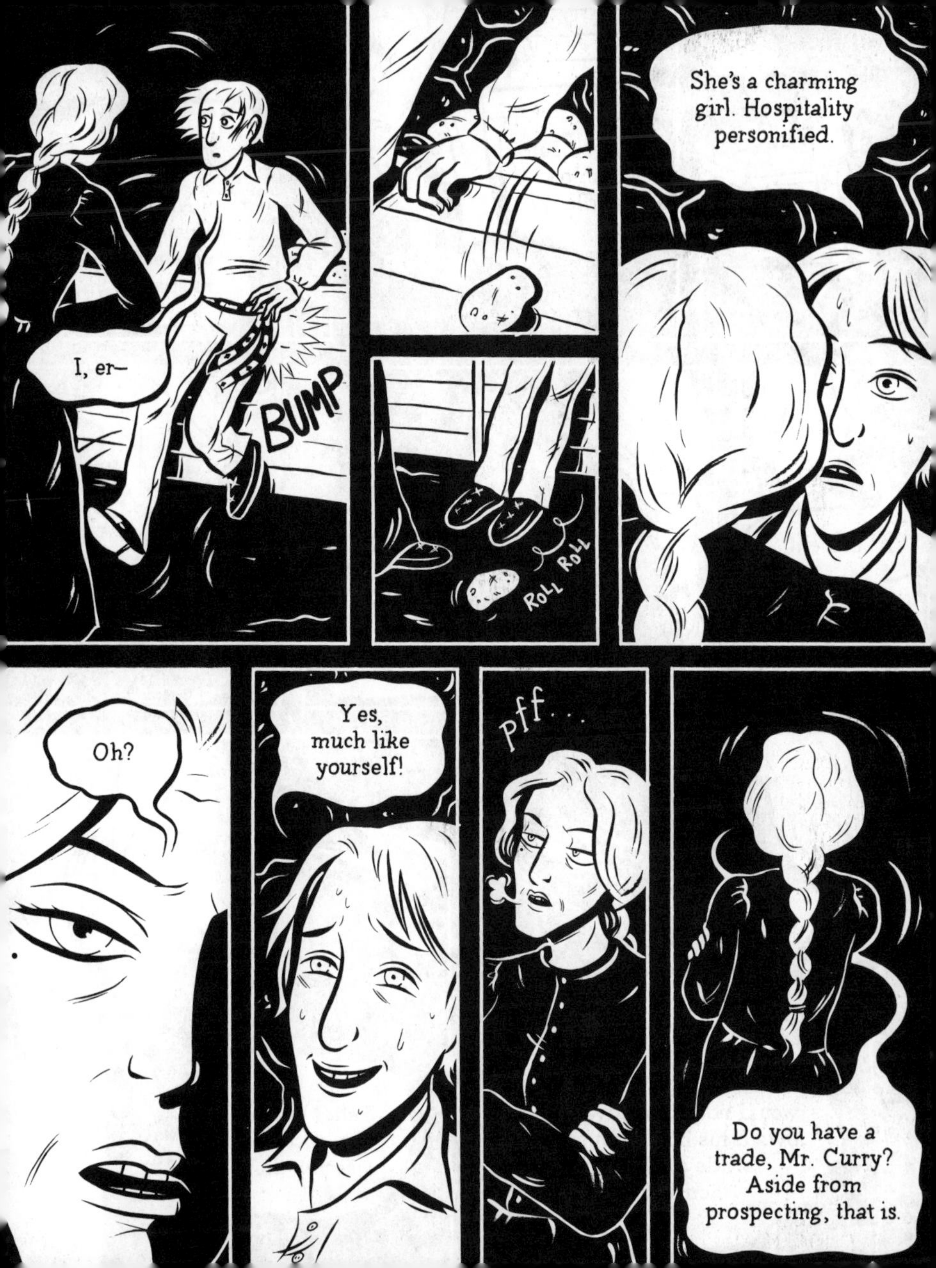
I, er–
BUMP
ROLL ROLL
She's a charming girl. Hospitality personified.
Oh?
Yes, much like yourself!
pff...
Do you have a trade, Mr. Curry? Aside from prospecting, that is.

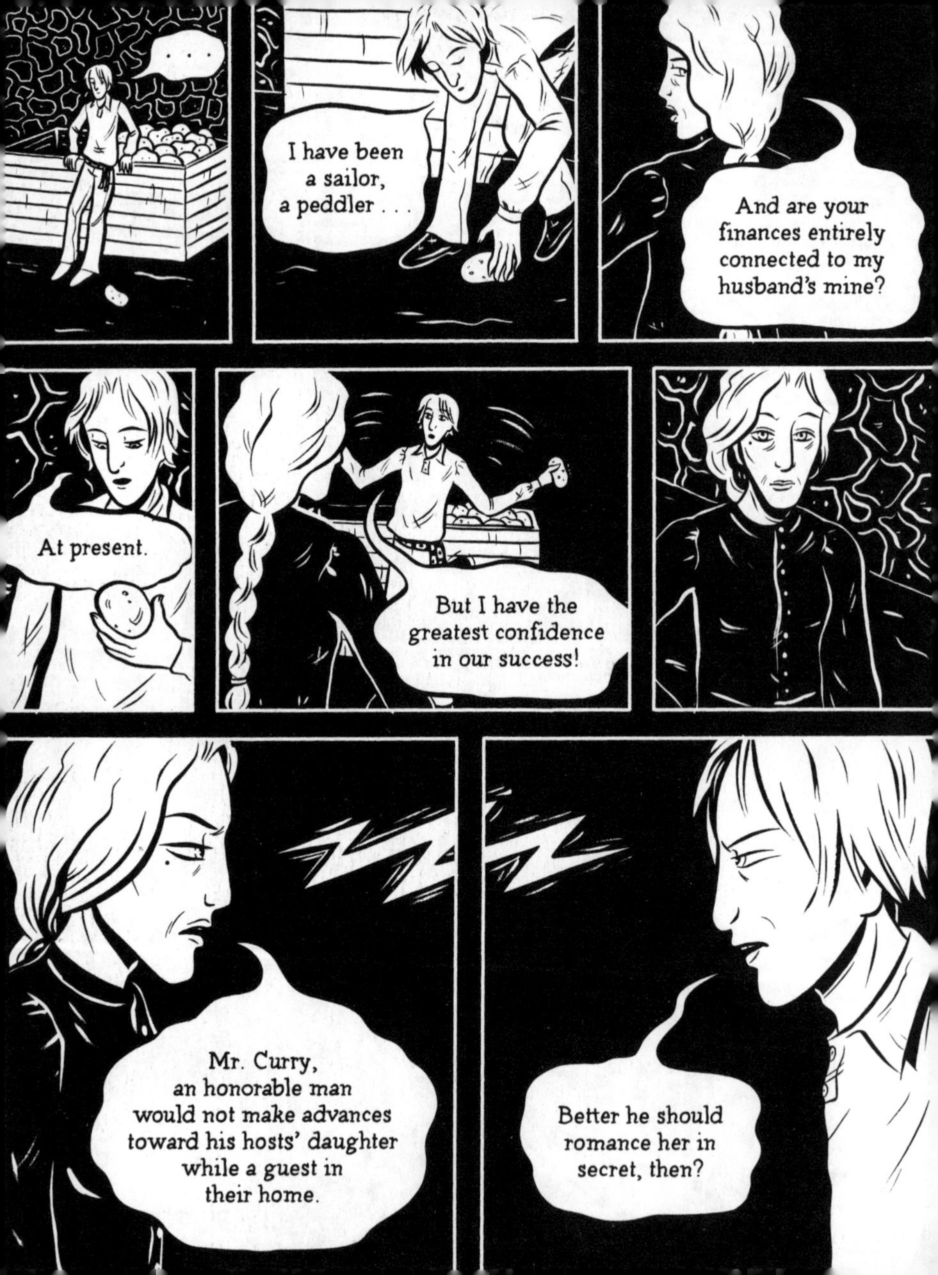
. . .
I have been a sailor, a peddler . . .
And are your finances entirely connected to my husband's mine?
At present.
But I have the greatest confidence in our success!
Mr. Curry, an honorable man would not make advances toward his hosts' daughter while a guest in their home.
Better he should romance her in secret, then?

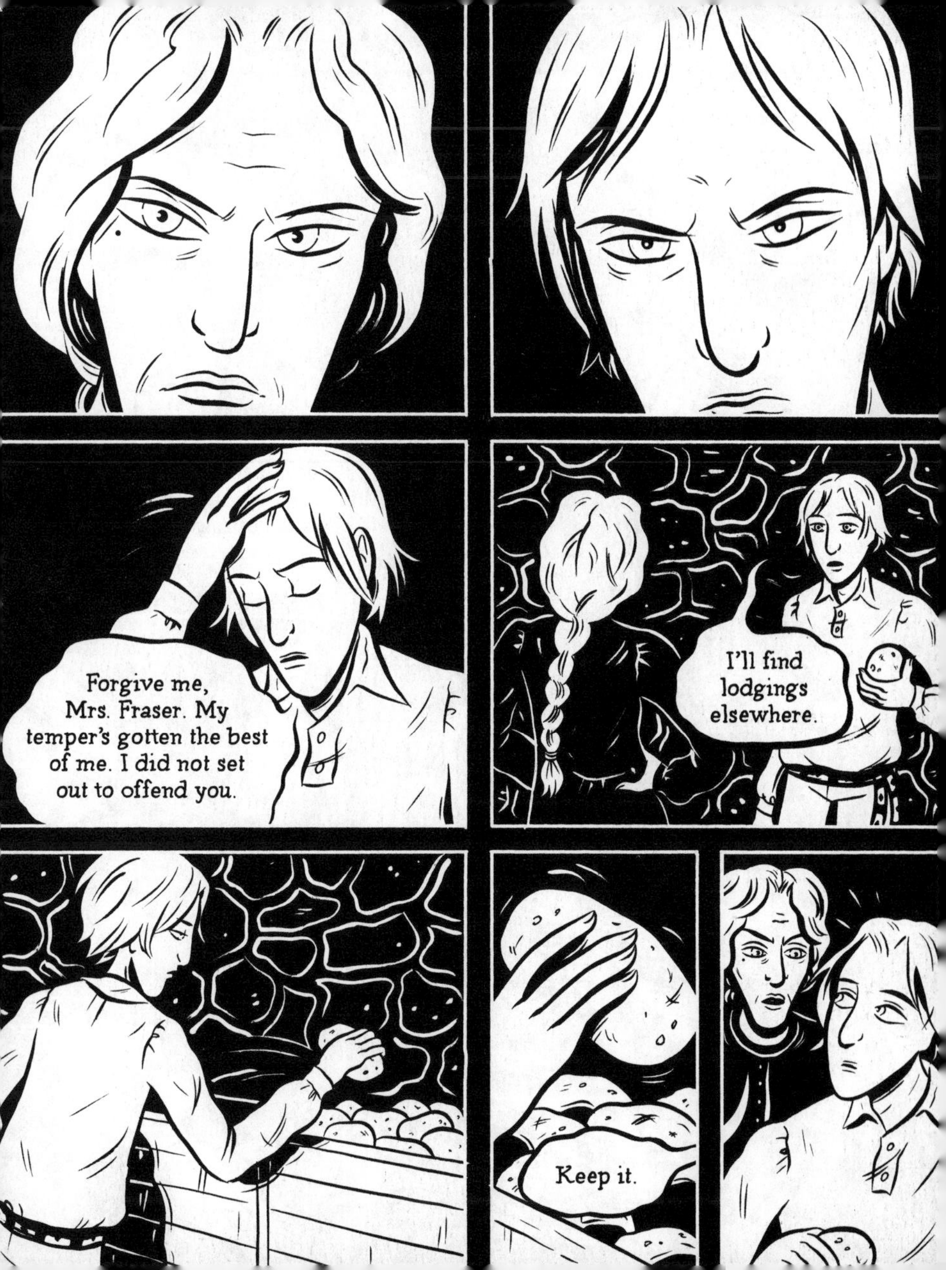
Forgive me, Mrs. Fraser. My temper's gotten the best of me. I did not set out to offend you.
I'll find lodgings elsewhere.
Keep it.

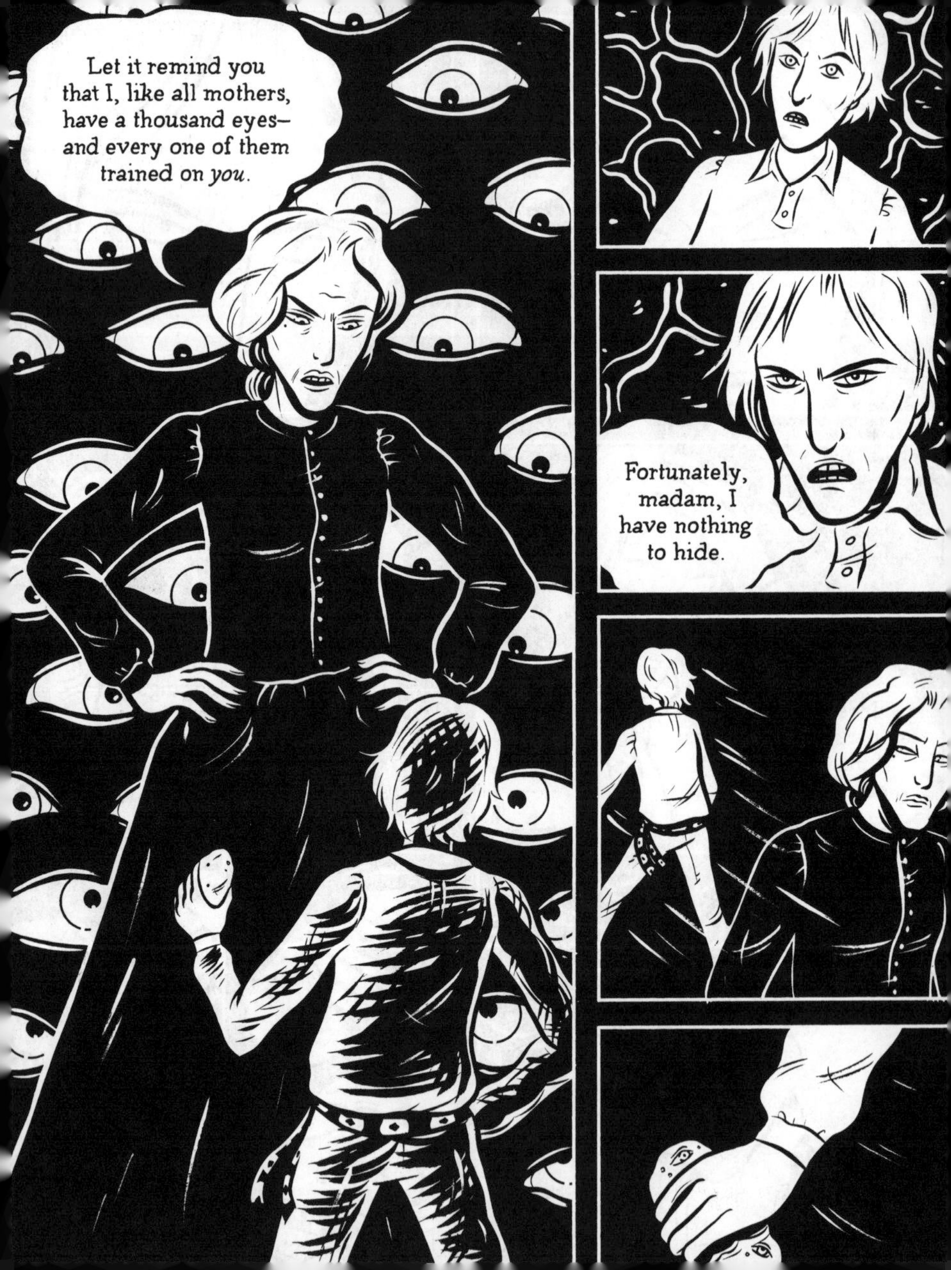
Let it remind you that I, like all mothers, have a thousand eyes— and every one of them trained on *you*.
Fortunately, madam, I have nothing to hide.

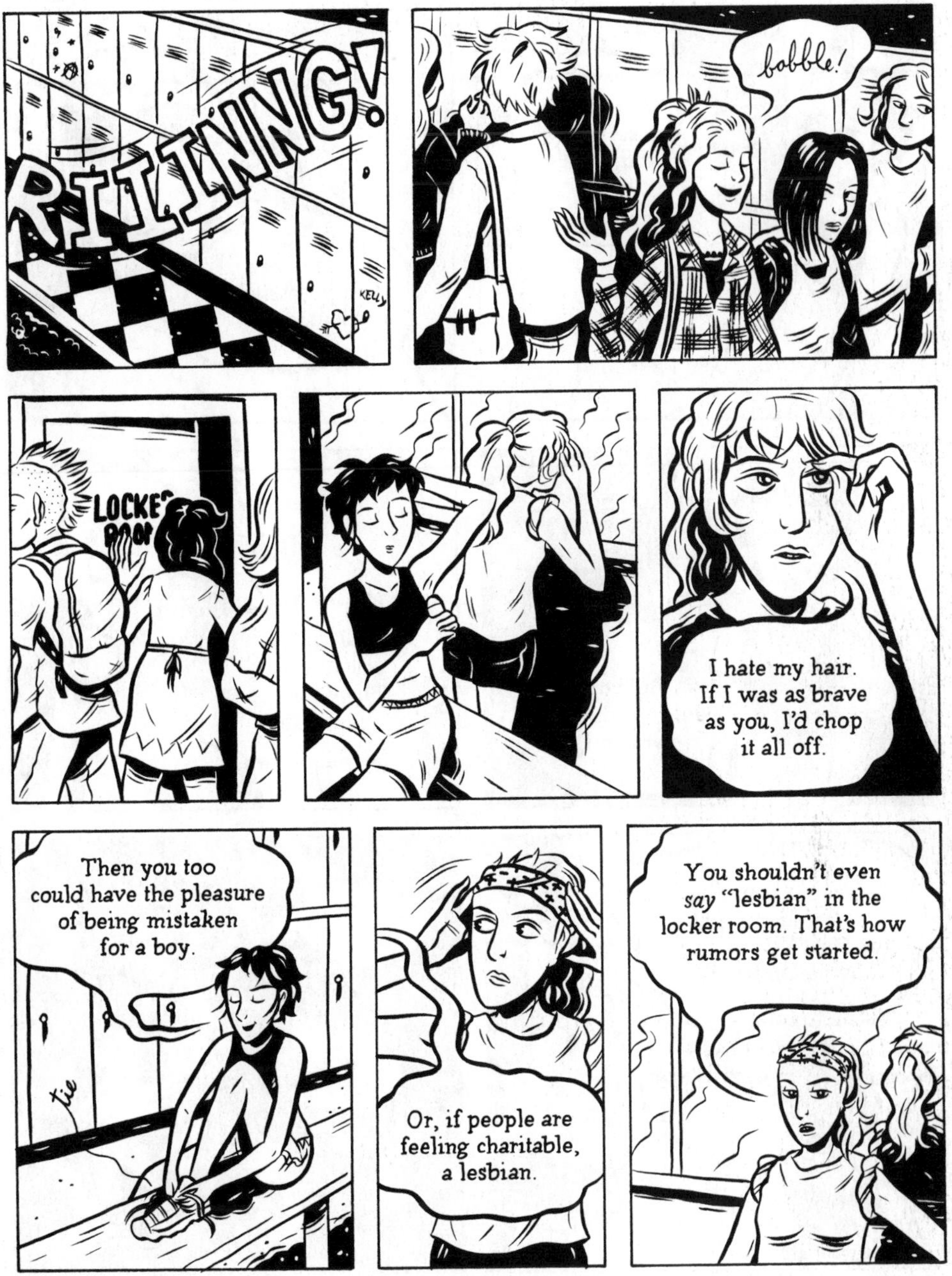
RIIINNG!
KELLY
bobble!
LOCKER ROOM
I hate my hair. If I was as brave as you, I'd chop it all off.
Then you too could have the pleasure of being mistaken for a boy.
tie
Or, if people are feeling charitable, a lesbian.
You shouldn't even *say* "lesbian" in the locker room. That's how rumors get started.

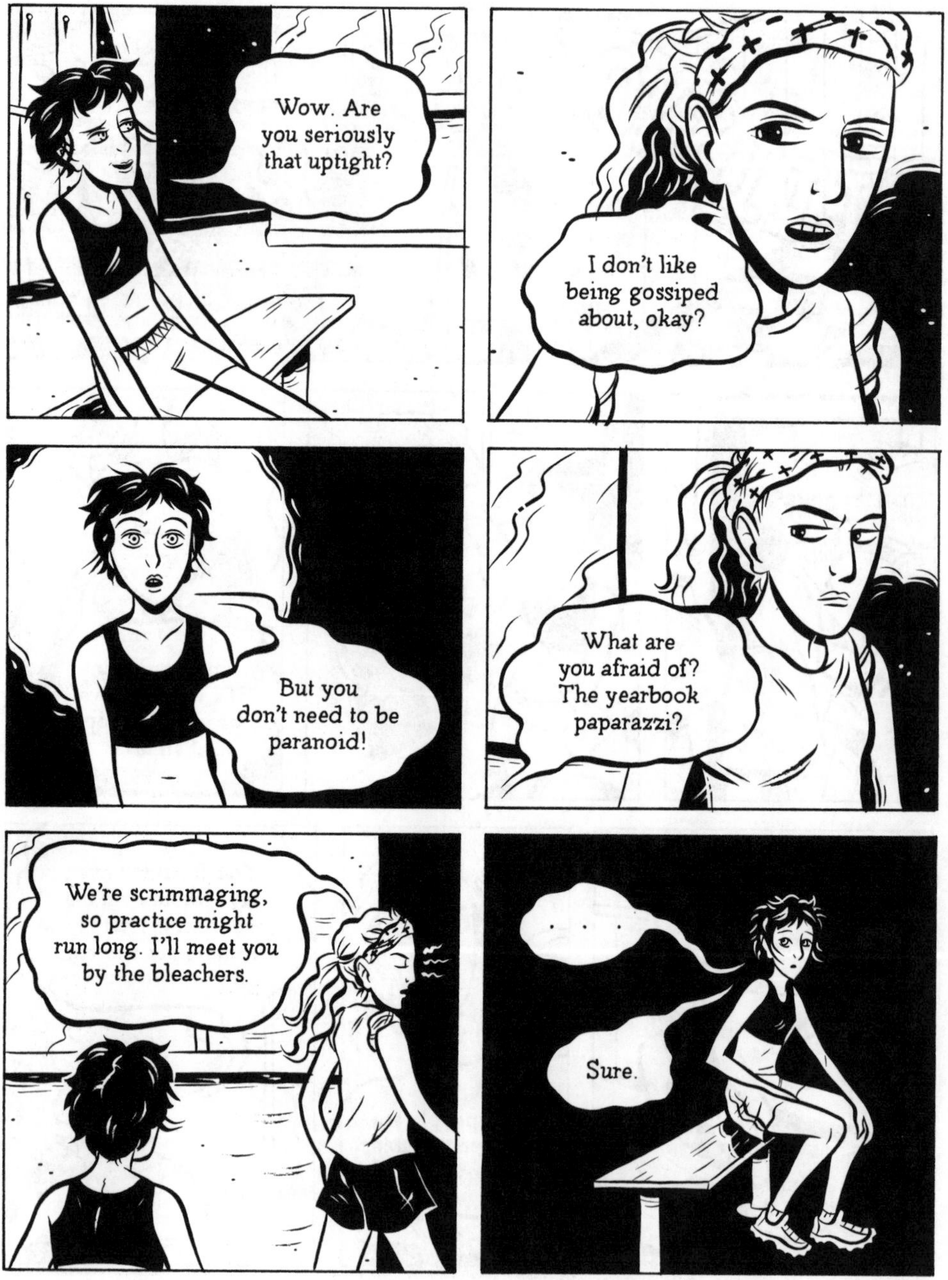
Wow. Are you seriously that uptight?
I don't like being gossiped about, okay?
But you don't need to be paranoid!
What are you afraid of? The yearbook paparazzi?
We're scrimmaging, so practice might run long. I'll meet you by the bleachers.
. . .
Sure.

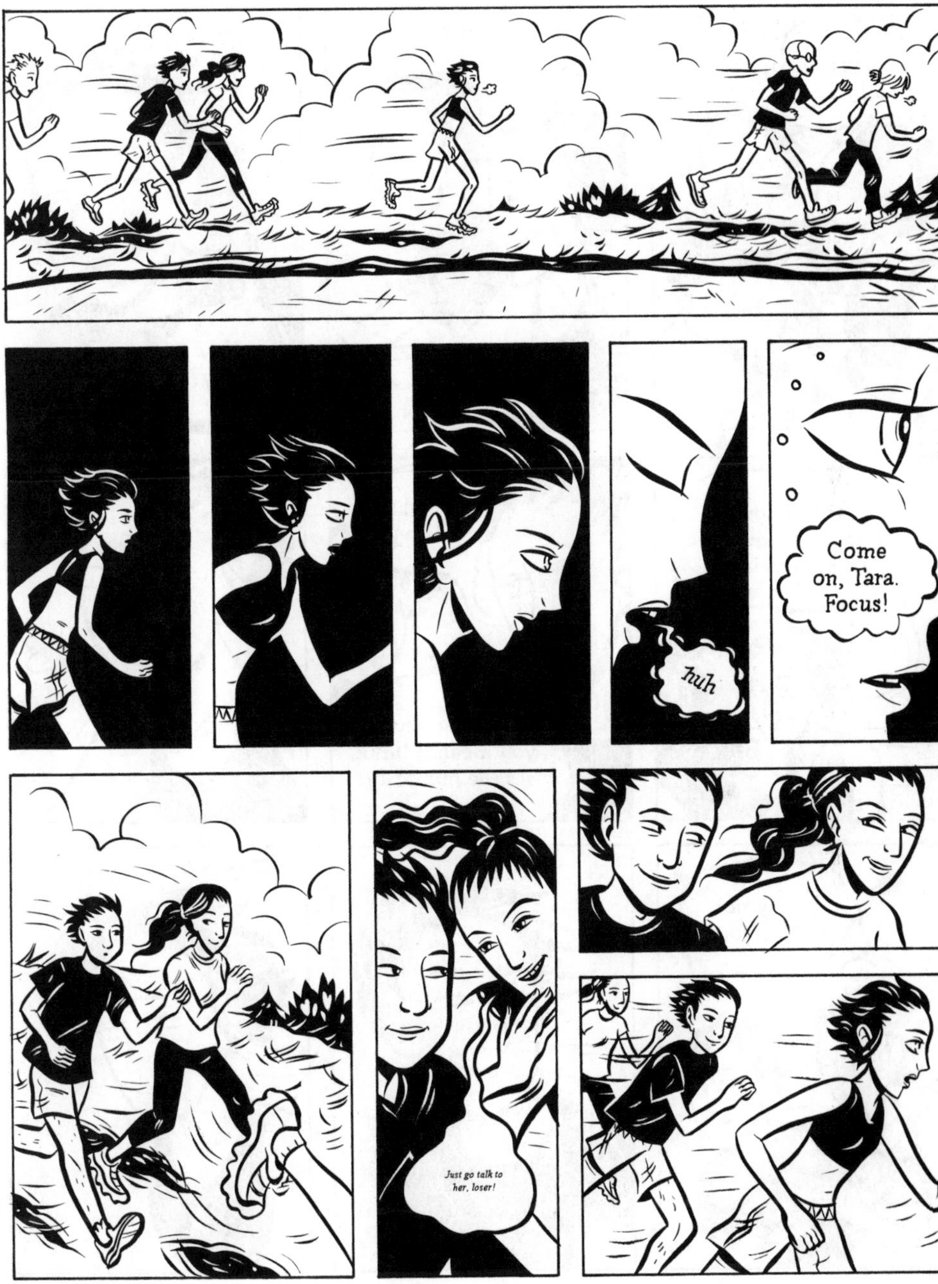
huh
Come on, Tara. Focus!
Just go talk to her, loser!

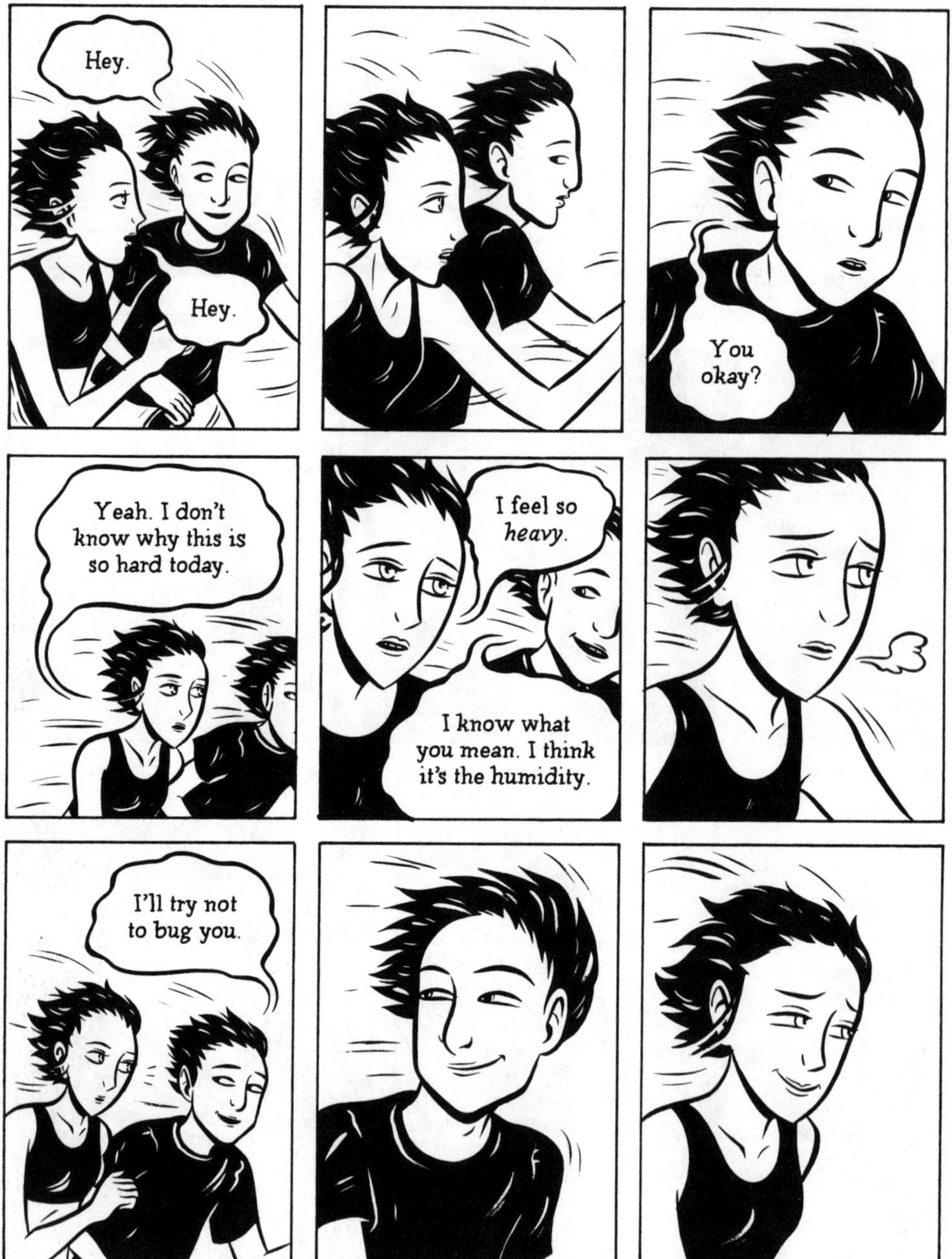
Hey.
Hey.
You okay?
Yeah. I don't know why this is so hard today.
I feel so *heavy*.
I know what you mean. I think it's the humidity.
I'll try not to bug you.

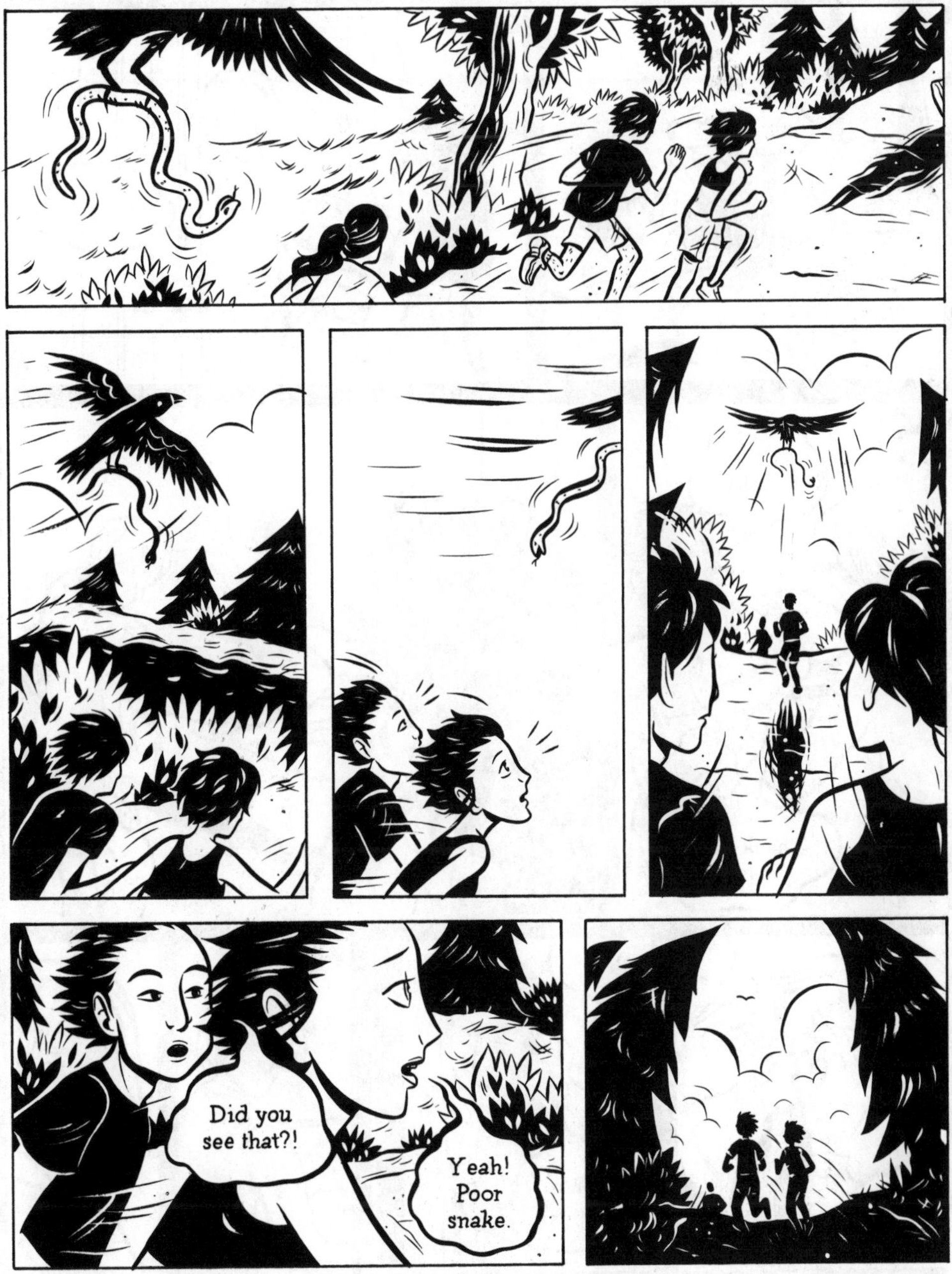
Did you see that?!
Yeah! Poor snake.

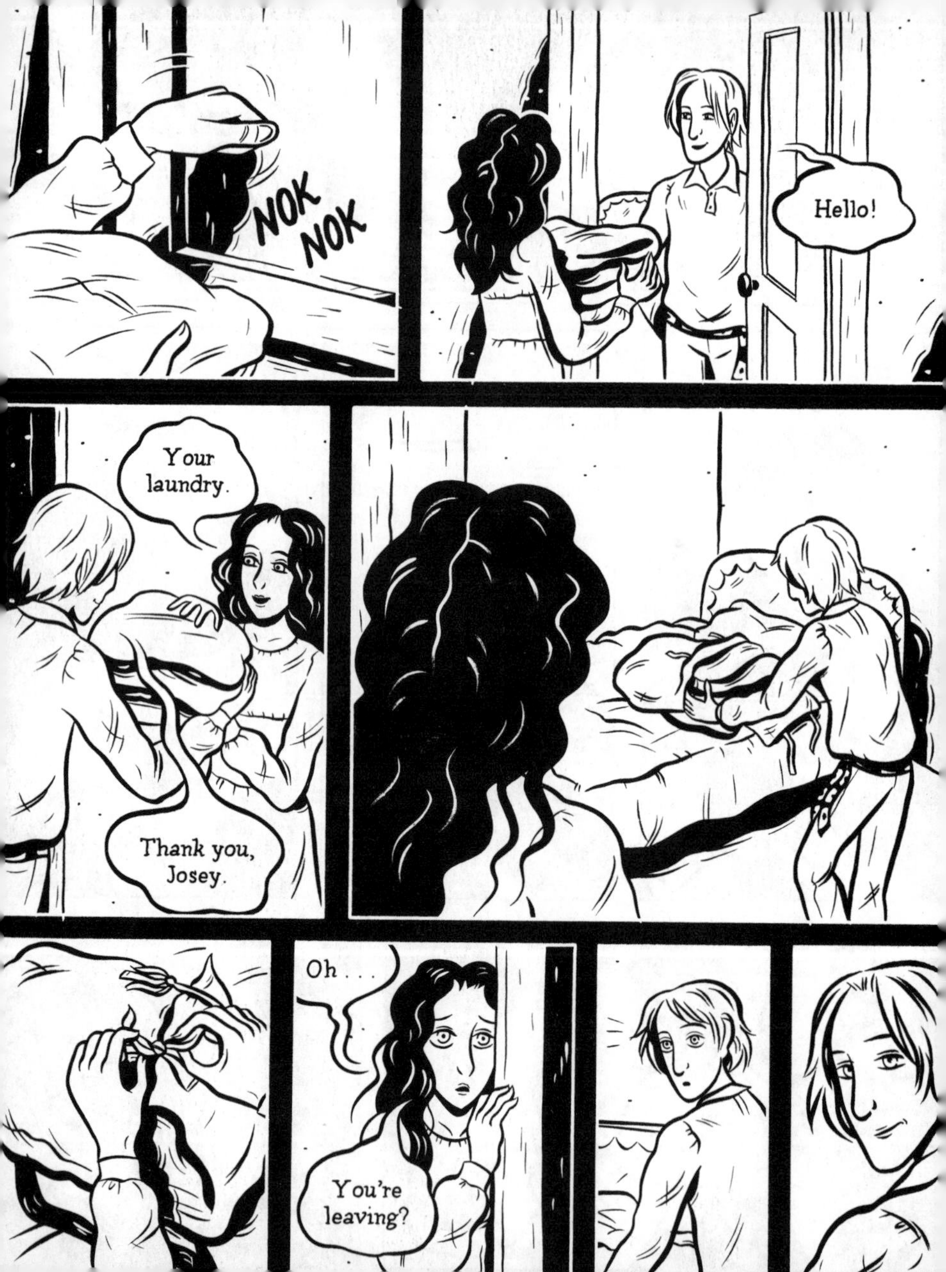
NOK NOK
Hello!
Your laundry.
Thank you, Josey.
Oh . . .
You're leaving?

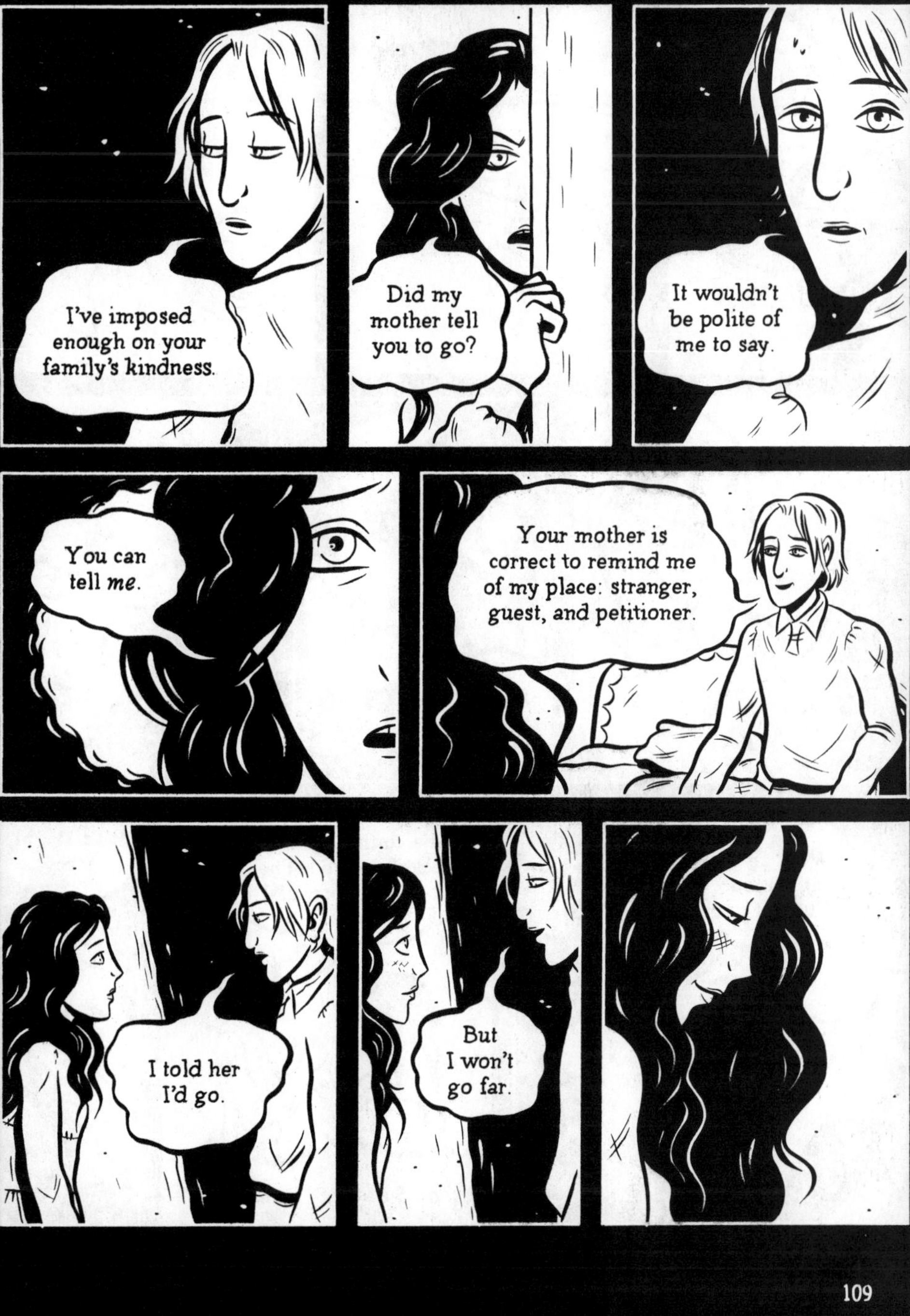
I've imposed enough on your family's kindness.
Did my mother tell you to go?
It wouldn't be polite of me to say.
You can tell *me*.
Your mother is correct to remind me of my place: stranger, guest, and petitioner.
I told her I'd go.
But I won't go far.

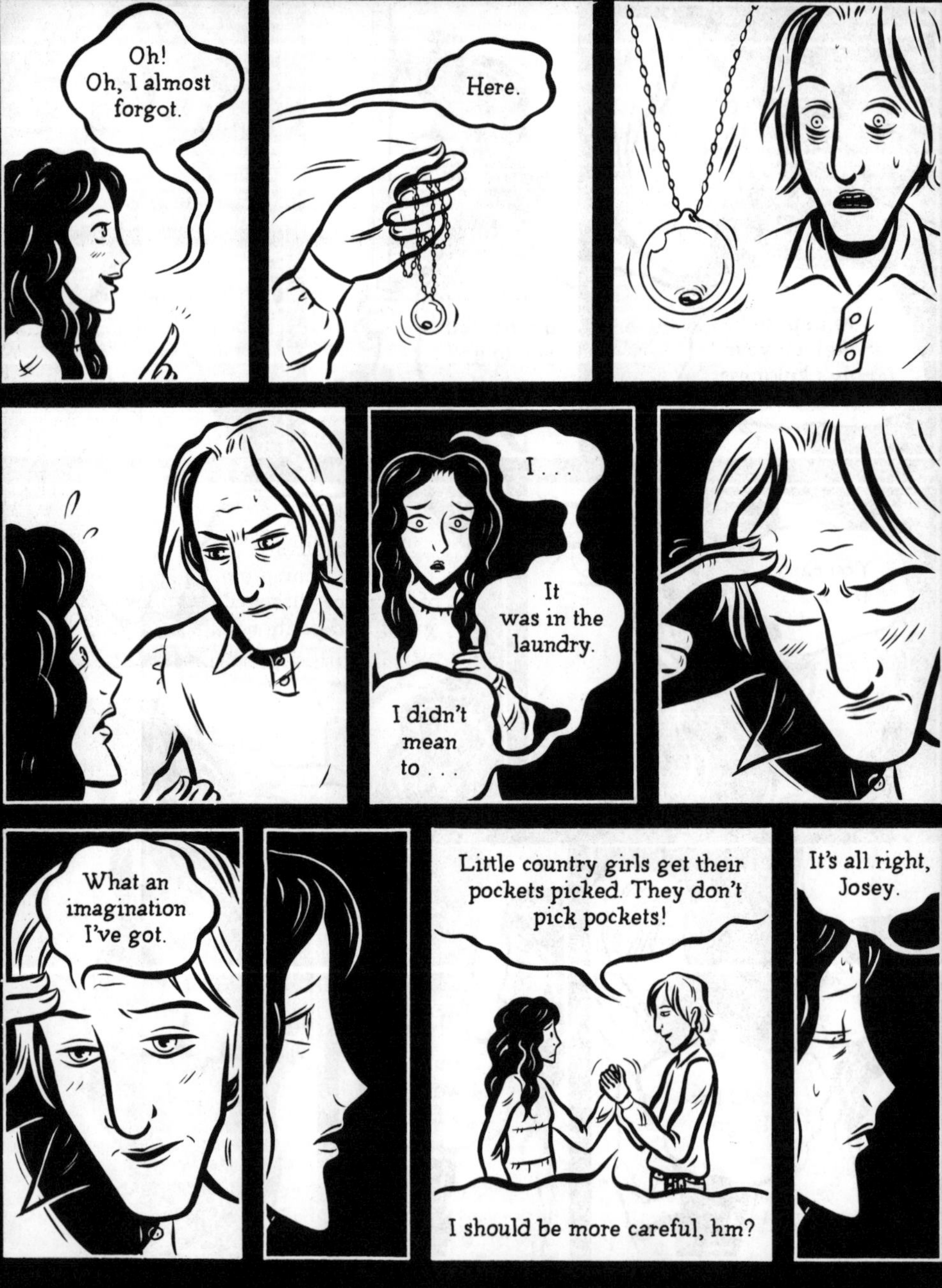
Oh!
Oh, I almost forgot.
Here.
I . . .
It was in the laundry.
I didn't mean to . . .
What an imagination I've got.
Little country girls get their pockets picked. They don't pick pockets!
I should be more careful, hm?
It's all right, Josey.

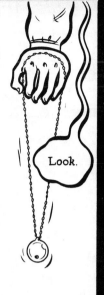

Look.

Quicksilver in glass. It's French*, very old.

*Acadian

It seeks out gold.

Or, maybe, gold seeks the quicksilver. Do you know how gold is purified, Josey?

No.

It's a simple process. Crush the ore, add mercury and a little heat . . .

Nothing to it.

Gold truly is a noble metal, Josey. It wants only to become pure.

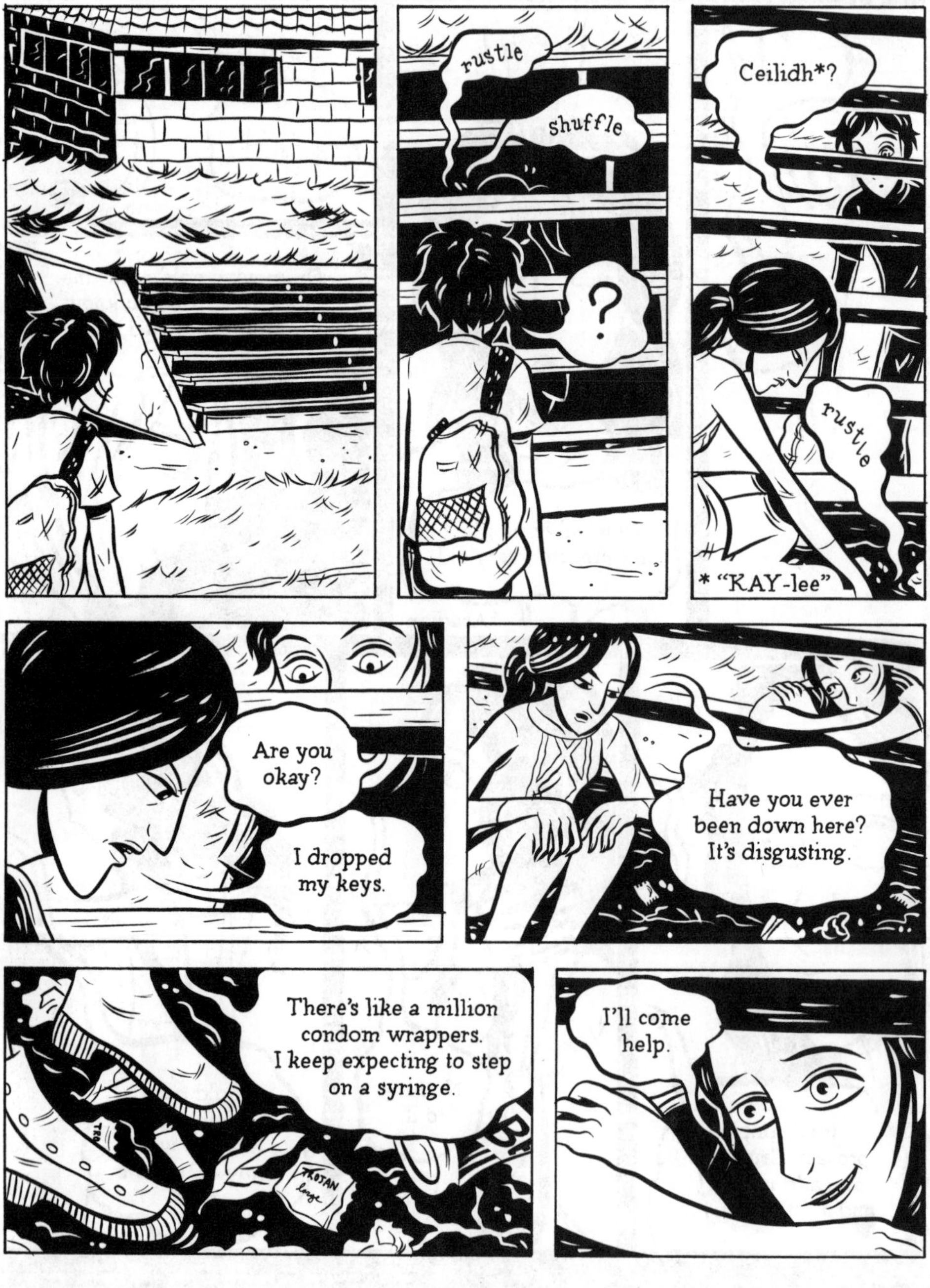
rustle
shuffle
?
Ceilidh*?
rustle
* "KAY-lee"
Are you okay?
I dropped my keys.
Have you ever been down here? It's disgusting.
There's like a million condom wrappers. I keep expecting to step on a syringe.
I'll come help.

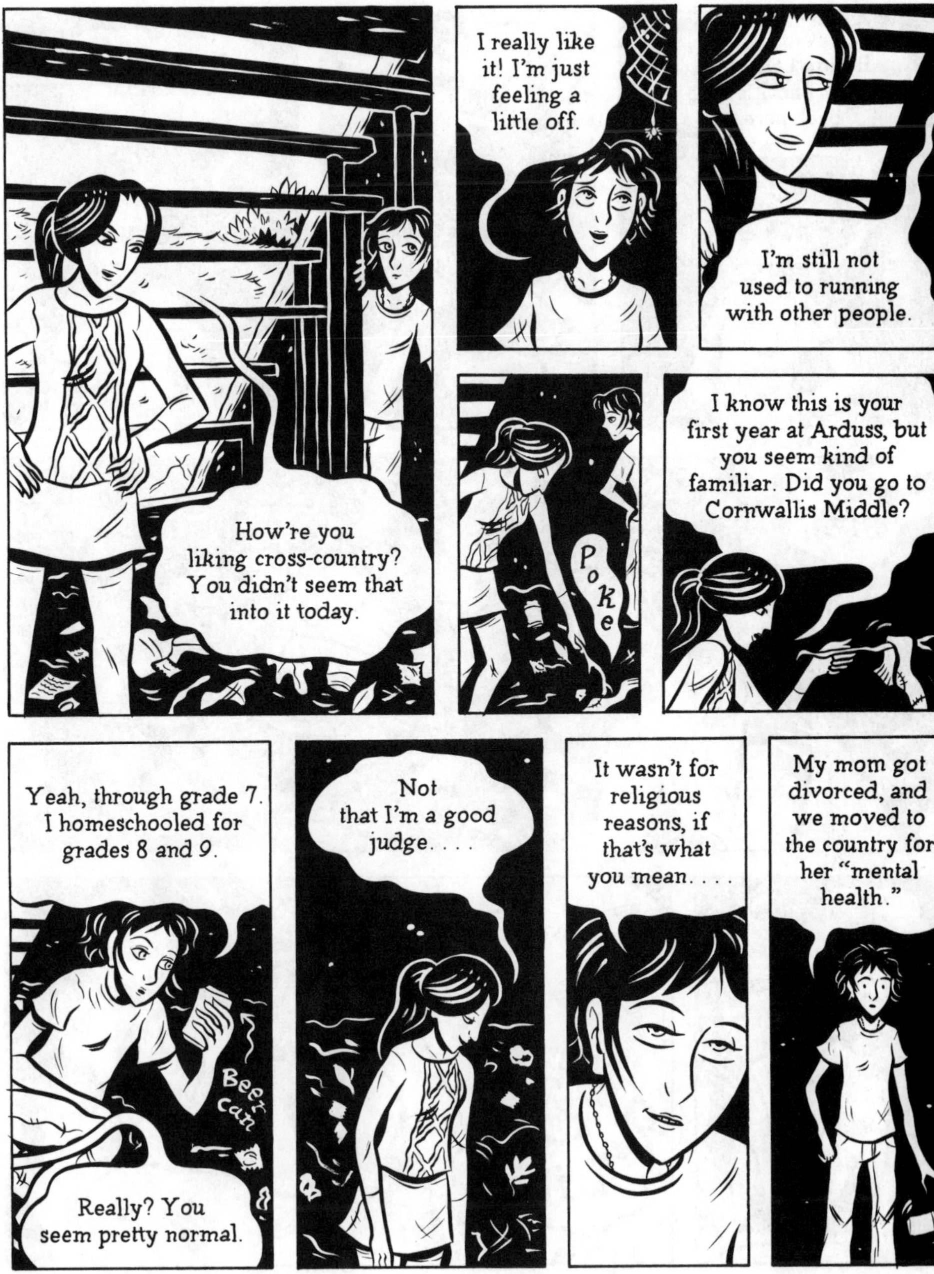
How're you liking cross-country? You didn't seem that into it today.
I really like it! I'm just feeling a little off.
I'm still not used to running with other people.
Poke
I know this is your first year at Arduss, but you seem kind of familiar. Did you go to Cornwallis Middle?
Yeah, through grade 7. I homeschooled for grades 8 and 9.
Beer can
Really? You seem pretty normal.
Not that I'm a good judge. . . .
It wasn't for religious reasons, if that's what you mean. . . .
My mom got divorced, and we moved to the country for her "mental health."

It's kind of, like, culture shock being back here.
Mmm.
That sucks.
No, it's good. I missed it here.
Sigh.
Keys, keys . . .
Twitch

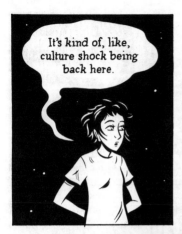

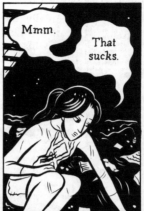

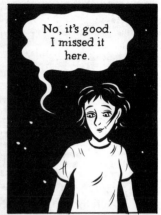

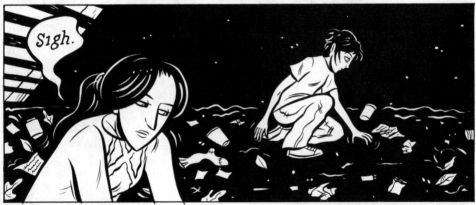

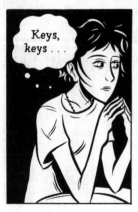

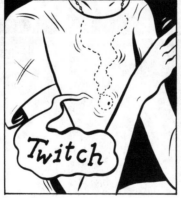

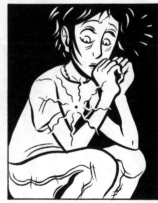

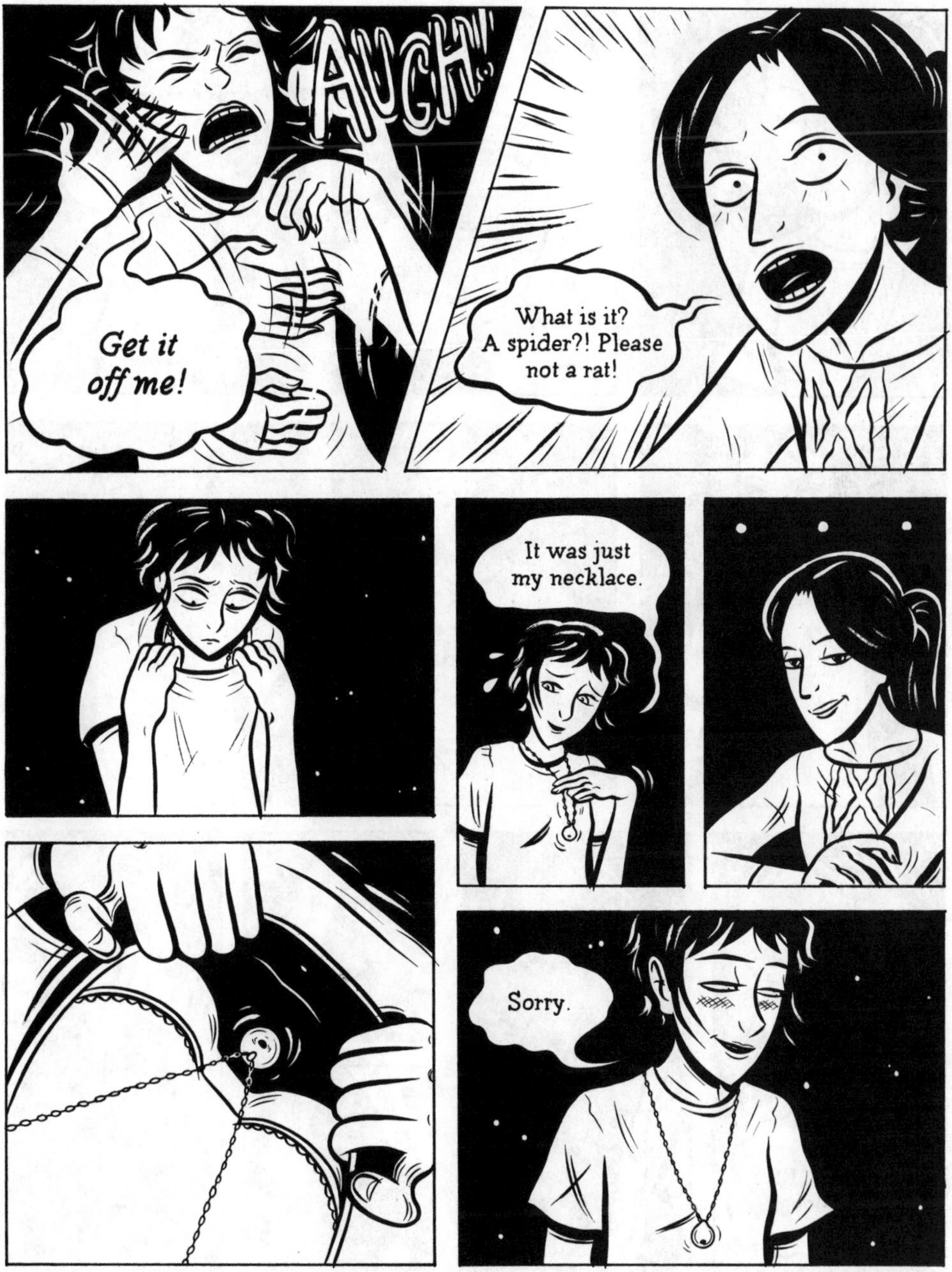
AUGH!
Get it off me!
What is it? A spider?! Please not a rat!
It was just my necklace.
Sorry.

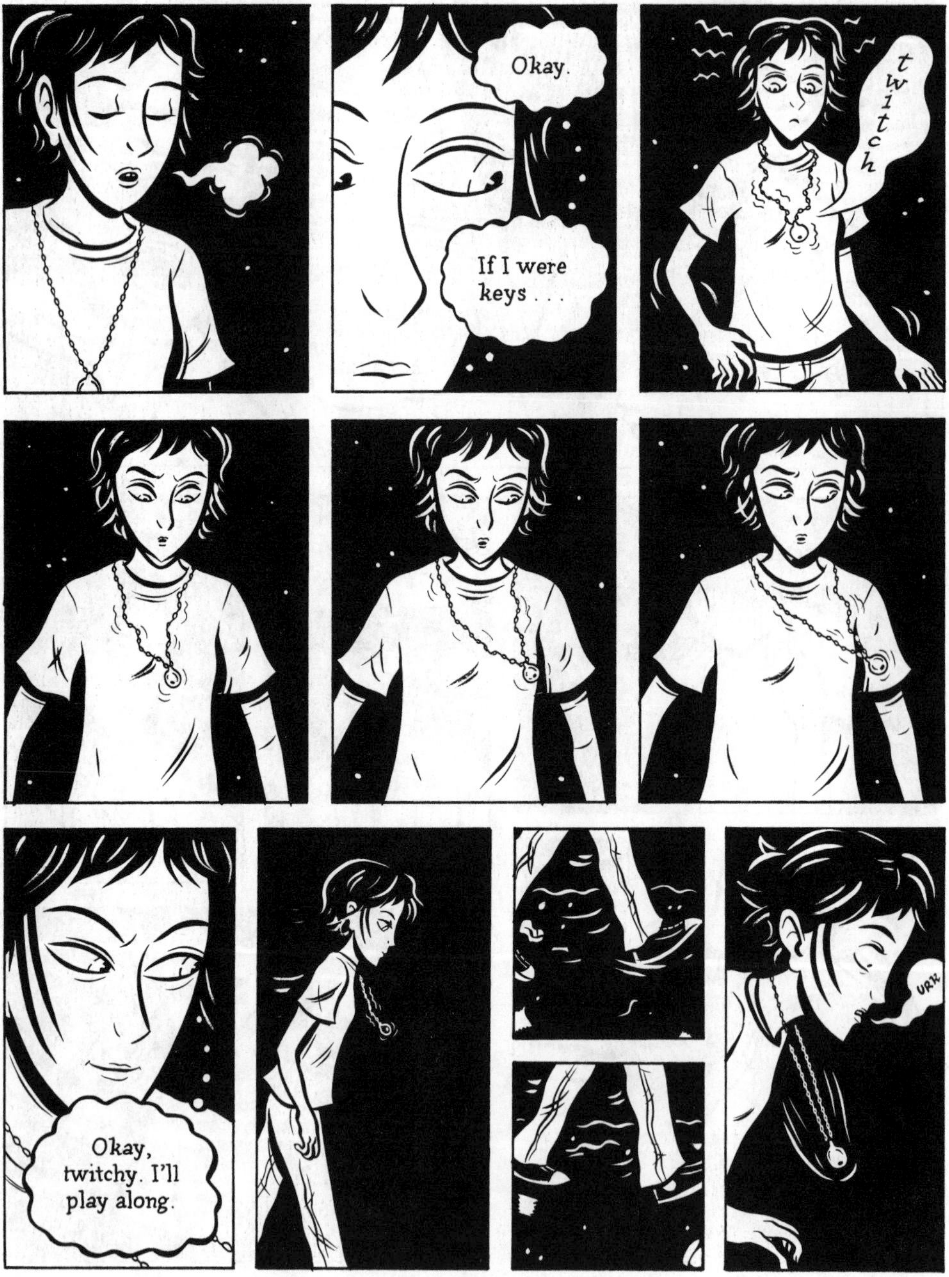
Okay.
If I were keys . . . .
twitch
Okay, twitchy. I'll play along.
URK

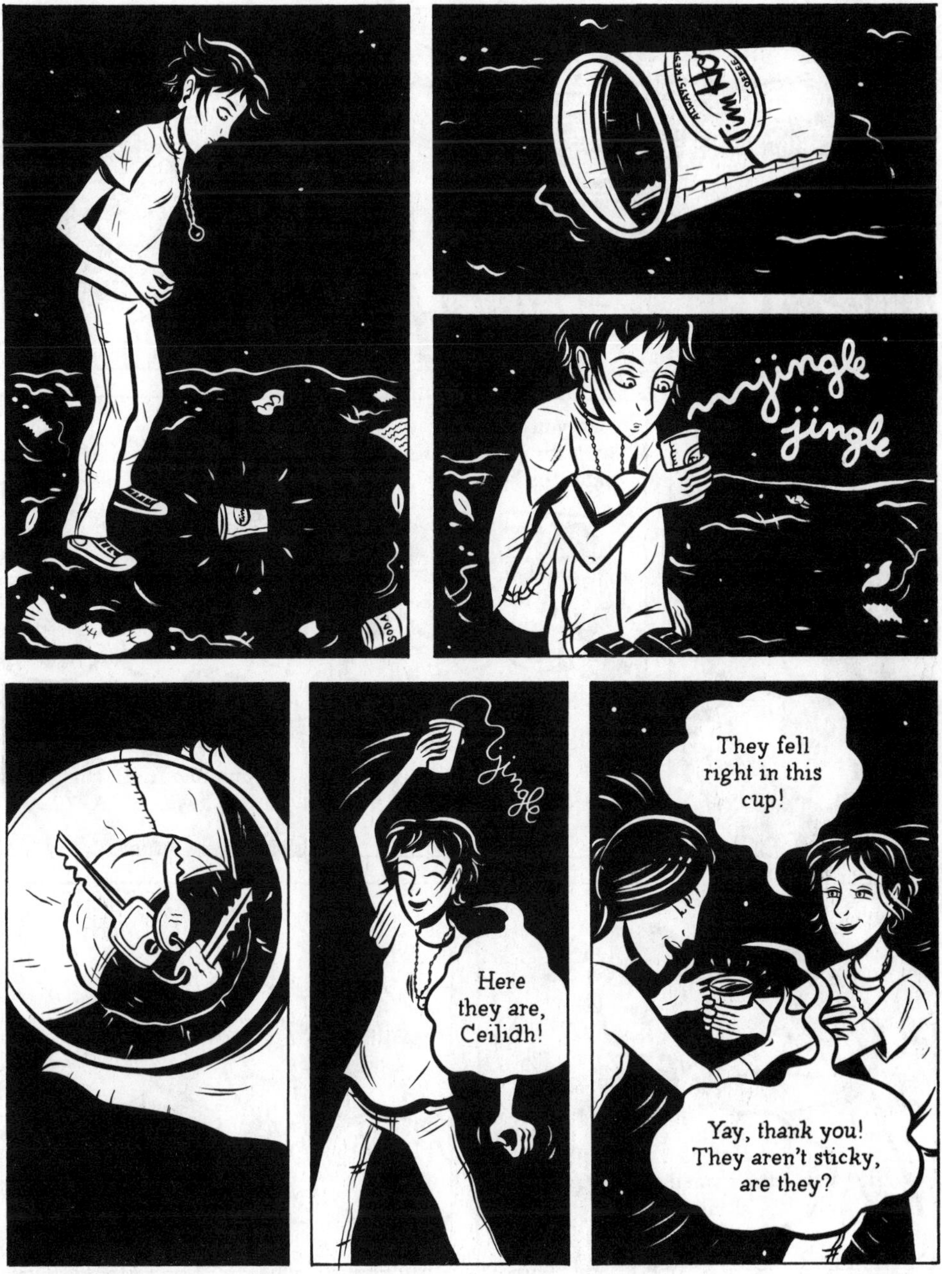
Tim Hortons
ALWAYS FRESH
COFFEE
SODA
jingle
jingle
jingle
Here they are, Ceilidh!
They fell right in this cup!
Yay, thank you! They aren't sticky, are they?

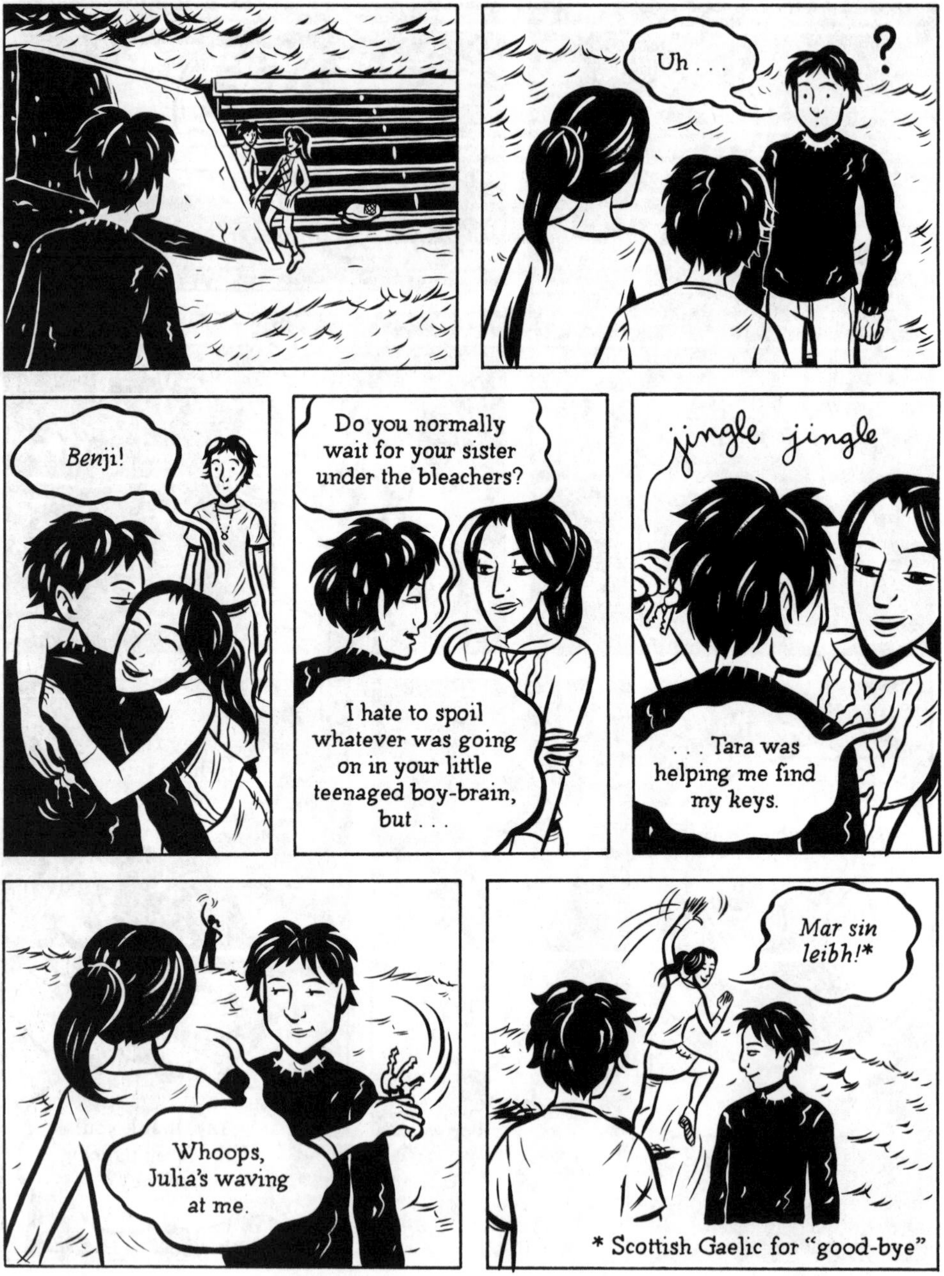
Uh . . .
?
Benji!
Do you normally wait for your sister under the bleachers?
I hate to spoil whatever was going on in your little teenaged boy-brain, but . . .
jingle jingle
. . . Tara was helping me find my keys.
Whoops, Julia's waving at me.
Mar sin leibh!*
* Scottish Gaelic for "good-bye"

She's funny.

Did she tell you a story about her crazy Cape Breton family?

No.

You dodged a bullet.

Are you waiting for someone, too?

Nooo . . .

. . . and I should get going.

Work.

119

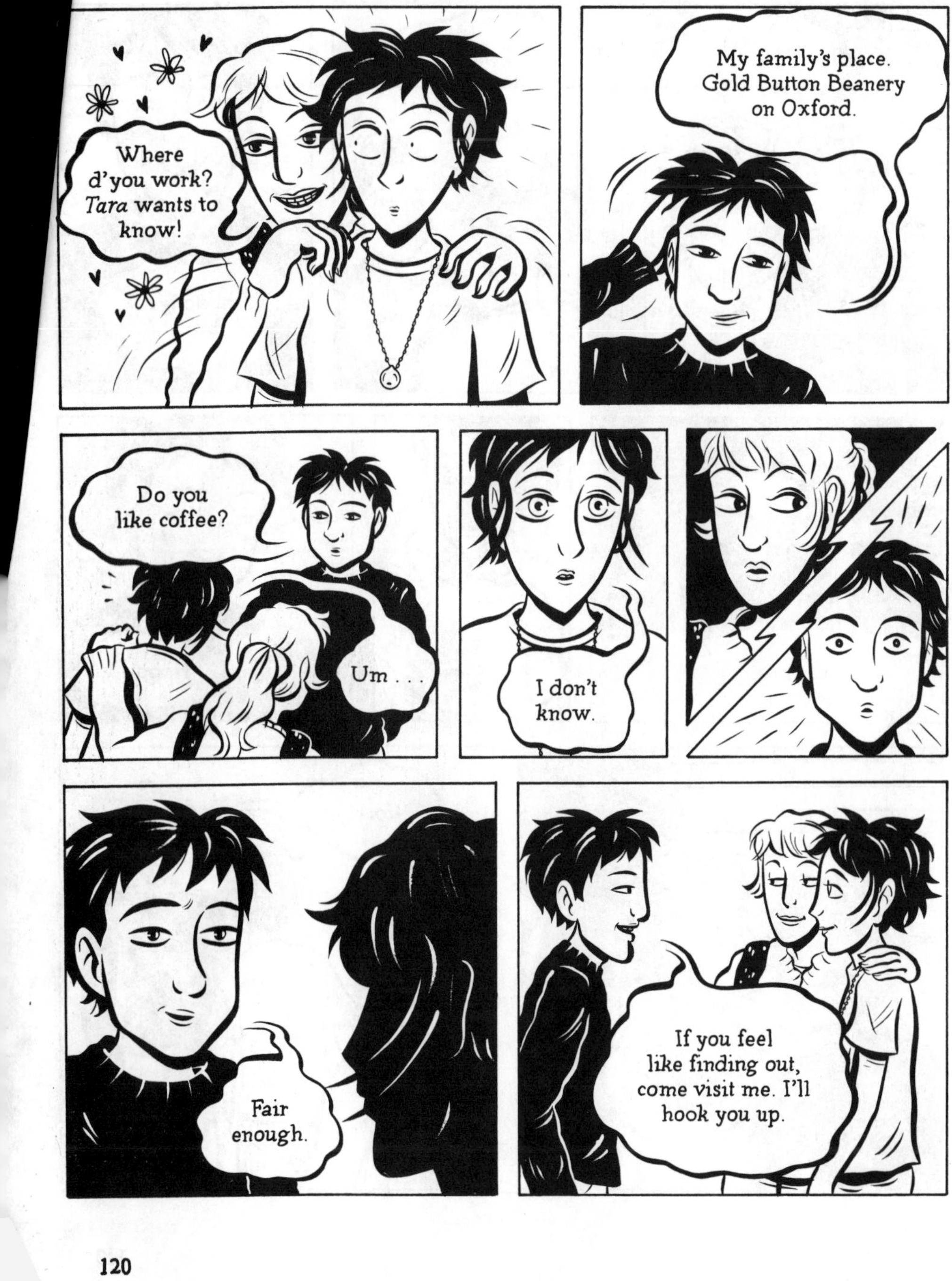
Where d'you work? *Tara* wants to know!
My family's place. Gold Button Beanery on Oxford.
Do you like coffee?
Um . . .
I don't know.
Fair enough.
If you feel like finding out, come visit me. I'll hook you up.

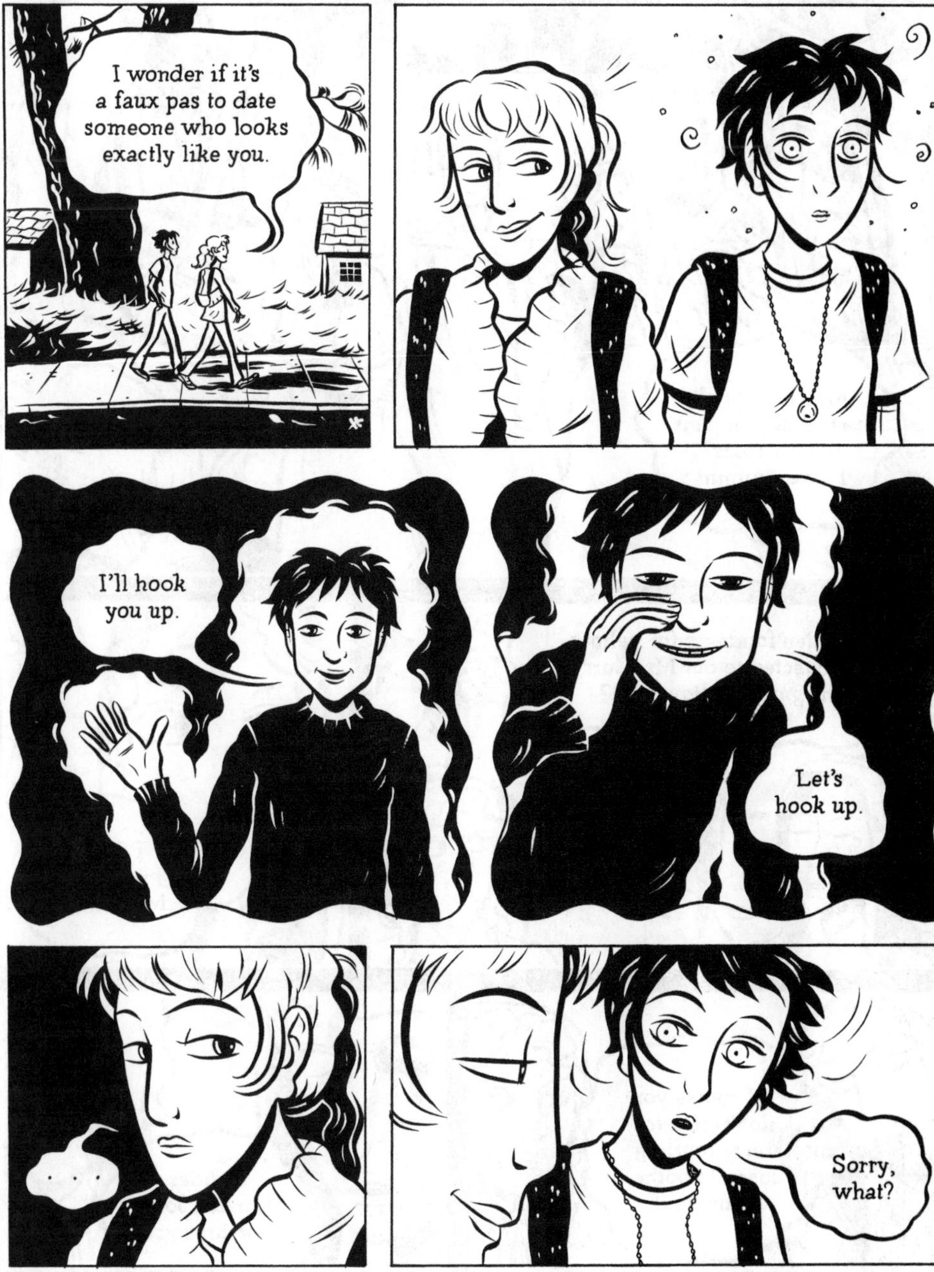
I wonder if it's a faux pas to date someone who looks exactly like you.
I'll hook you up.
Let's hook up.
. . .
Sorry, what?

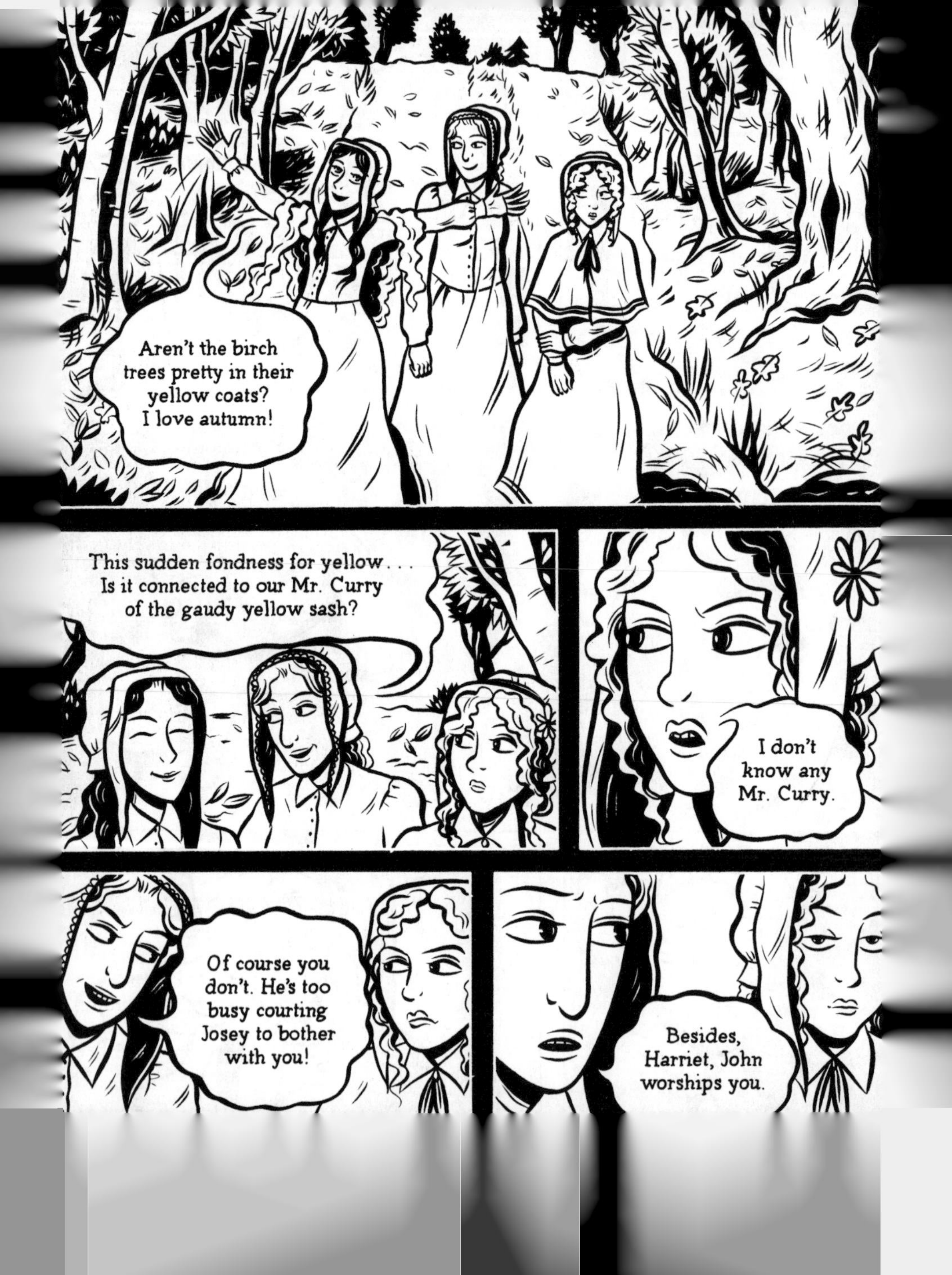
Aren't the birch trees pretty in their yellow coats? I love autumn!
This sudden fondness for yellow . . . Is it connected to our Mr. Curry of the gaudy yellow sash?
I don't know any Mr. Curry.
Of course you don't. He's too busy courting Josey to bother with you!
Besides, Harriet, John worships you.

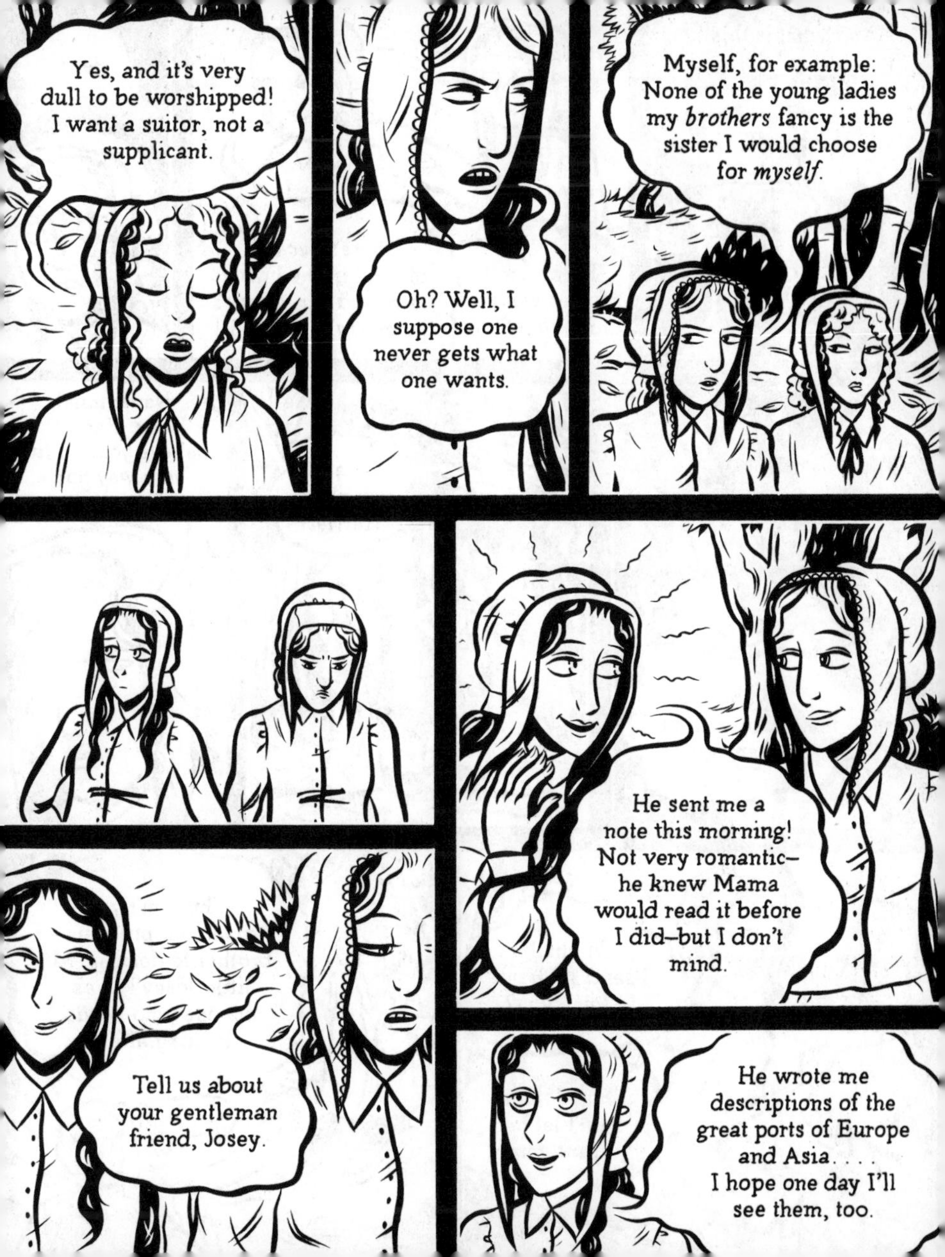
Yes, and it's very dull to be worshipped! I want a suitor, not a supplicant.
Oh? Well, I suppose one never gets what one wants.
Myself, for example: None of the young ladies my *brothers* fancy is the sister I would choose for *myself*.
He sent me a note this morning! Not very romantic—he knew Mama would read it before I did—but I don't mind.
Tell us about your gentleman friend, Josey.
He wrote me descriptions of the great ports of Europe and Asia. . . . I hope one day I'll see them, too.

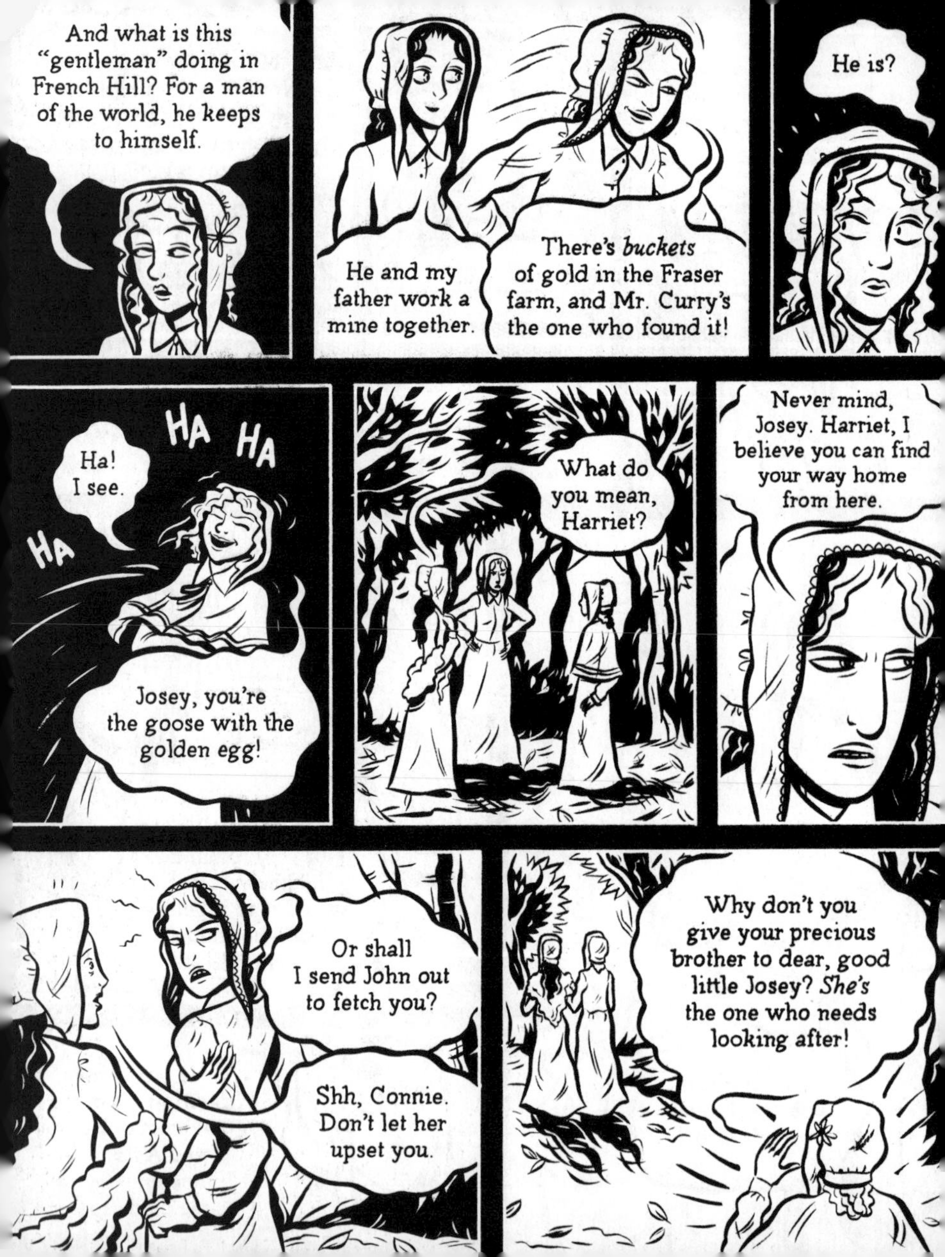

And what is this "gentleman" doing in French Hill? For a man of the world, he keeps to himself.
He and my father work a mine together.
There's *buckets* of gold in the Fraser farm, and Mr. Curry's the one who found it!
He is?
Ha! I see.
HA HA
HA
Josey, you're the goose with the golden egg!
What do you mean, Harriet?
Never mind, Josey. Harriet, I believe you can find your way home from here.
Or shall I send John out to fetch you?
Shh, Connie. Don't let her upset you.
Why don't you give your precious brother to dear, good little Josey? *She's* the one who needs looking after!

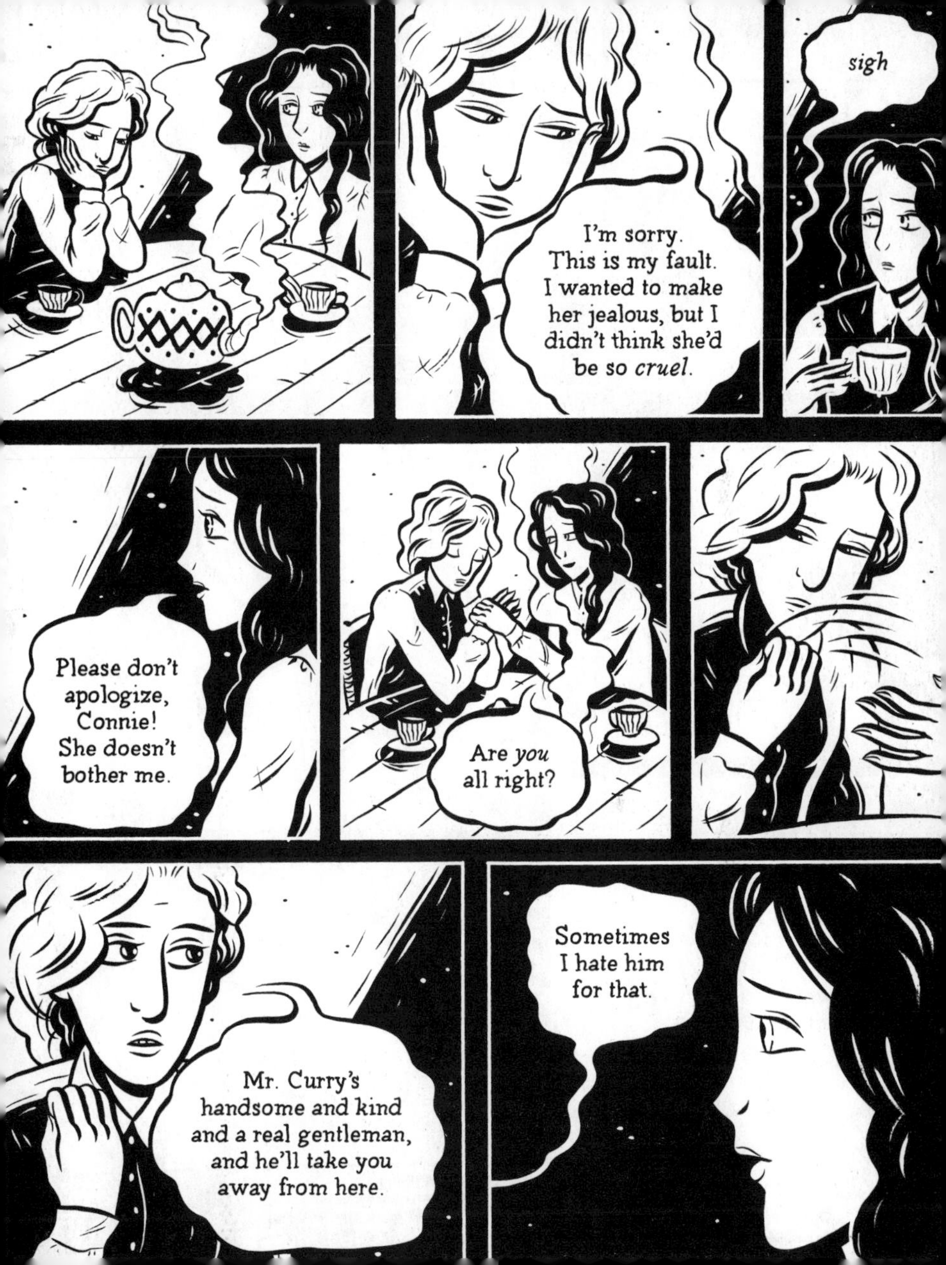

sigh
I'm sorry. This is my fault. I wanted to make her jealous, but I didn't think she'd be so *cruel*.
Please don't apologize, Connie! She doesn't bother me.
Are *you* all right?
Mr. Curry's handsome and kind and a real gentleman, and he'll take you away from here.
Sometimes I hate him for that.

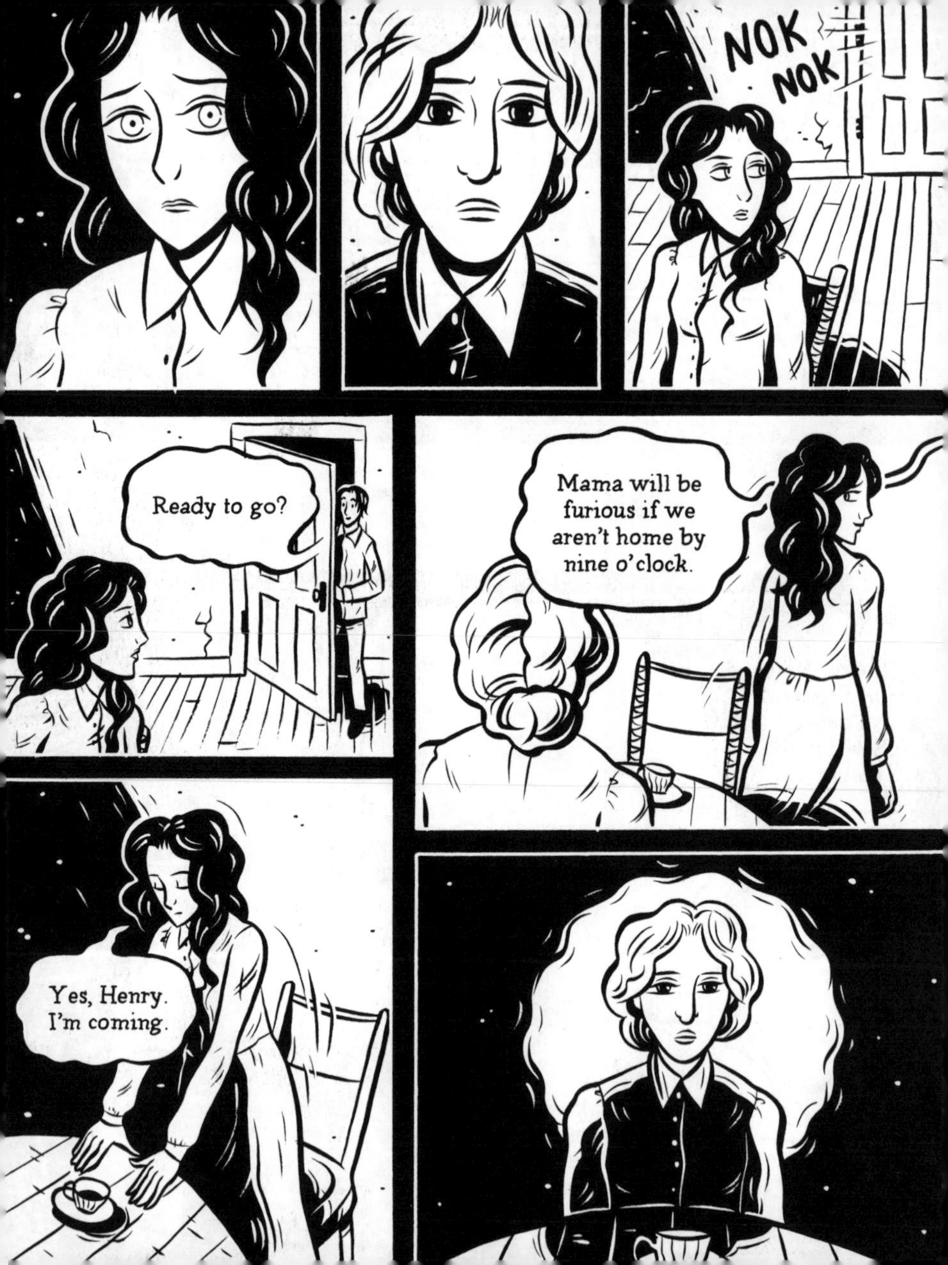
NOK
NOK
Ready to go?
Mama will be furious if we aren't home by nine o'clock.
Yes, Henry. I'm coming.

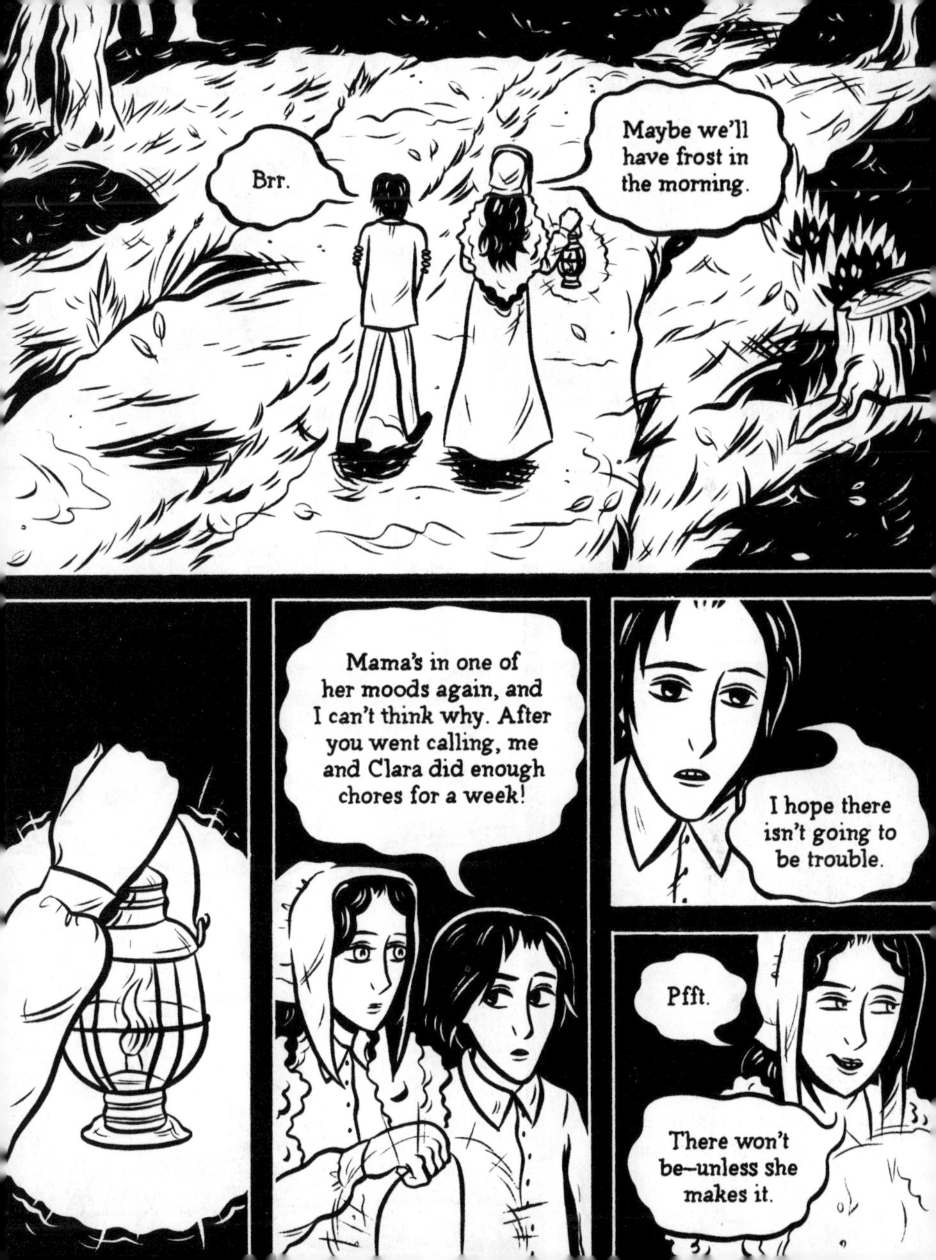
Brr.
Maybe we'll have frost in the morning.
Mama's in one of her moods again, and I can't think why. After you went calling, me and Clara did enough chores for a week!
I hope there isn't going to be trouble.
Pfft.
There won't be—unless she makes it.

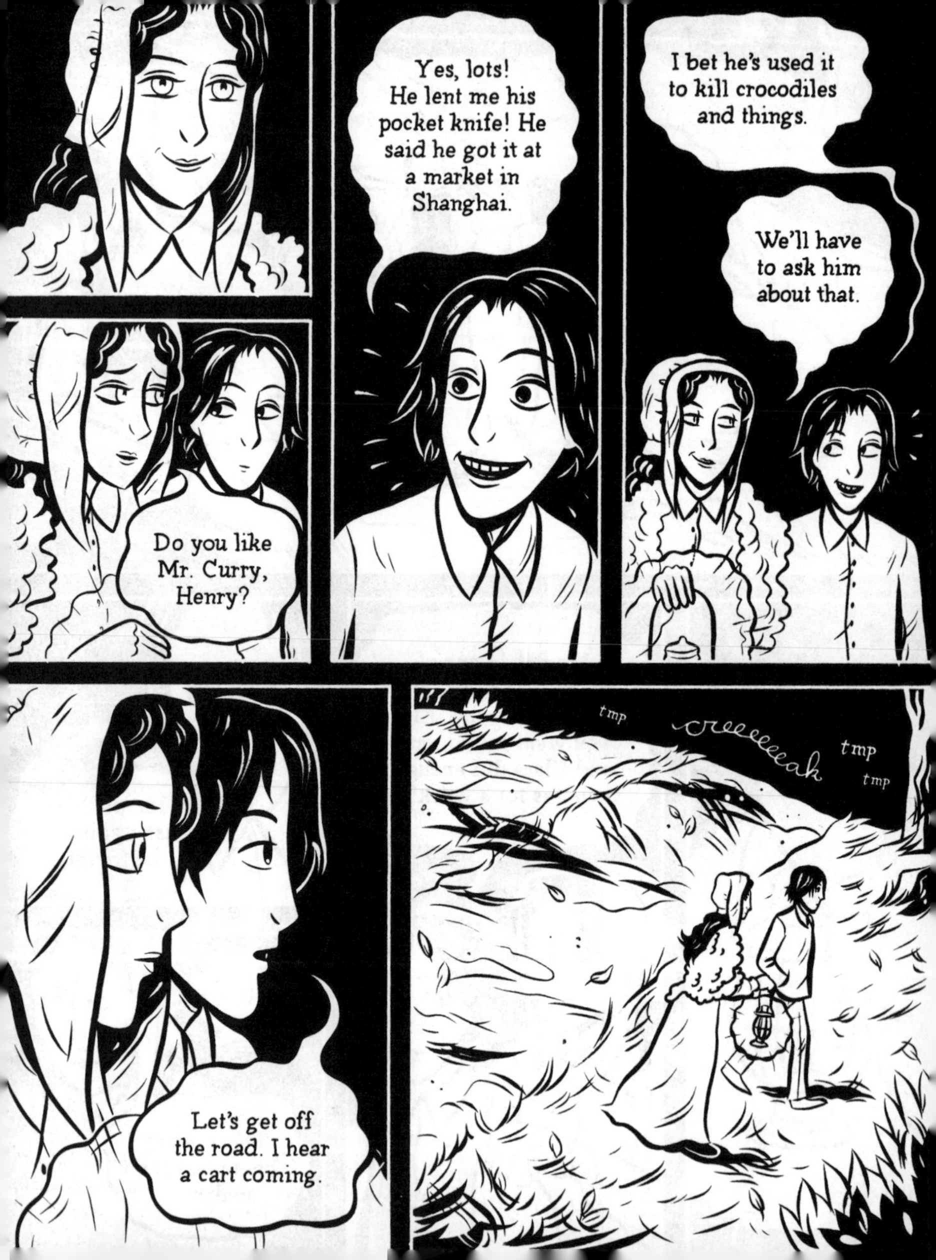
Do you like Mr. Curry, Henry?
Yes, lots! He lent me his pocket knife! He said he got it at a market in Shanghai.
I bet he's used it to kill crocodiles and things.
We'll have to ask him about that.
Let's get off the road. I hear a cart coming.
tmp
creeeeeeak
tmp
tmp

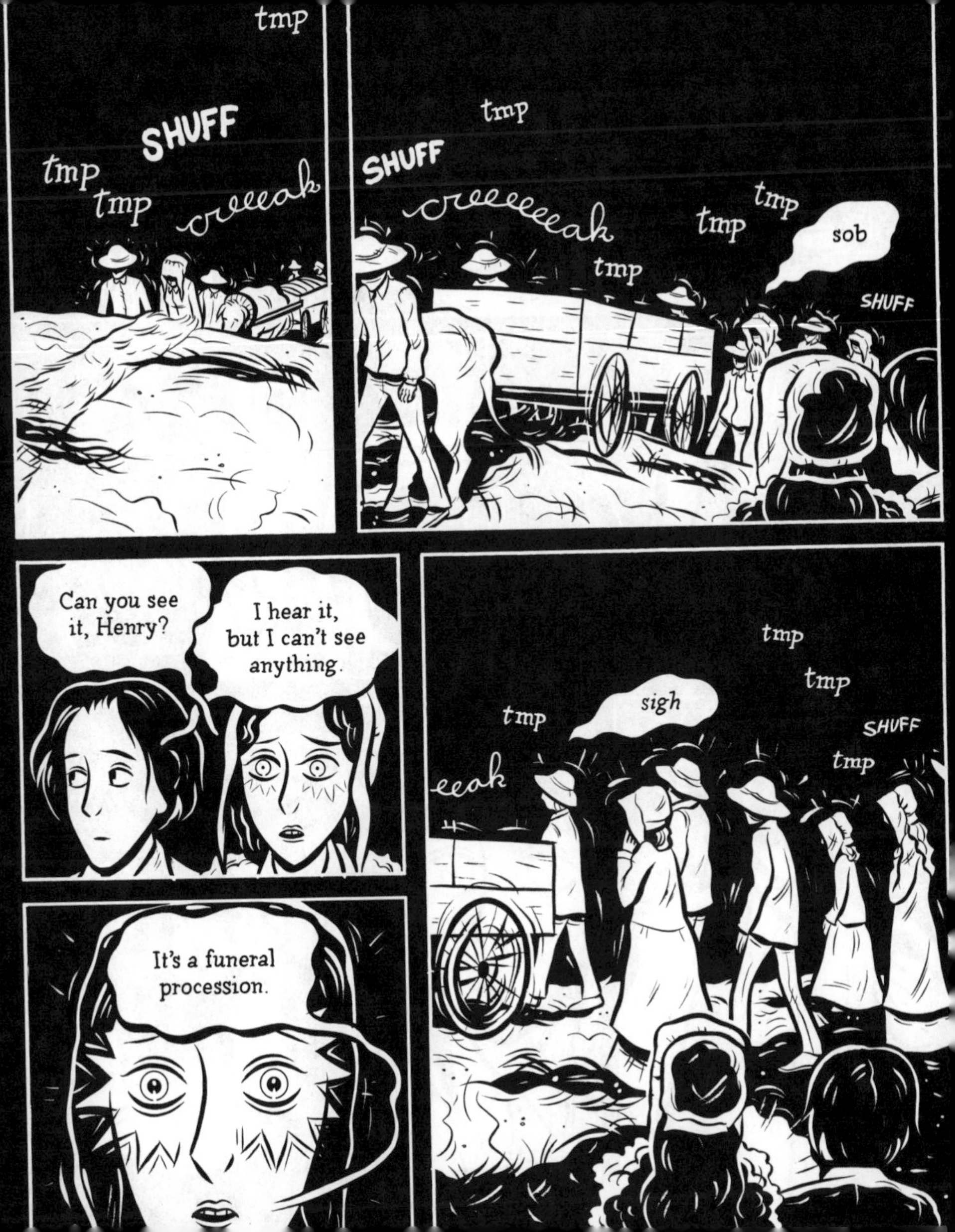
tmp
SHUFF
tmp
tmp
creeak
tmp
SHUFF
creeeeeak
tmp
tmp
tmp
sob
SHUFF
Can you see it, Henry?
I hear it, but I can't see anything.
It's a funeral procession.
tmp
tmp
sigh
tmp
SHUFF
eeak
tmp

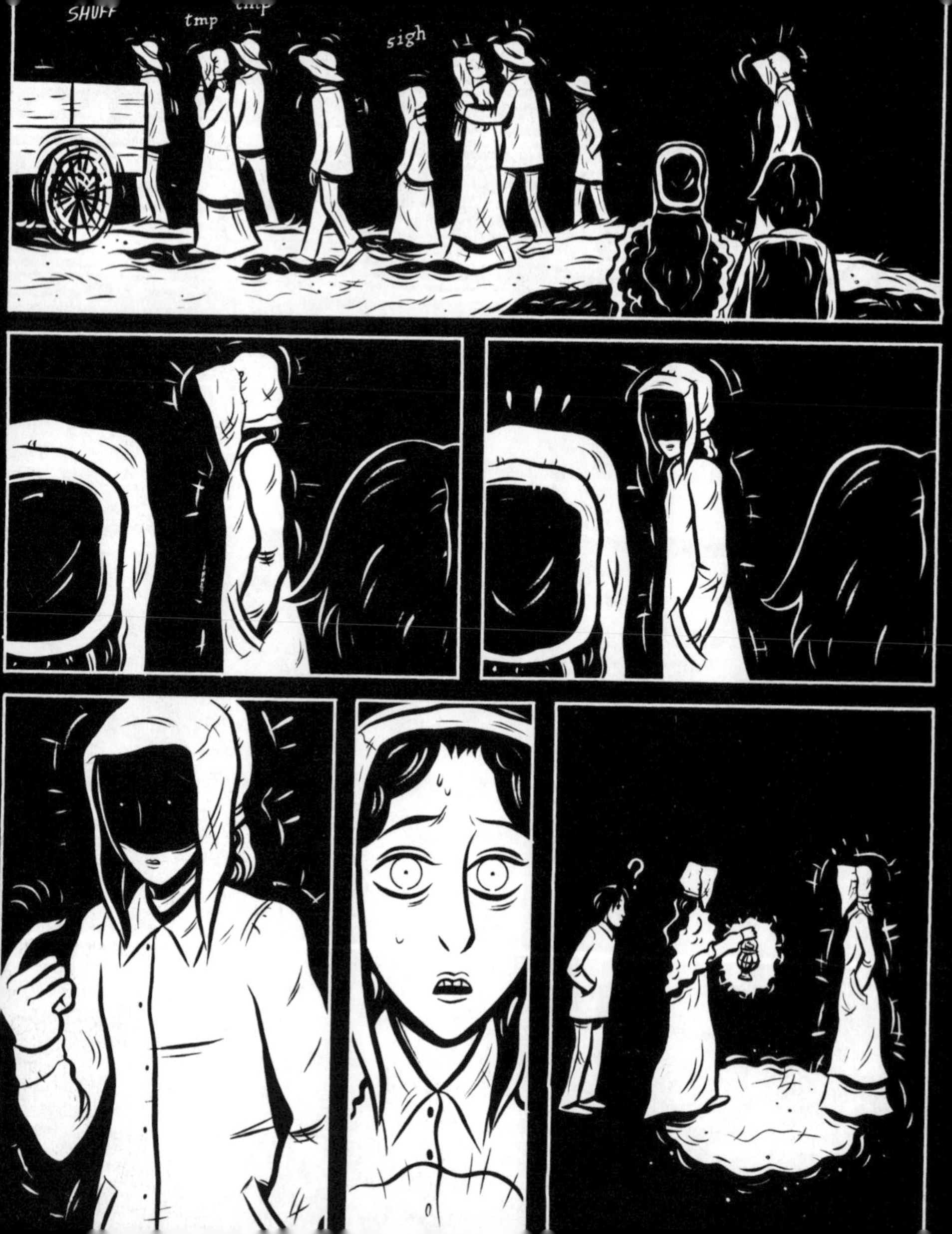

SHUFF
tmp
sigh
?

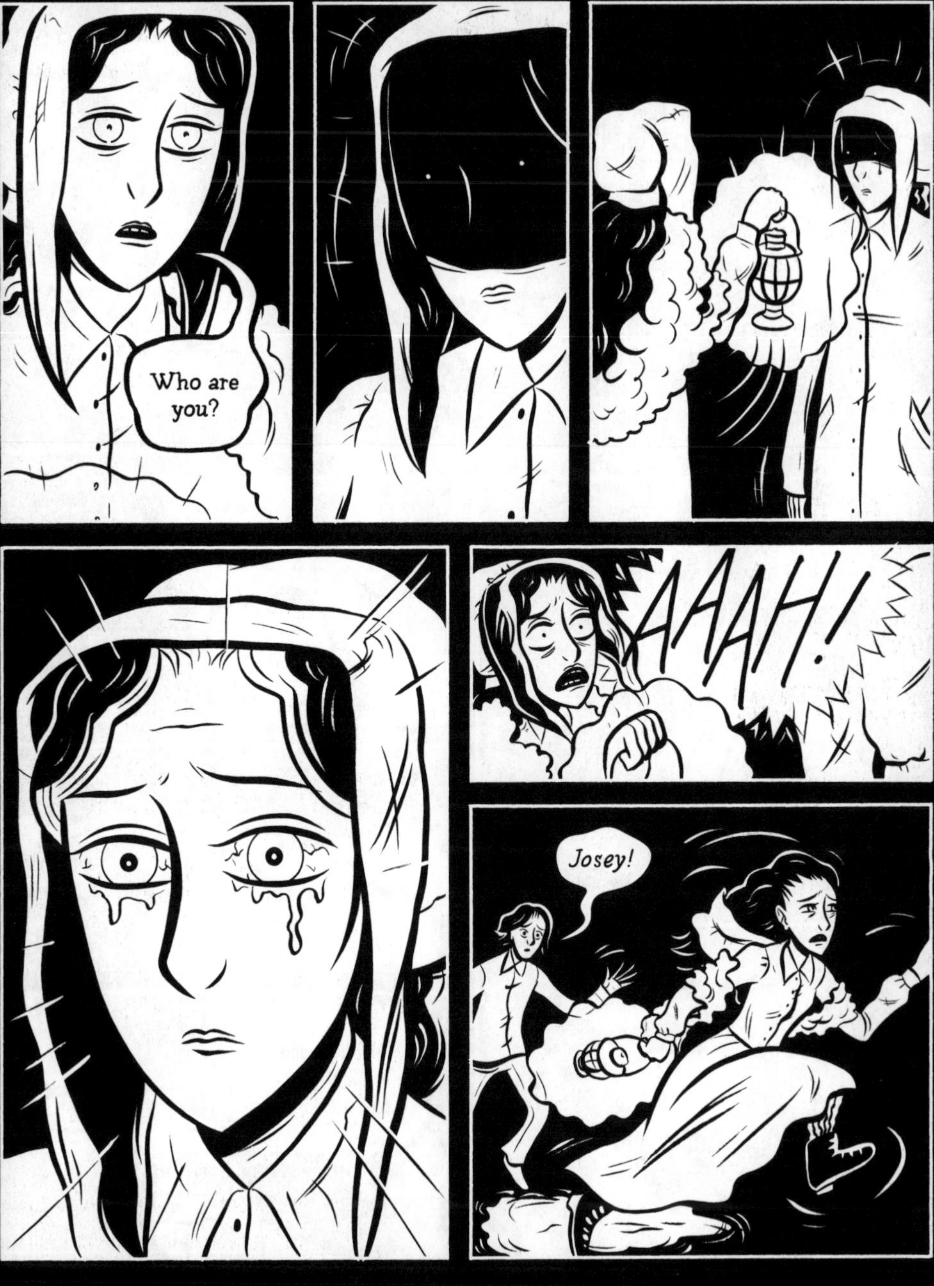
Who are you?
AAAH!
Josey!

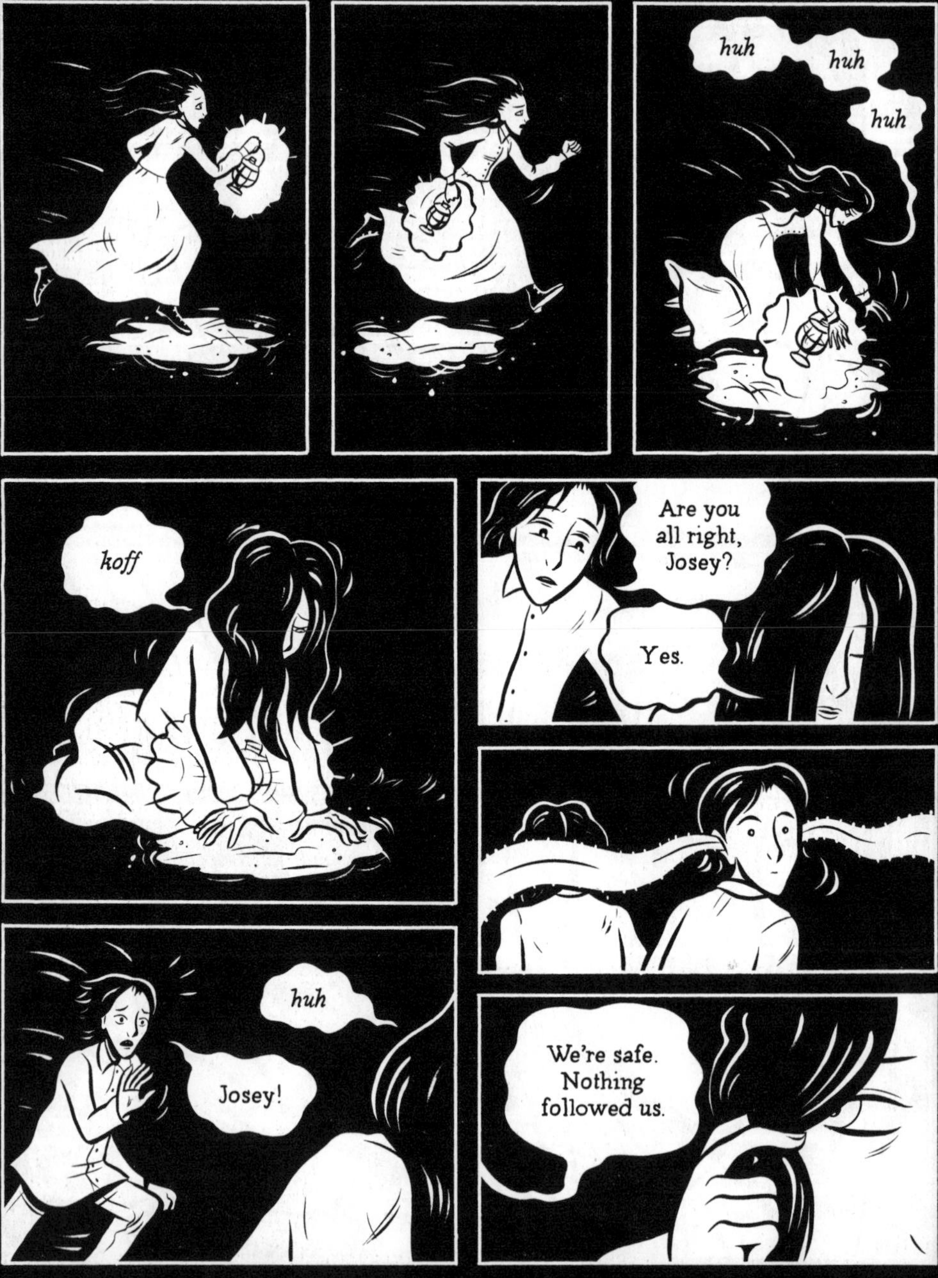
huh
huh
huh
koff
Are you all right, Josey?
Yes.
huh
Josey!
We're safe. Nothing followed us.

Josey?
Promise!
You can't tell Mama about this! You know how she goes on about ghosts. She'll never let me out of the house again!
I won't, Josey!
I'm no snitch.

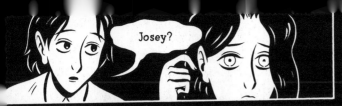

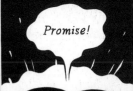

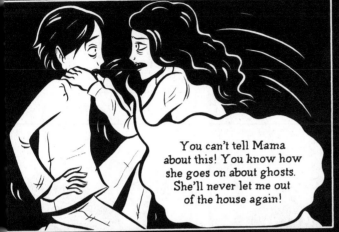

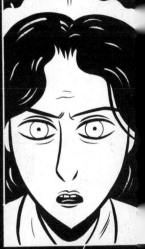

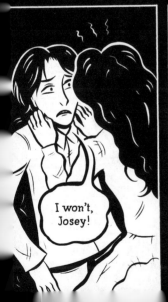

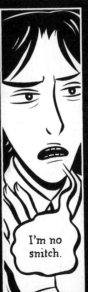

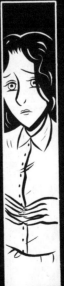

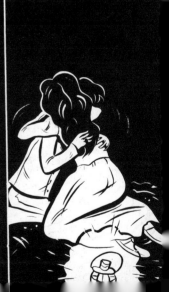

BLARE
Well, good morning!
Looks like you two have the day off.
ARDUSS TRIBUNE
ARDUSS T
Arduss High Cancels Classes
Officials point to contaminated water supply
WHAAAT?!

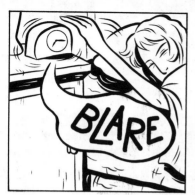

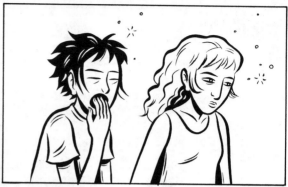

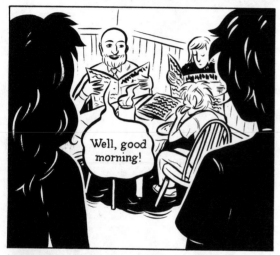

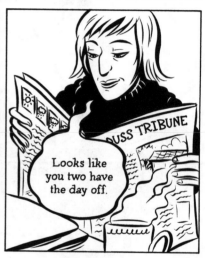

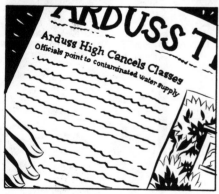

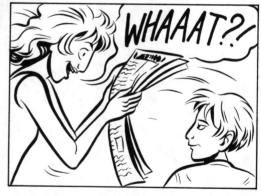

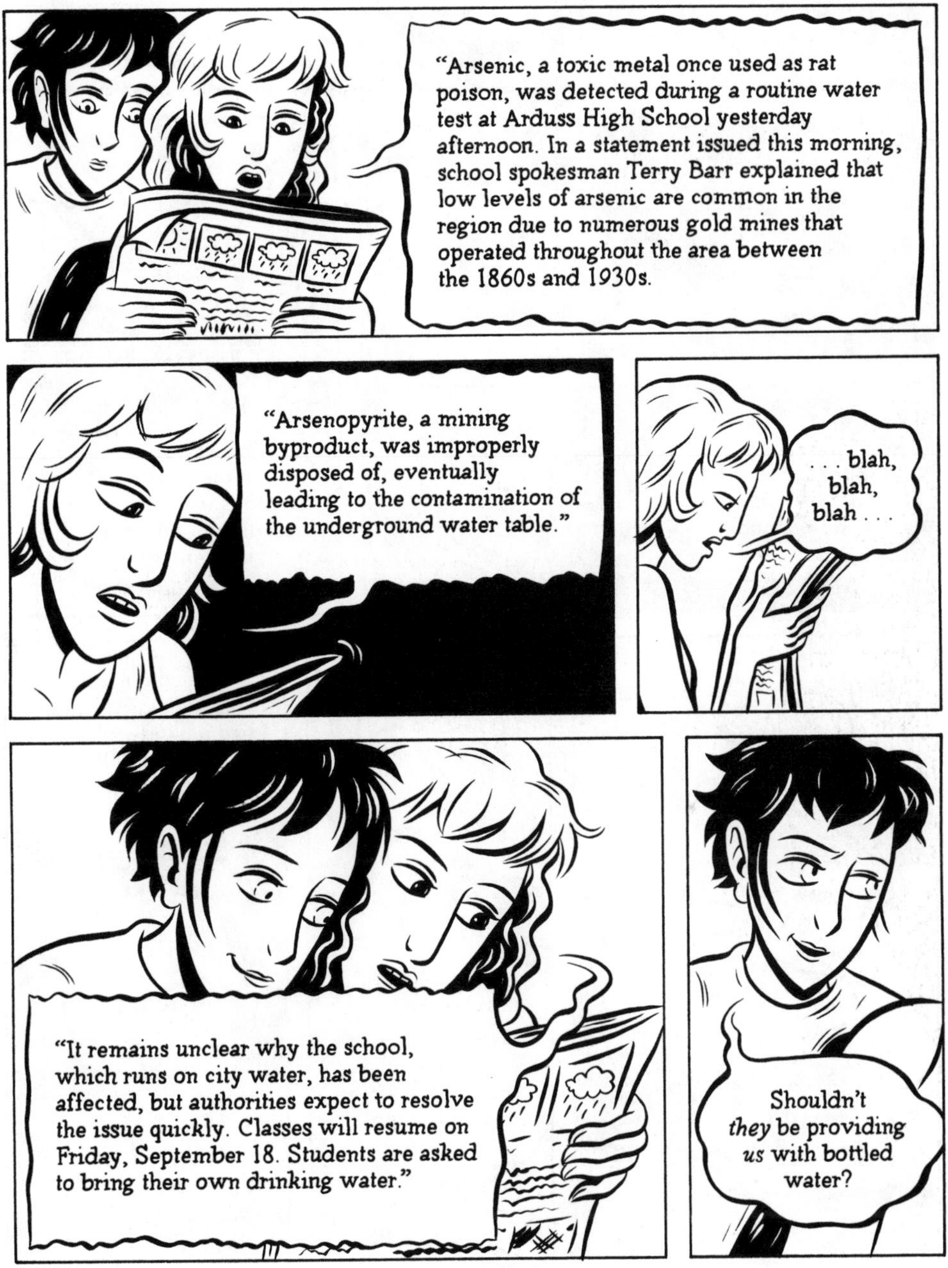
"Arsenic, a toxic metal once used as rat poison, was detected during a routine water test at Arduss High School yesterday afternoon. In a statement issued this morning, school spokesman Terry Barr explained that low levels of arsenic are common in the region due to numerous gold mines that operated throughout the area between the 1860s and 1930s.
"Arsenopyrite, a mining byproduct, was improperly disposed of, eventually leading to the contamination of the underground water table."
. . . blah, blah, blah . . .
"It remains unclear why the school, which runs on city water, has been affected, but authorities expect to resolve the issue quickly. Classes will resume on Friday, September 18. Students are asked to bring their own drinking water."
Shouldn't *they* be providing *us* with bottled water?

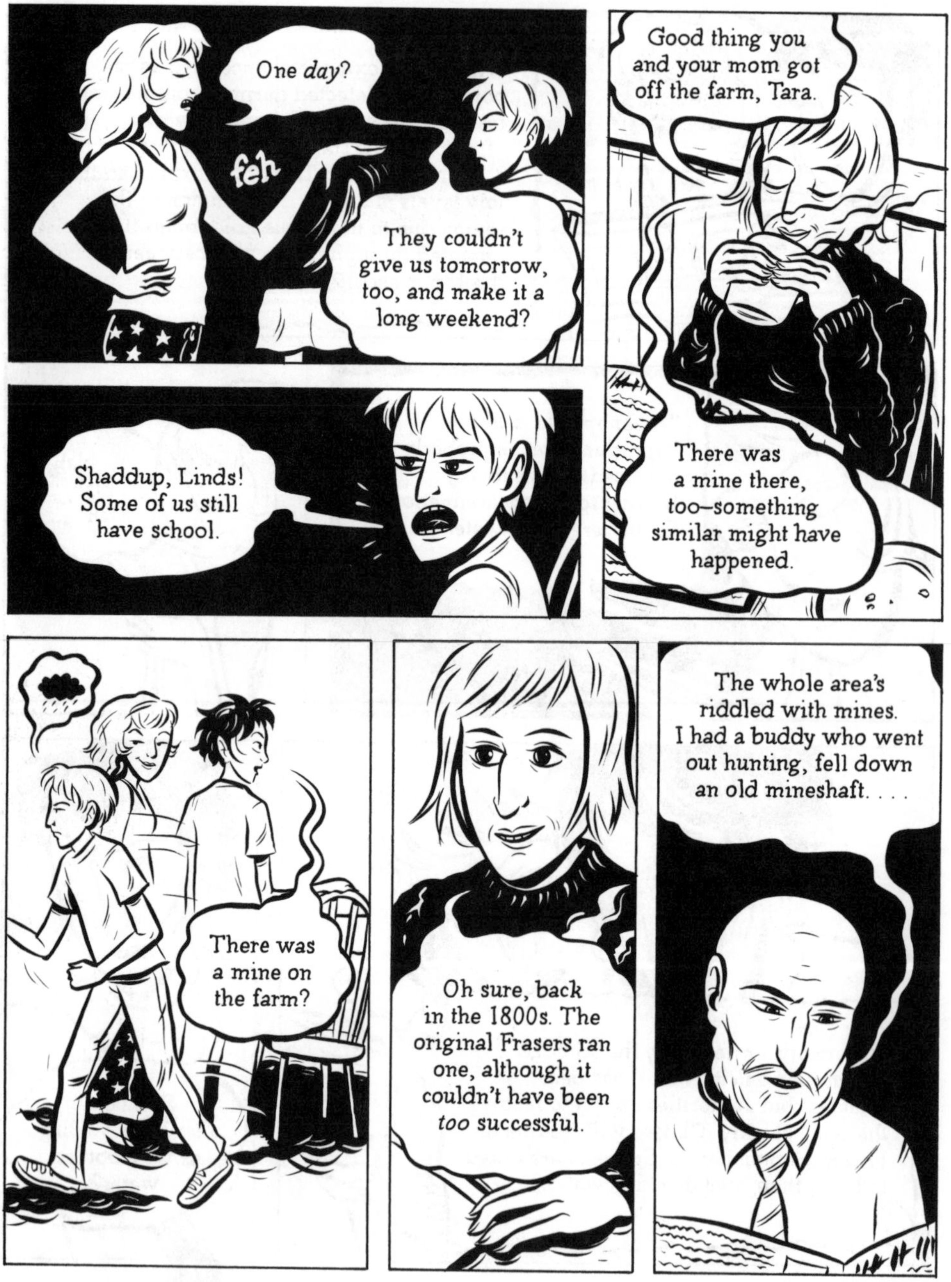
One *day*?
feh
They couldn't give us tomorrow, too, and make it a long weekend?
Shaddup, Linds! Some of us still have school.
Good thing you and your mom got off the farm, Tara.
There was a mine there, too—something similar might have happened.
There was a mine on the farm?
Oh sure, back in the 1800s. The original Frasers ran one, although it couldn't have been *too* successful.
The whole area's riddled with mines. I had a buddy who went out hunting, fell down an old mineshaft. . . .

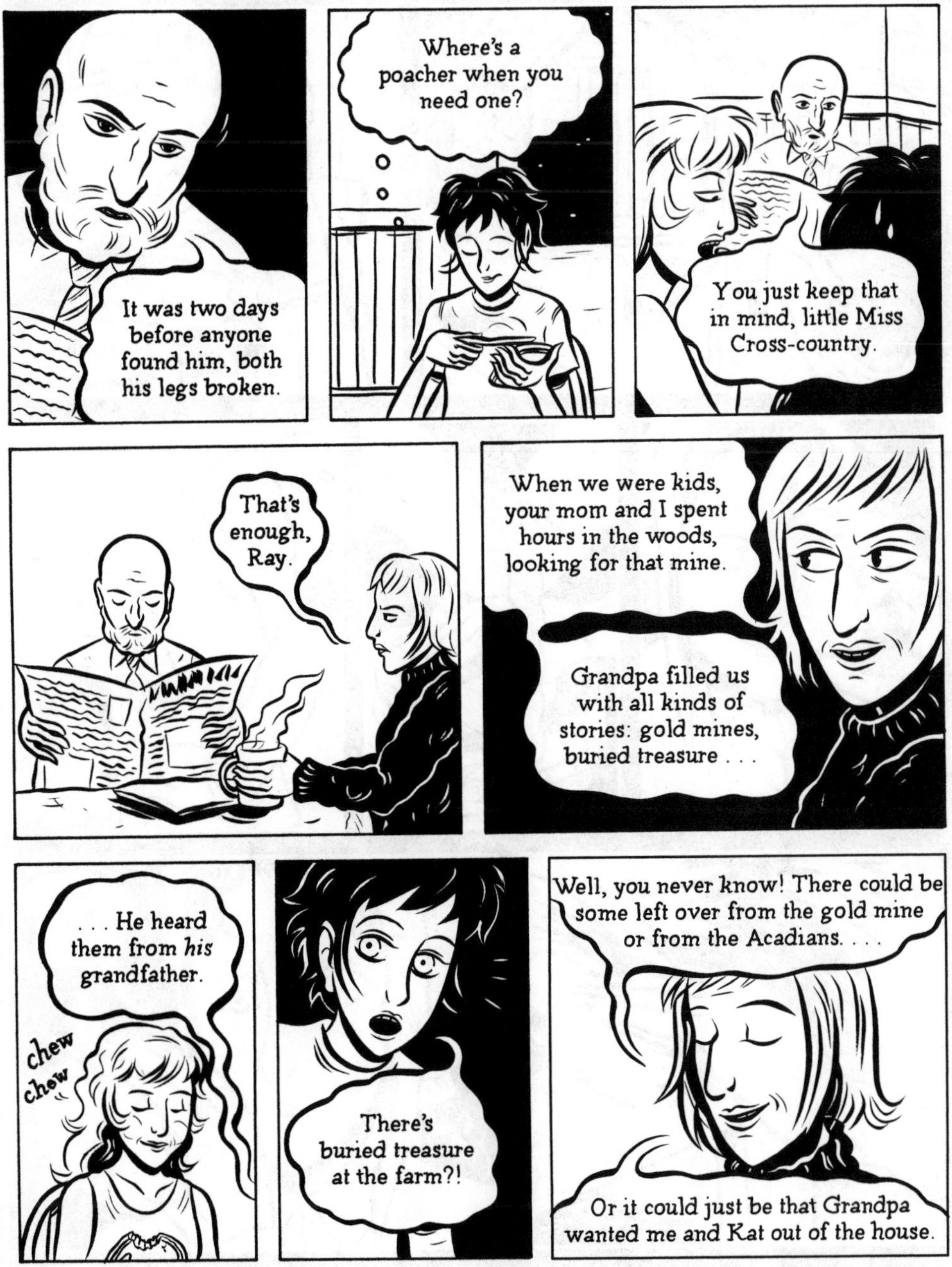
It was two days before anyone found him, both his legs broken.
Where's a poacher when you need one?
You just keep that in mind, little Miss Cross-country.
That's enough, Ray.
When we were kids, your mom and I spent hours in the woods, looking for that mine.
Grandpa filled us with all kinds of stories: gold mines, buried treasure . . .
. . . He heard them from *his* grandfather.
chew chew
There's buried treasure at the farm?!
Well, you never know! There could be some left over from the gold mine or from the Acadians. . . .
Or it could just be that Grandpa wanted me and Kat out of the house.

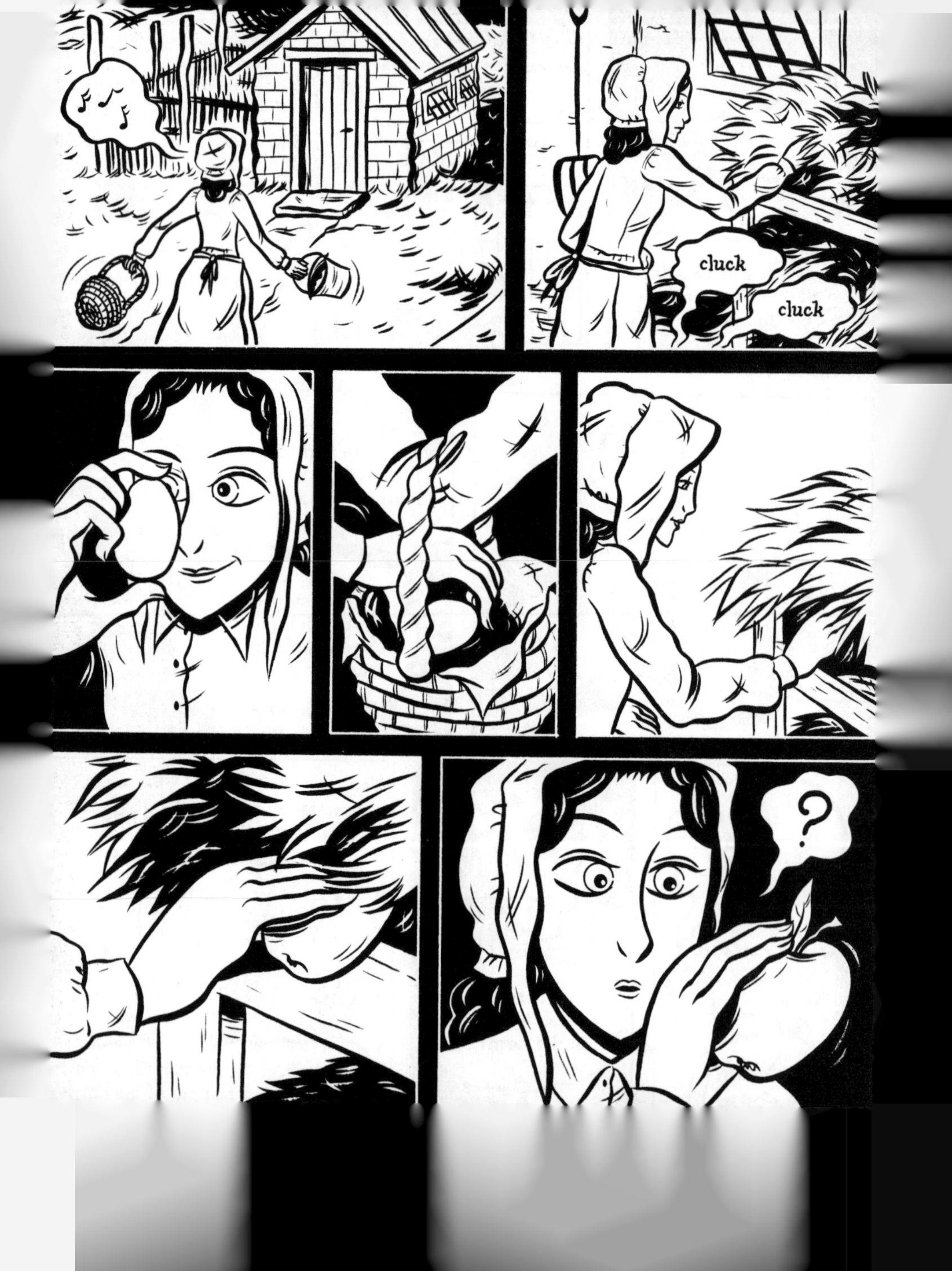

cluck
cluck
?

A & J

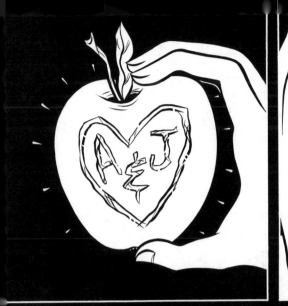

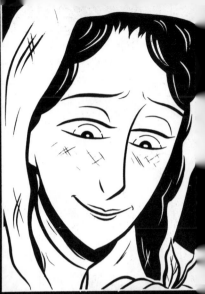

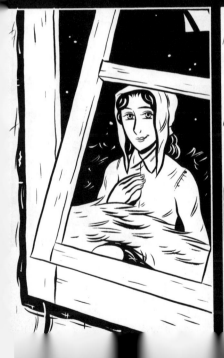

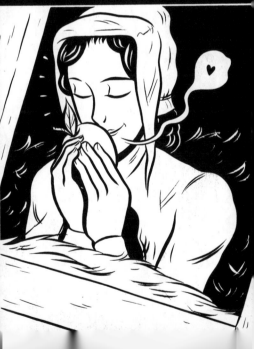

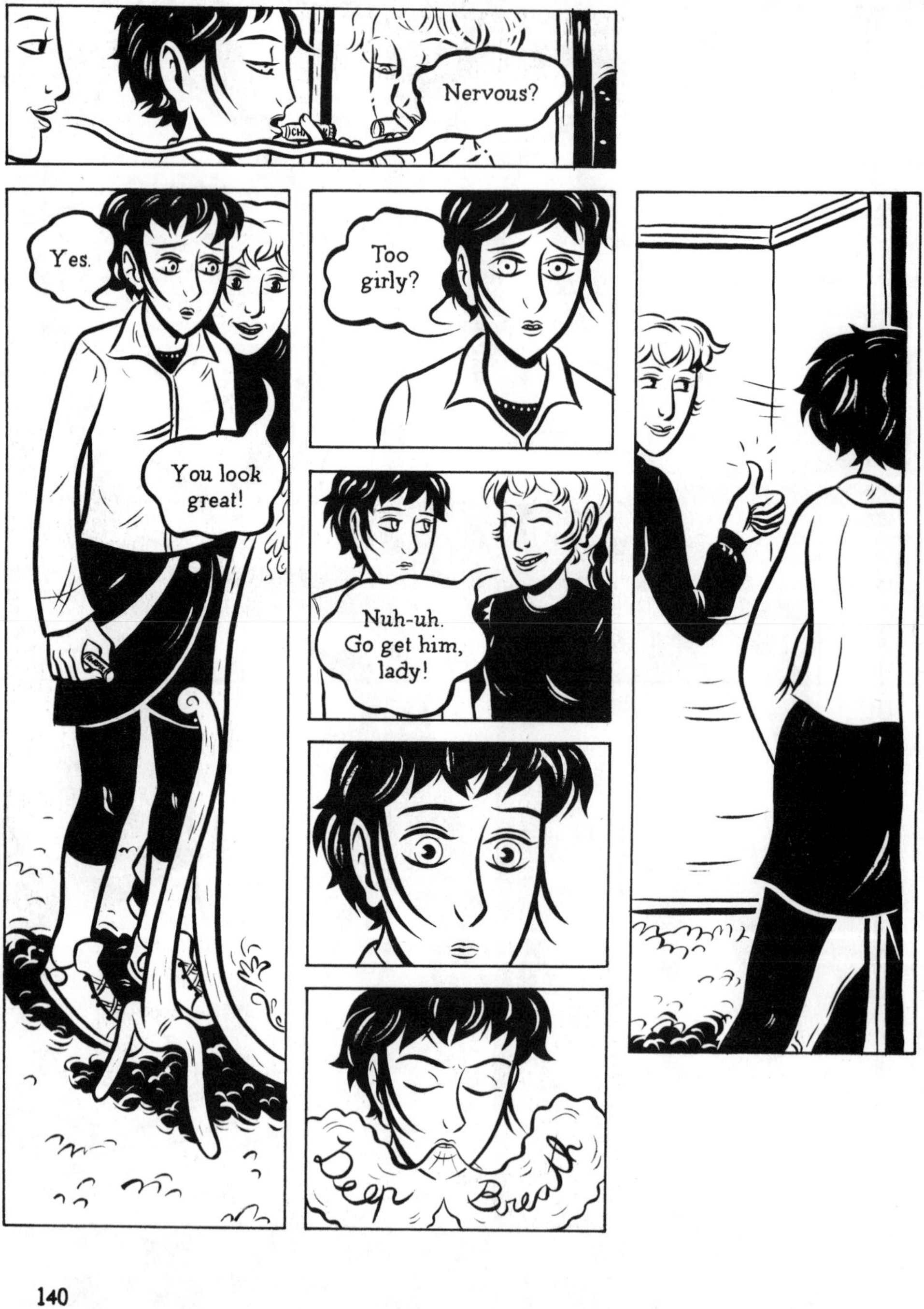
Nervous?
Yes.
You look great!
Too girly?
Nuh-uh. Go get him, lady!
Deep Breath

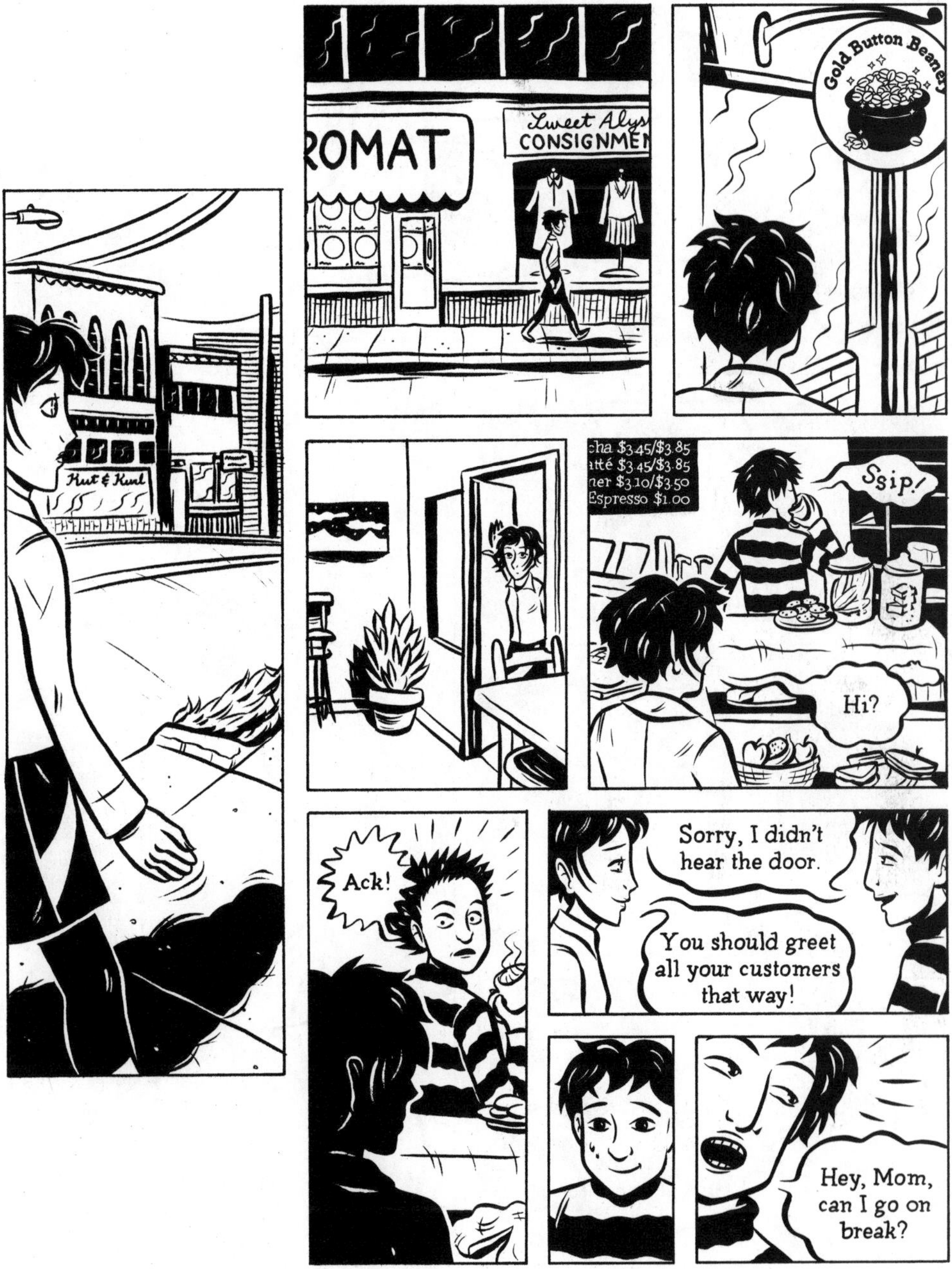
Kut & Kurl
ROMAT
Sweet Alys
CONSIGNMEN
Gold Button Beanery
cha $3.45/$3.85
atté $3.45/$3.85
ner $3.10/$3.50
Espresso $1.00
Ssip!
Hi?
Ack!
Sorry, I didn't hear the door.
You should greet all your customers that way!
Hey, Mom, can I go on break?

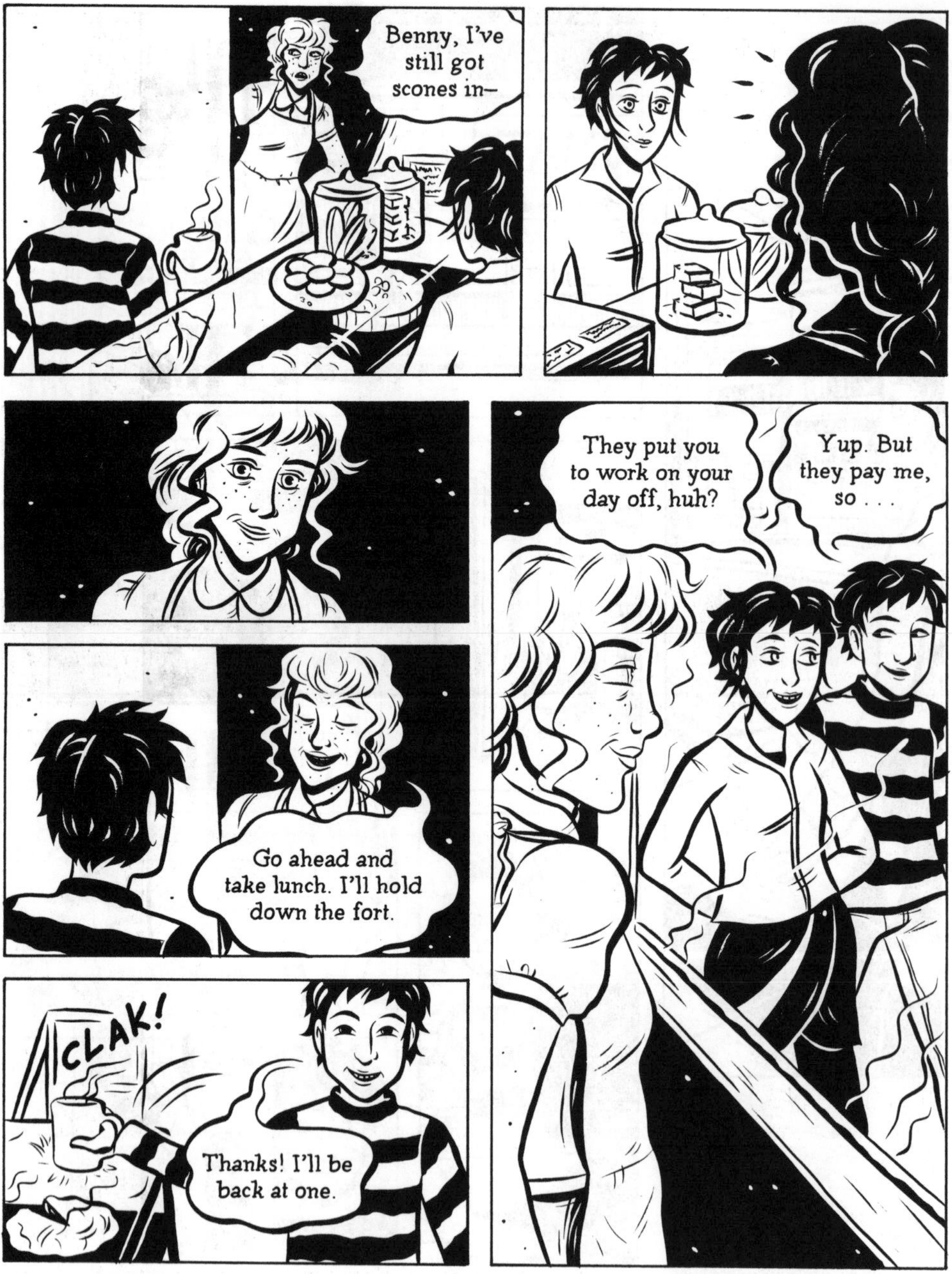
Benny, I've still got scones in—
They put you to work on your day off, huh?
Yup. But they pay me, so . . .
Go ahead and take lunch. I'll hold down the fort.
CLAK!
Thanks! I'll be back at one.

Are you hungry? Did you eat already?
I could go for some lunch.
King of Donair?*
Sure.
Five minutes later . . .
This way!

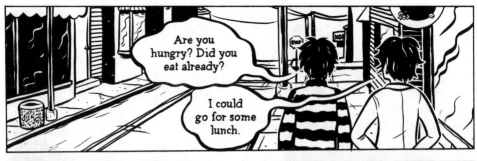

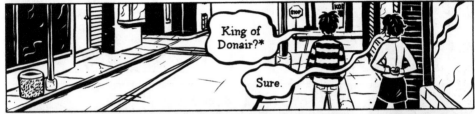

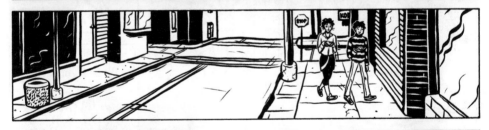

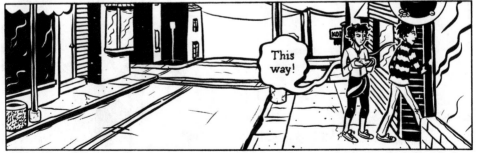

*Nova Scotian chain that serves pizza and donairs (greasy pseduo-Lebanese sandwiches popular in the region).

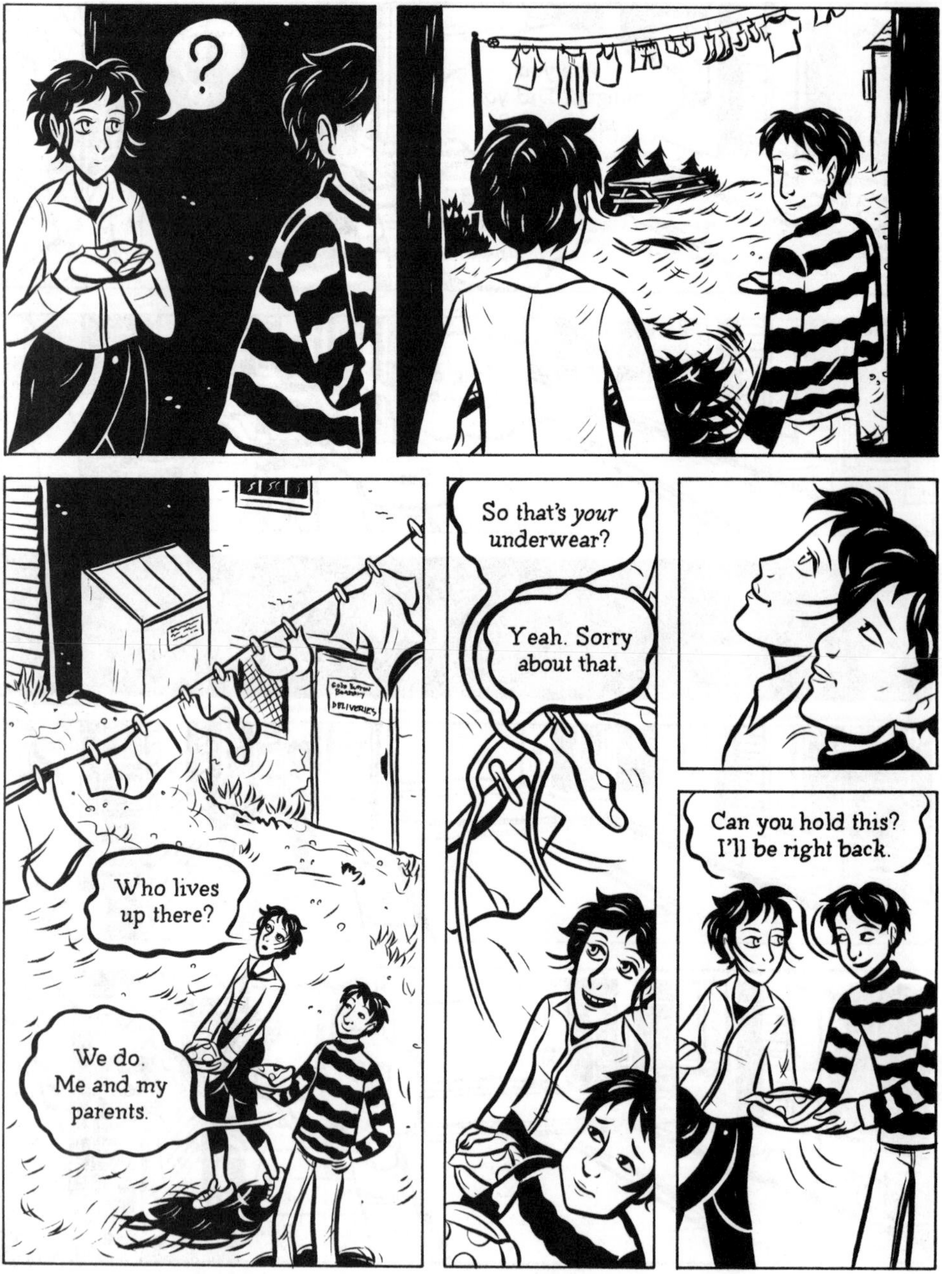
?
Who lives up there?
We do. Me and my parents.
So that's *your* underwear?
Yeah. Sorry about that.
Can you hold this? I'll be right back.

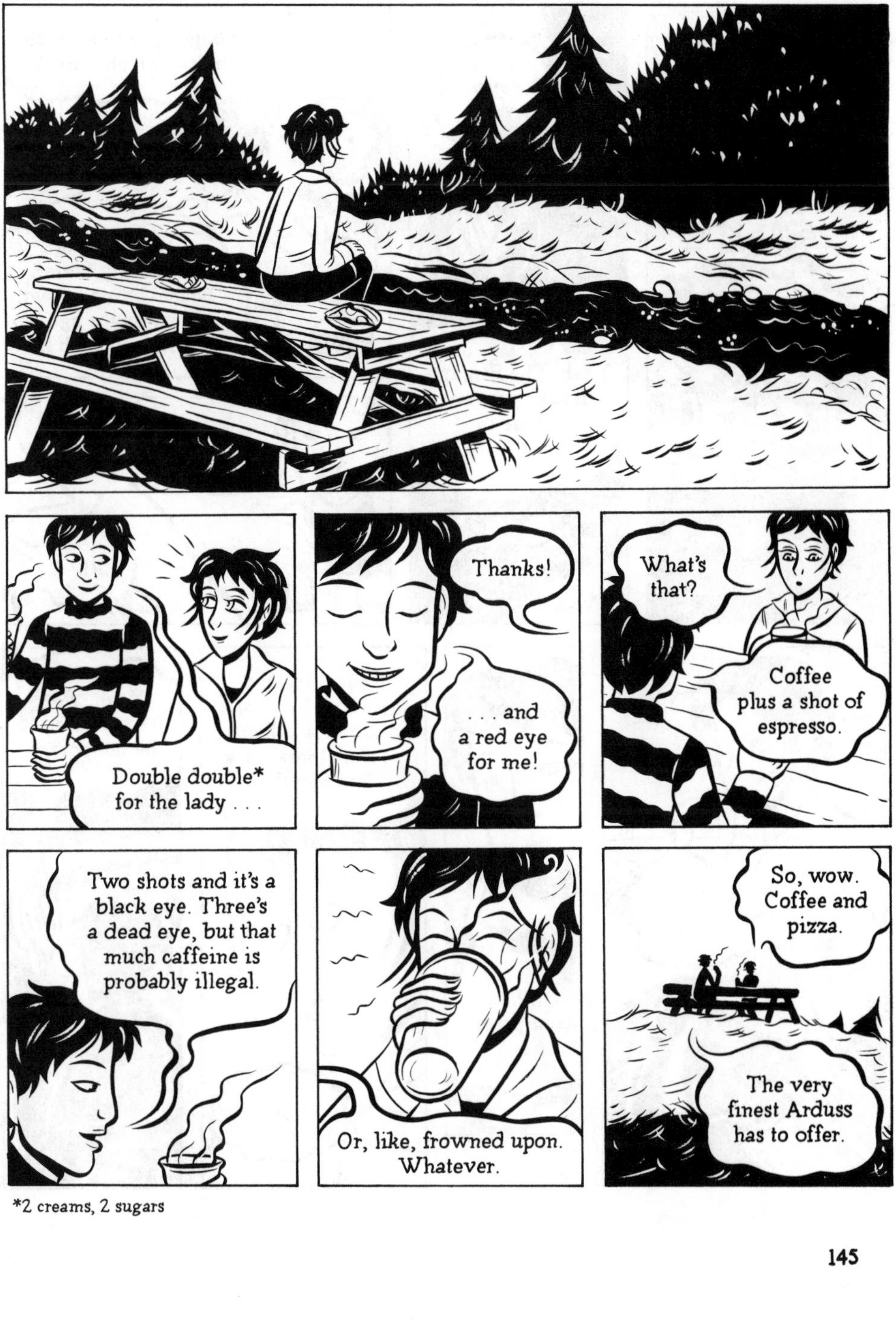
Double double*
for the lady . . .
Thanks!
. . . and
a red eye
for me!
What's
that?
Coffee
plus a shot of
espresso.
Two shots and it's a
black eye. Three's
a dead eye, but that
much caffeine is
probably illegal.
Or, like, frowned upon.
Whatever.
So, wow.
Coffee and
pizza.
The very
finest Arduss
has to offer.

*2 creams, 2 sugars

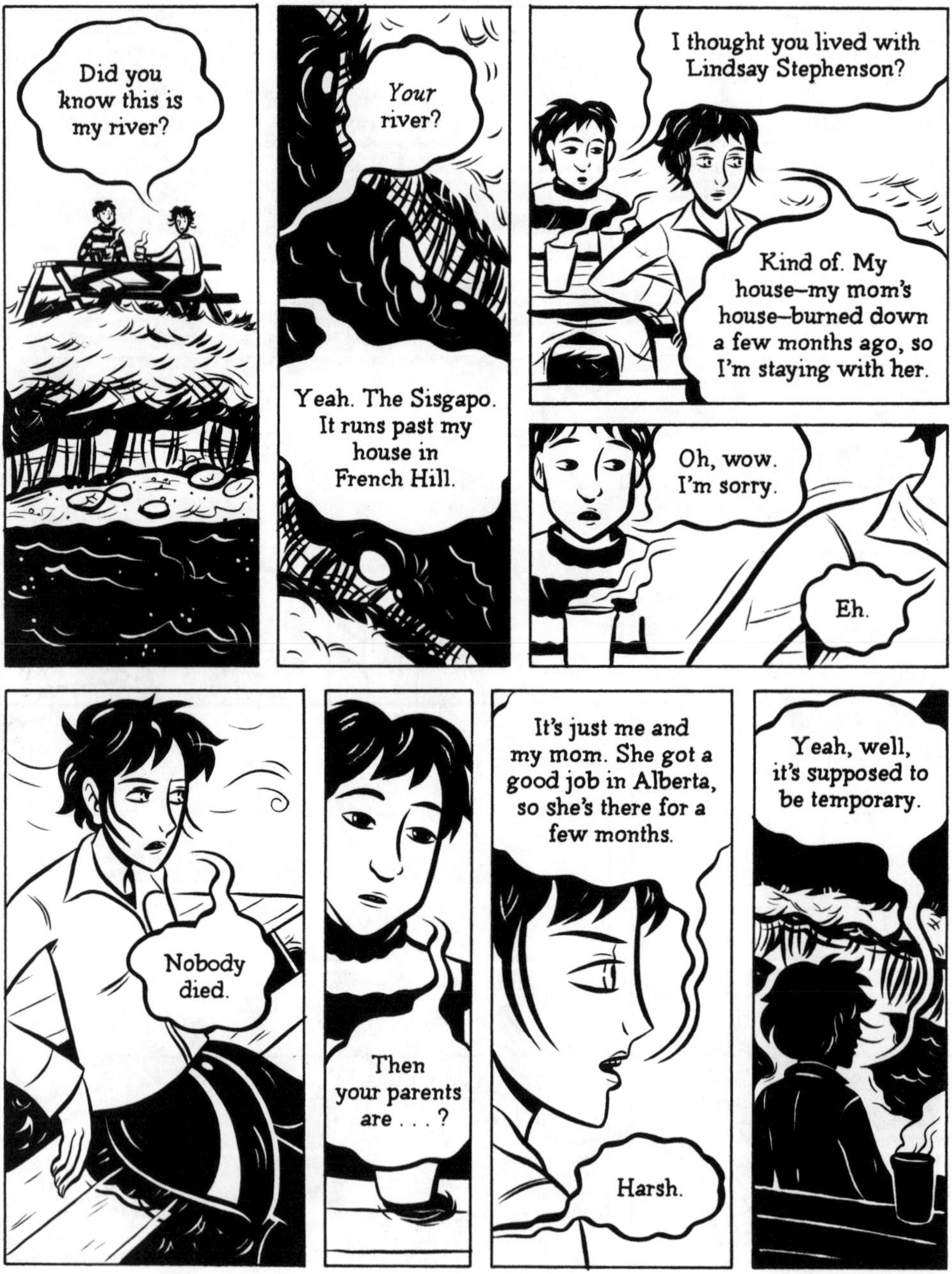
Did you know this is my river?
Your river?
Yeah. The Sisgapo. It runs past my house in French Hill.
I thought you lived with Lindsay Stephenson?
Kind of. My house—my mom's house—burned down a few months ago, so I'm staying with her.
Oh, wow. I'm sorry.
Eh.
Nobody died.
Then your parents are . . . ?
It's just me and my mom. She got a good job in Alberta, so she's there for a few months.
Harsh.
Yeah, well, it's supposed to be temporary.

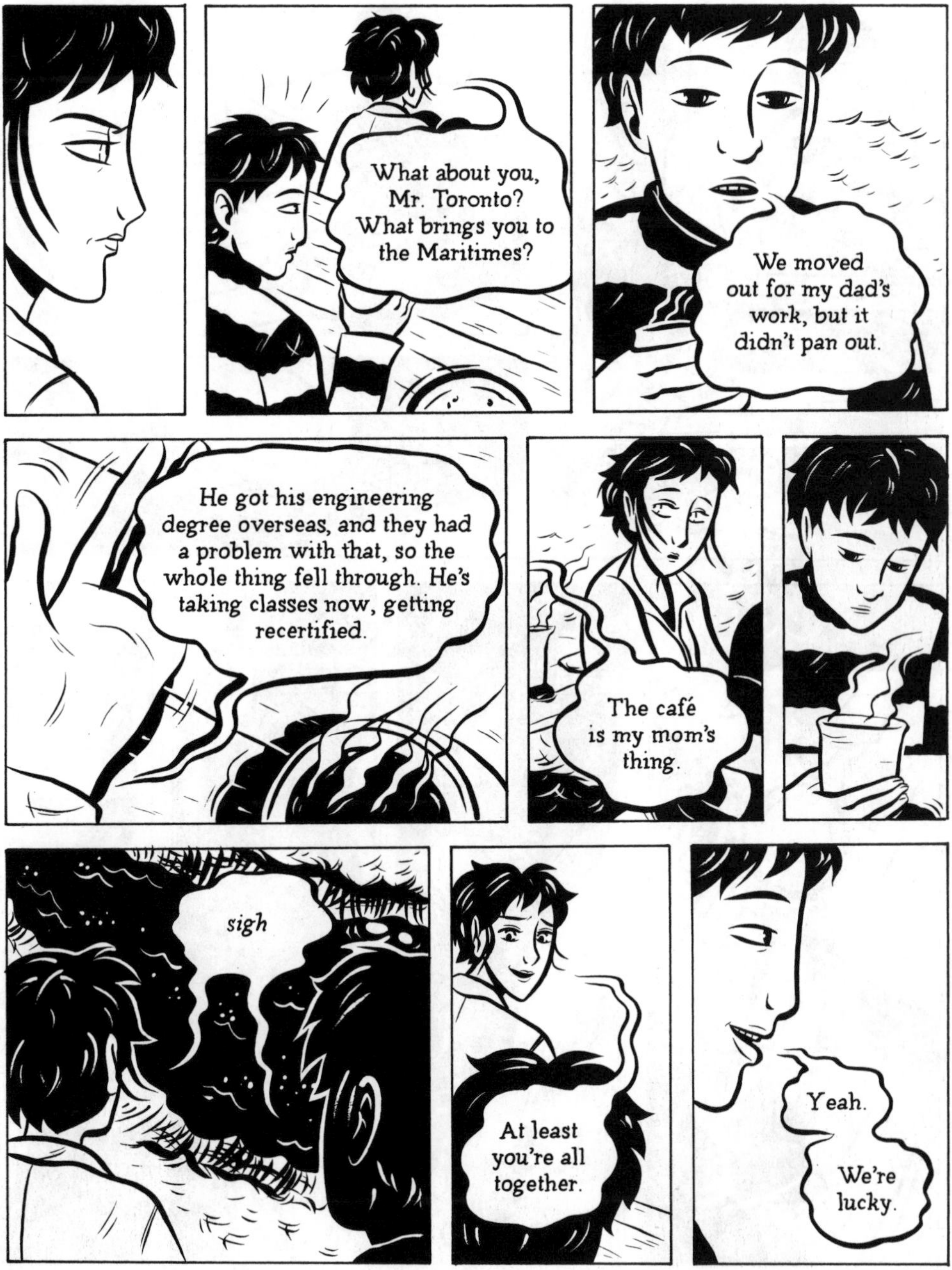
What about you, Mr. Toronto? What brings you to the Maritimes?
We moved out for my dad's work, but it didn't pan out.
He got his engineering degree overseas, and they had a problem with that, so the whole thing fell through. He's taking classes now, getting recertified.
The café is my mom's thing.
sigh
At least you're all together.
Yeah.
We're lucky.

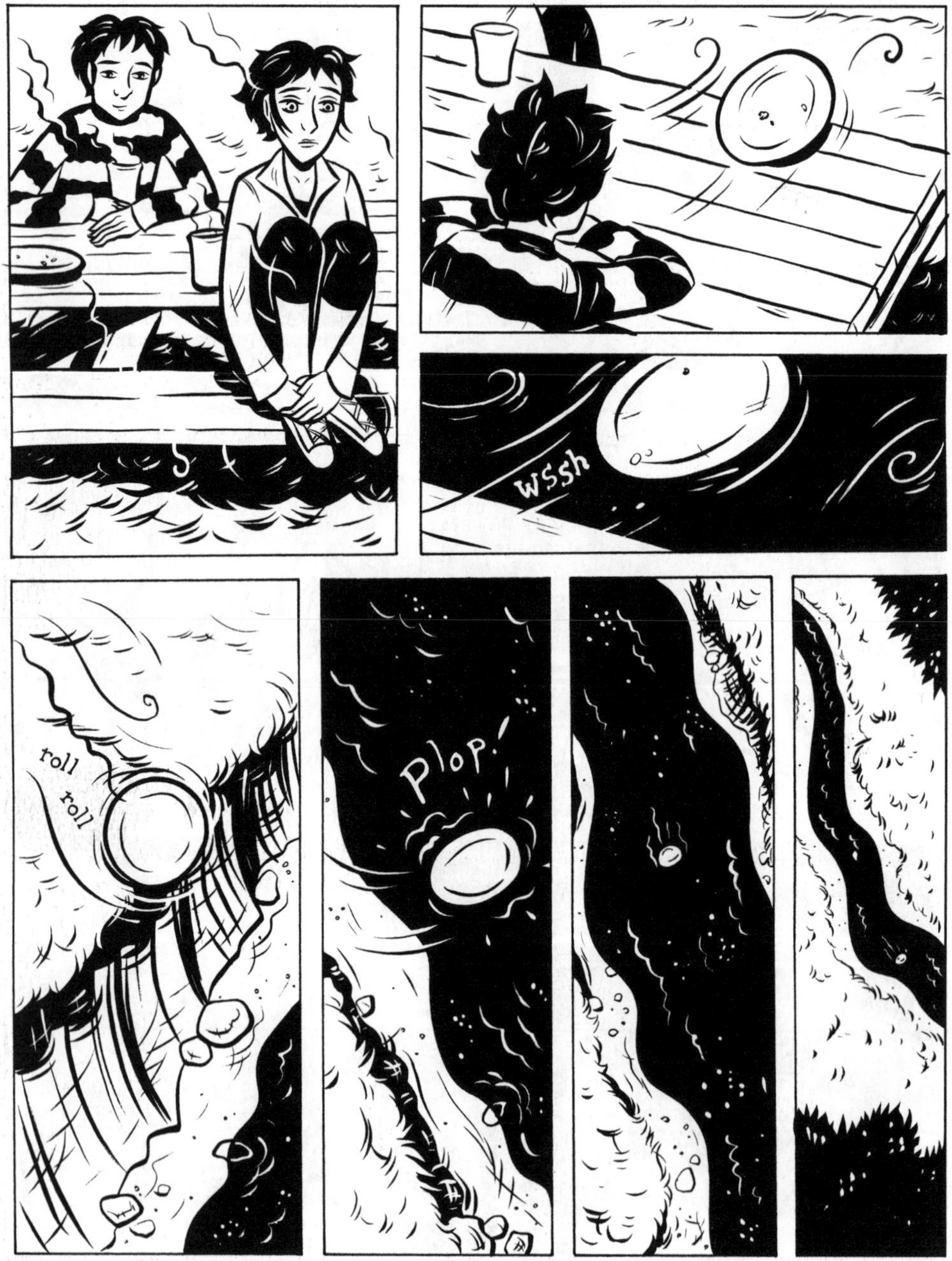
wssh
roll
roll
Plop!

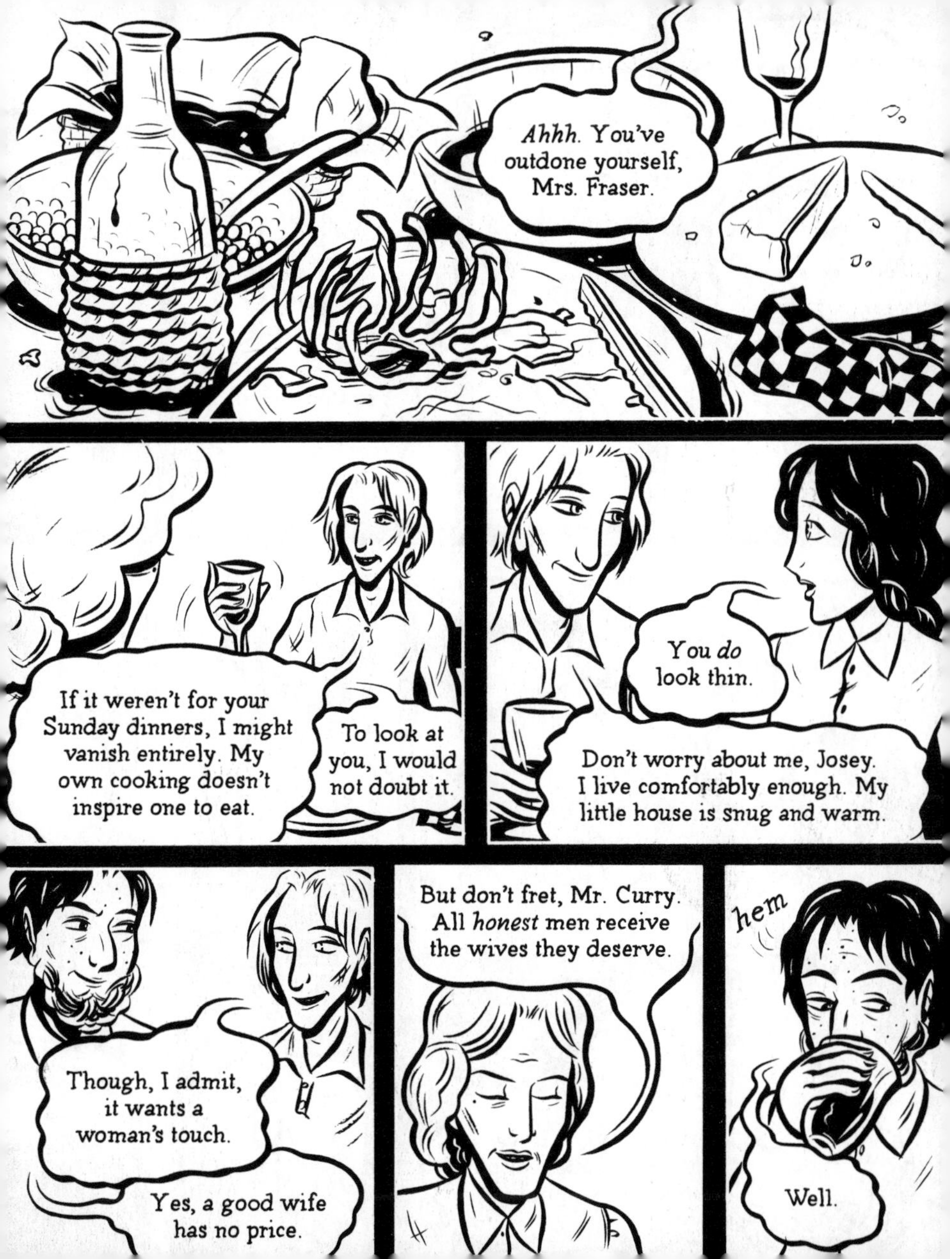
Ahhh. You've outdone yourself, Mrs. Fraser.
If it weren't for your Sunday dinners, I might vanish entirely. My own cooking doesn't inspire one to eat.
To look at you, I would not doubt it.
You do look thin.
Don't worry about me, Josey. I live comfortably enough. My little house is snug and warm.
Though, I admit, it wants a woman's touch.
Yes, a good wife has no price.
But don't fret, Mr. Curry. All honest men receive the wives they deserve.
hem
Well.

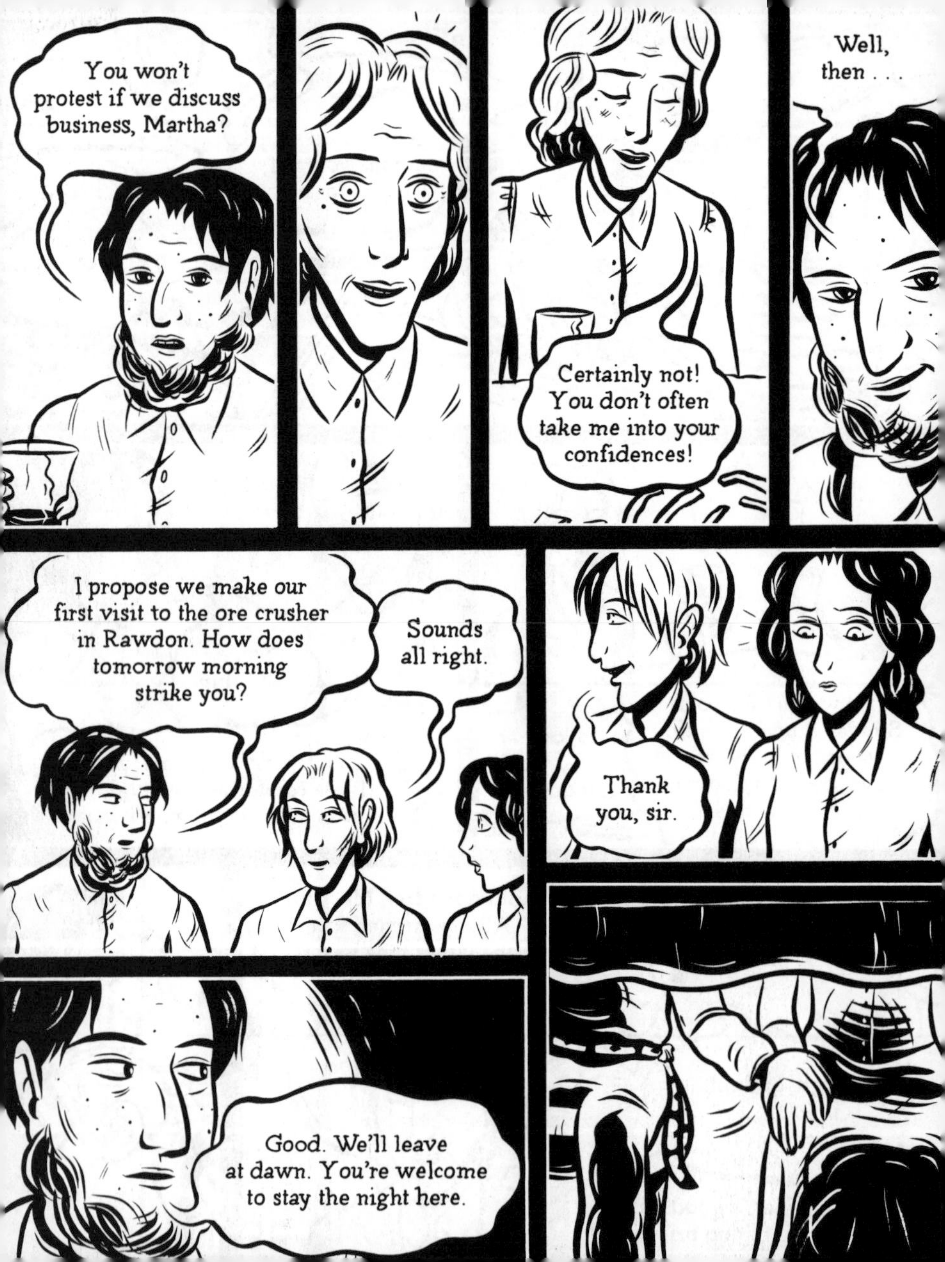
You won't protest if we discuss business, Martha?
Certainly not! You don't often take me into your confidences!
Well, then . . .
I propose we make our first visit to the ore crusher in Rawdon. How does tomorrow morning strike you?
Sounds all right.
Thank you, sir.
Good. We'll leave at dawn. You're welcome to stay the night here.

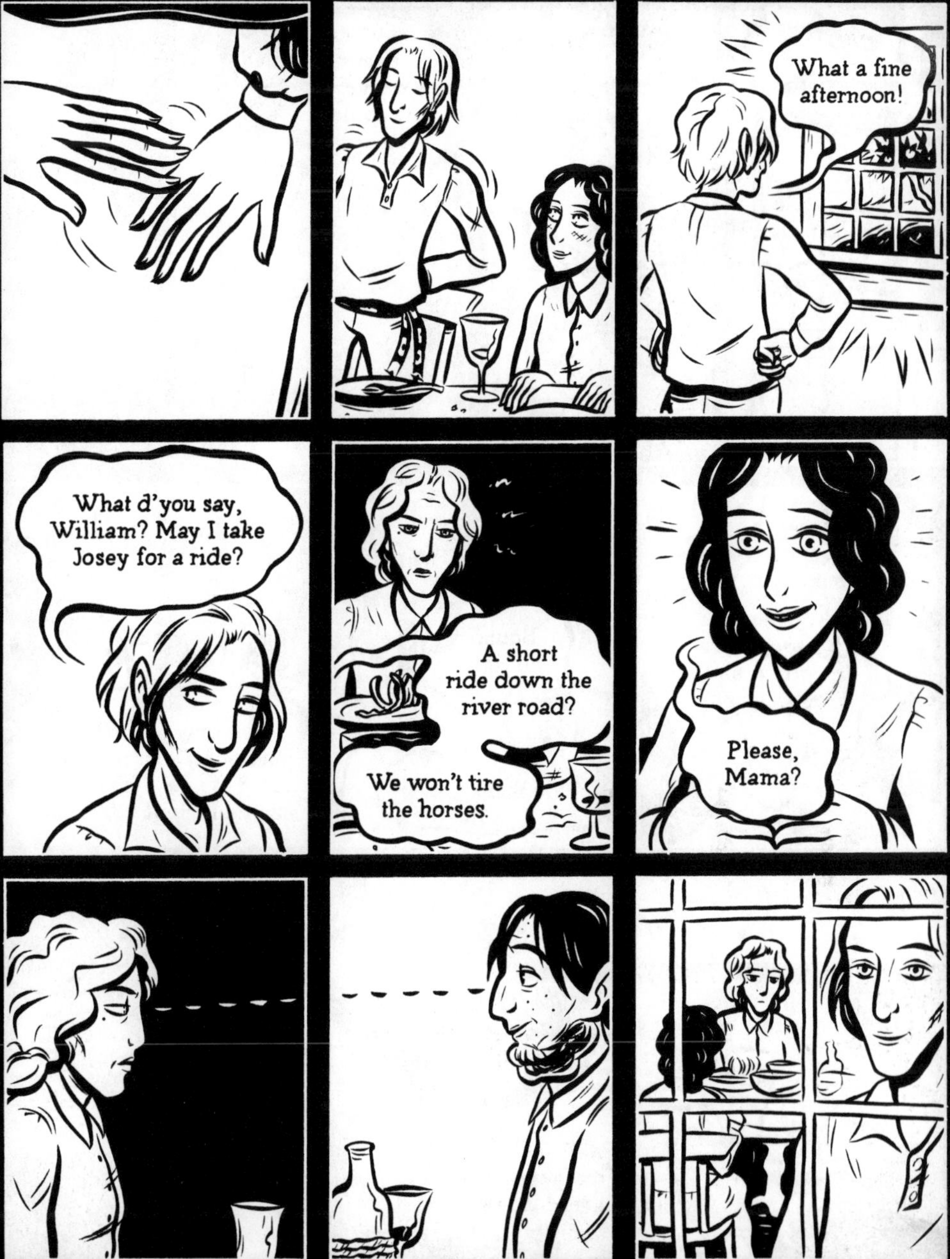
What a fine afternoon!
What d'you say, William? May I take Josey for a ride?
A short ride down the river road?
We won't tire the horses.
Please, Mama?

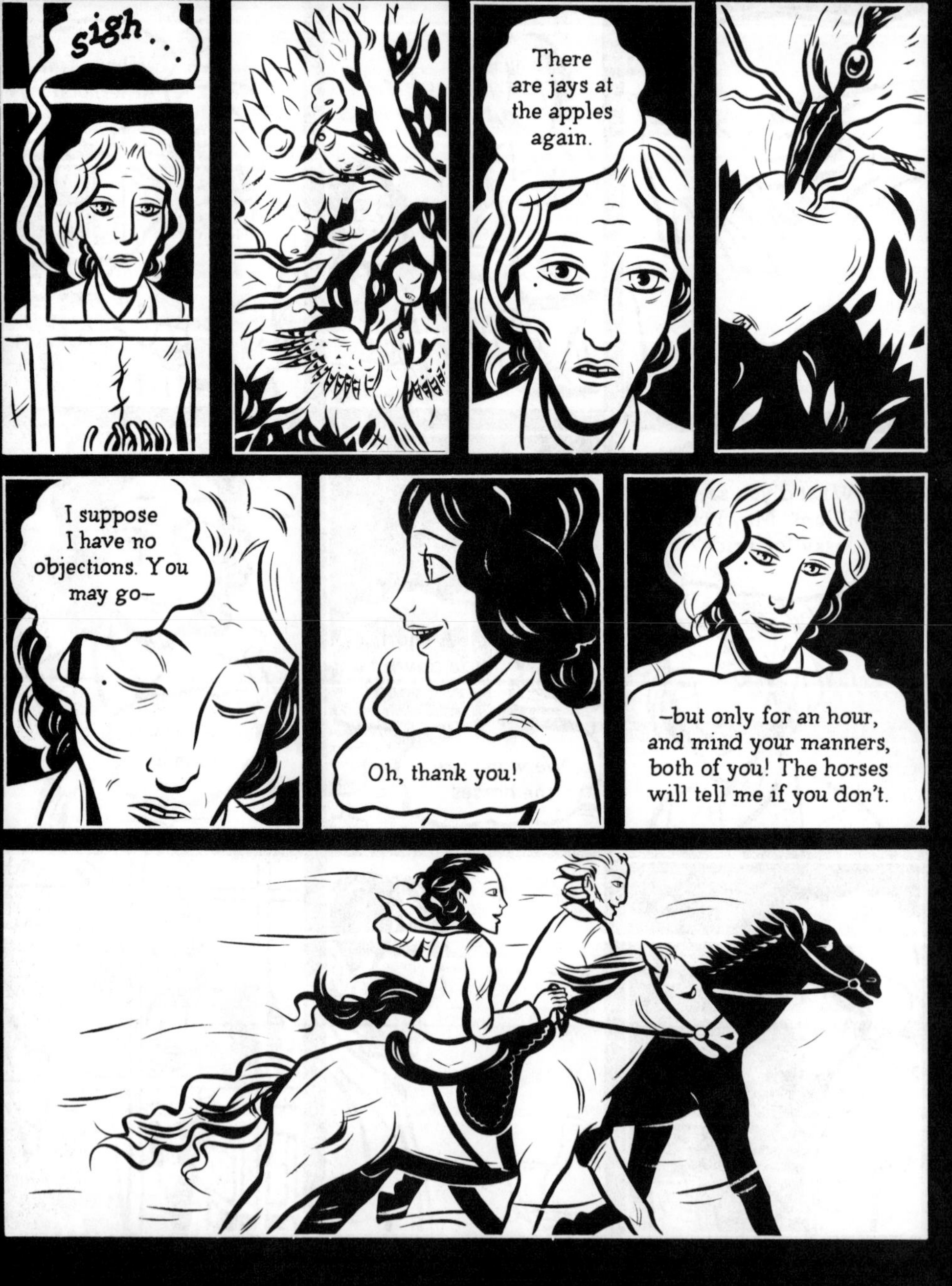
sigh...
There are jays at the apples again.
I suppose I have no objections. You may go–
Oh, thank you!
–but only for an hour, and mind your manners, both of you! The horses will tell me if you don't.

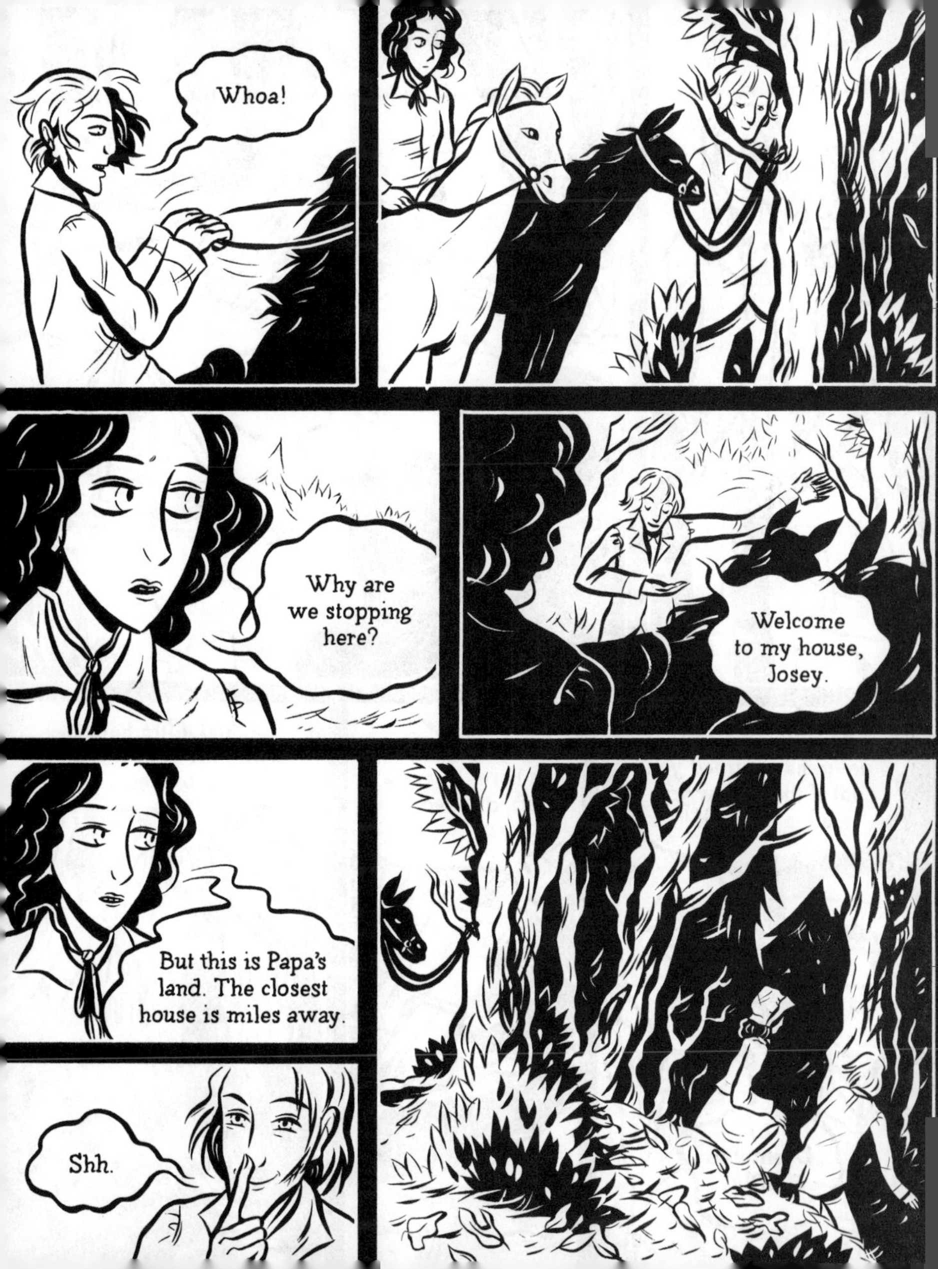

Whoa!
Why are we stopping here?
Welcome to my house, Josey.
But this is Papa's land. The closest house is miles away.
Shh.

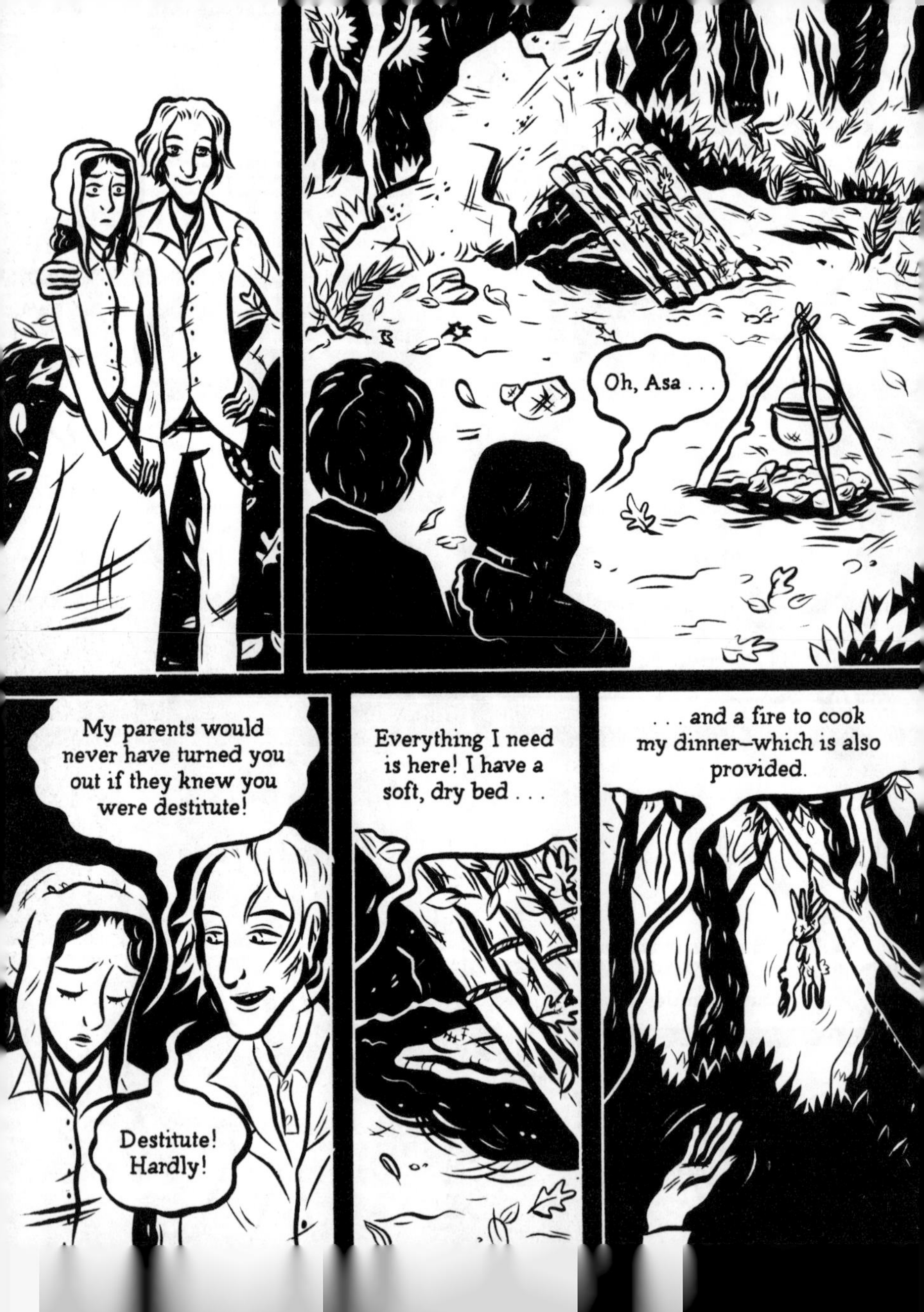

Oh, Asa . . .
My parents would never have turned you out if they knew you were destitute!
Destitute! Hardly!
Everything I need is here! I have a soft, dry bed . . .
. . . and a fire to cook my dinner—which is also provided.

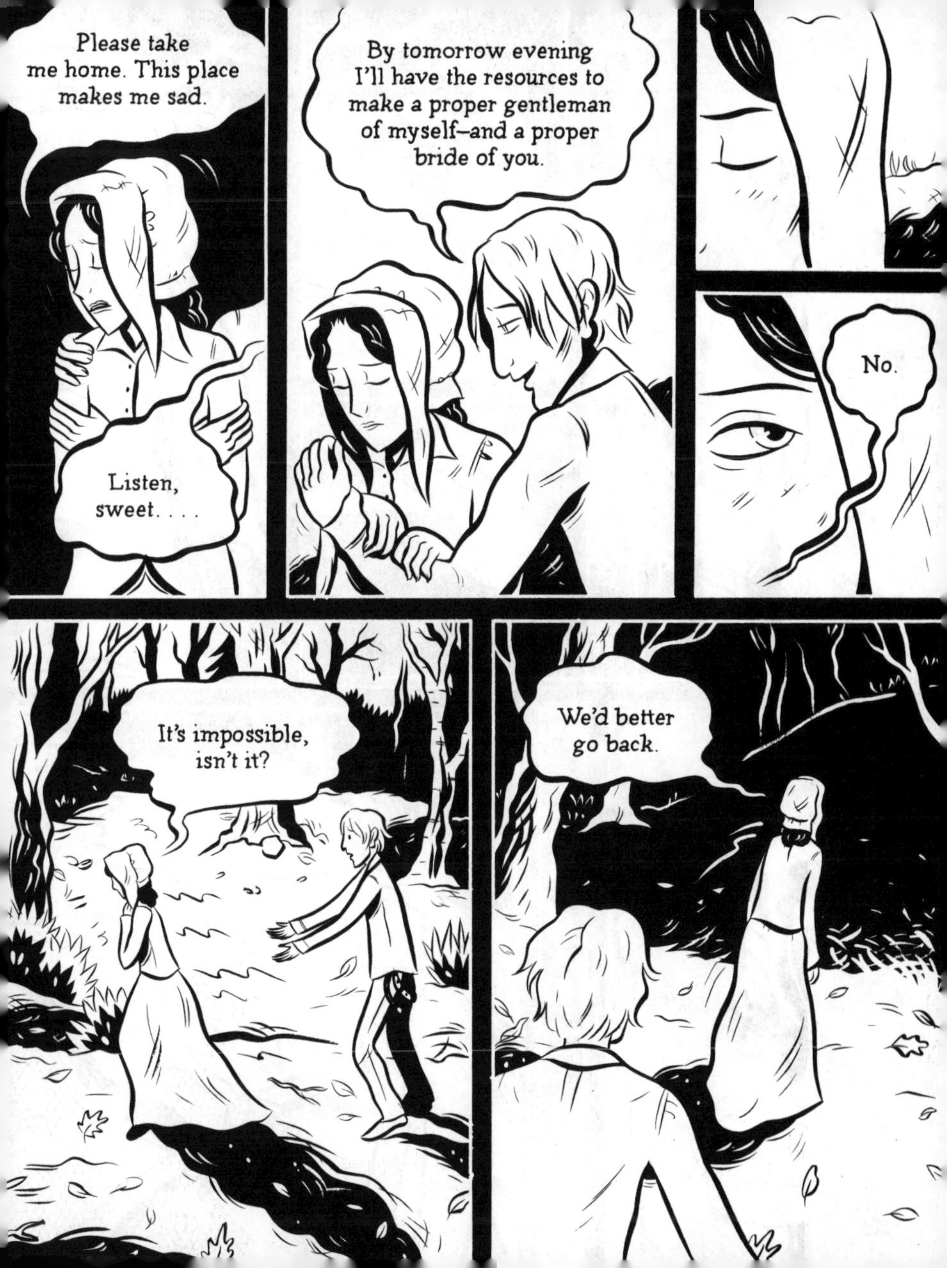
Please take me home. This place makes me sad.
Listen, sweet. . . .
By tomorrow evening I'll have the resources to make a proper gentleman of myself—and a proper bride of you.
No.
It's impossible, isn't it?
We'd better go back.

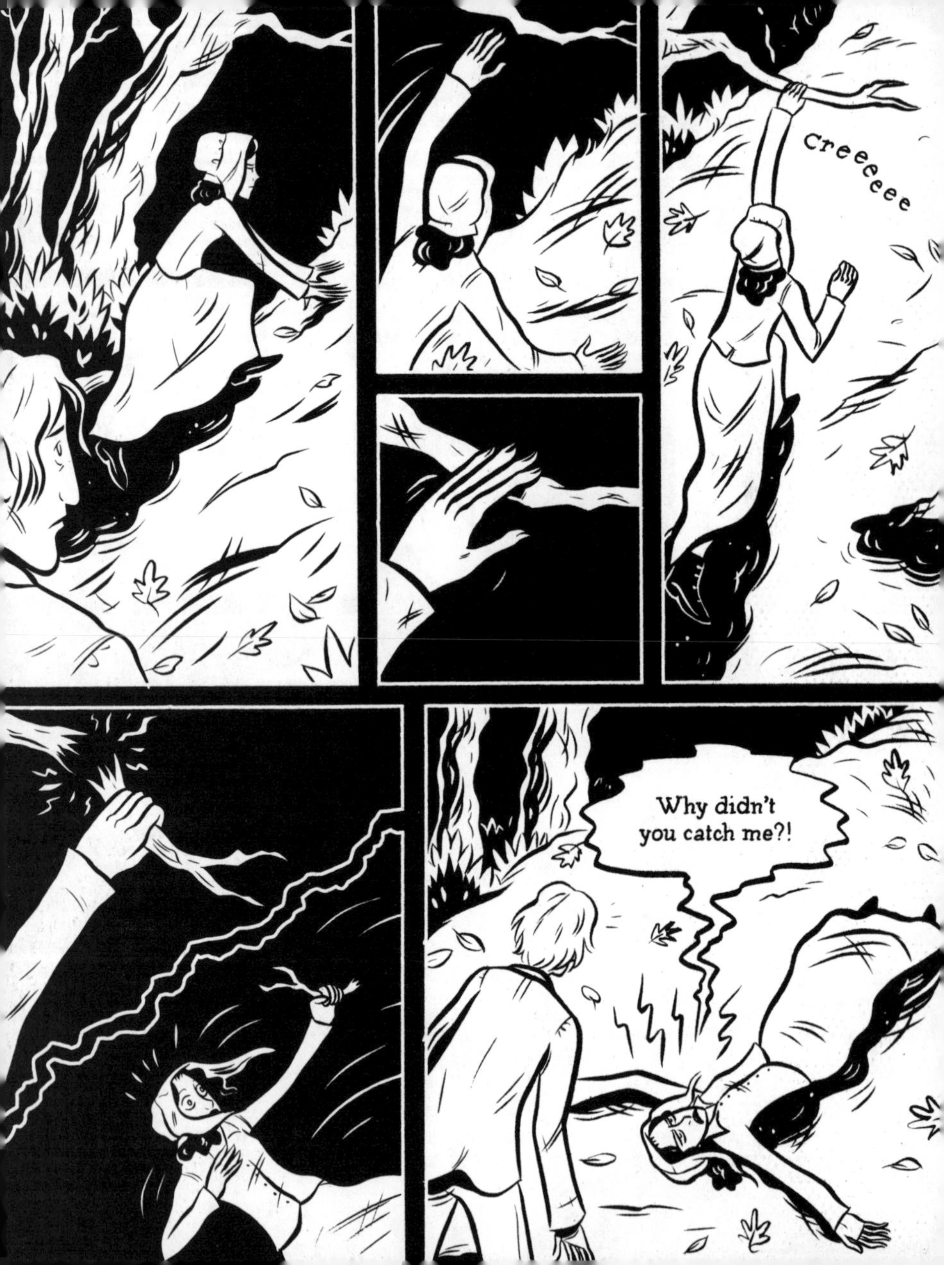
Creeeeeee
Why didn't you catch me?!

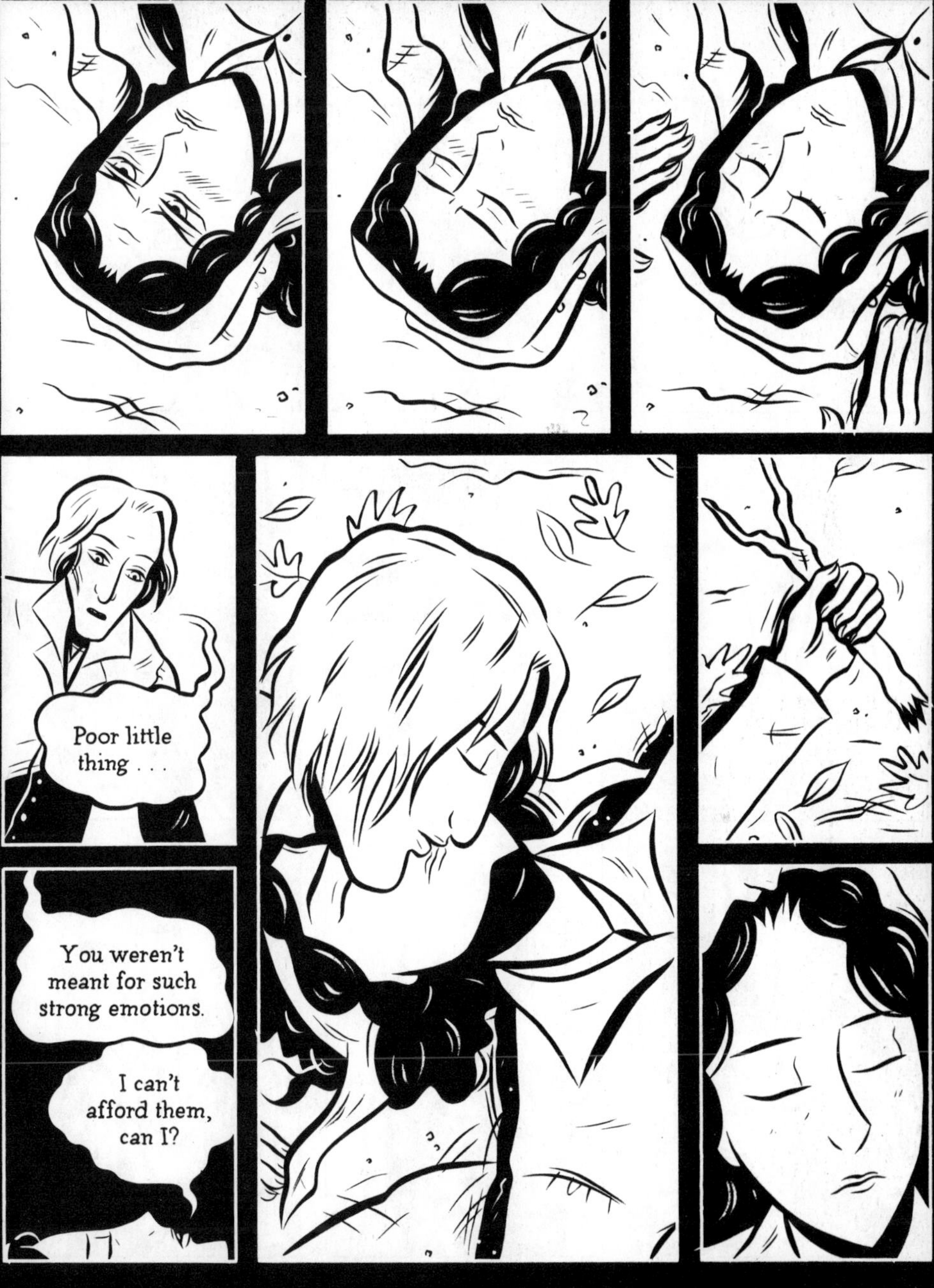
Poor little thing . . .
You weren't meant for such strong emotions.
I can't afford them, can I?

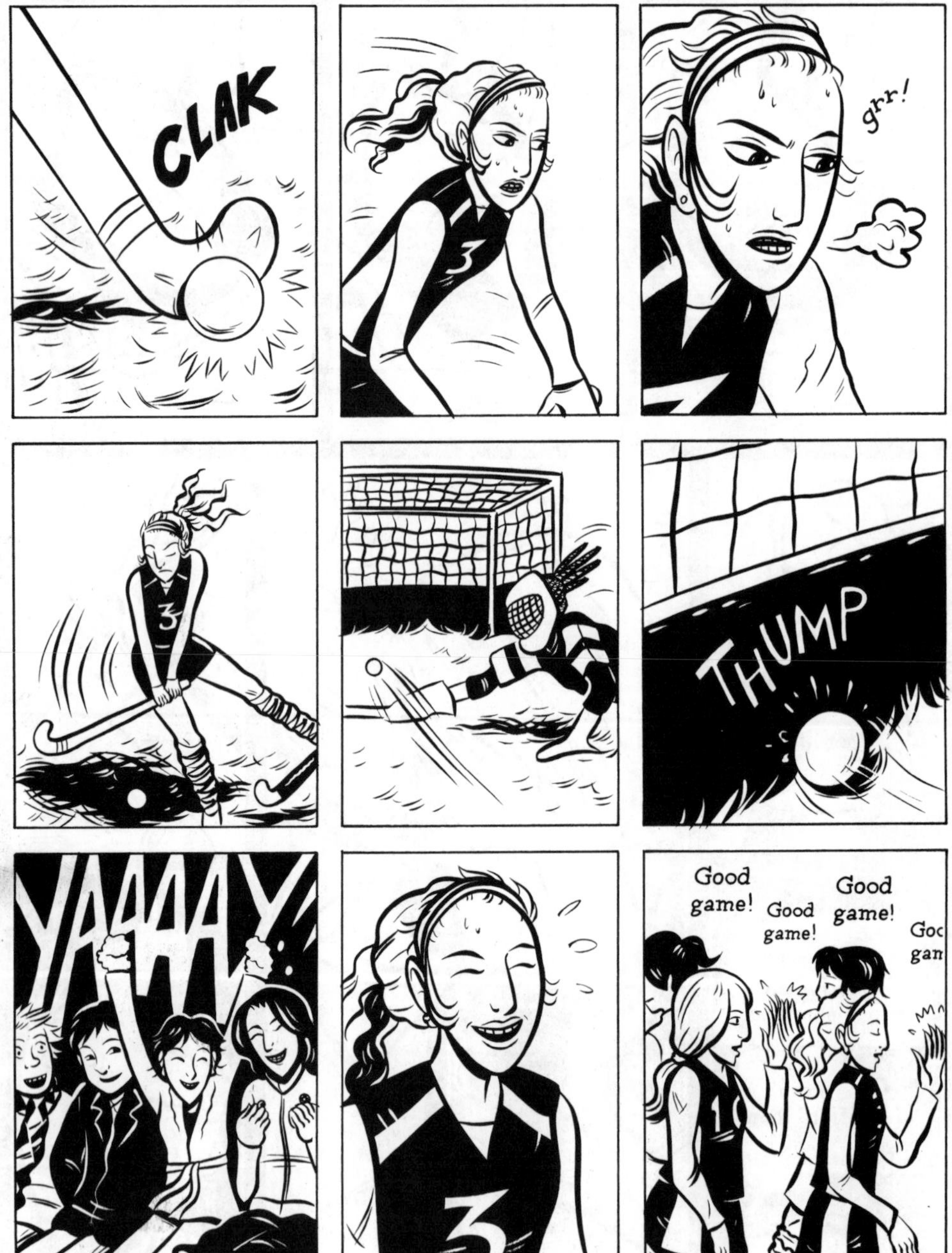
CLAK
grr!
THUMP
YAAAAY!
Good game!
Good game!
Good game!

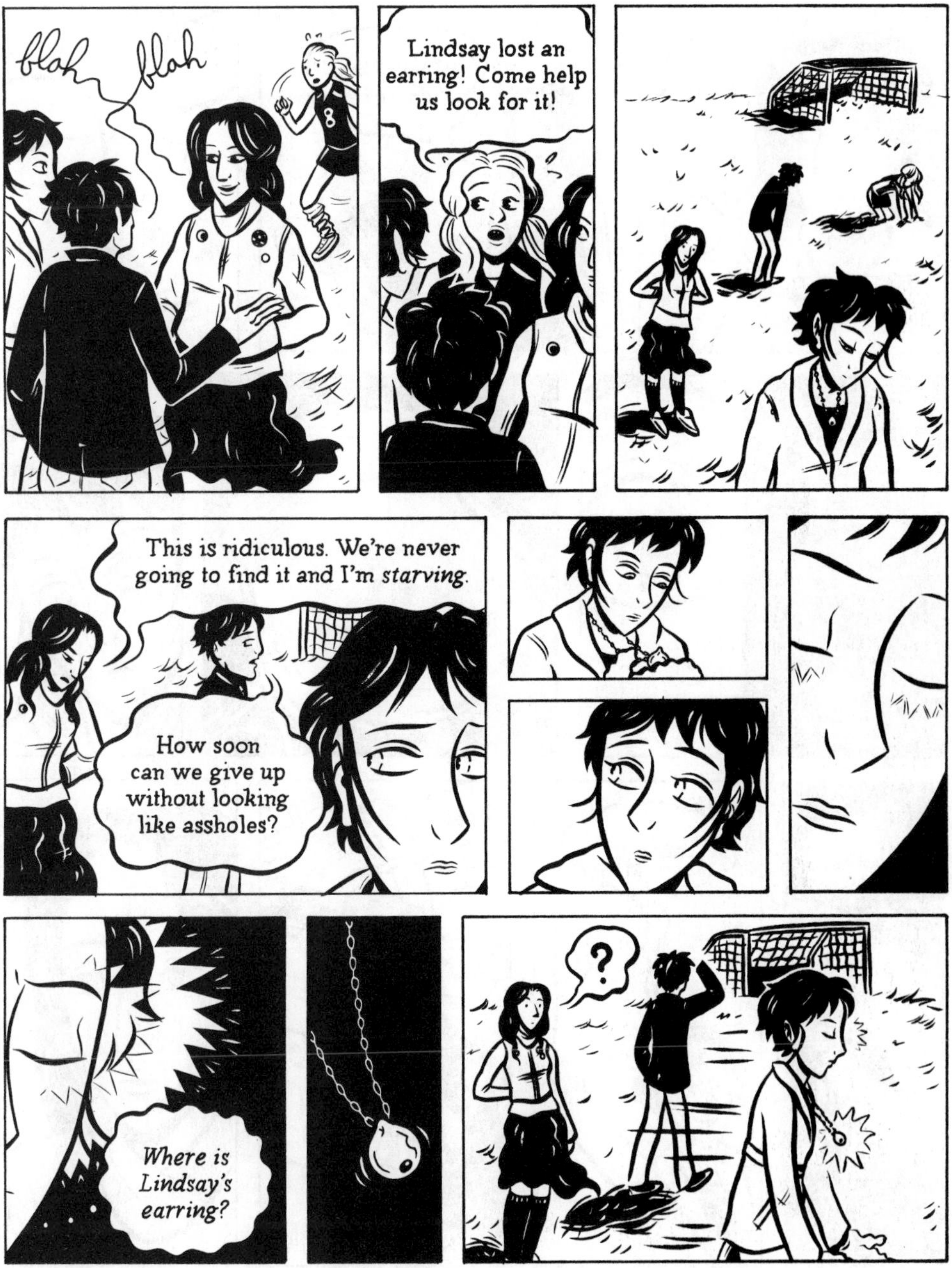
blah blah
Lindsay lost an earring! Come help us look for it!
This is ridiculous. We're never going to find it and I'm *starving*.
How soon can we give up without looking like assholes?
Where is Lindsay's earring?
?

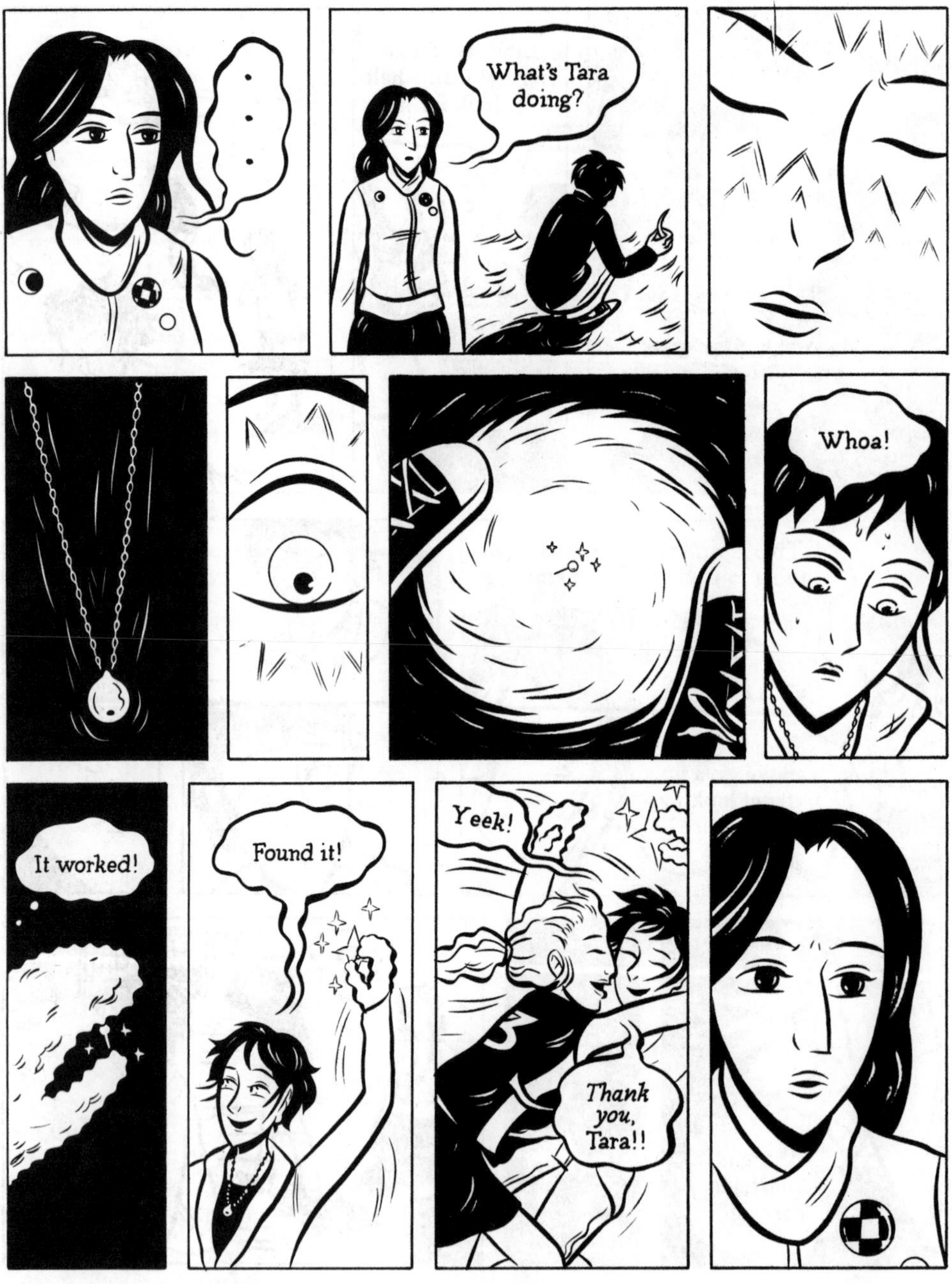
. . .
What's Tara doing?
Whoa!
It worked!
Found it!
Yeek!
Thank you, Tara!!

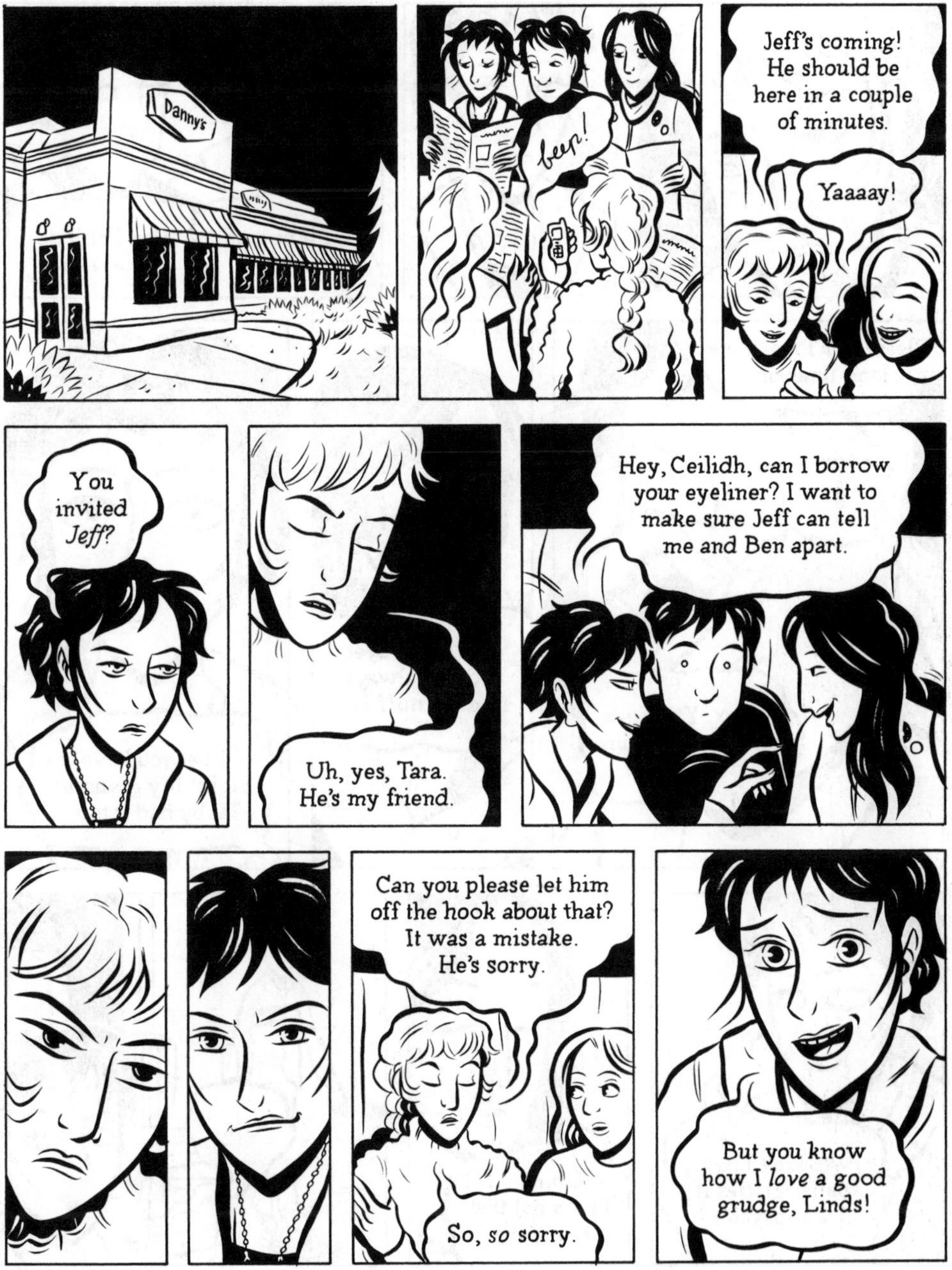
Danny's
beep!
Jeff's coming! He should be here in a couple of minutes.
Yaaaay!
You invited *Jeff*?
Uh, yes, Tara. He's my friend.
Hey, Ceilidh, can I borrow your eyeliner? I want to make sure Jeff can tell me and Ben apart.
Can you please let him off the hook about that? It was a mistake. He's sorry.
So, *so* sorry.
But you know how I *love* a good grudge, Linds!

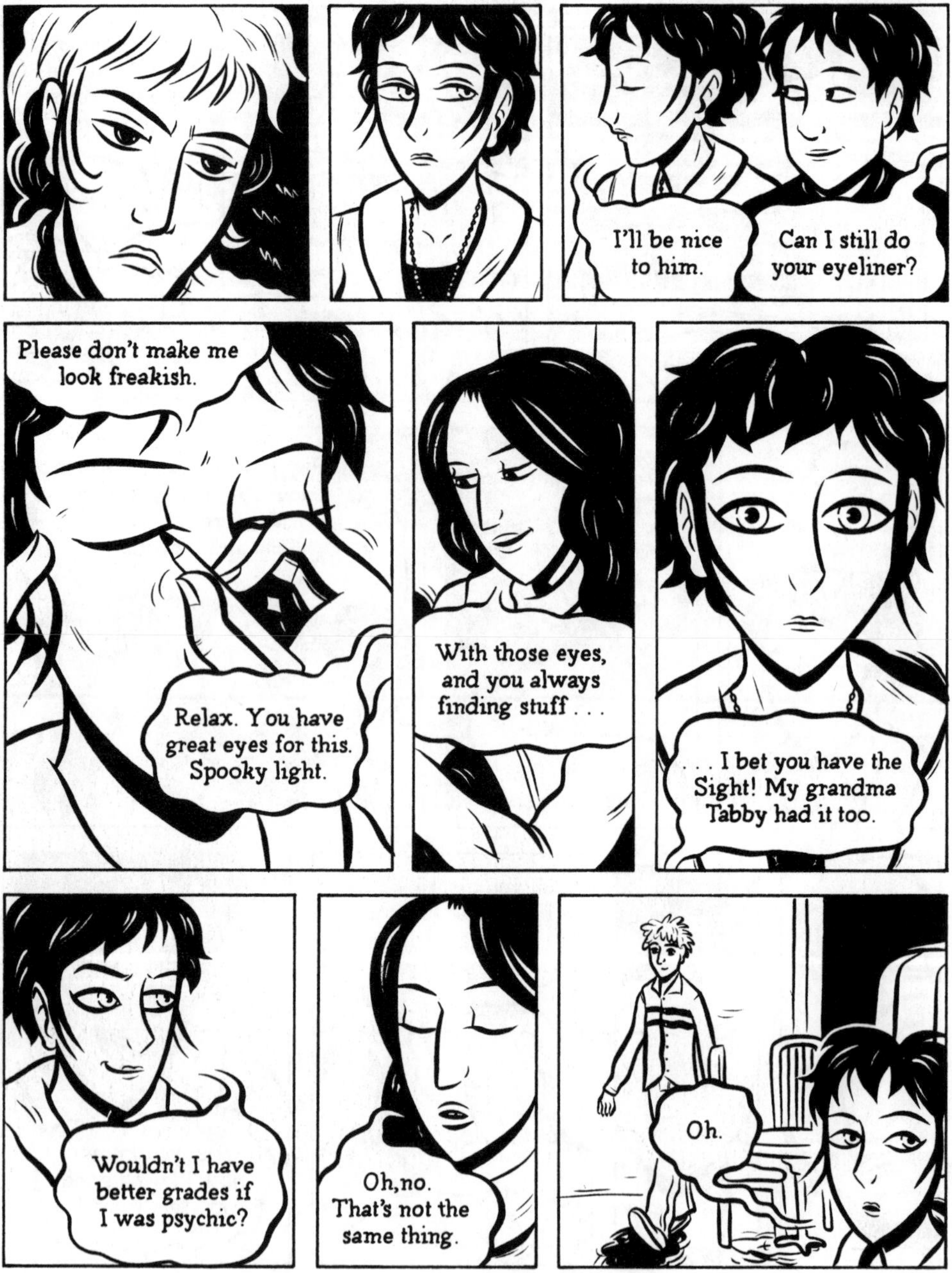
I'll be nice to him.
Can I still do your eyeliner?
Please don't make me look freakish.
Relax. You have great eyes for this. Spooky light.
With those eyes, and you always finding stuff . . .
. . . I bet you have the Sight! My grandma Tabby had it too.
Wouldn't I have better grades if I was psychic?
Oh,no. That's not the same thing.
Oh.

Jeff!
Hi, Jeff!
Hi, Julia. Lindsay. Everybody.
Ahem.
menu
?
Oh! Uh, hi, Tara.
You look nice.
Thanks.

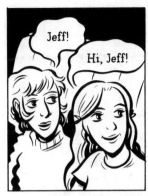

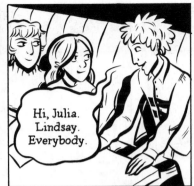

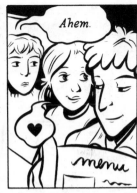

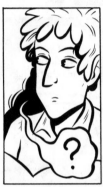

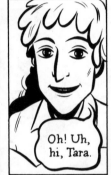

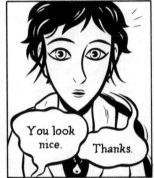

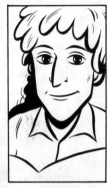

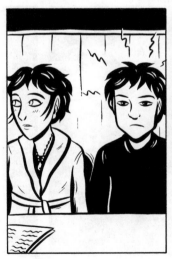

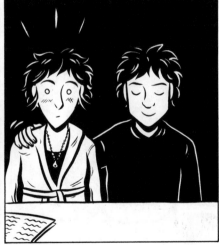

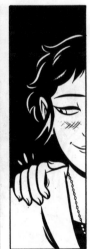

Good night!

Bye!

Are you guys dating or what?

I don't know.

We haven't really talked about it.

Ah.

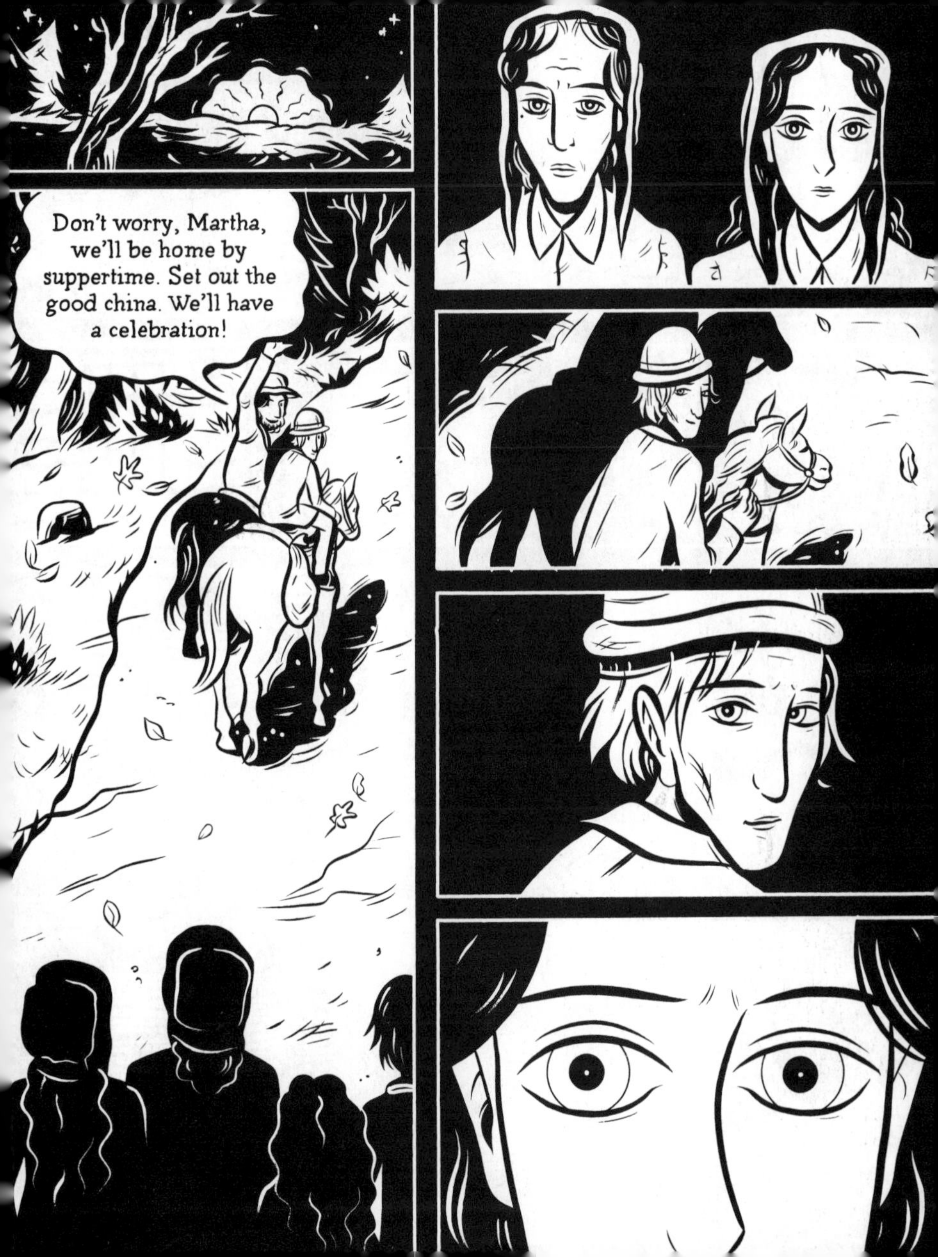
Don't worry, Martha, we'll be home by suppertime. Set out the good china. We'll have a celebration!

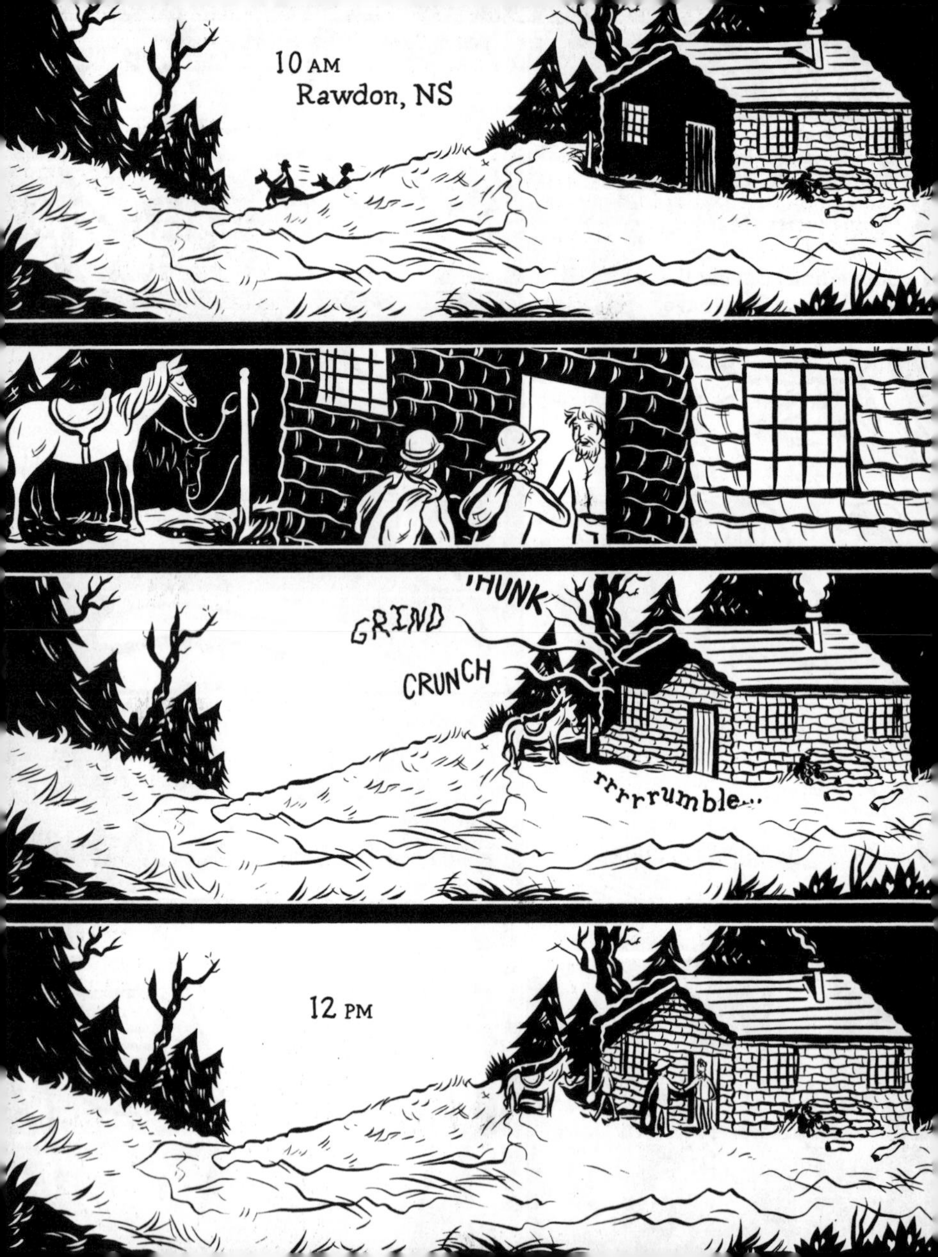
10 AM
Rawdon, NS
THUNK
GRIND
CRUNCH
rrrrrumble...
12 PM

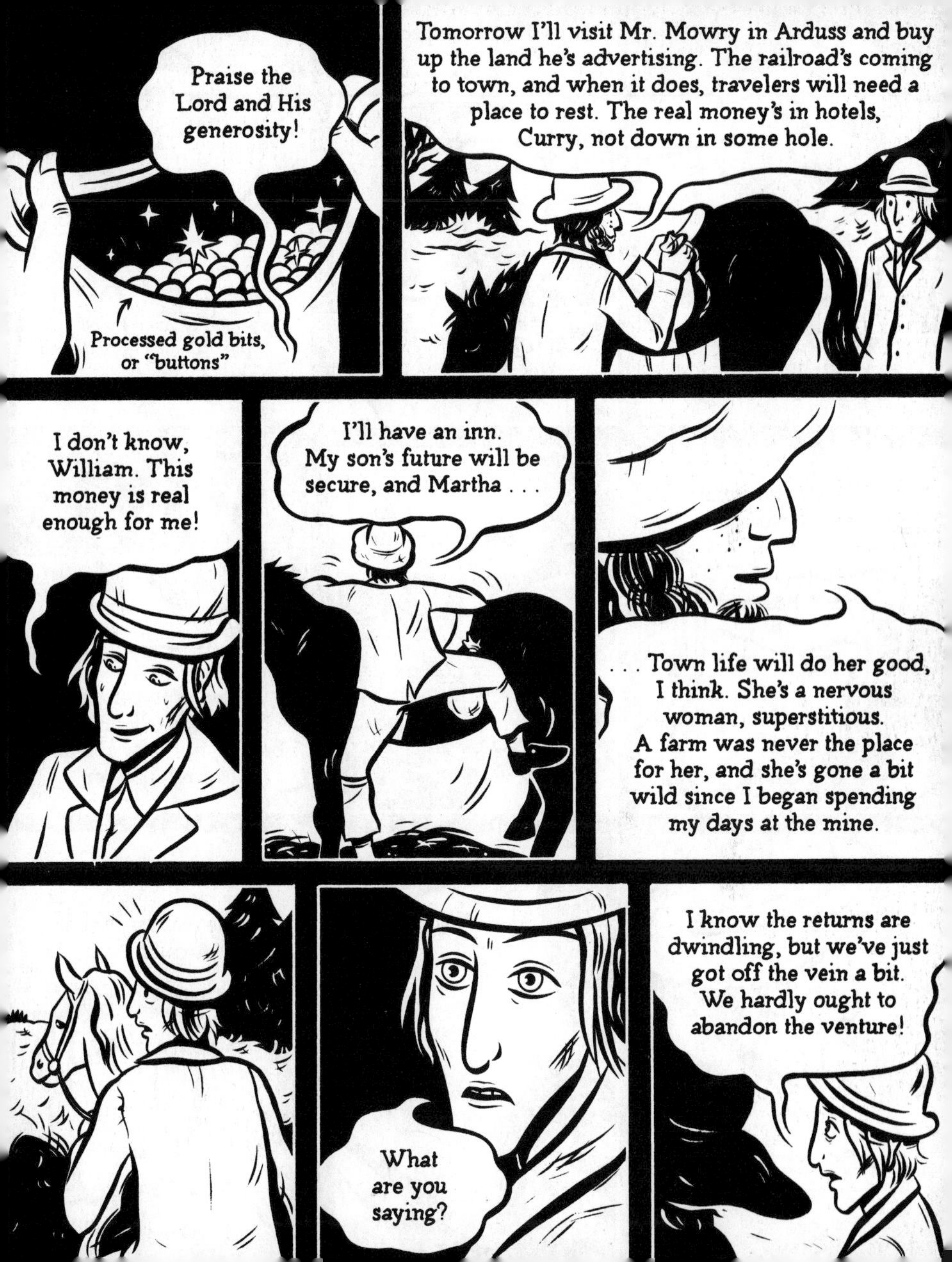
Praise the Lord and His generosity!
Processed gold bits, or "buttons"
Tomorrow I'll visit Mr. Mowry in Arduss and buy up the land he's advertising. The railroad's coming to town, and when it does, travelers will need a place to rest. The real money's in hotels, Curry, not down in some hole.
I don't know, William. This money is real enough for me!
I'll have an inn. My son's future will be secure, and Martha . . .
. . . Town life will do her good, I think. She's a nervous woman, superstitious. A farm was never the place for her, and she's gone a bit wild since I began spending my days at the mine.
What are you saying?
I know the returns are dwindling, but we've just got off the vein a bit. We hardly ought to abandon the venture!

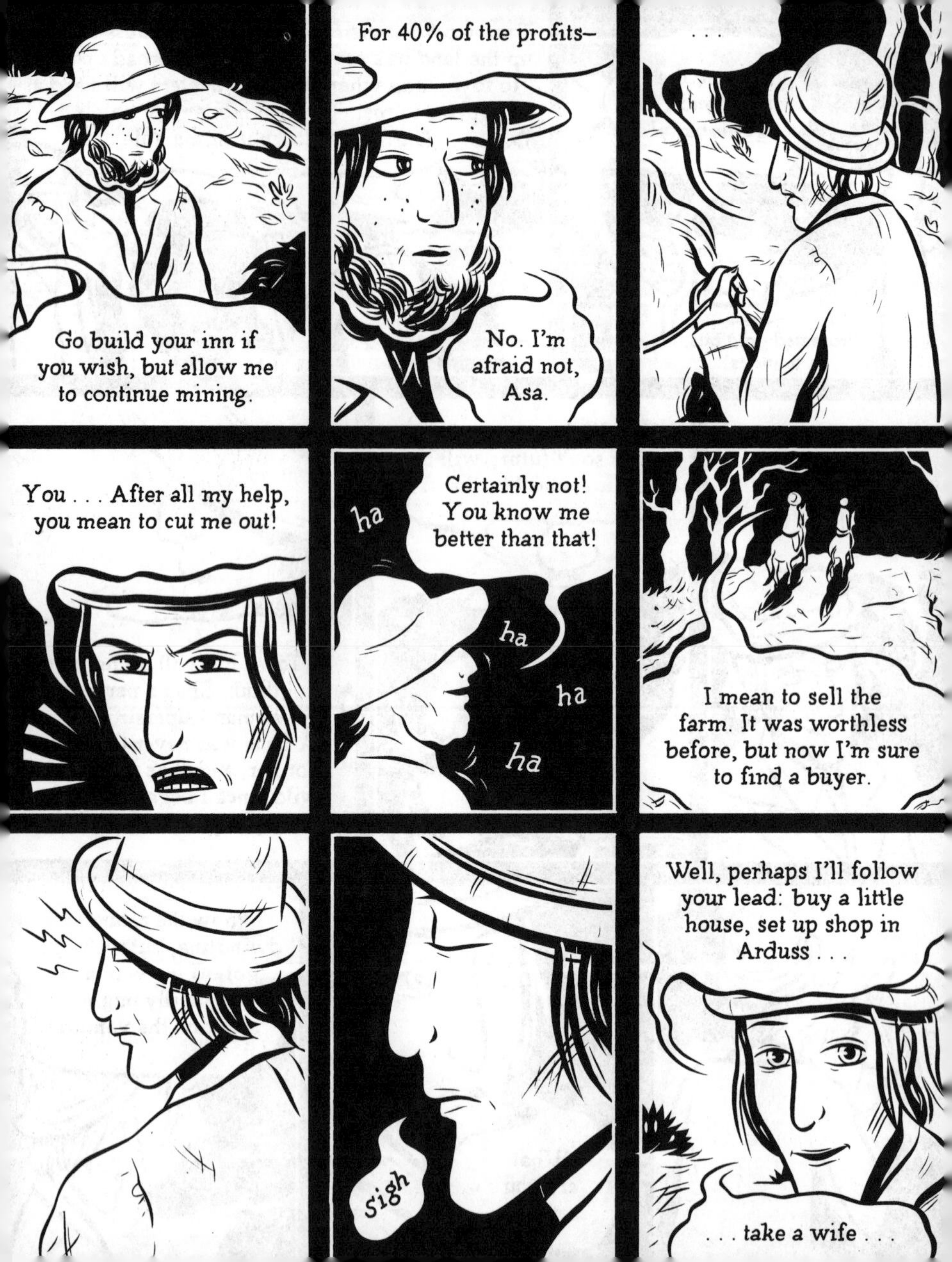
Go build your inn if you wish, but allow me to continue mining.
For 40% of the profits–
No. I'm afraid not, Asa.
. . .
You . . . After all my help, you mean to cut me out!
Certainly not! You know me better than that!
ha
ha
ha
ha
I mean to sell the farm. It was worthless before, but now I'm sure to find a buyer.
sigh
Well, perhaps I'll follow your lead: buy a little house, set up shop in Arduss . . .
. . . take a wife . . .

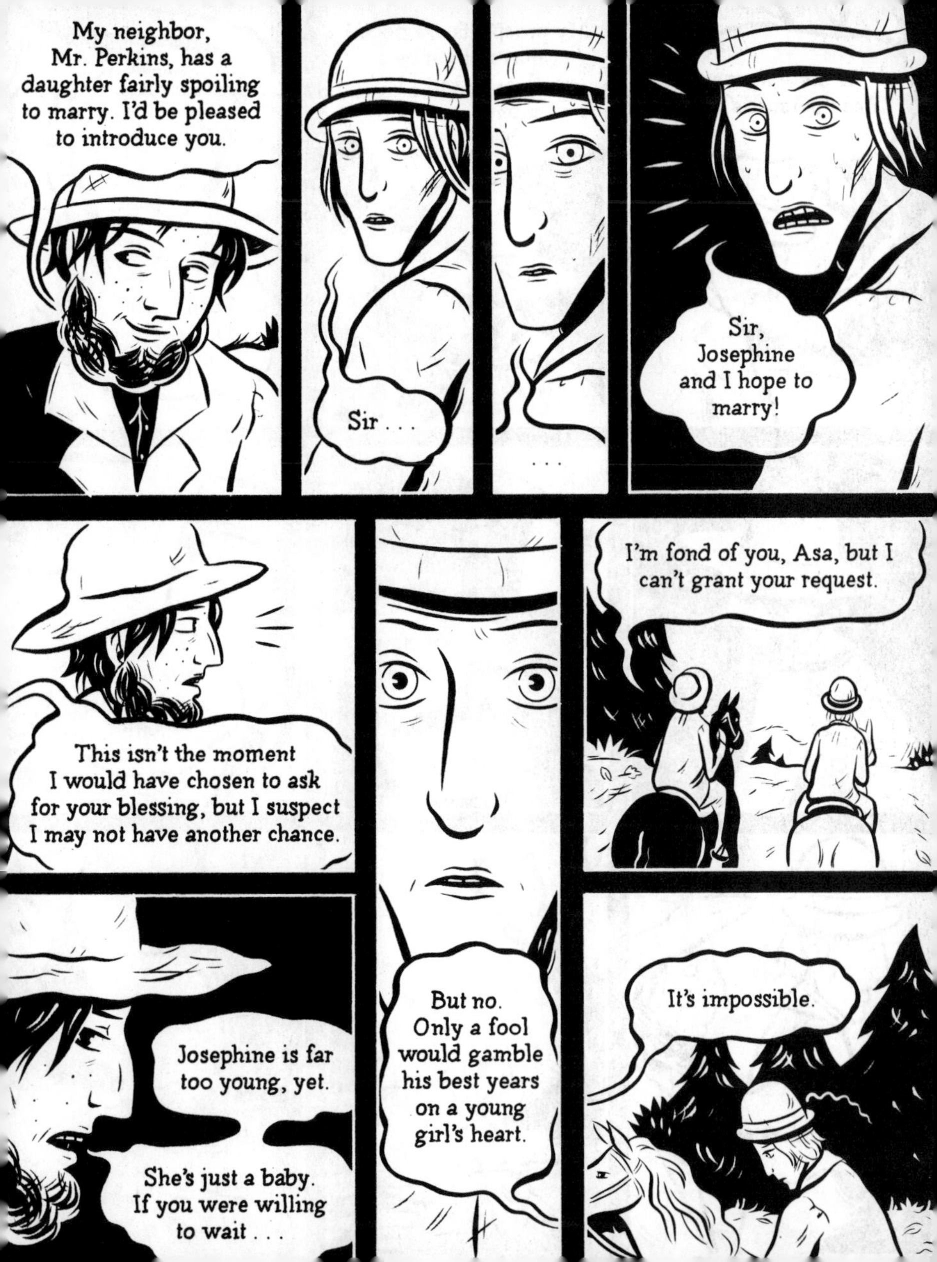
My neighbor, Mr. Perkins, has a daughter fairly spoiling to marry. I'd be pleased to introduce you.
Sir . . .
. . .
Sir, Josephine and I hope to marry!
This isn't the moment I would have chosen to ask for your blessing, but I suspect I may not have another chance.
I'm fond of you, Asa, but I can't grant your request.
Josephine is far too young, yet.
She's just a baby. If you were willing to wait . . .
But no. Only a fool would gamble his best years on a young girl's heart.
It's impossible.

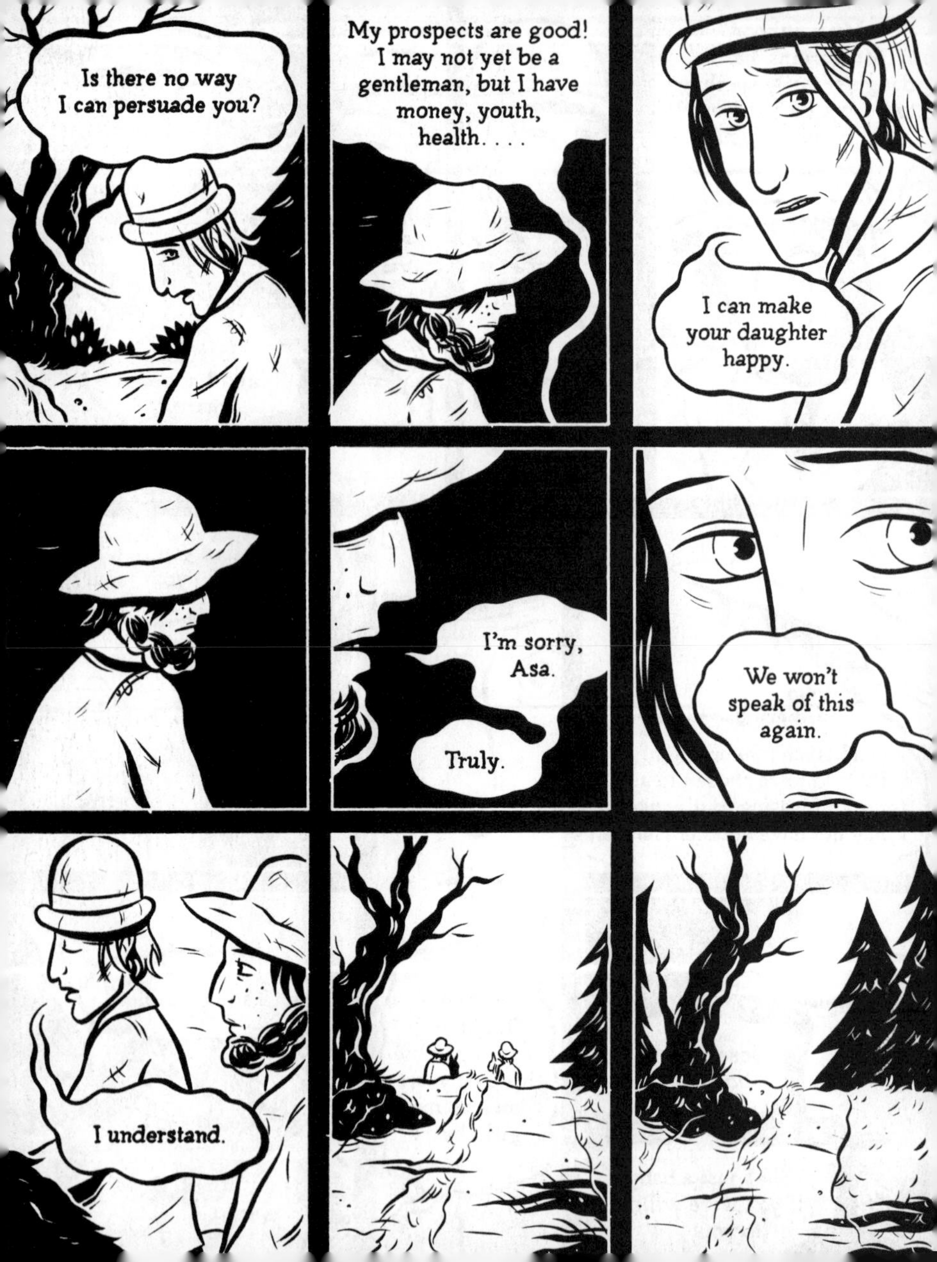
Is there no way I can persuade you?
My prospects are good! I may not yet be a gentleman, but I have money, youth, health. . . .
I can make your daughter happy.
I'm sorry, Asa.
Truly.
We won't speak of this again.
I understand.

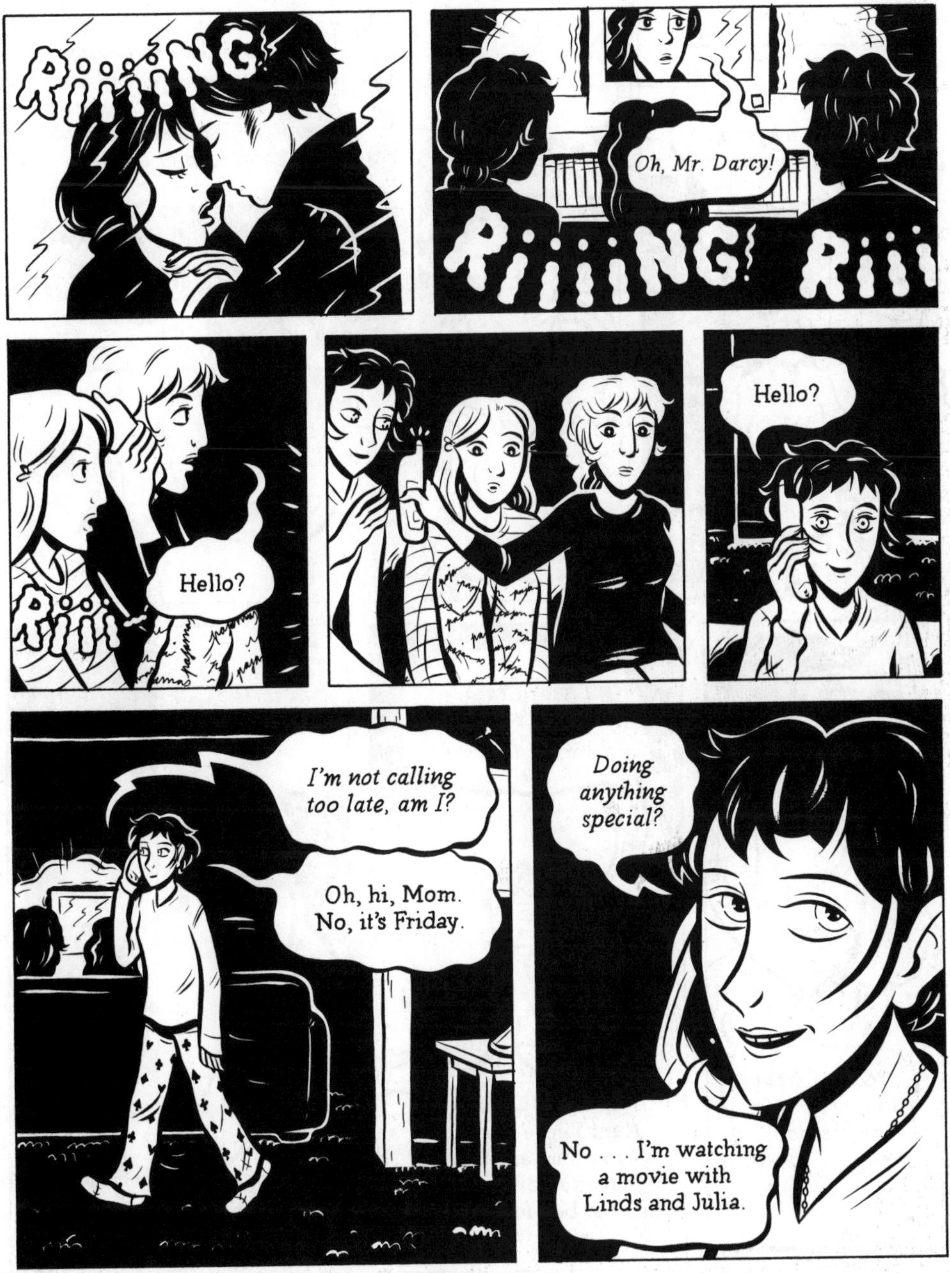
RiiiiNG!
Oh, Mr. Darcy!
RiiiNG! Riii
Hello?
Riii
Hello?
I'm not calling too late, am I?
Oh, hi, Mom. No, it's Friday.
Doing anything special?
No . . . I'm watching a movie with Linds and Julia.

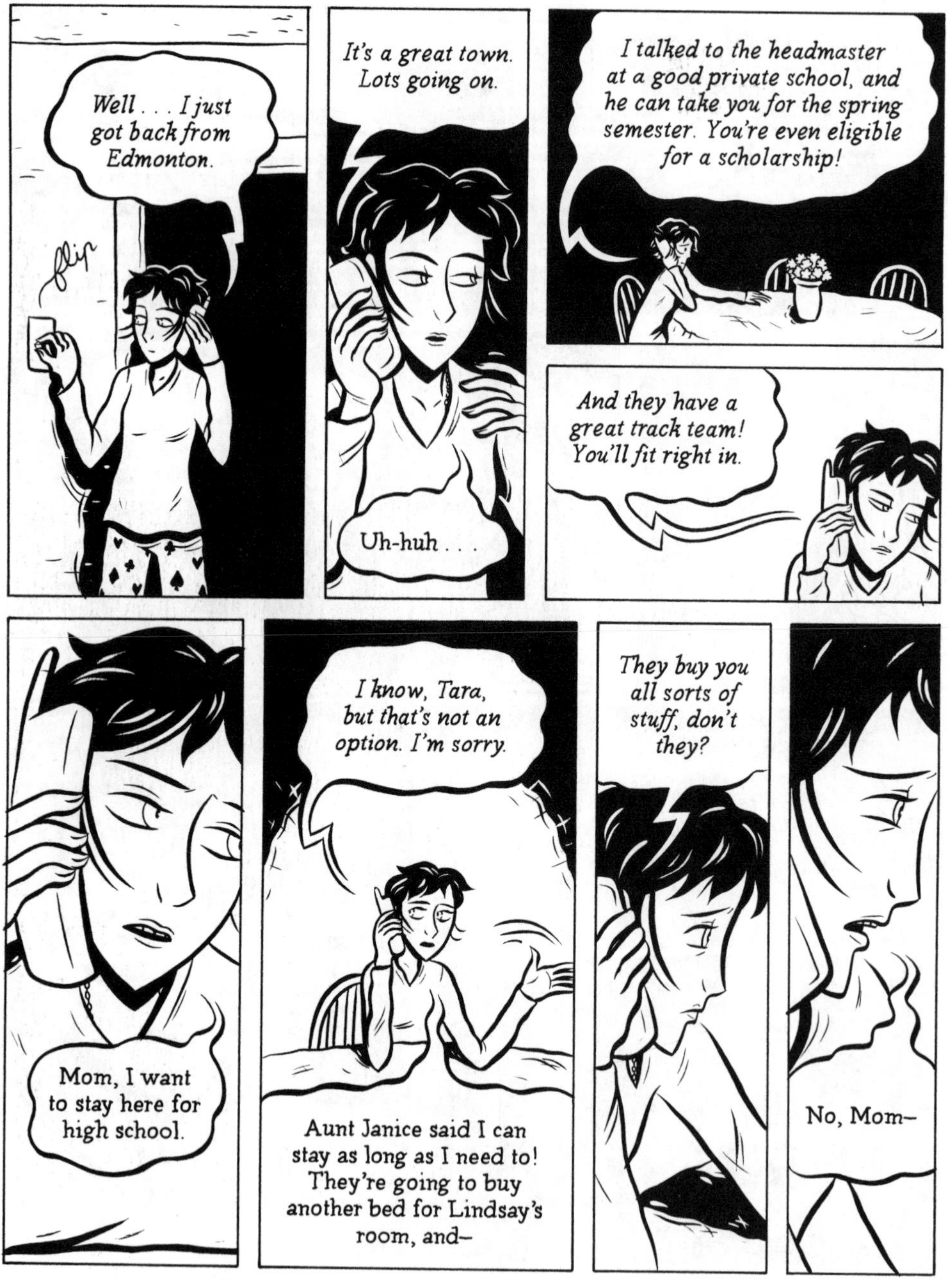
Well . . . I just got back from Edmonton.
flip
It's a great town. Lots going on.
Uh-huh . . .
I talked to the headmaster at a good private school, and he can take you for the spring semester. You're even eligible for a scholarship!
And they have a great track team! You'll fit right in.
Mom, I want to stay here for high school.
I know, Tara, but that's not an option. I'm sorry.
Aunt Janice said I can stay as long as I need to! They're going to buy another bed for Lindsay's room, and–
They buy you all sorts of stuff, don't they?
No, Mom–

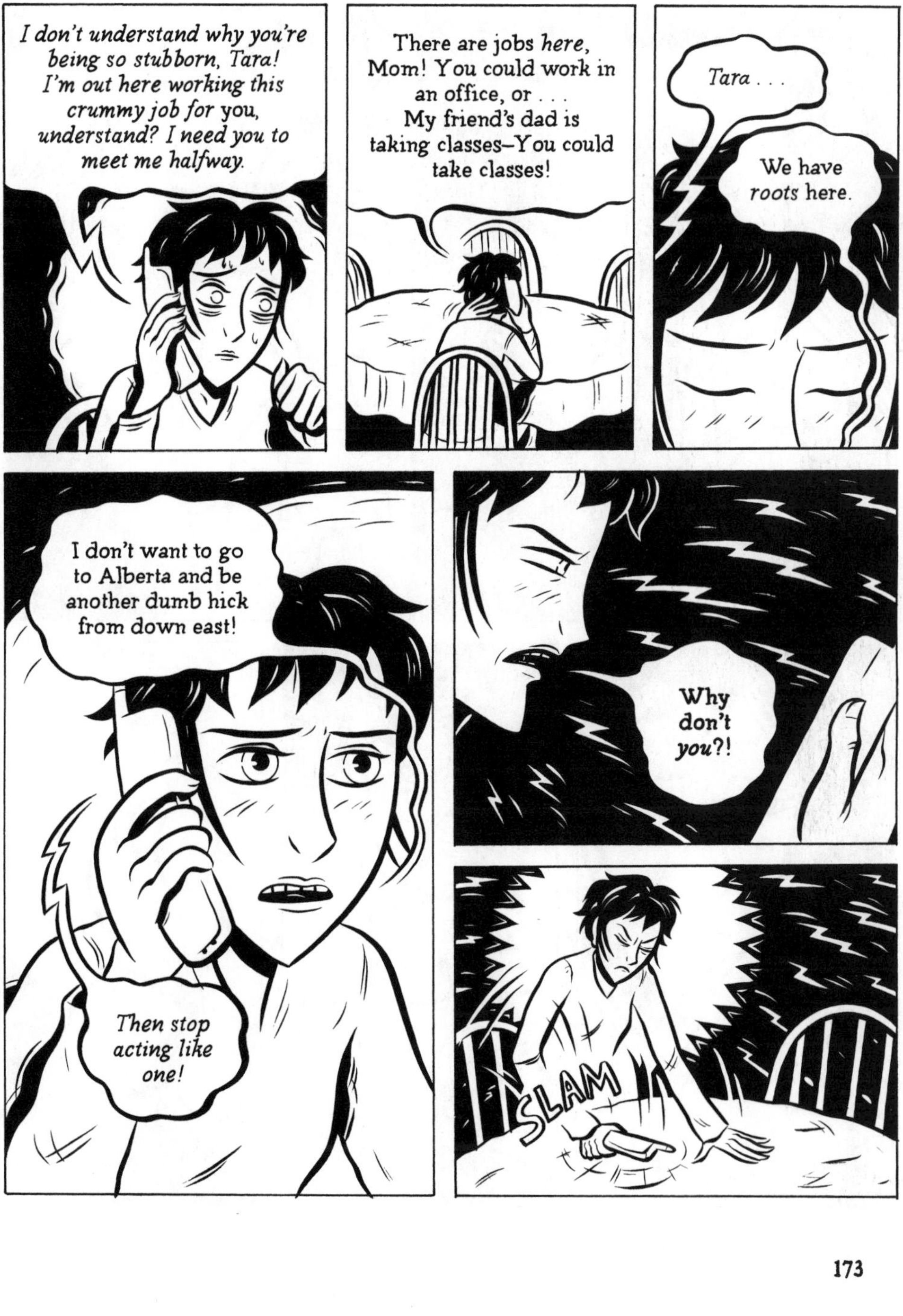
I don't understand why you're being so stubborn, Tara! I'm out here working this crummy job for you, understand? I need you to meet me halfway.
There are jobs here, Mom! You could work in an office, or . . . My friend's dad is taking classes–You could take classes!
Tara . . .
We have roots here.
I don't want to go to Alberta and be another dumb hick from down east!
Then stop acting like one!
Why don't you?!
SLAM

huff huff
huh huh huh

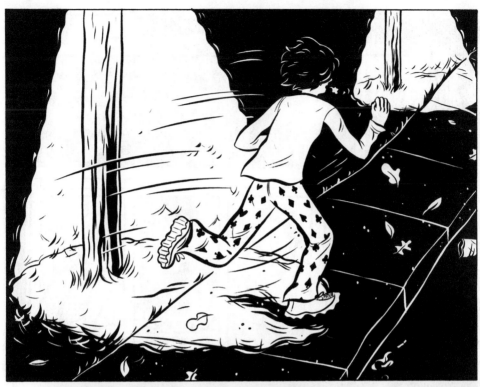

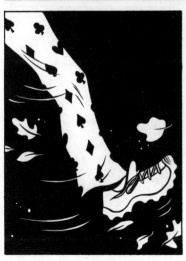

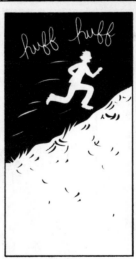

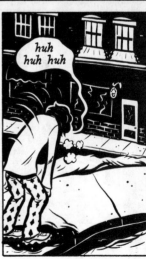

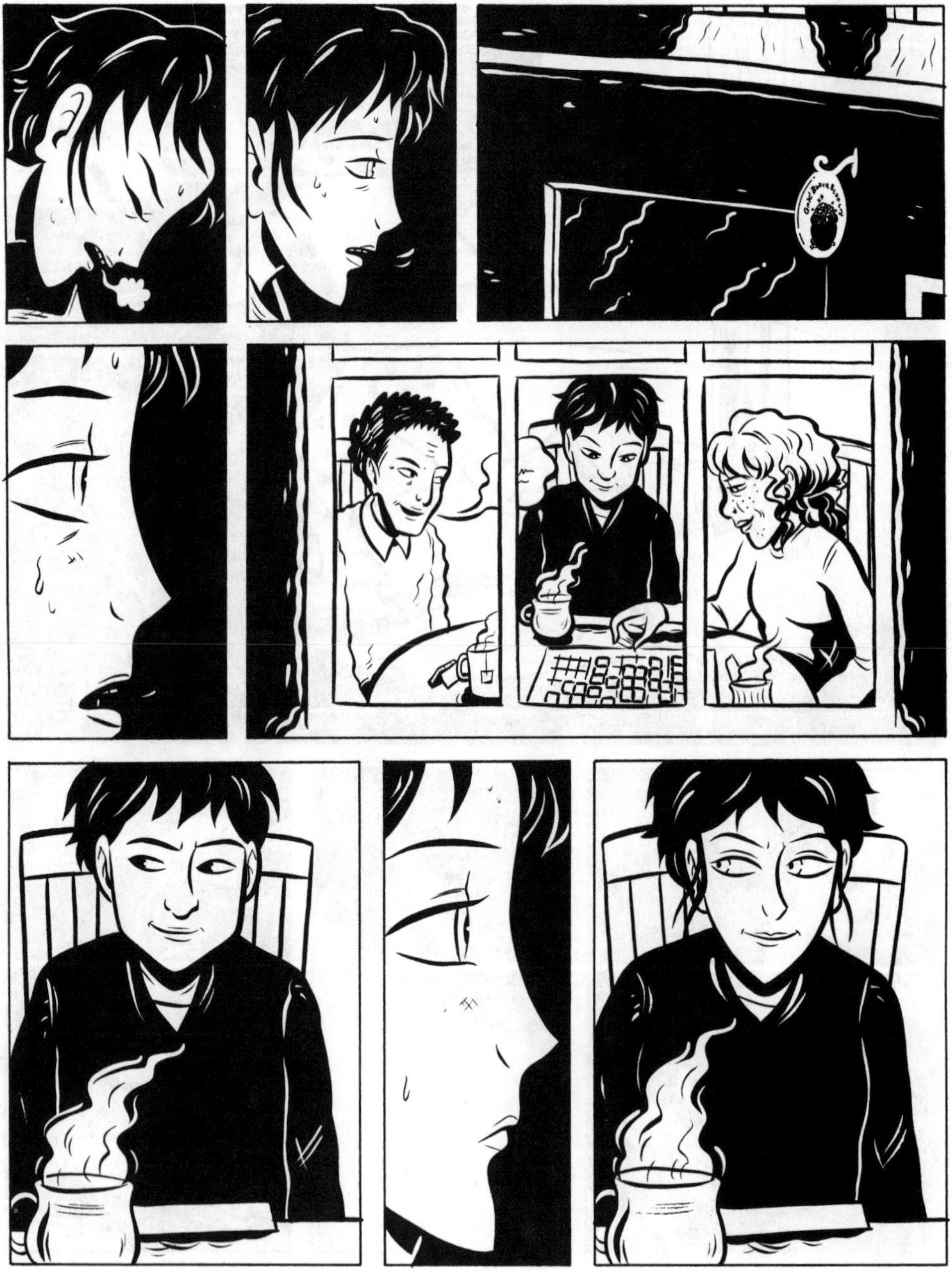

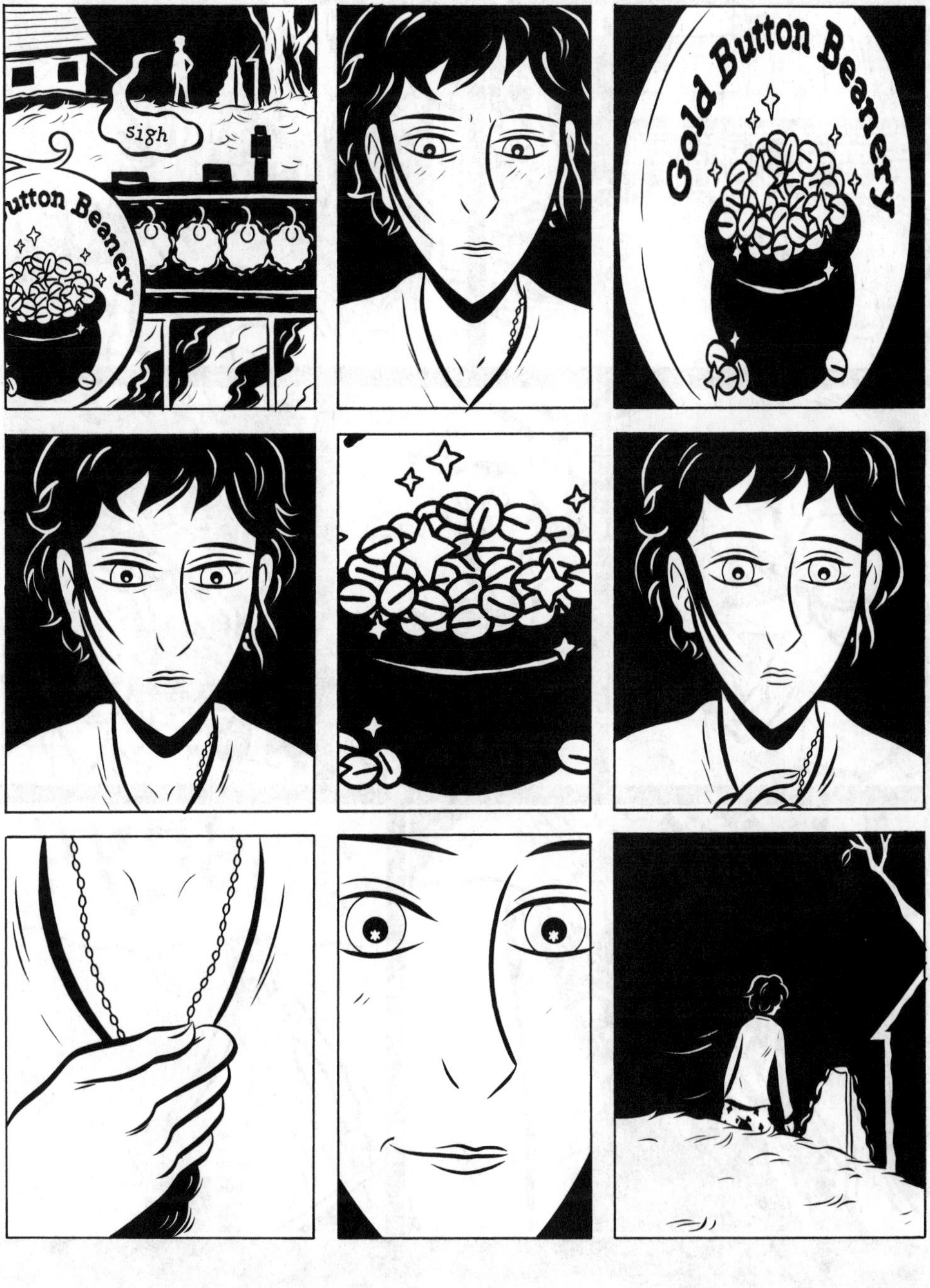
sigh
utton Beanery
Gold Button Beanery

CAW
CAW
CAW
CAW
CAW
CAW
CAW
JOSEY!!

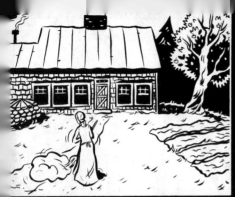

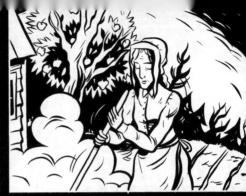

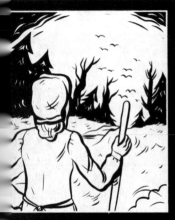

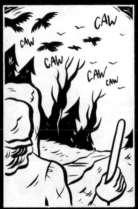

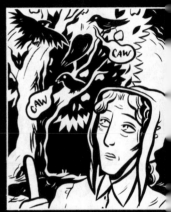

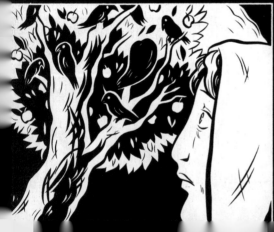

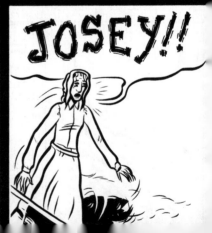

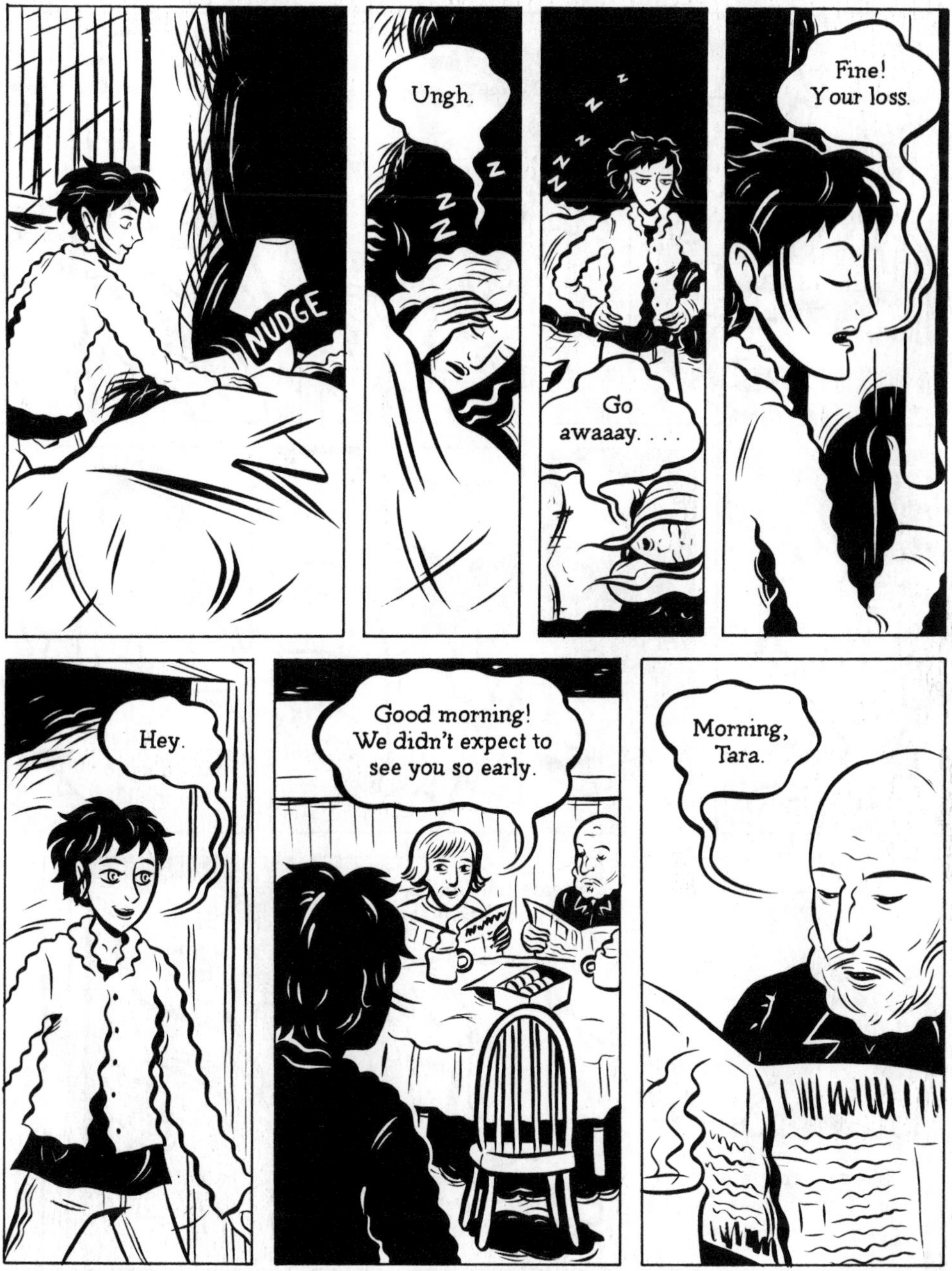
NUDGE
Ungh.
Go awaaay. . . .
Fine! Your loss.
Hey.
Good morning! We didn't expect to see you so early.
Morning, Tara.

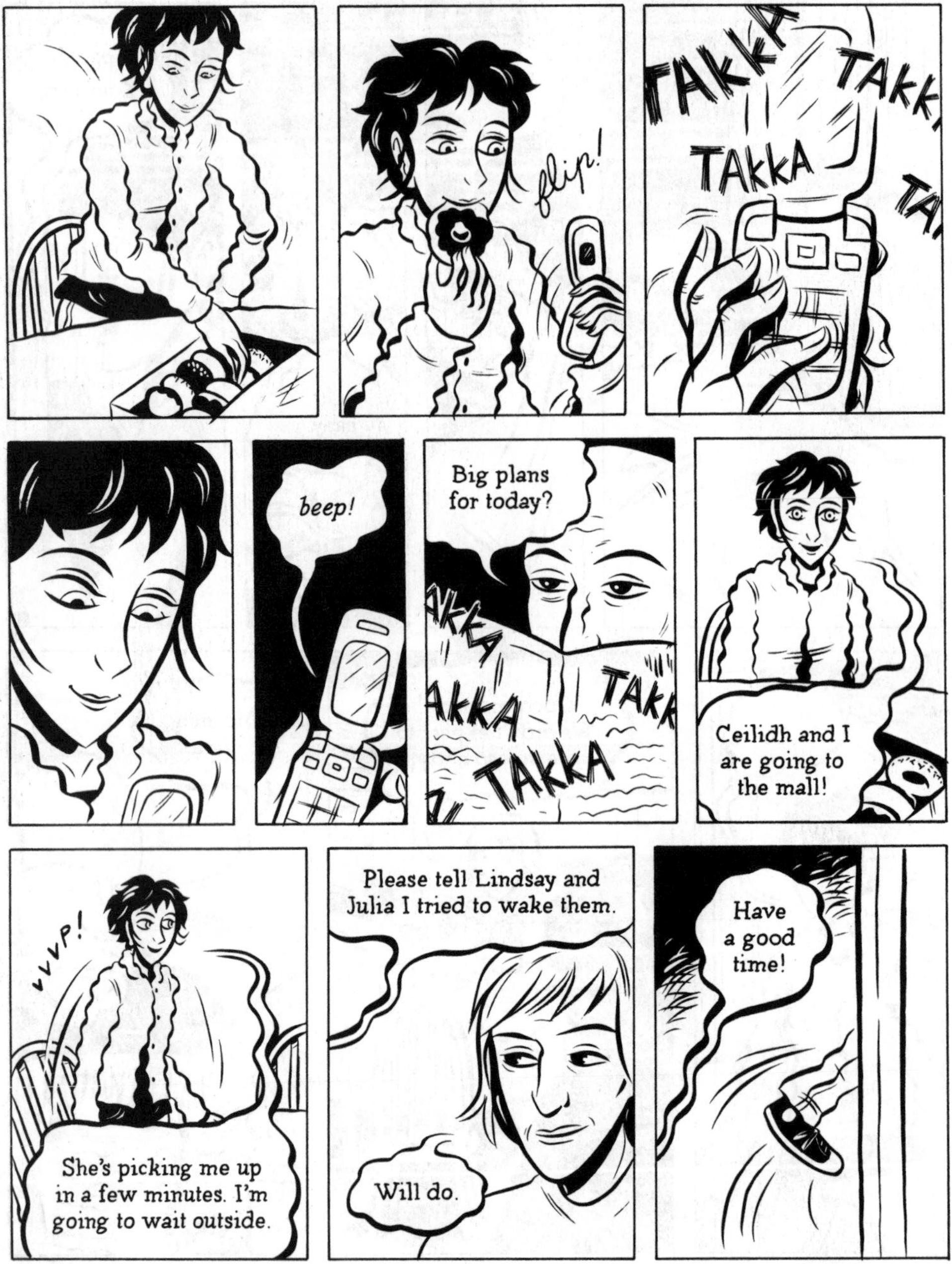
flip!
TAKKA
TAKKA
TAKKA
beep!
Big plans for today?
TAKKA
TAKKA
TAKKA
TAKKA
Ceilidh and I are going to the mall!
vvvP!
She's picking me up in a few minutes. I'm going to wait outside.
Please tell Lindsay and Julia I tried to wake them.
Will do.
Have a good time!

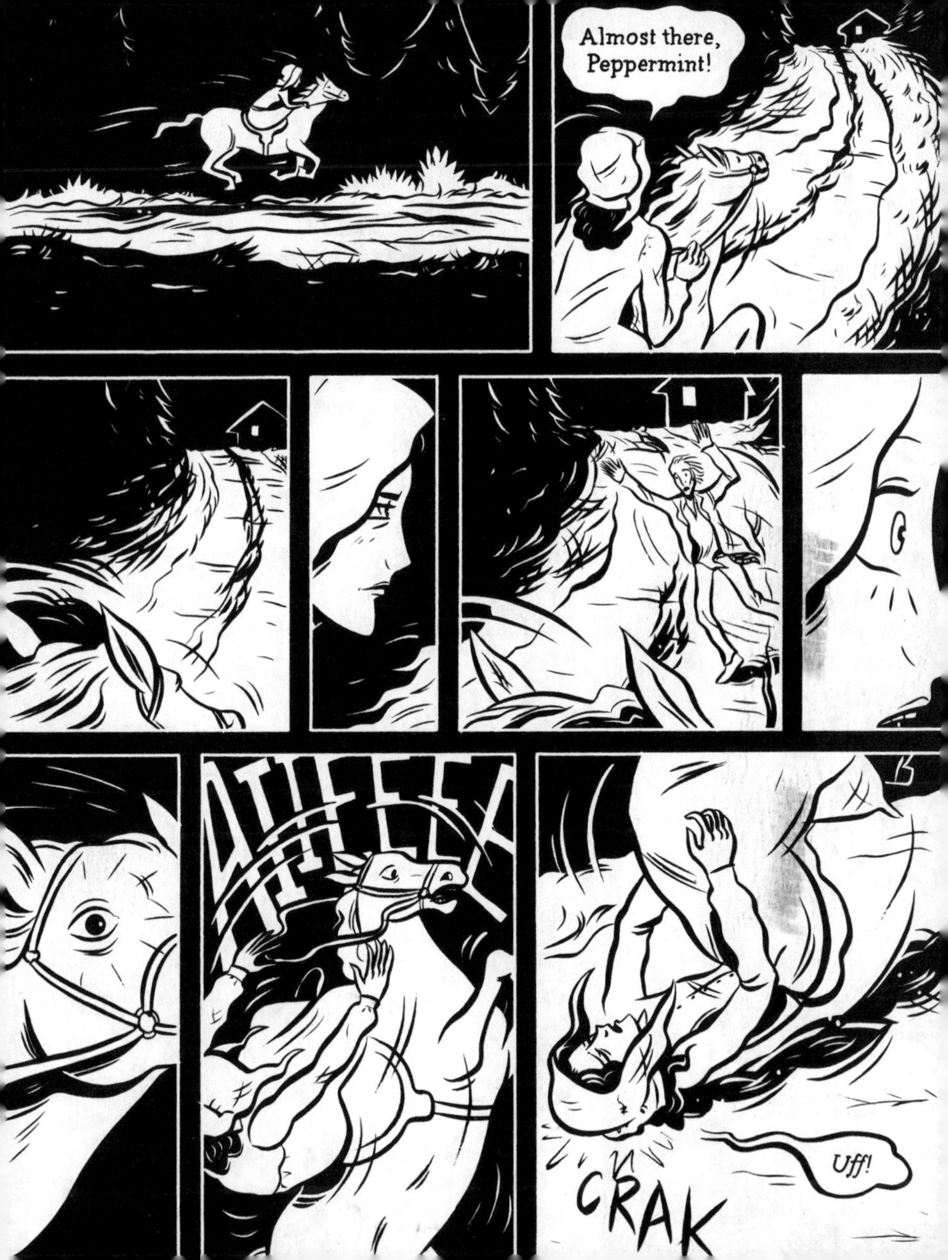
Almost there, Peppermint!
Uff!
CRAK

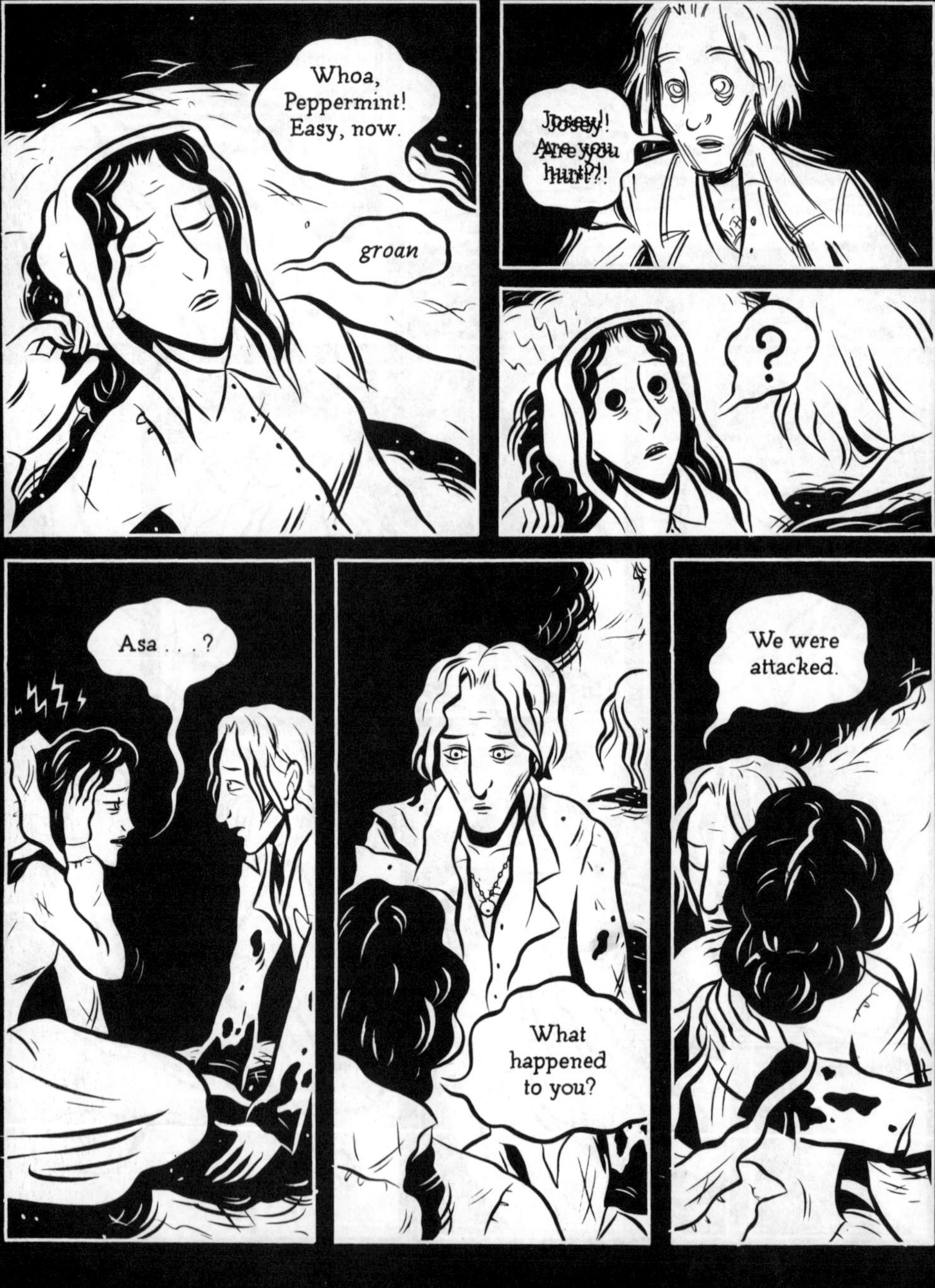
Whoa, Peppermint! Easy, now.
groan
Josey! Are you hurt?!
?
Asa . . . ?
What happened to you?
We were attacked.

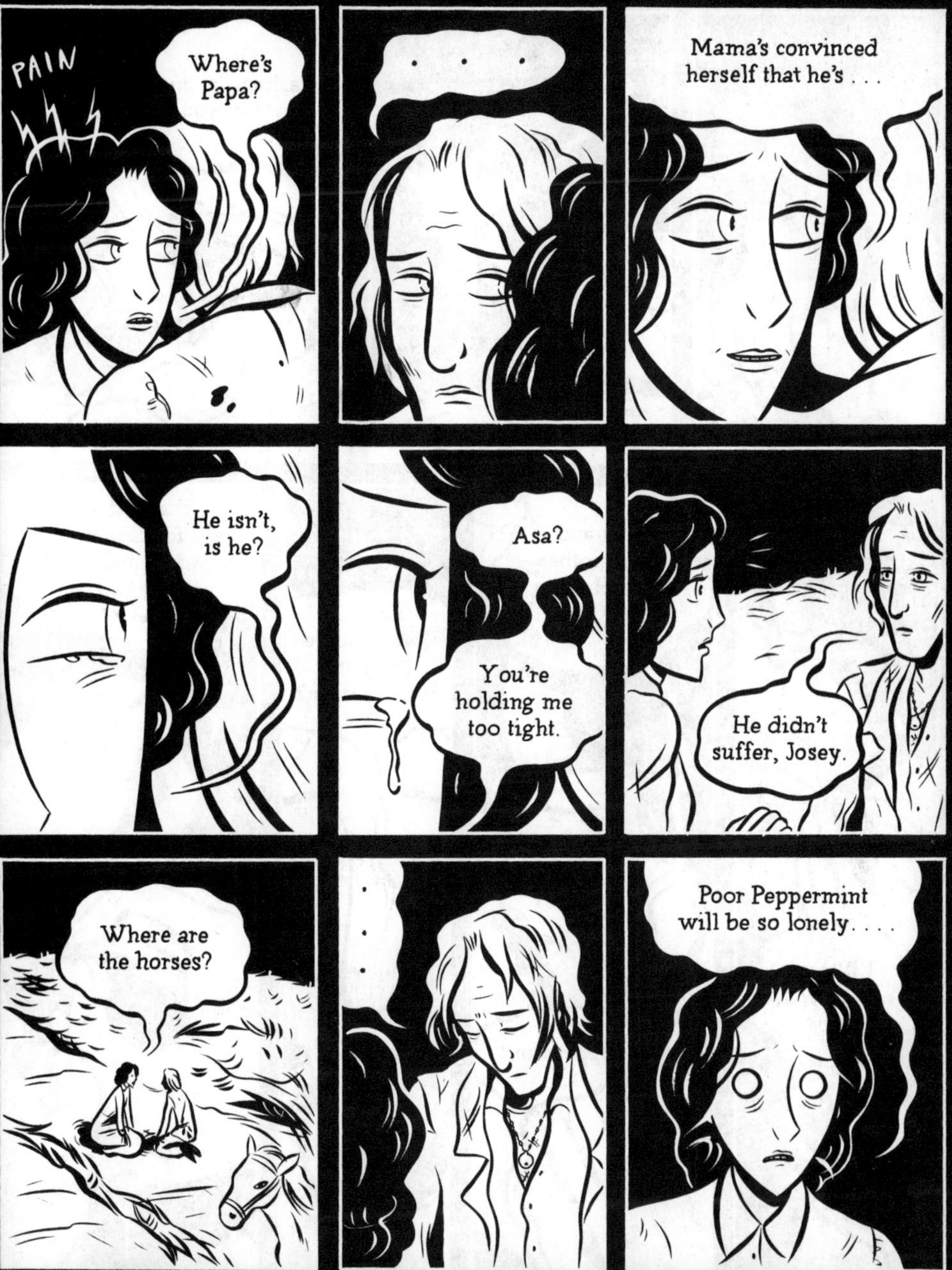
PAIN
Where's Papa?
. . .
Mama's convinced herself that he's . . .
He isn't, is he?
Asa?
You're holding me too tight.
He didn't suffer, Josey.
Where are the horses?
. . .
Poor Peppermint will be so lonely. . . .

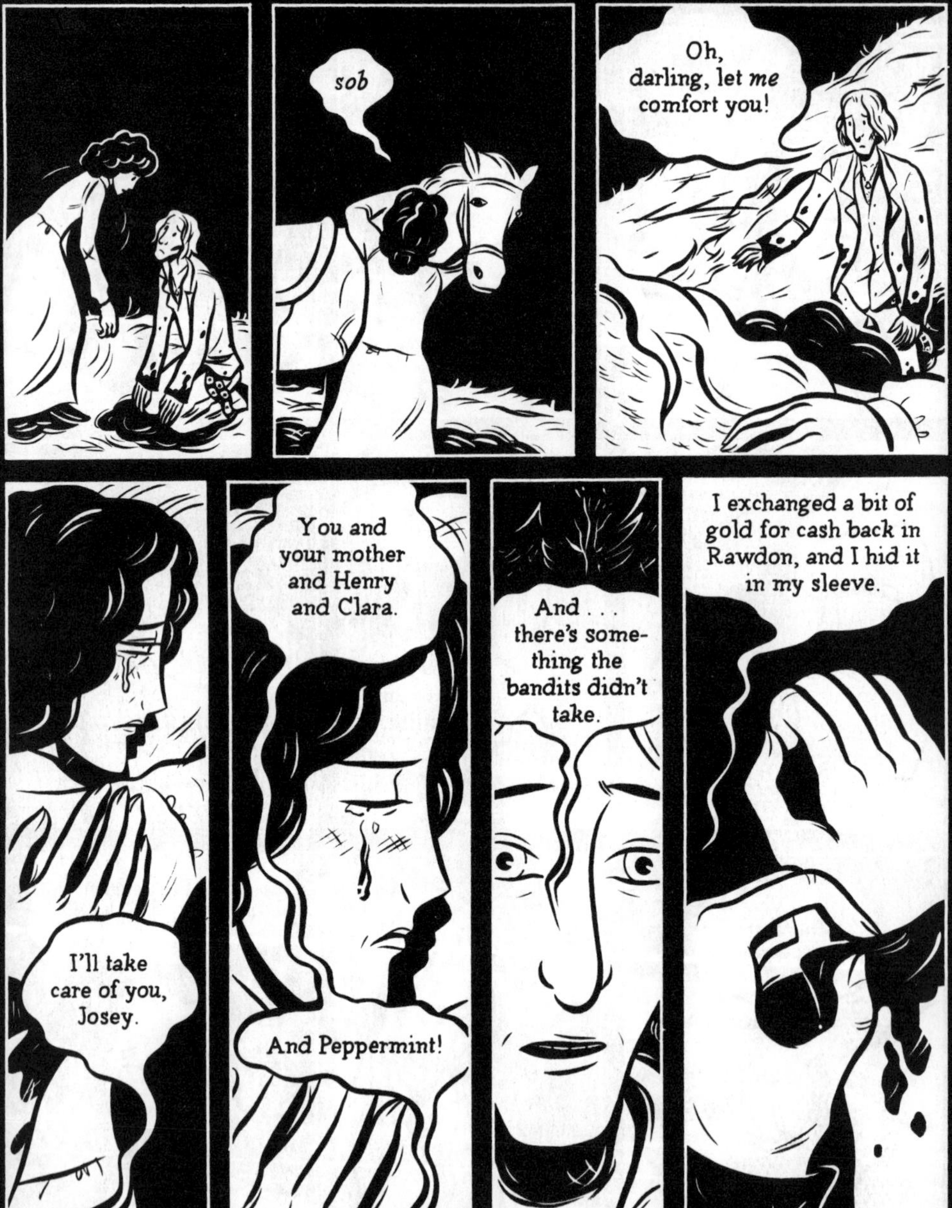
sob
Oh, darling, let *me* comfort you!
I'll take care of you, Josey.
You and your mother and Henry and Clara.
And Peppermint!
And . . . there's something the bandits didn't take.
I exchanged a bit of gold for cash back in Rawdon, and I hid it in my sleeve.

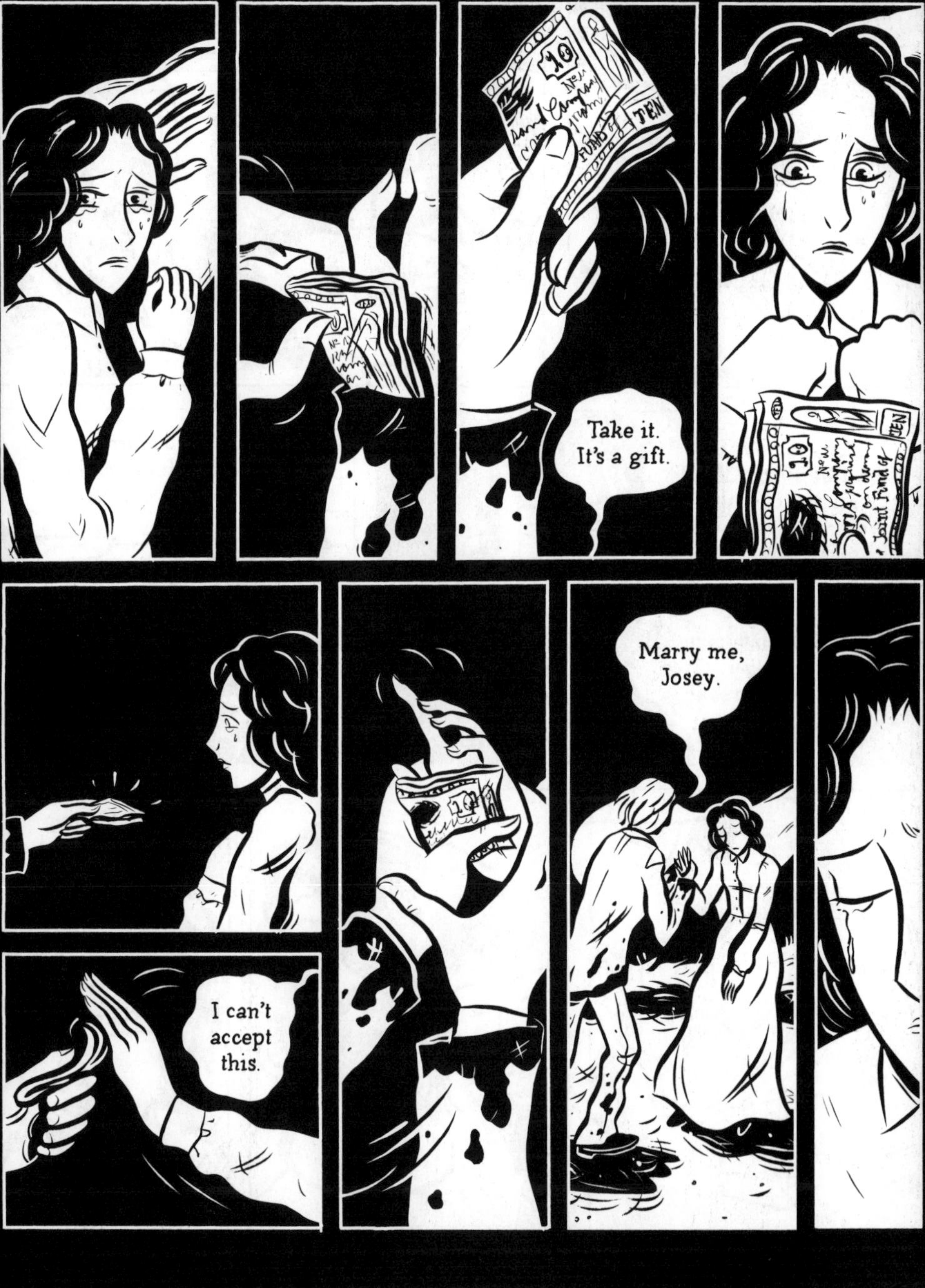
Take it.
It's a gift.
I can't accept this.
Marry me, Josey.

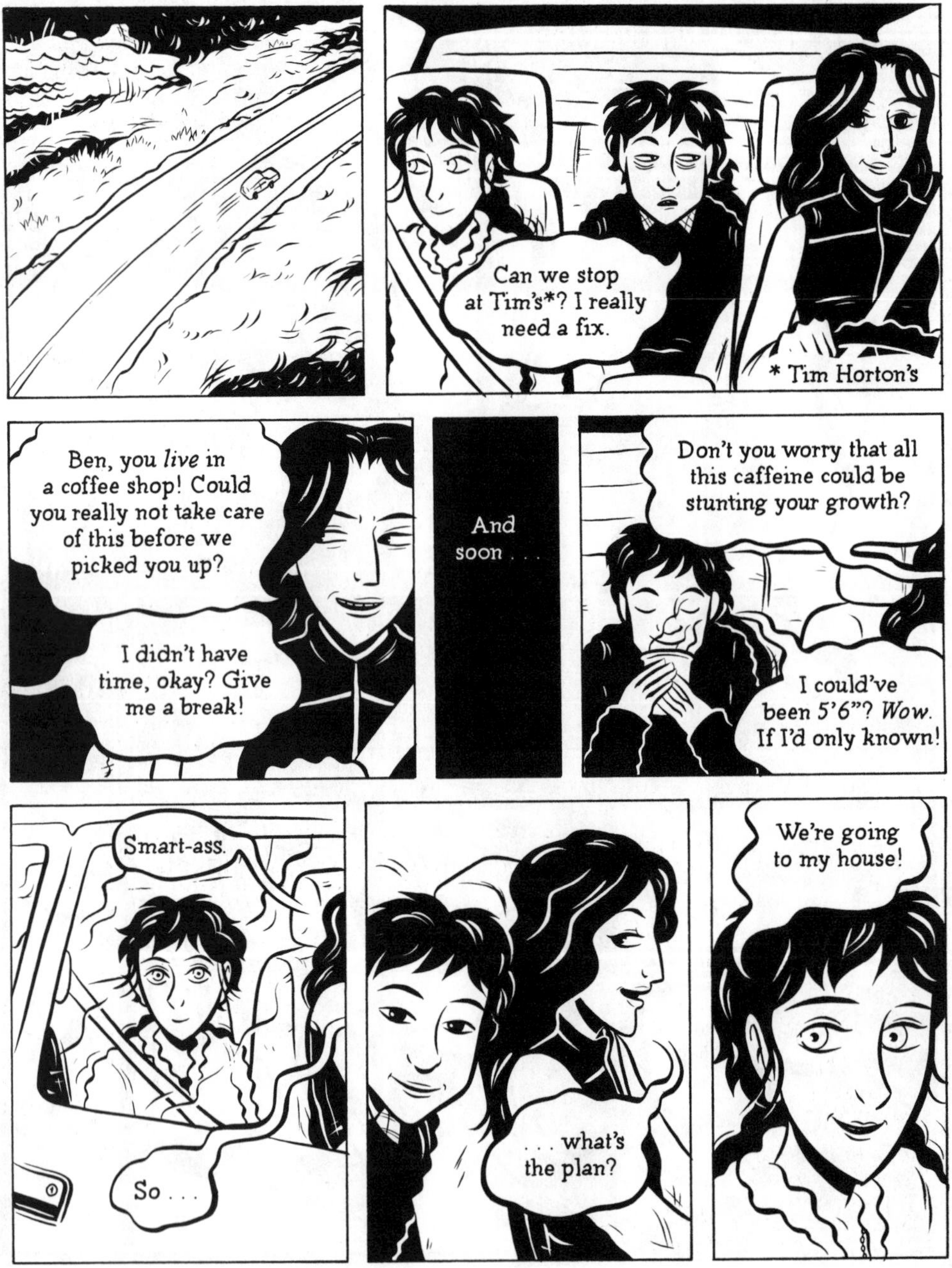
Can we stop at Tim's*? I really need a fix.
* Tim Horton's
Ben, you *live* in a coffee shop! Could you really not take care of this before we picked you up?
I didn't have time, okay? Give me a break!
And soon . . .
Don't you worry that all this caffeine could be stunting your growth?
I could've been 5'6"? *Wow.* If I'd only known!
Smart-ass.
So . . .
. . . what's the plan?
We're going to my house!

And when
we get there?

We find
the gold and
dig it up.

Don't take this the wrong
way, Tara, but are you serious?

Nova Scotia had pirates,
Acadians, *and* a gold rush.

As buried
treasure goes,
you can't top
those odds.

Right. . . .

But how
are we going
to find it?

You'll see.

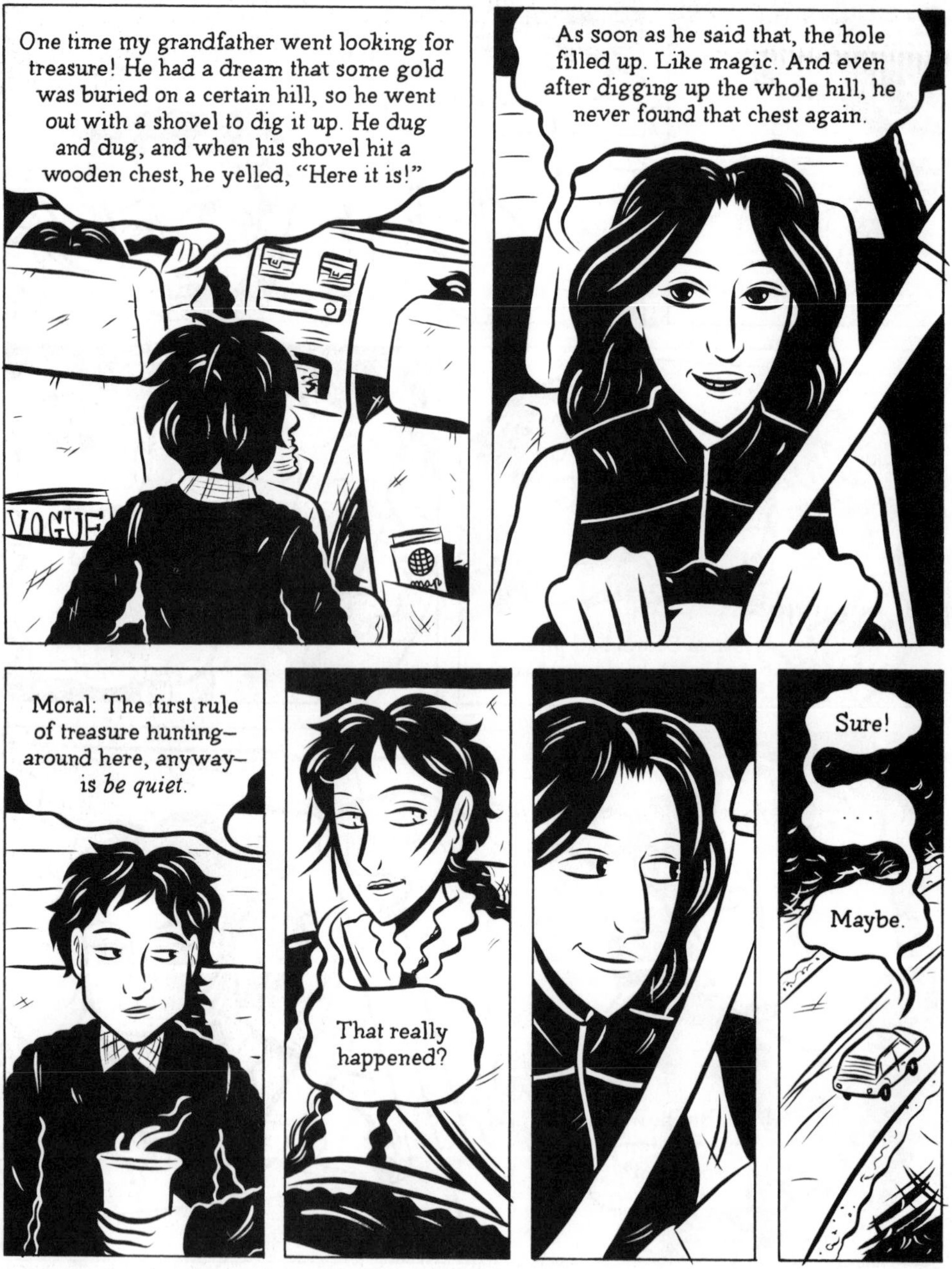
One time my grandfather went looking for treasure! He had a dream that some gold was buried on a certain hill, so he went out with a shovel to dig it up. He dug and dug, and when his shovel hit a wooden chest, he yelled, "Here it is!"
VOGUE
As soon as he said that, the hole filled up. Like magic. And even after digging up the whole hill, he never found that chest again.
Moral: The first rule of treasure hunting—around here, anyway—is *be quiet*.
That really happened?
Sure!
. . .
Maybe.

sob

Go for Sheriff Drake, Mr. Curry. He may still have time to apprehend the robbers.

They'll be halfway to Yarmouth by now, the way they were riding.

Then *I'll go!*

No, Mrs. Fraser, you're in a delicate state. I'll go.

Take good care of them, Henry. You're man of the house, now.

Wait!

Leave us proof that you'll return.

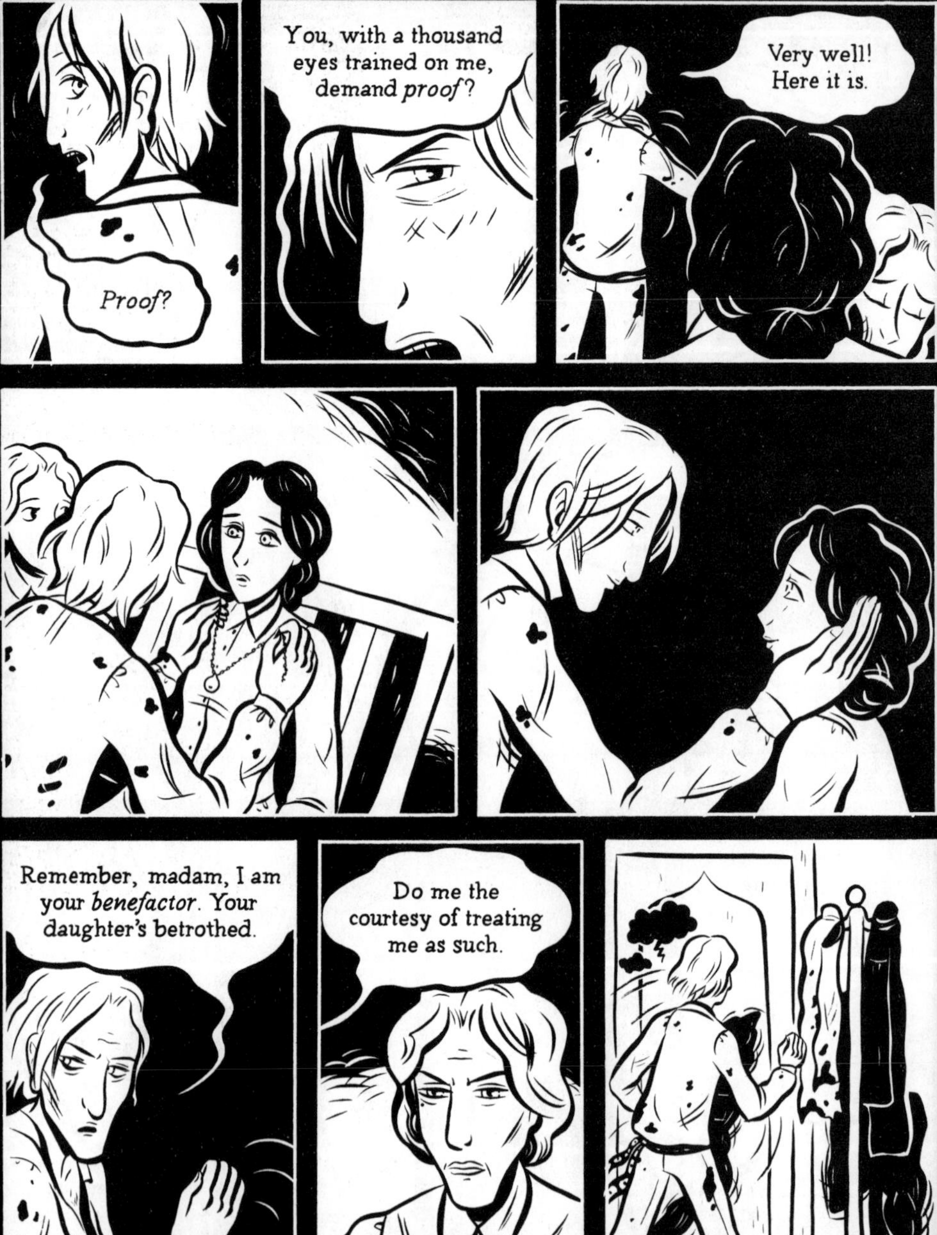
Proof?
You, with a thousand eyes trained on me, demand *proof*?
Very well! Here it is.
Remember, madam, I am your *benefactor*. Your daughter's betrothed.
Do me the courtesy of treating me as such.

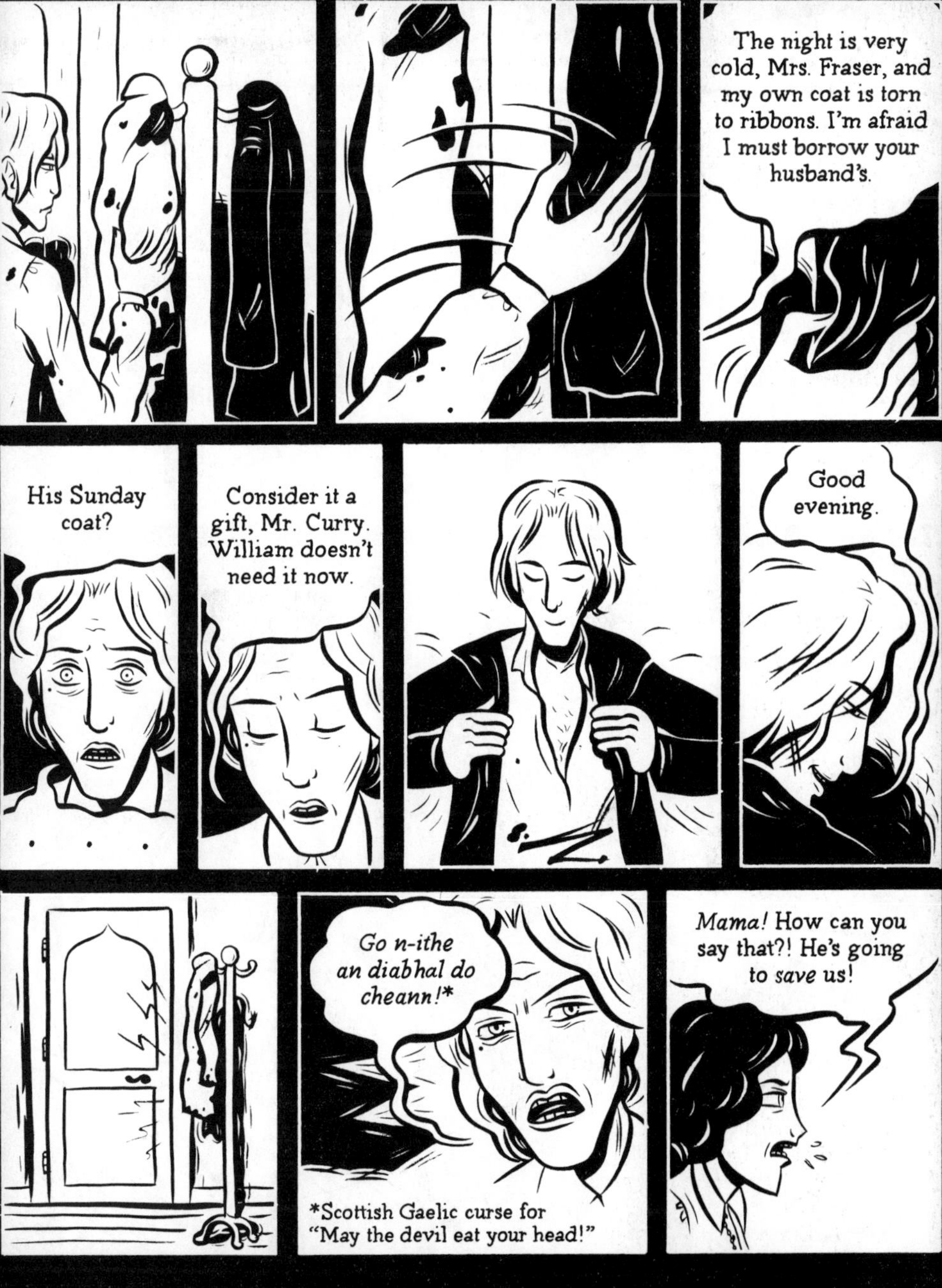

The night is very cold, Mrs. Fraser, and my own coat is torn to ribbons. I'm afraid I must borrow your husband's.
His Sunday coat?
Consider it a gift, Mr. Curry. William doesn't need it now.
Good evening.
Go n-ithe an diabhal do cheann!*
*Scottish Gaelic curse for "May the devil eat your head!"
Mama! How can you say that?! He's going to *save* us!

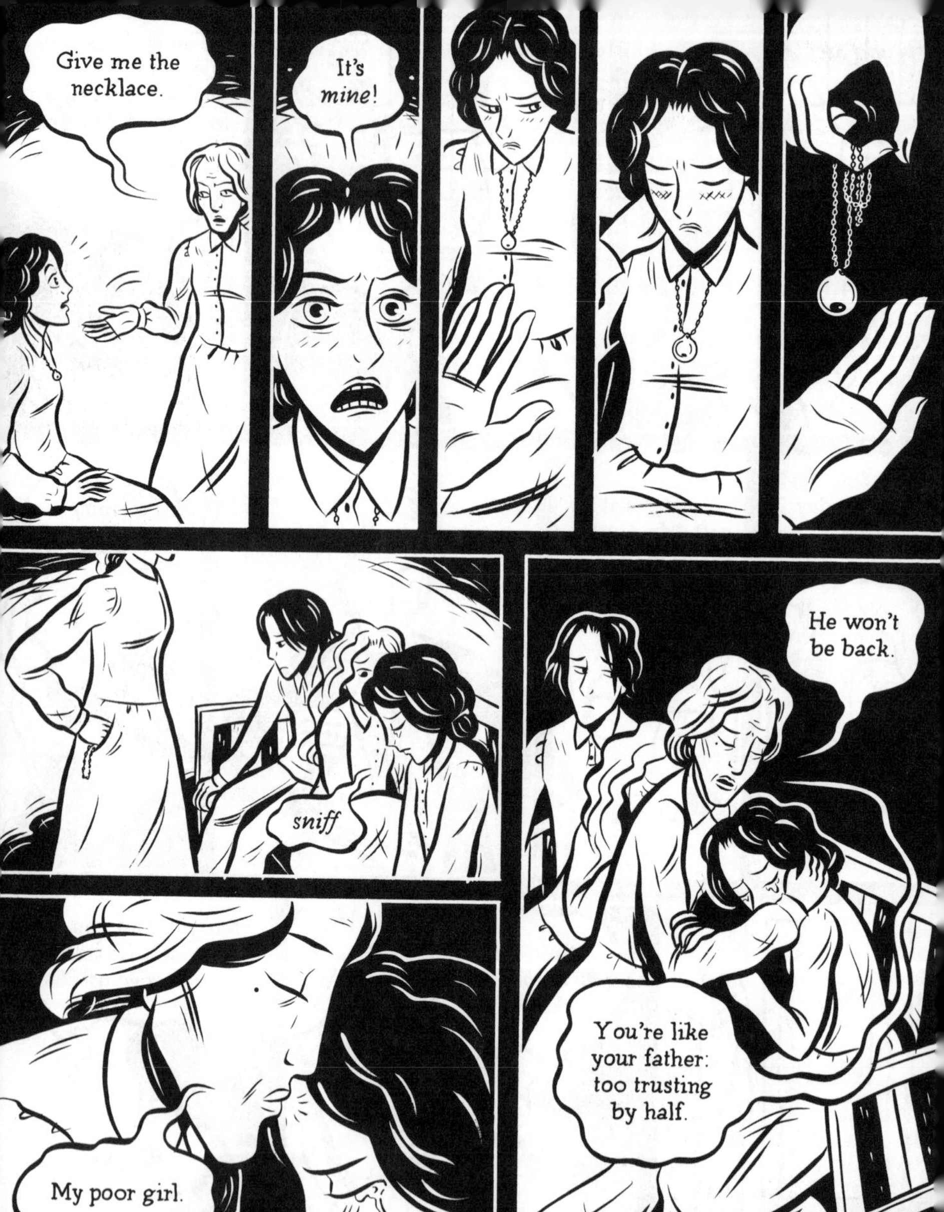
Give me the necklace.
It's *mine*!
sniff
He won't be back.
My poor girl.
You're like your father: too trusting by half.

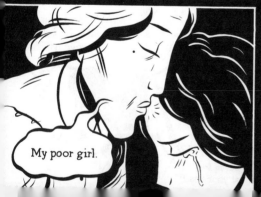

This is your house, huh?

Aw, Tara . . . This really sucks.

It's okay. Really.

Well . . .

Let's get going.

Okay.

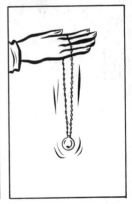

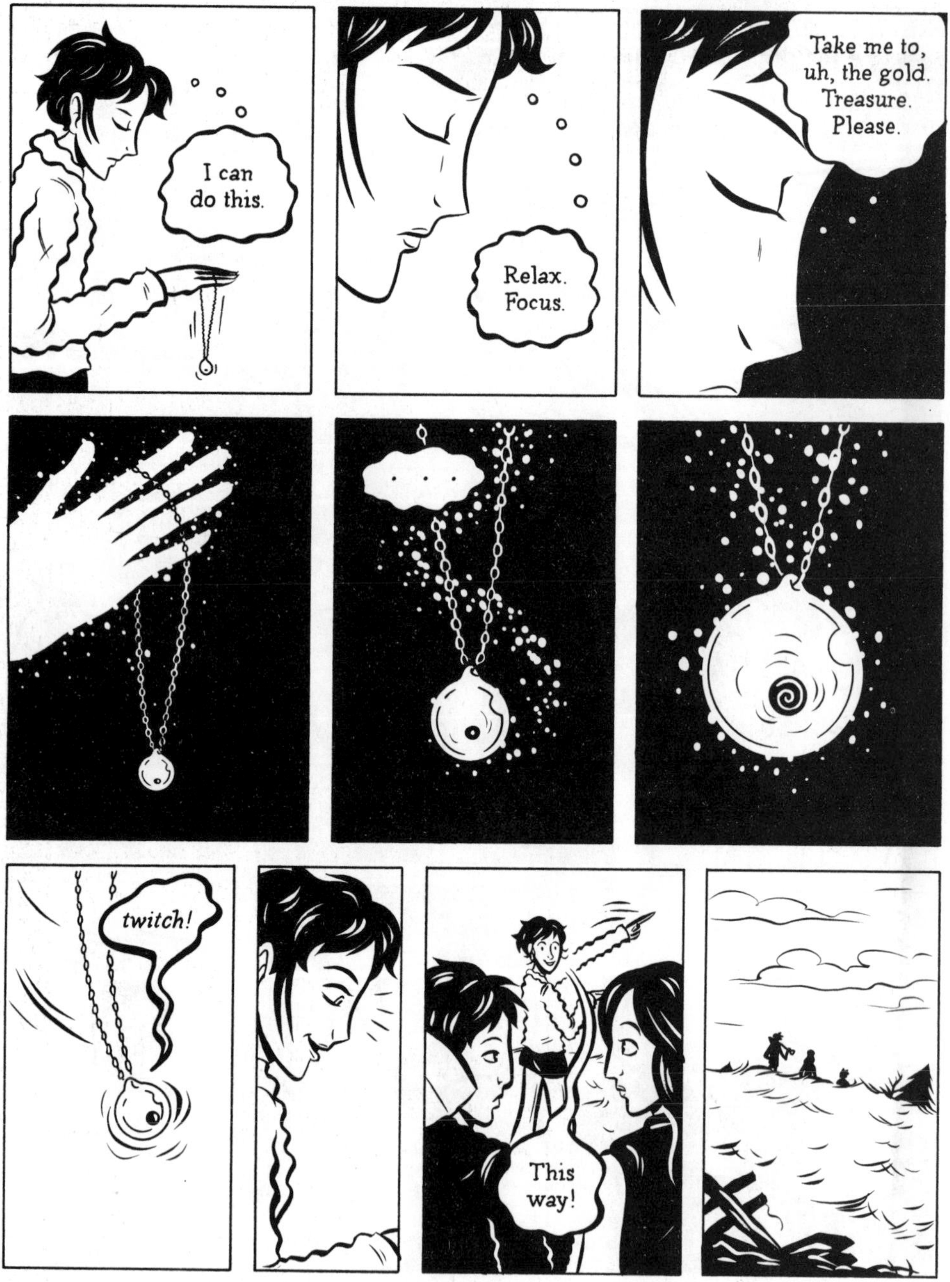
I can do this.
Relax. Focus.
Take me to, uh, the gold. Treasure. Please.
. . .
twitch!
This way!

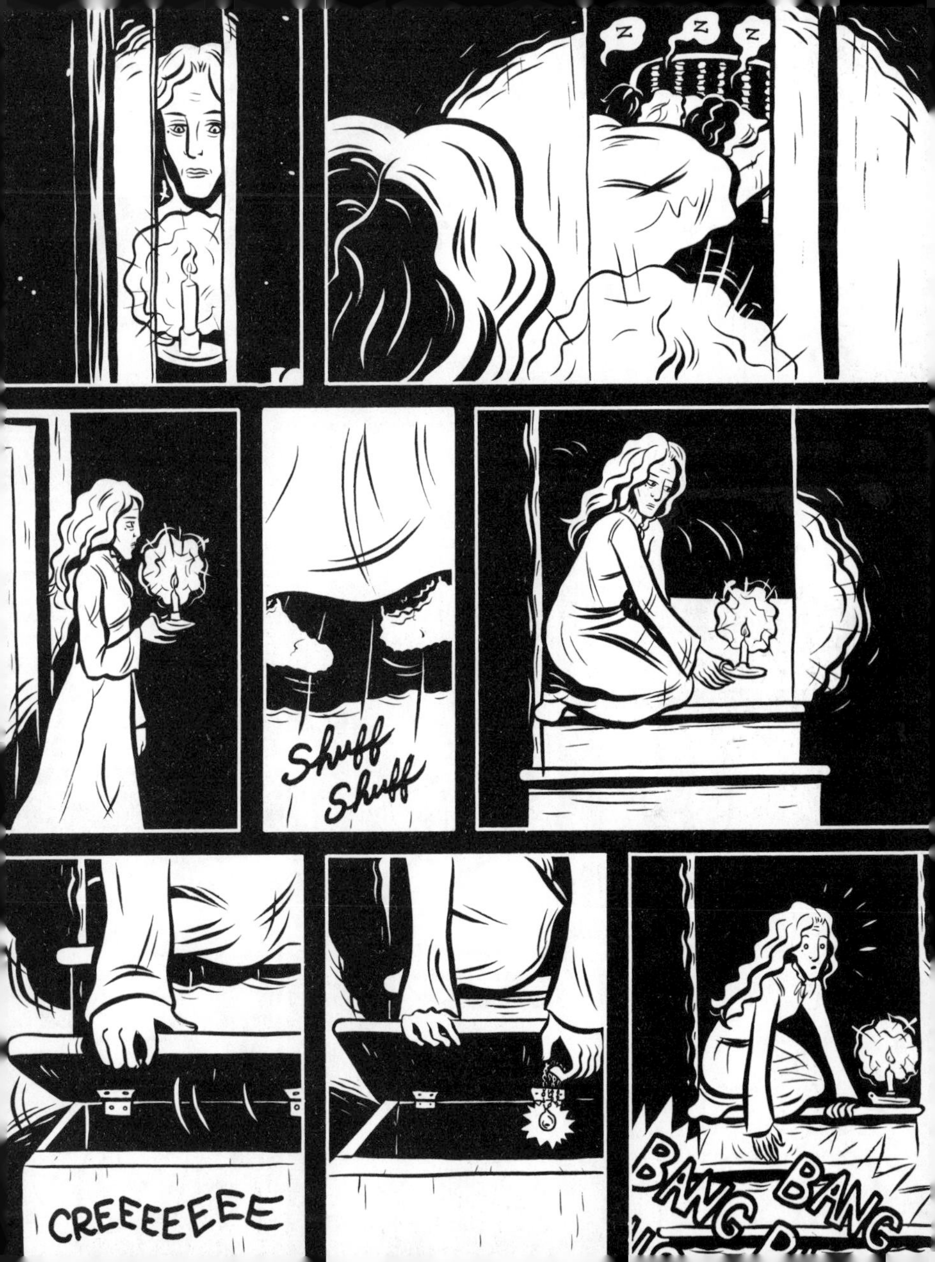
Z Z Z
Shuff Shuff
CREEEEEEEE
BANG BANG

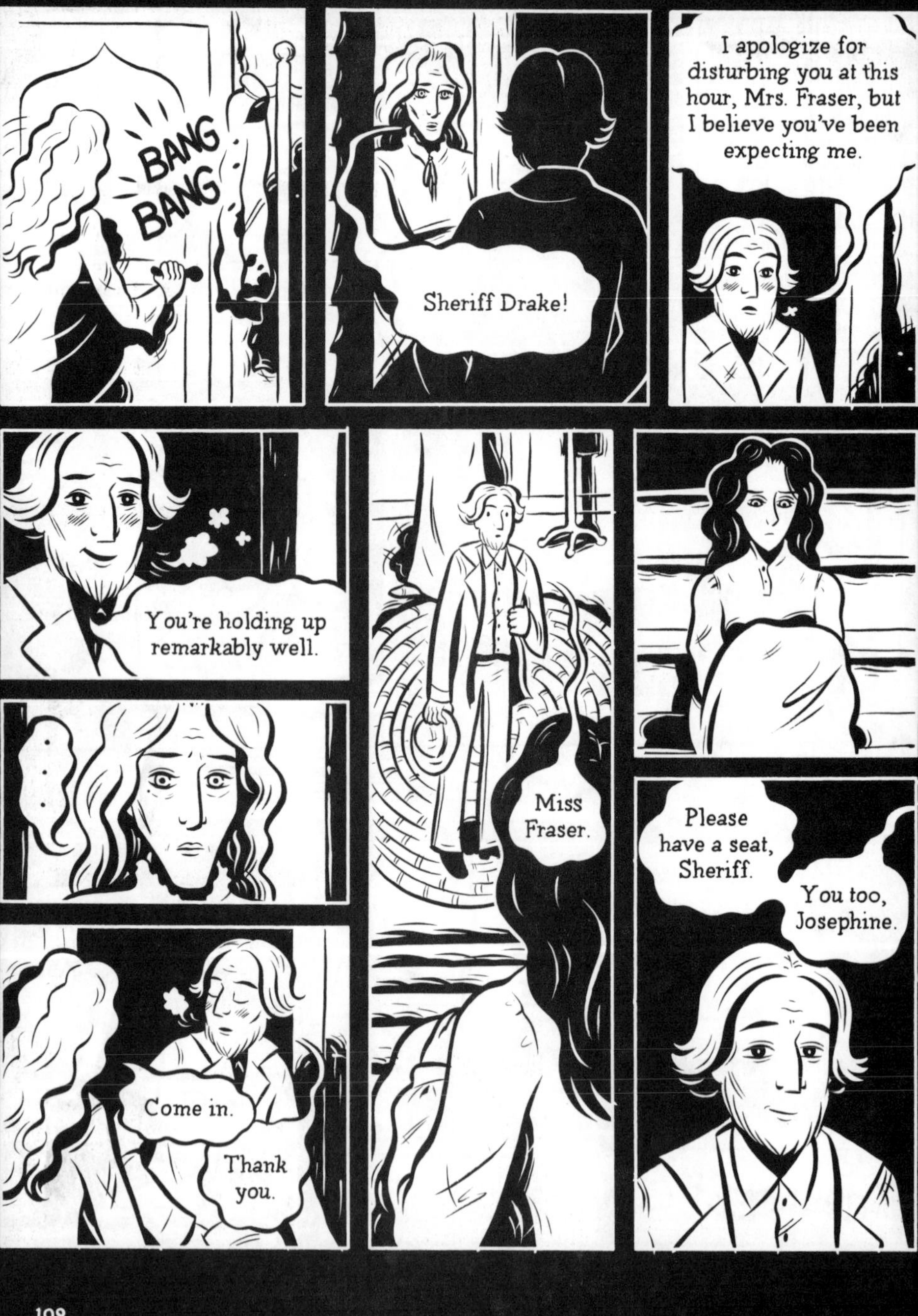
BANG
BANG
Sheriff Drake!
I apologize for disturbing you at this hour, Mrs. Fraser, but I believe you've been expecting me.
You're holding up remarkably well.
Come in.
Thank you.
Miss Fraser.
Please have a seat, Sheriff.
You too, Josephine.

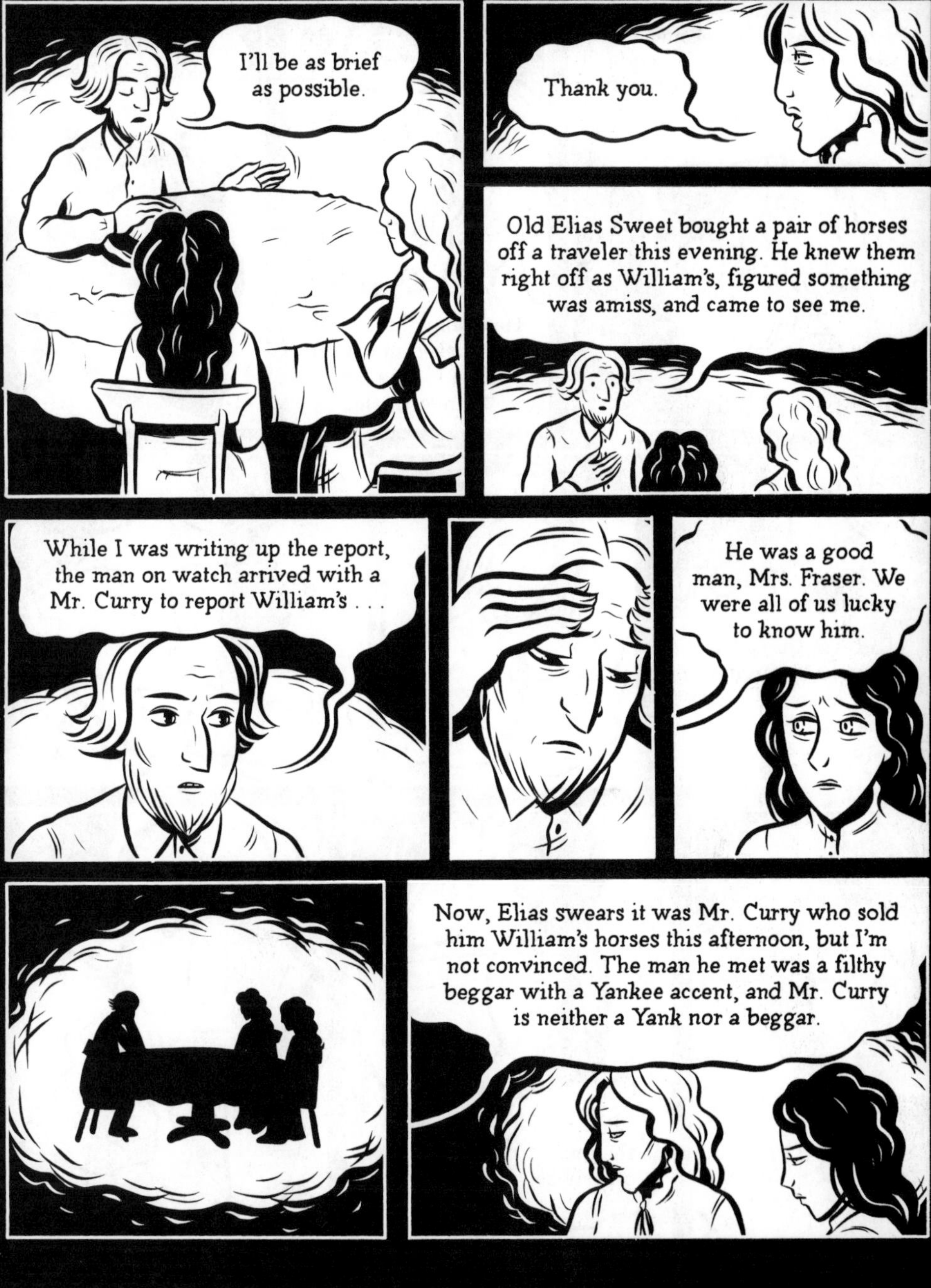
I'll be as brief as possible.
Thank you.
Old Elias Sweet bought a pair of horses off a traveler this evening. He knew them right off as William's, figured something was amiss, and came to see me.
While I was writing up the report, the man on watch arrived with a Mr. Curry to report William's . . .
He was a good man, Mrs. Fraser. We were all of us lucky to know him.
Now, Elias swears it was Mr. Curry who sold him William's horses this afternoon, but I'm not convinced. The man he met was a filthy beggar with a Yankee accent, and Mr. Curry is neither a Yank nor a beggar.

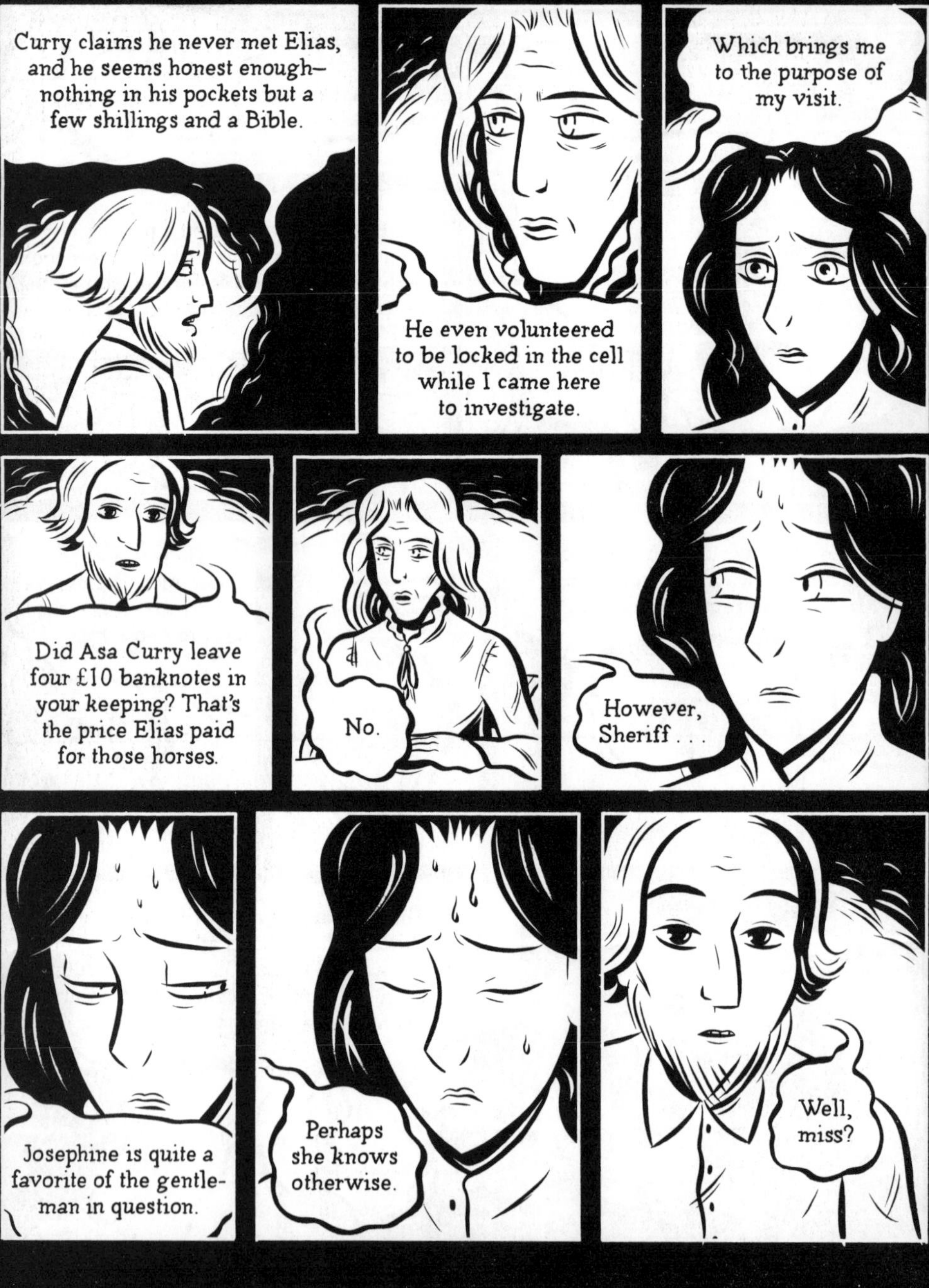

Curry claims he never met Elias, and he seems honest enough— nothing in his pockets but a few shillings and a Bible.
He even volunteered to be locked in the cell while I came here to investigate.
Which brings me to the purpose of my visit.
Did Asa Curry leave four £10 banknotes in your keeping? That's the price Elias paid for those horses.
No.
However, Sheriff . . .
Josephine is quite a favorite of the gentle- man in question.
Perhaps she knows otherwise.
Well, miss?

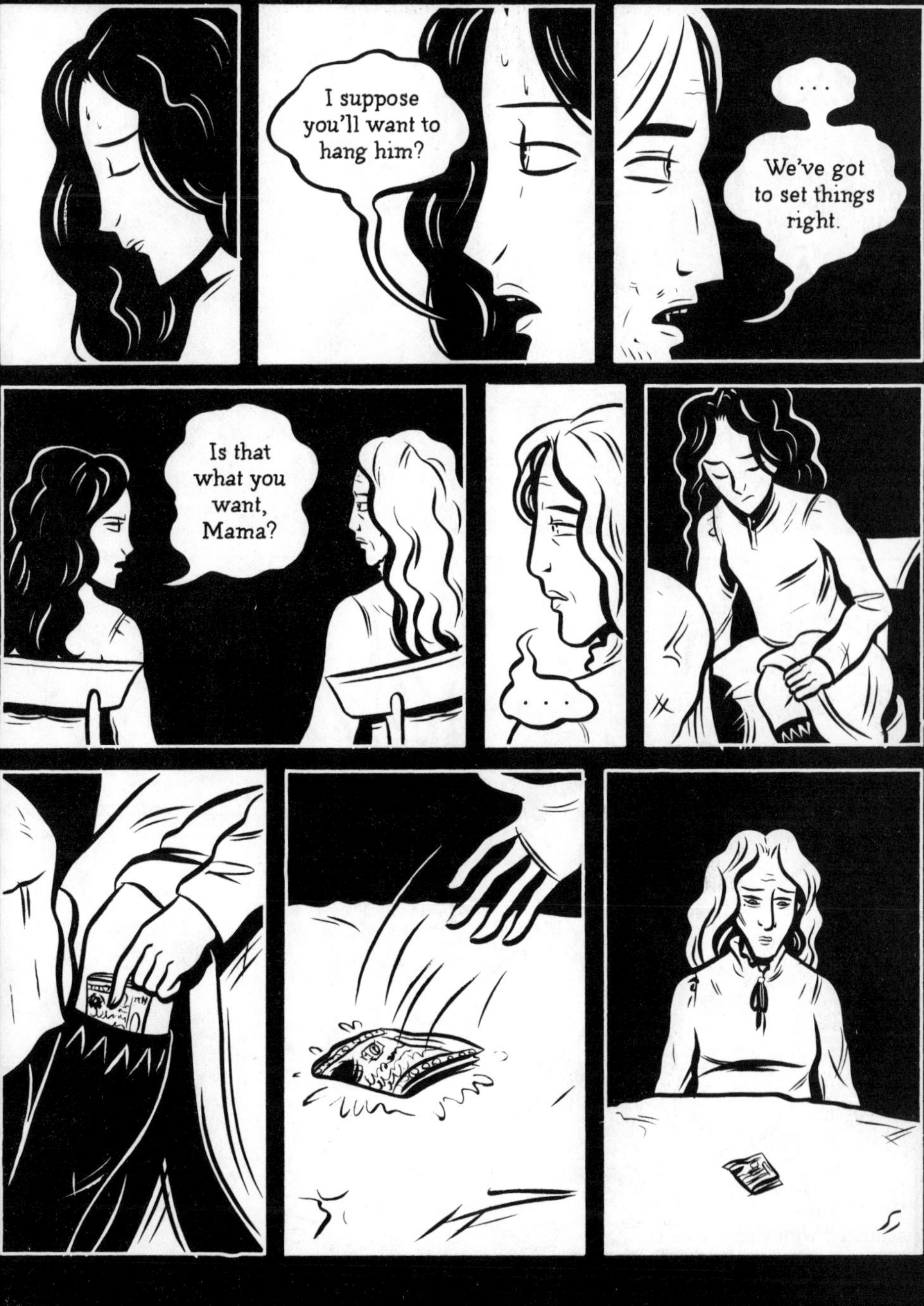
I suppose you'll want to hang him?
. . .
We've got to set things right.
Is that what you want, Mama?
. . .

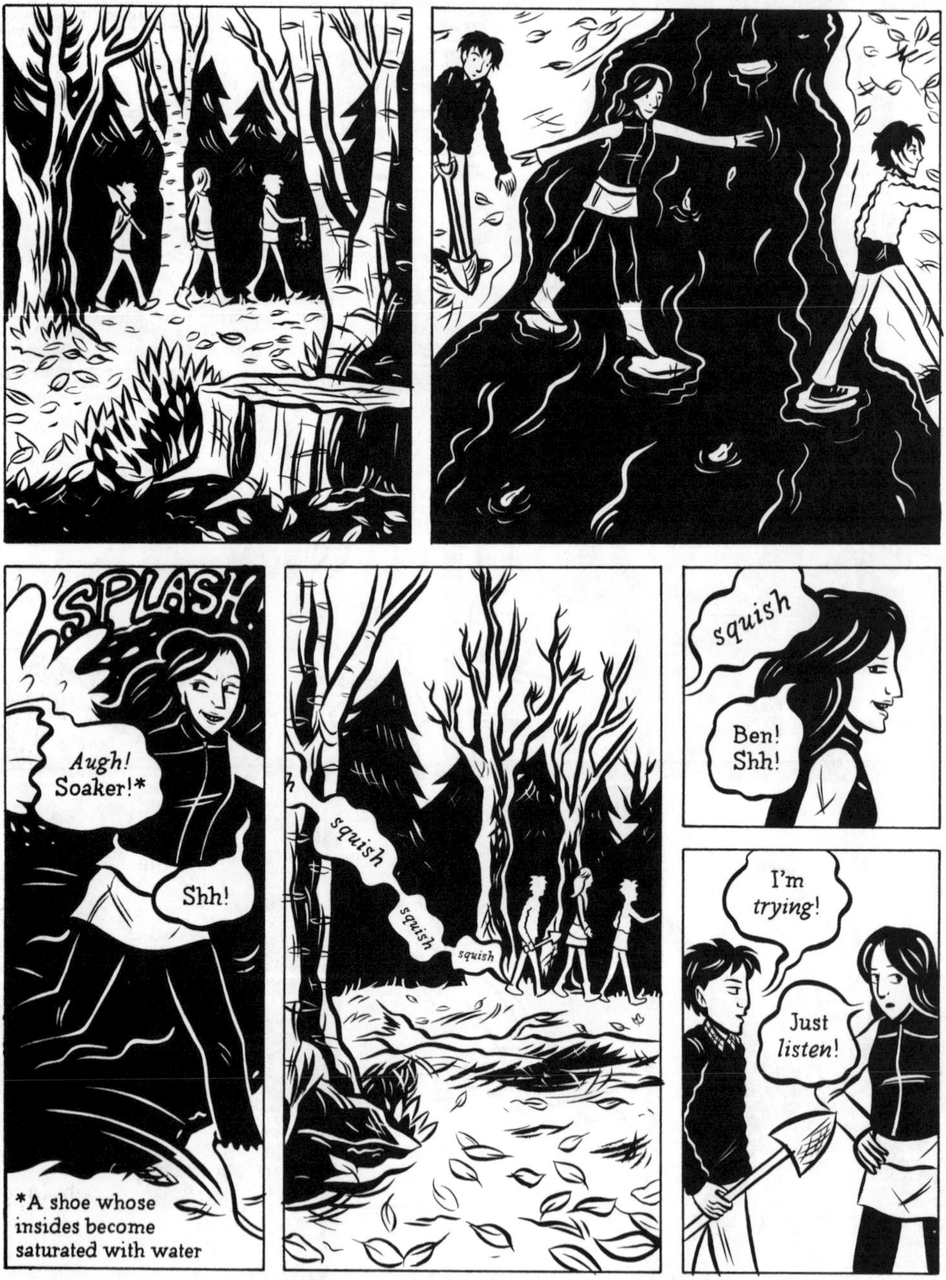
SPLASH
Augh! Soaker!*
Shh!
*A shoe whose insides become saturated with water
squish
squish
squish
squish
Ben! Shh!
I'm trying!
Just listen!

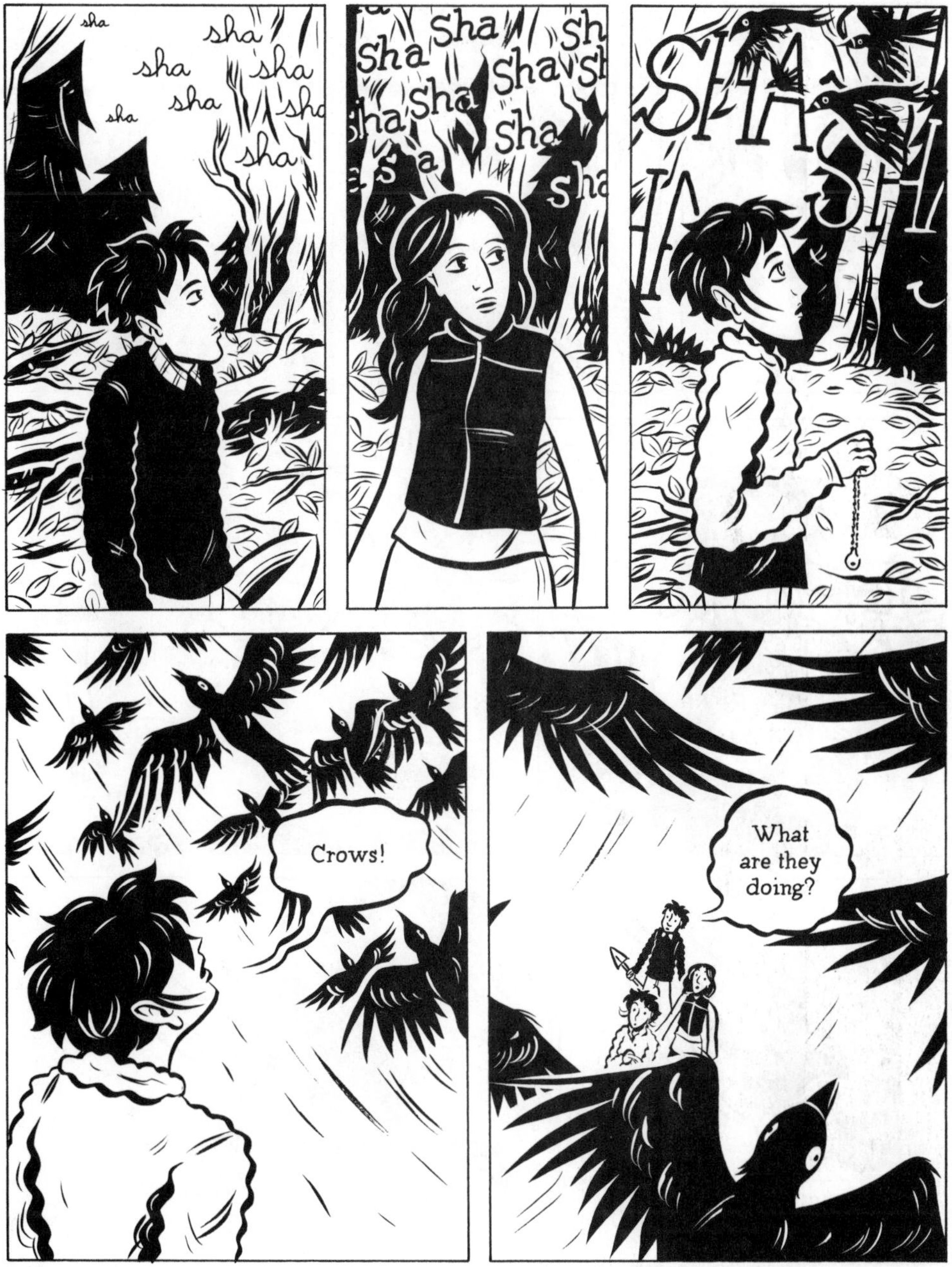

sha
sha
sha
sha
sha
sha
sha
Sha
Sha
Sha
Sha
Sha
sha
SHA
SHA
Crows!
What are they doing?

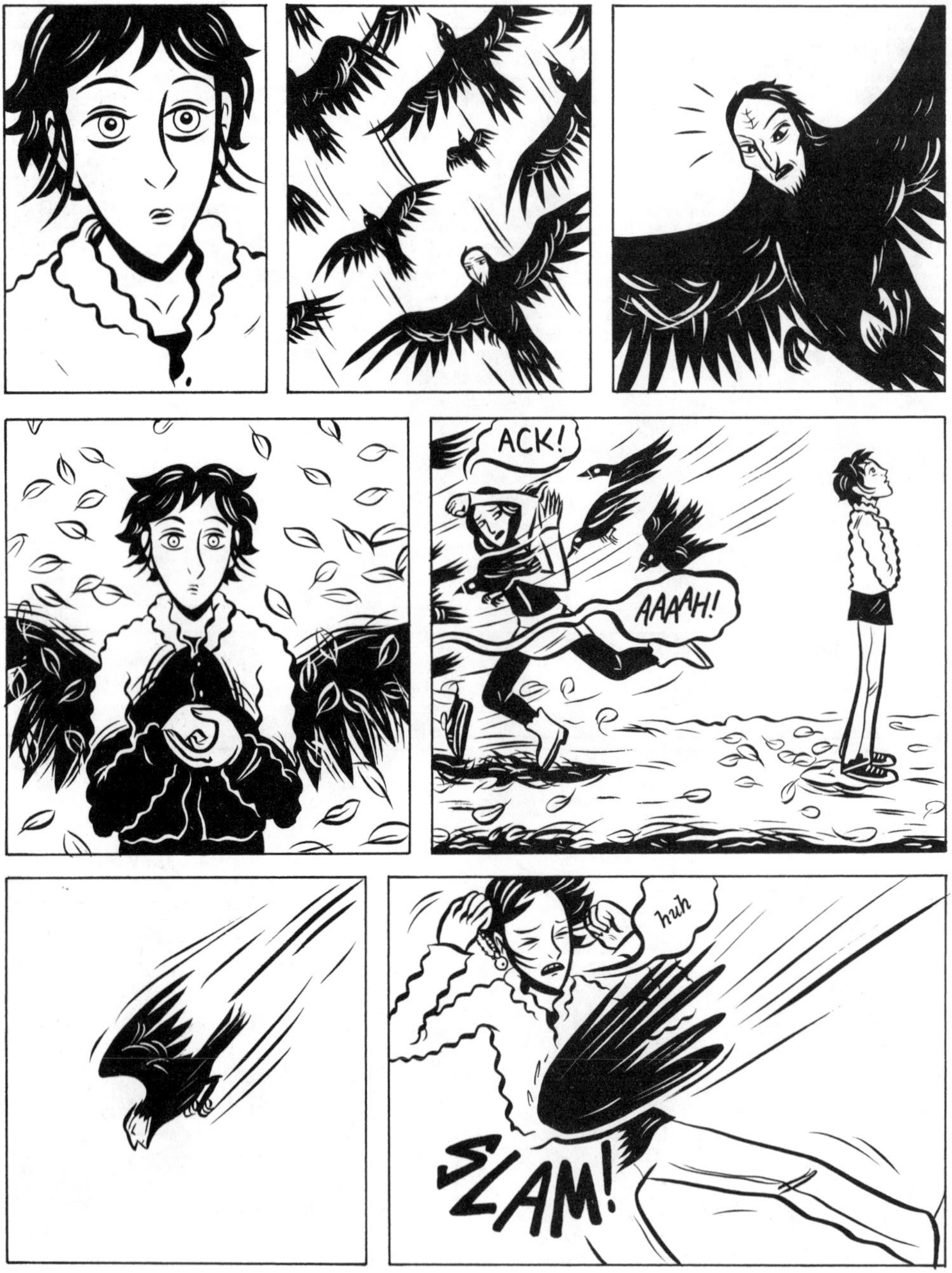
ACK!
AAAAH!
huh
SLAM!

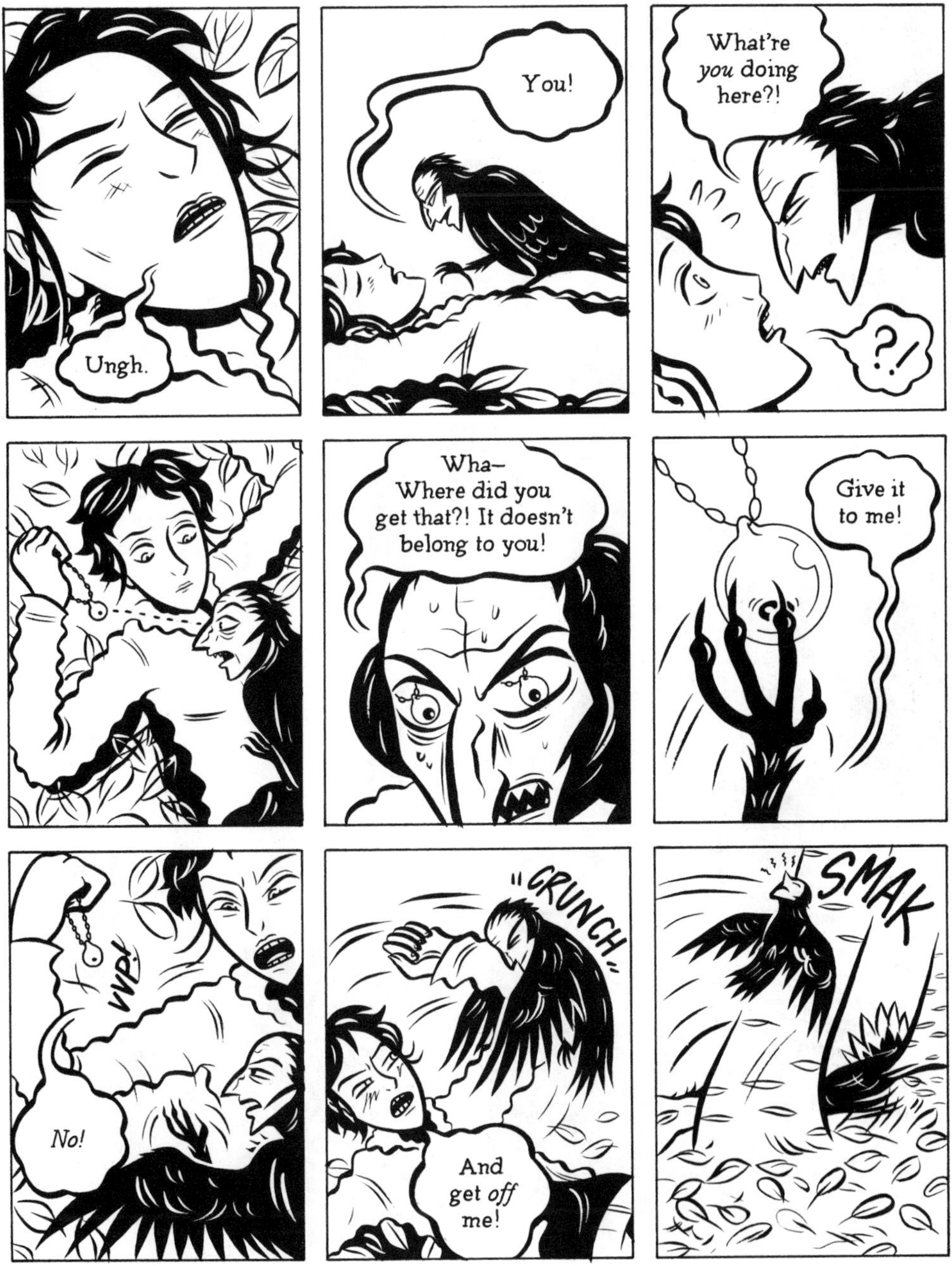
Ungh.
You!
What're *you* doing here?!
?!
Wha– Where did you get that?! It doesn't belong to you!
Give it to me!
VVP!
No!
"CRUNCH"
And get *off* me!
SMAK

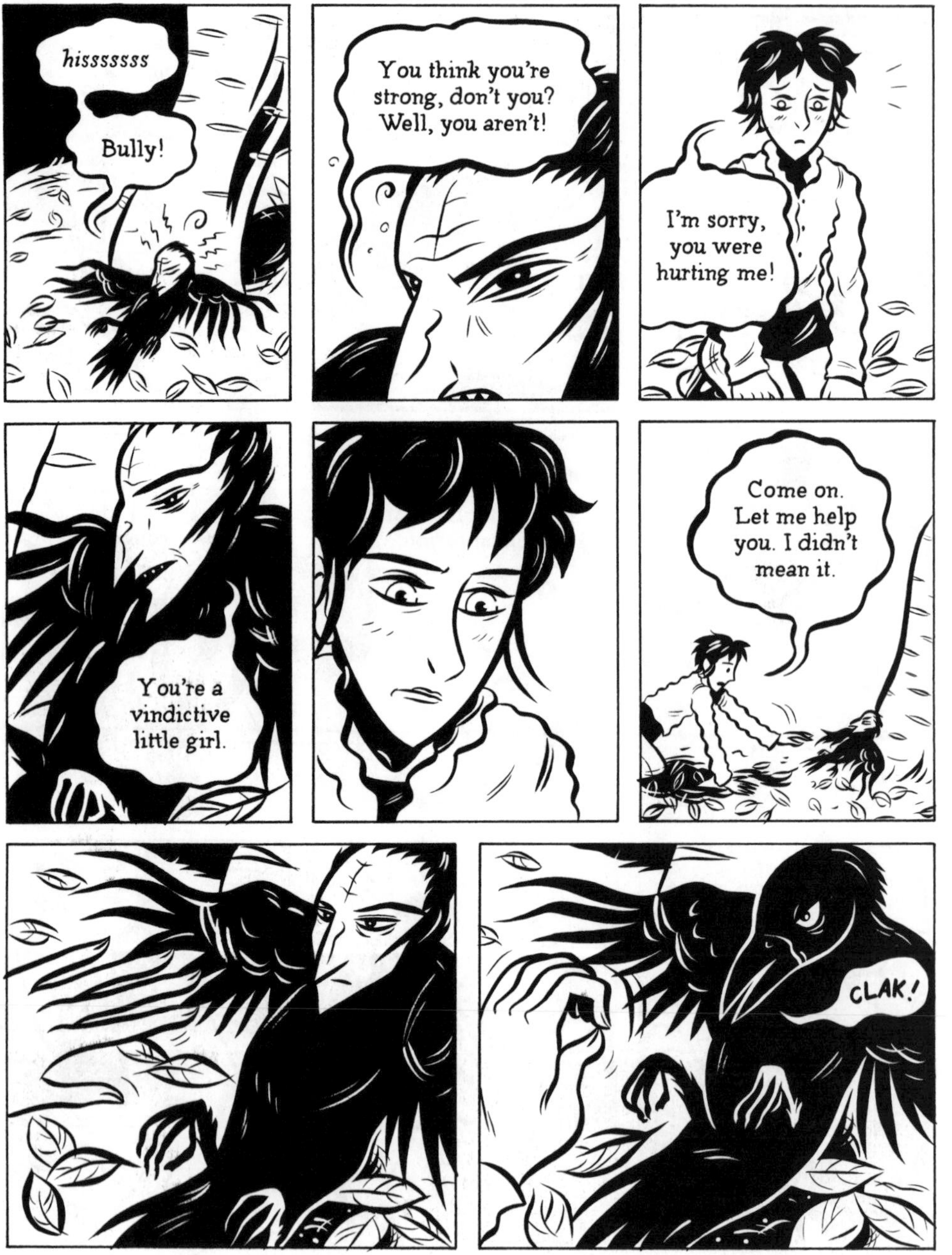
hissssssss
Bully!
You think you're strong, don't you? Well, you aren't!
I'm sorry, you were hurting me!
You're a vindictive little girl.
Come on. Let me help you. I didn't mean it.
CLAK!

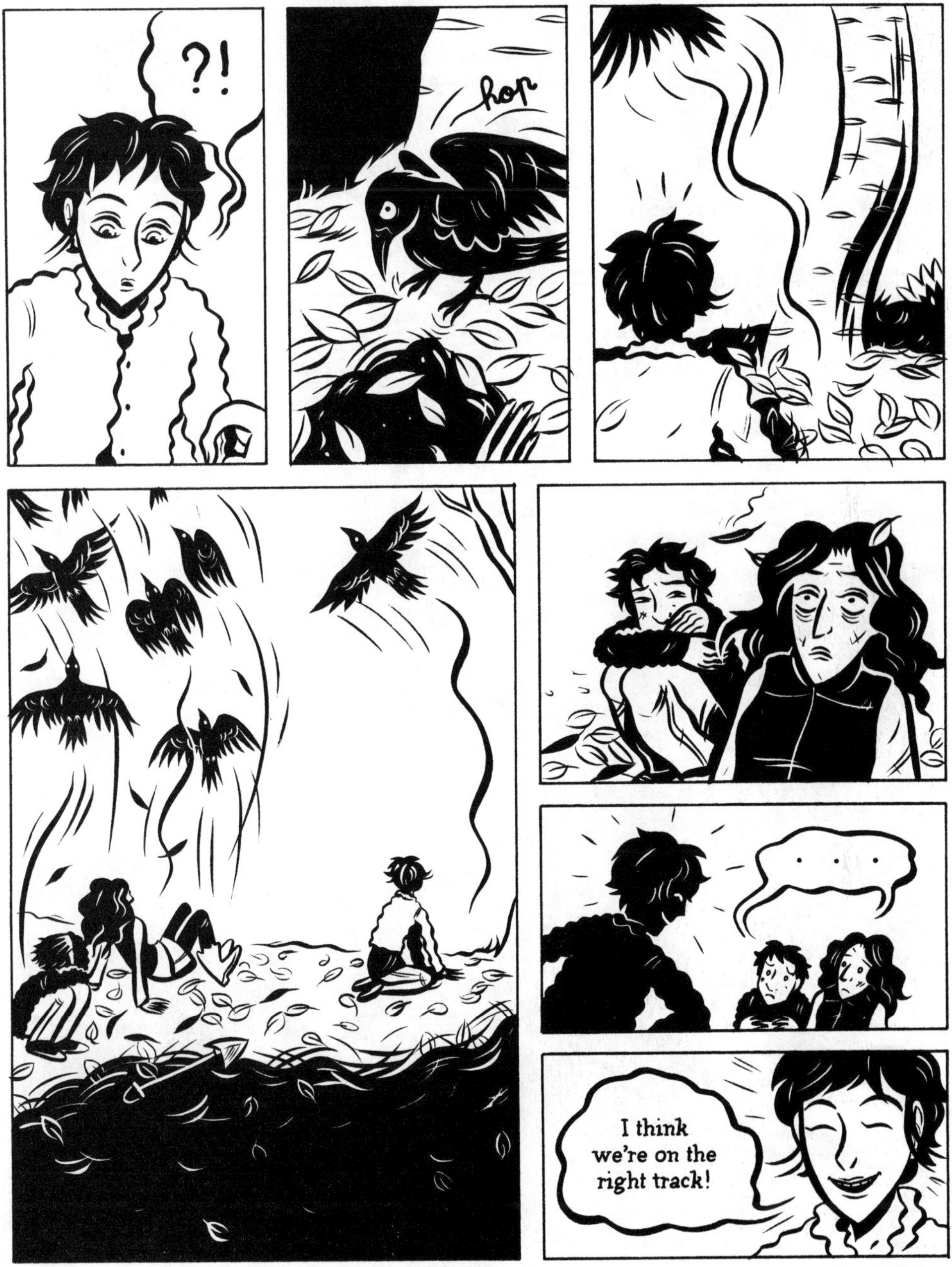
?!
hop
. . .
I think we're on the right track!

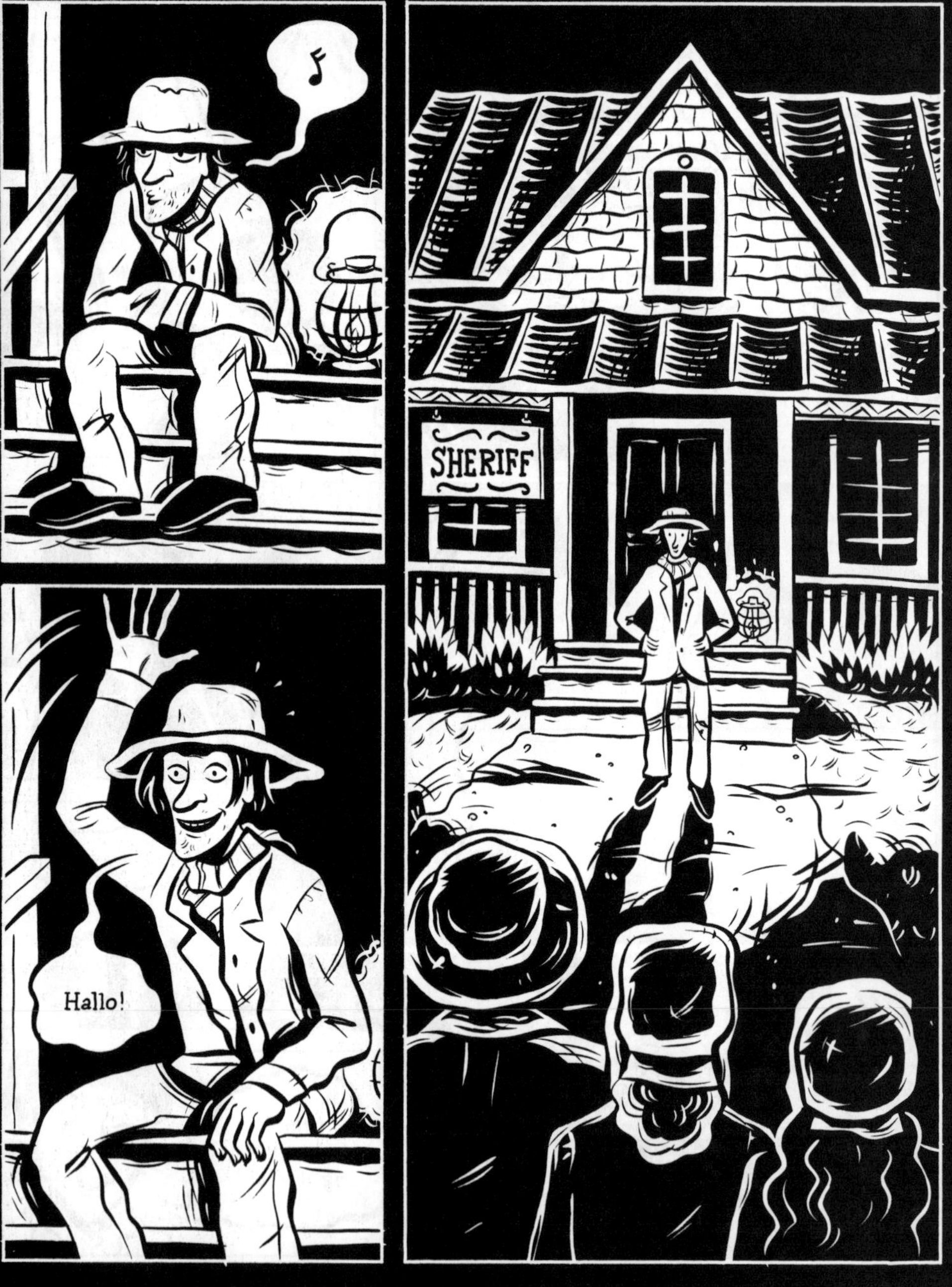
Hallo!
SHERIFF

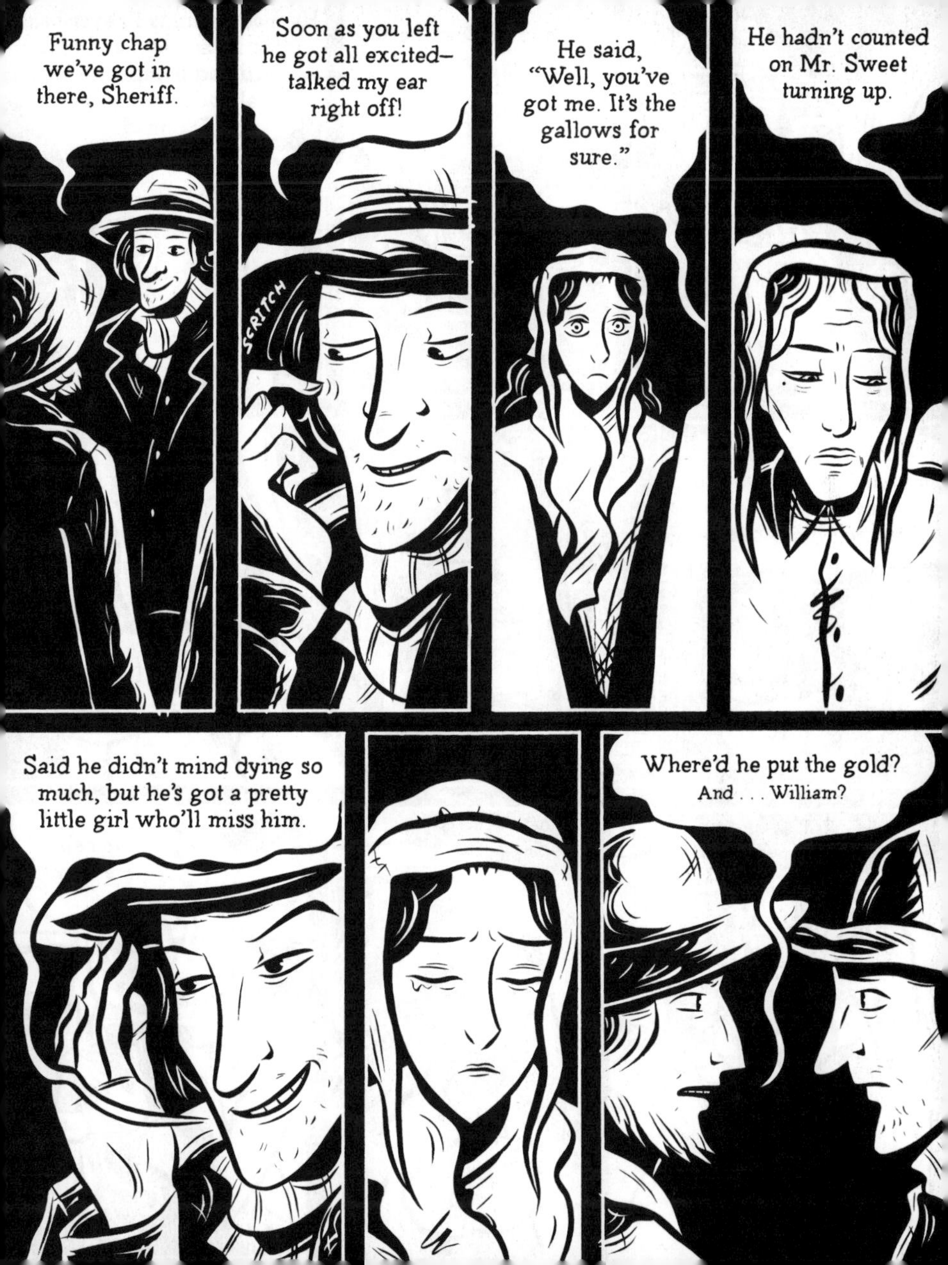
Funny chap we've got in there, Sheriff.
Soon as you left he got all excited— talked my ear right off!
SCRITCH
He said, "Well, you've got me. It's the gallows for sure."
He hadn't counted on Mr. Sweet turning up.
Said he didn't mind dying so much, but he's got a pretty little girl who'll miss him.
Where'd he put the gold?
And . . . William?

Don't know.

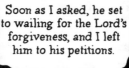
Soon as I asked, he set to wailing for the Lord's forgiveness, and I left him to his petitions.

He made sounds I never heard issue from a human being. You'd had thought he was already among the Damned.

He let off a few minutes ago, and when I put my head in, he was sleeping like a babe.

Hm.

I want to see him!

Very well.

The cell's this way.

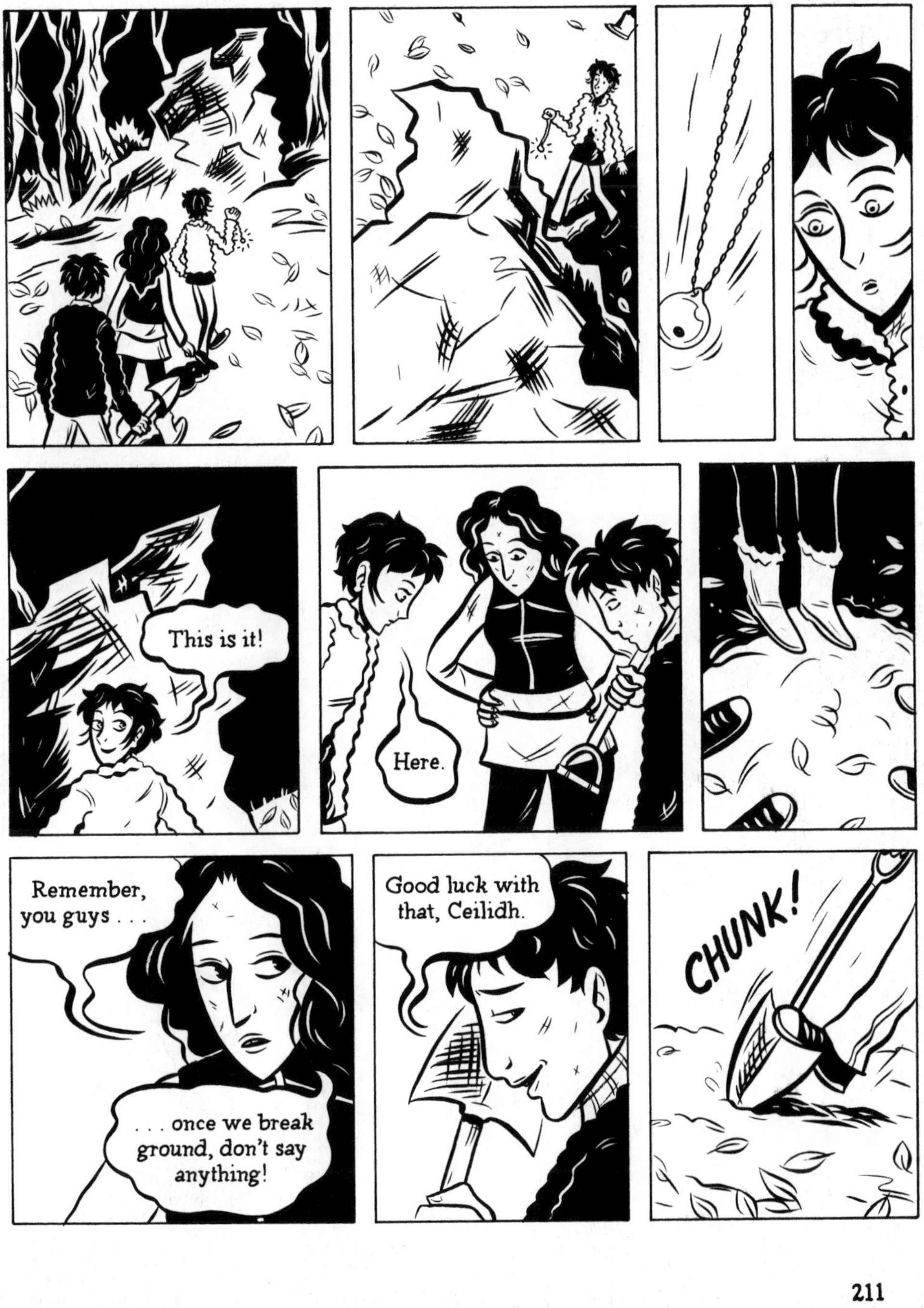
This is it!
Here.
Remember, you guys . . .
. . . once we break ground, don't say anything!
Good luck with that, Ceilidh.
CHUNK!

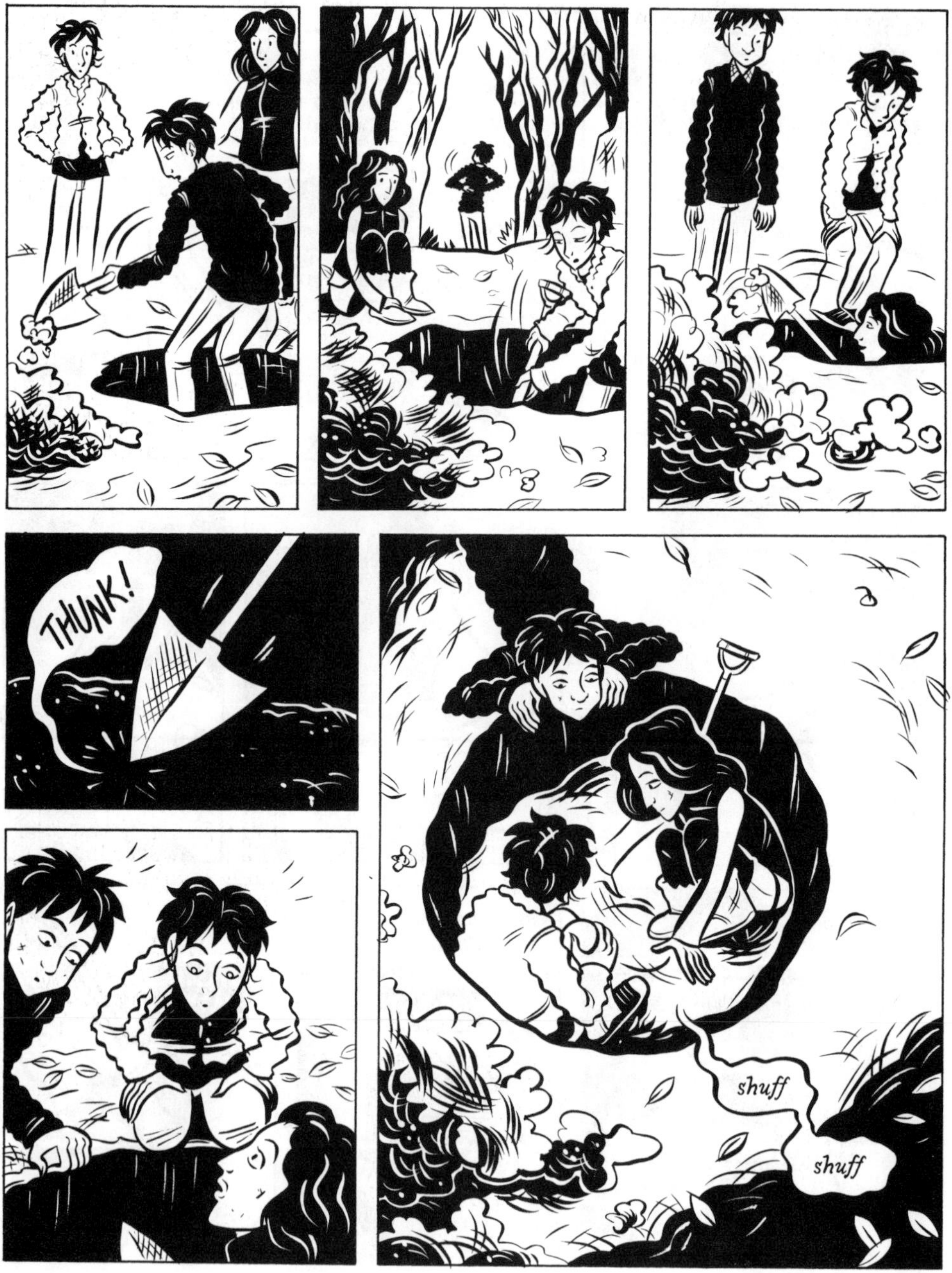
THUNK!
shuff
shuff

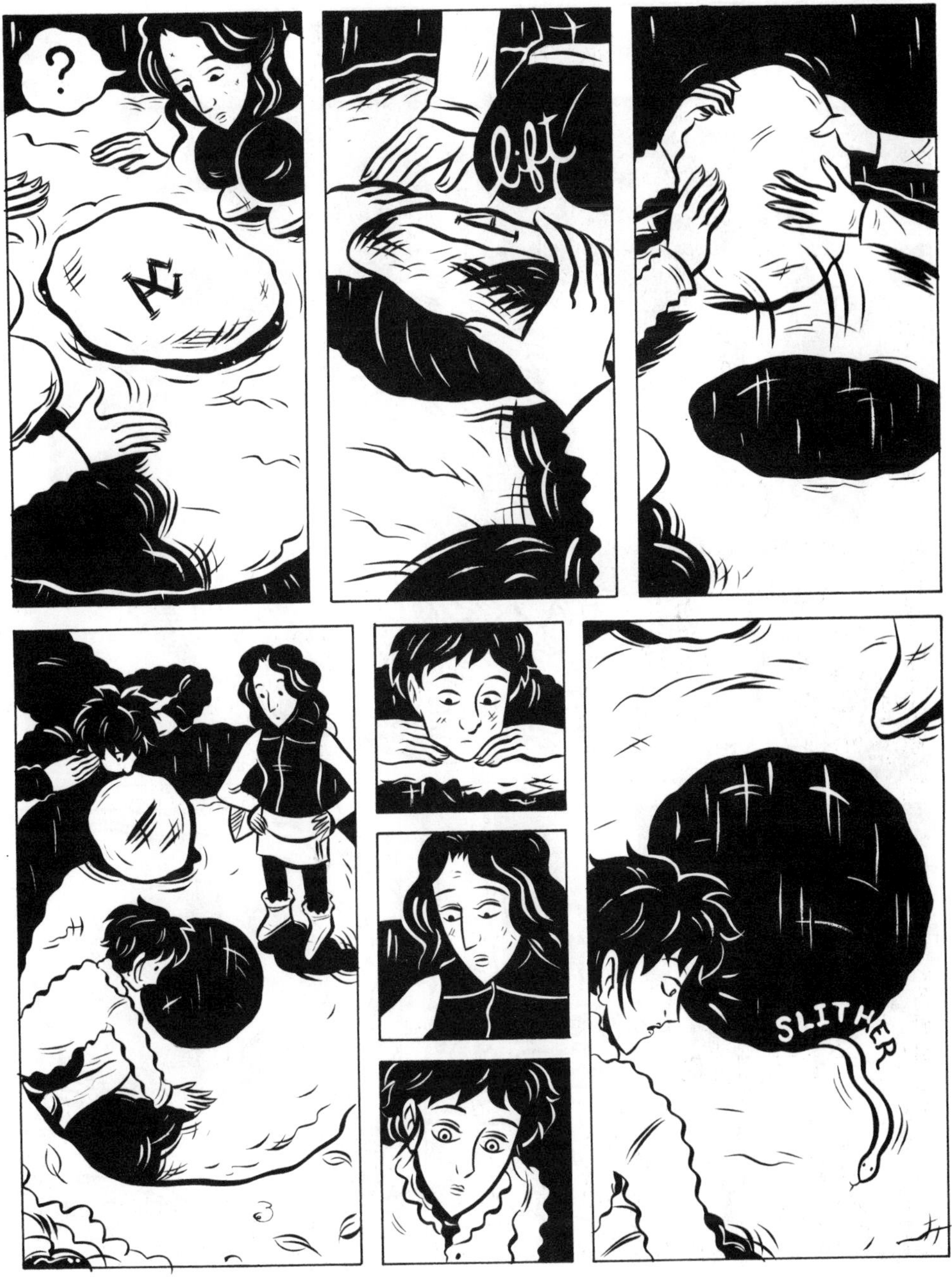
?
lift
SLITHER

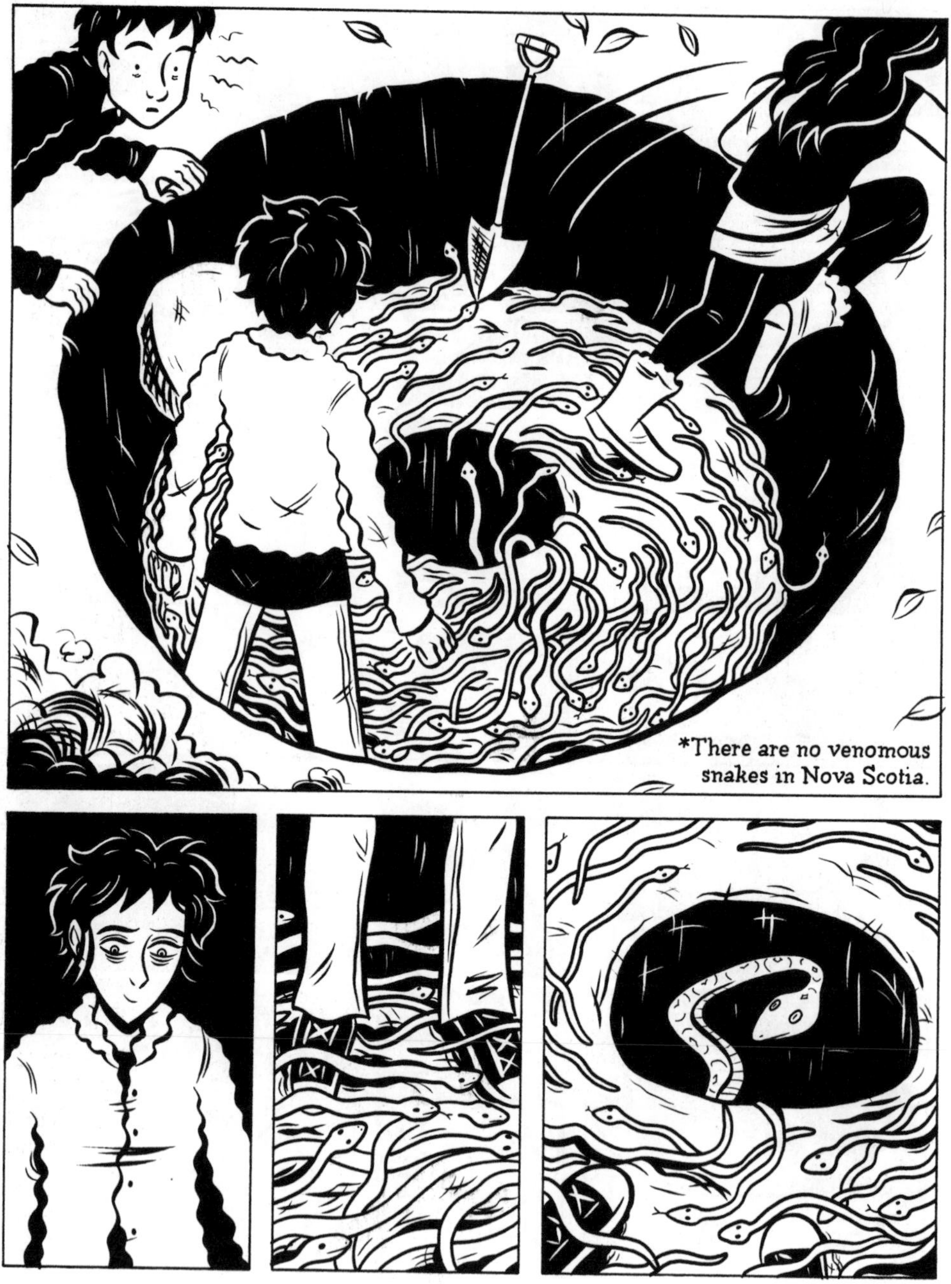
*There are no venomous snakes in Nova Scotia.

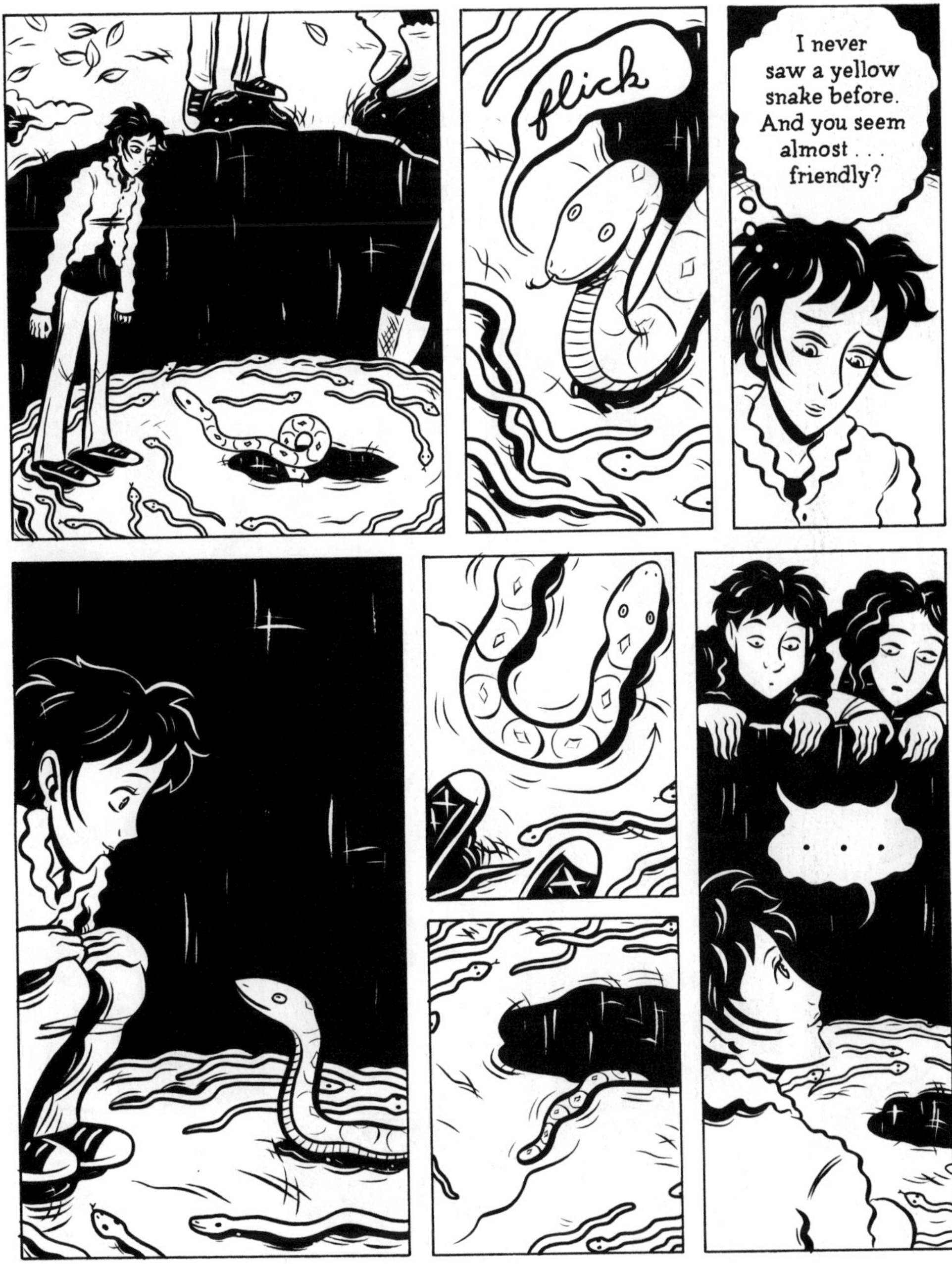
flick
I never saw a yellow snake before. And you seem almost . . . friendly?
• • •

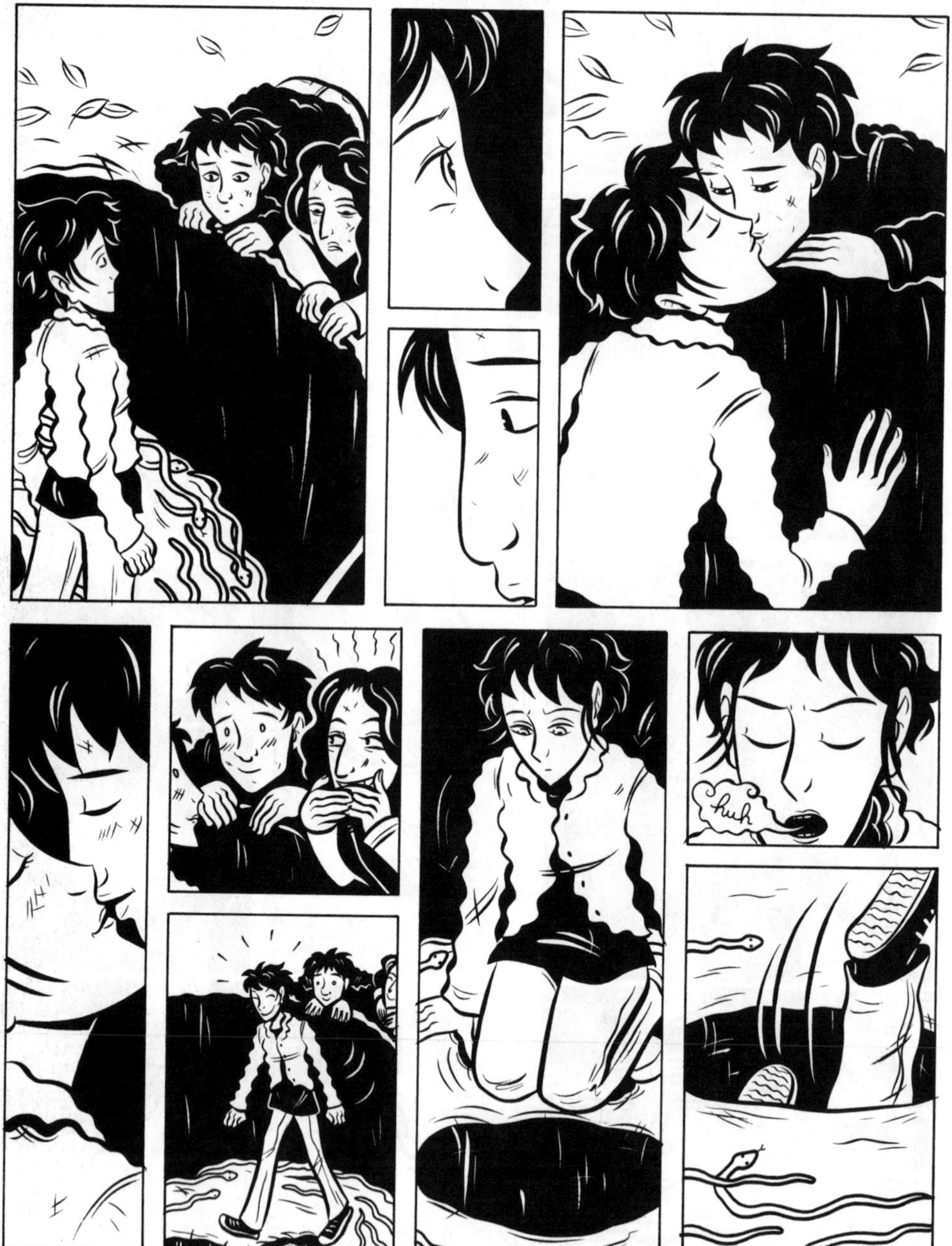
huh

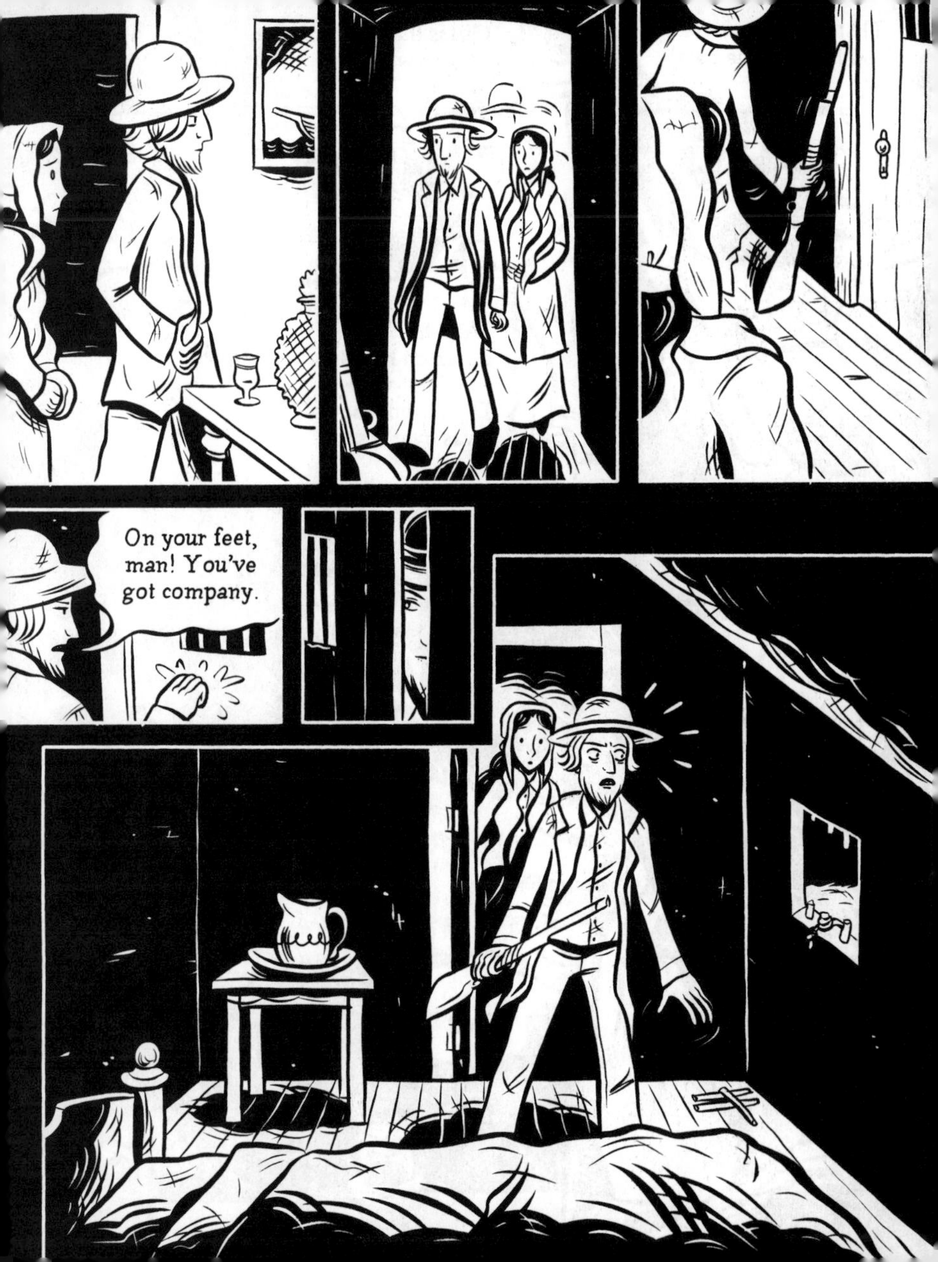
On your feet, man! You've got company.

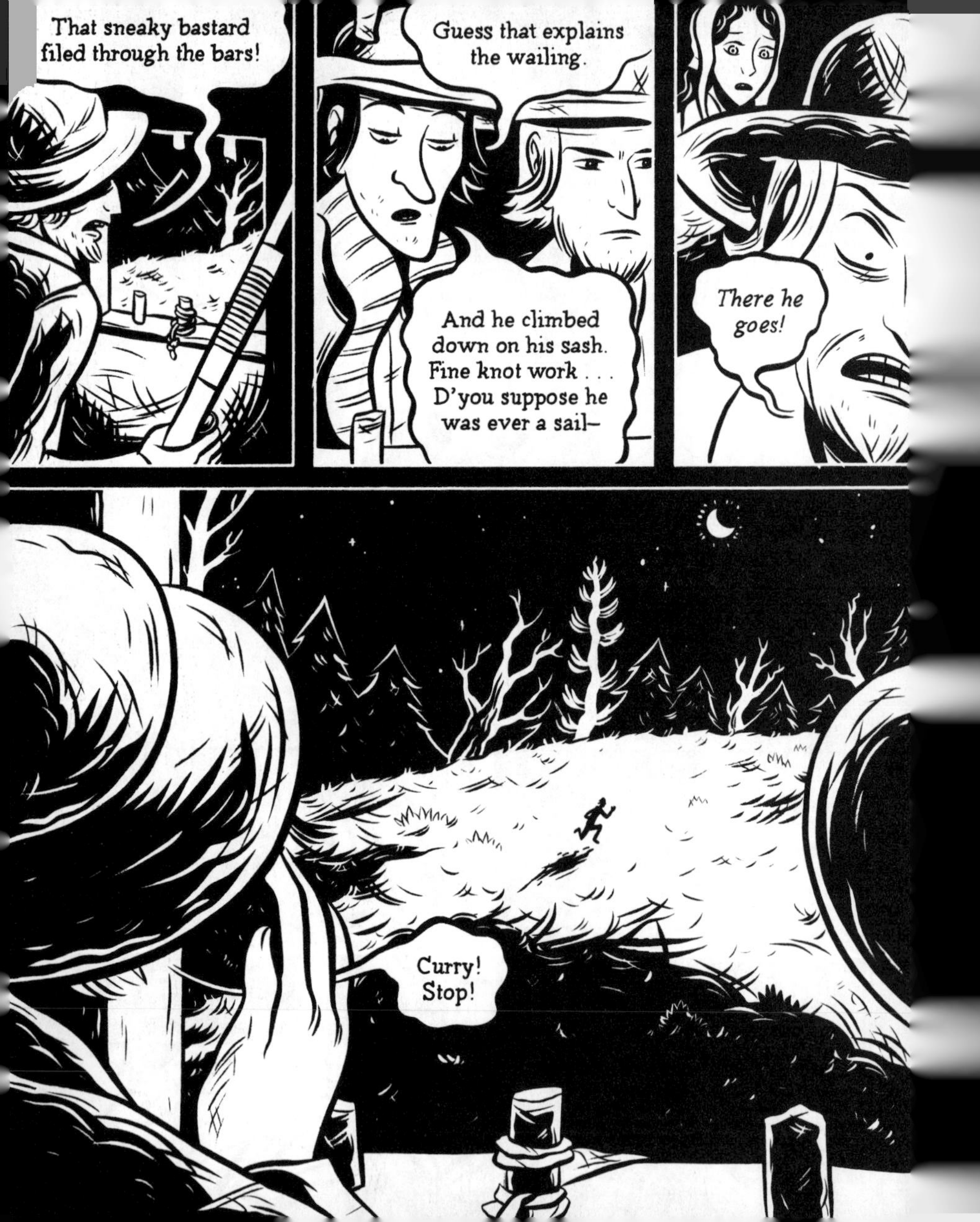
That sneaky bastard filed through the bars!
Guess that explains the wailing.
And he climbed down on his sash. Fine knot work . . . D'you suppose he was ever a sail–
There he goes!
Curry! Stop!

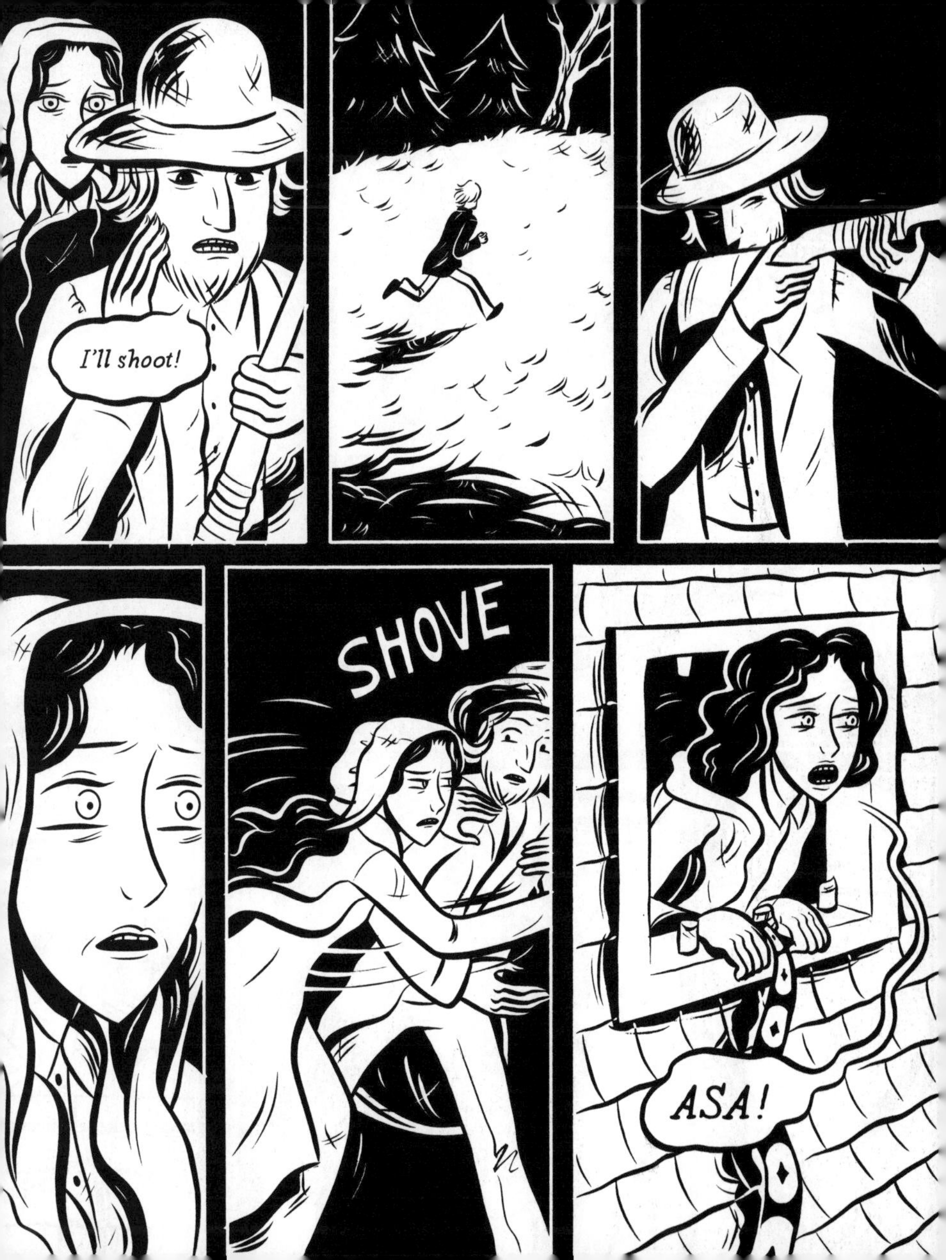

I'll shoot!
SHOVE
ASA!

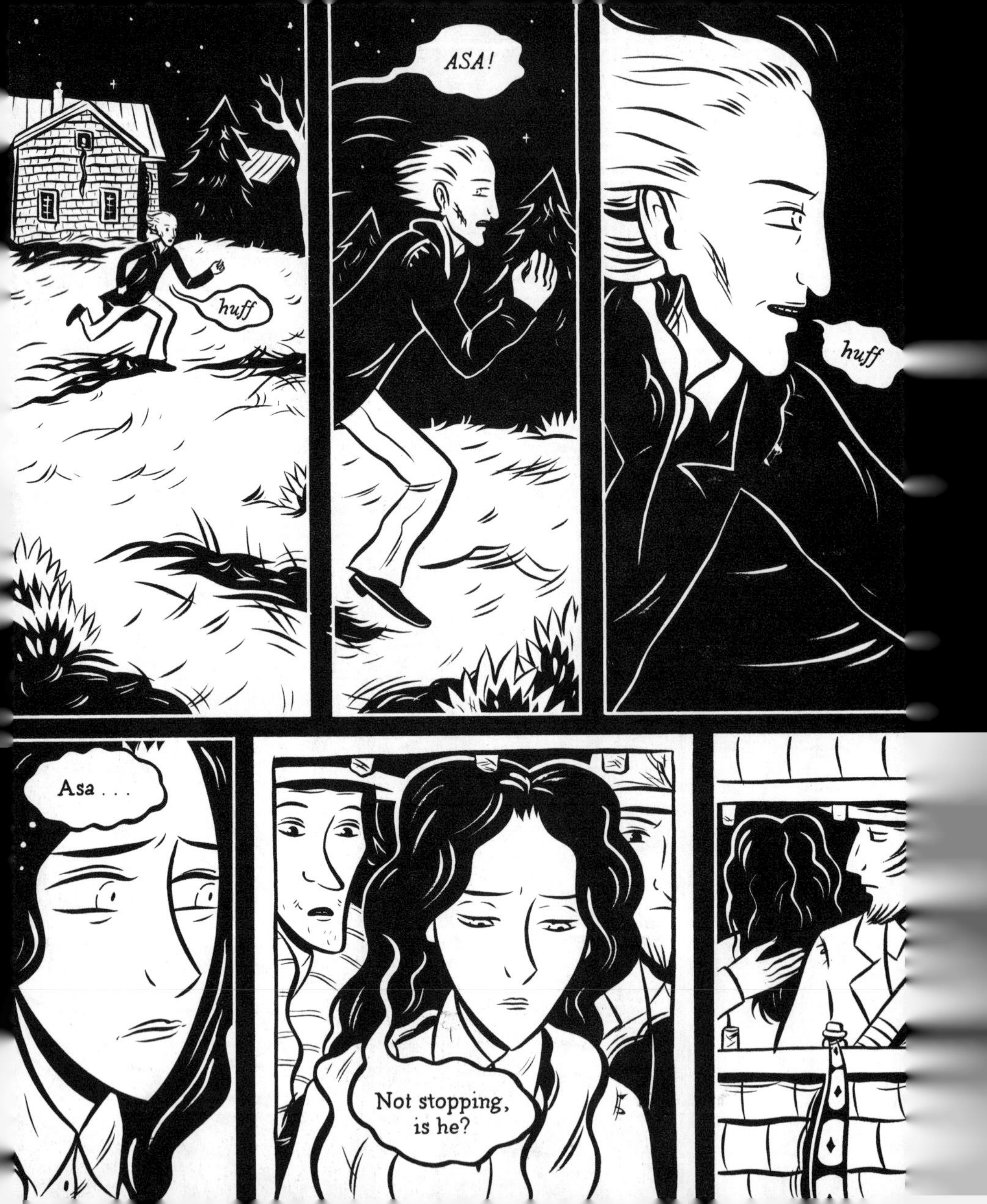
huff
ASA!
huff
Asa . . .
Not stopping, is he?

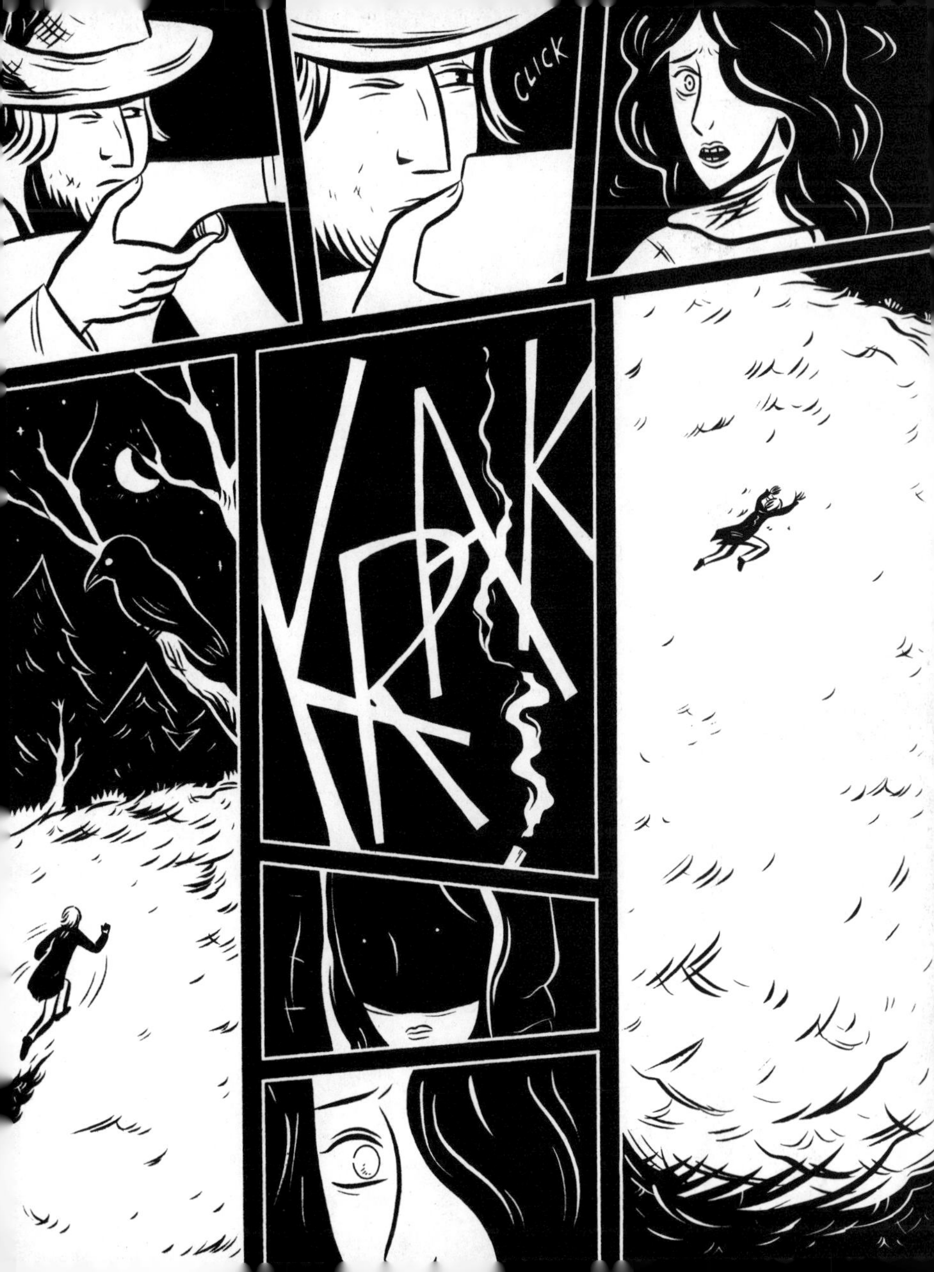
CLICK

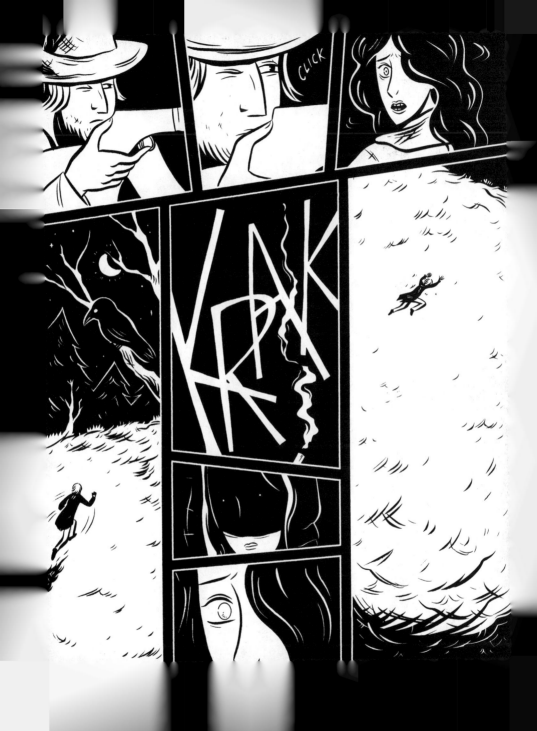

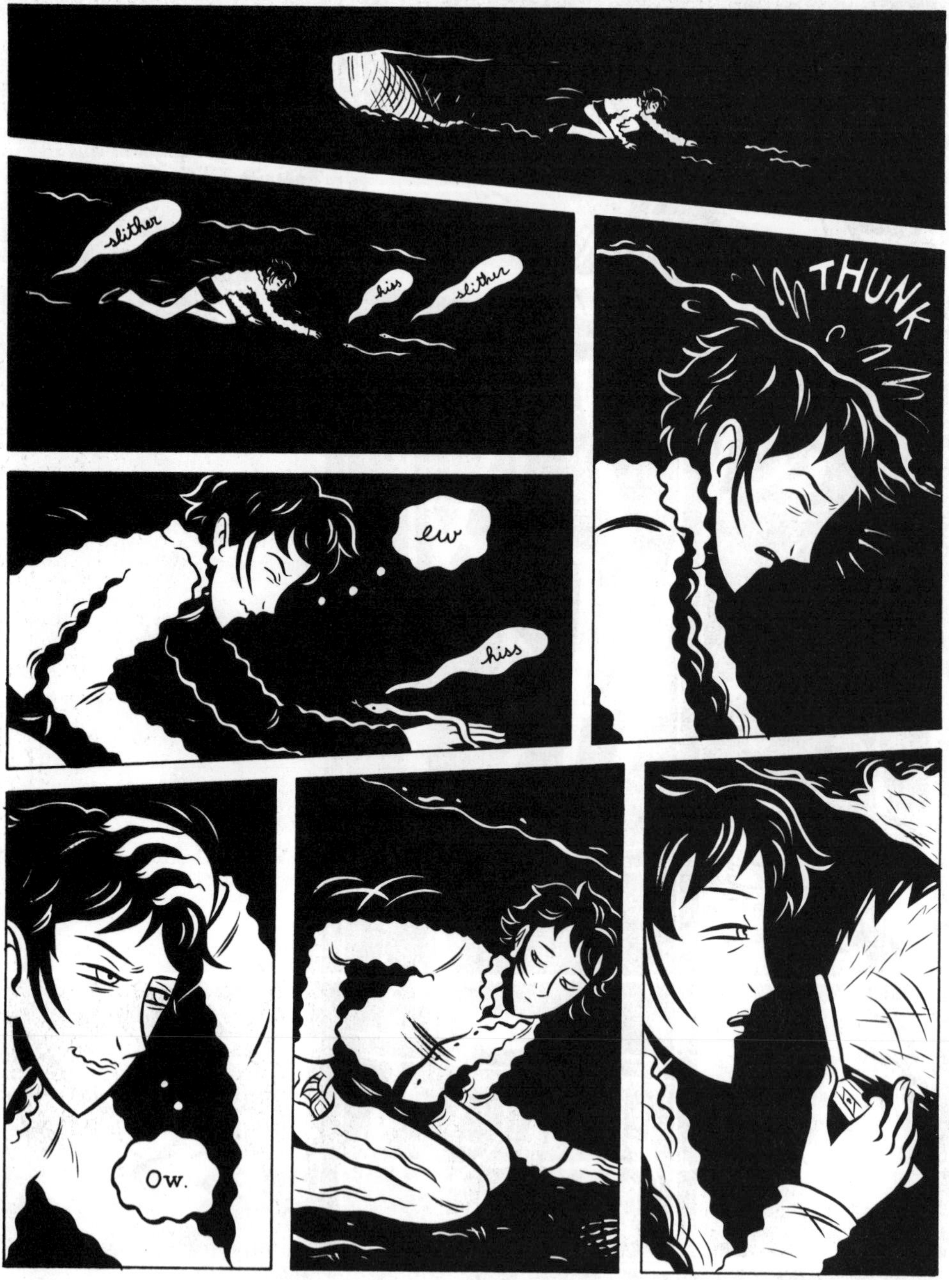
slither
hiss
slither
THUNK
ew
hiss
Ow.

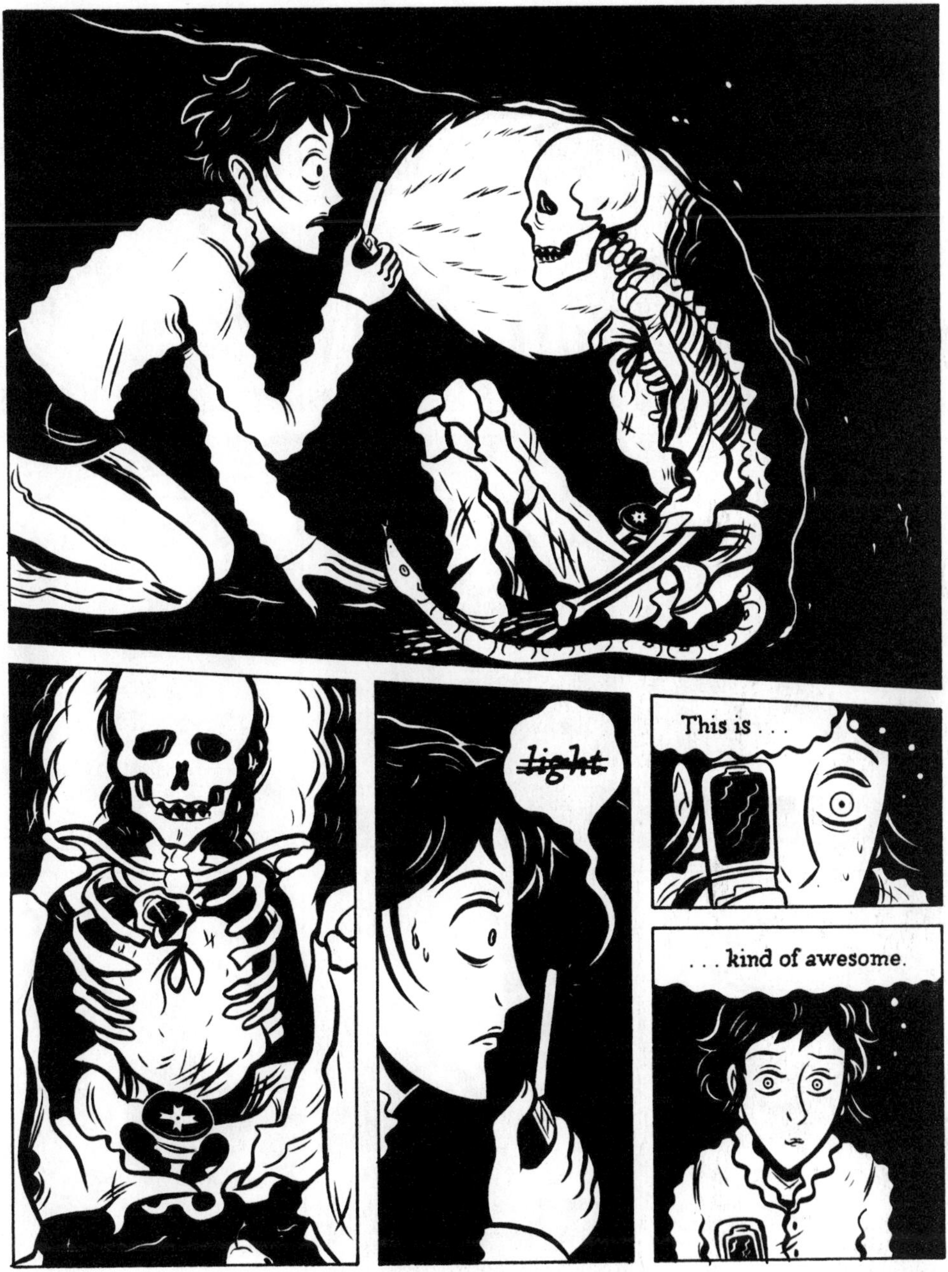

light
This is . . .
. . . kind of awesome.

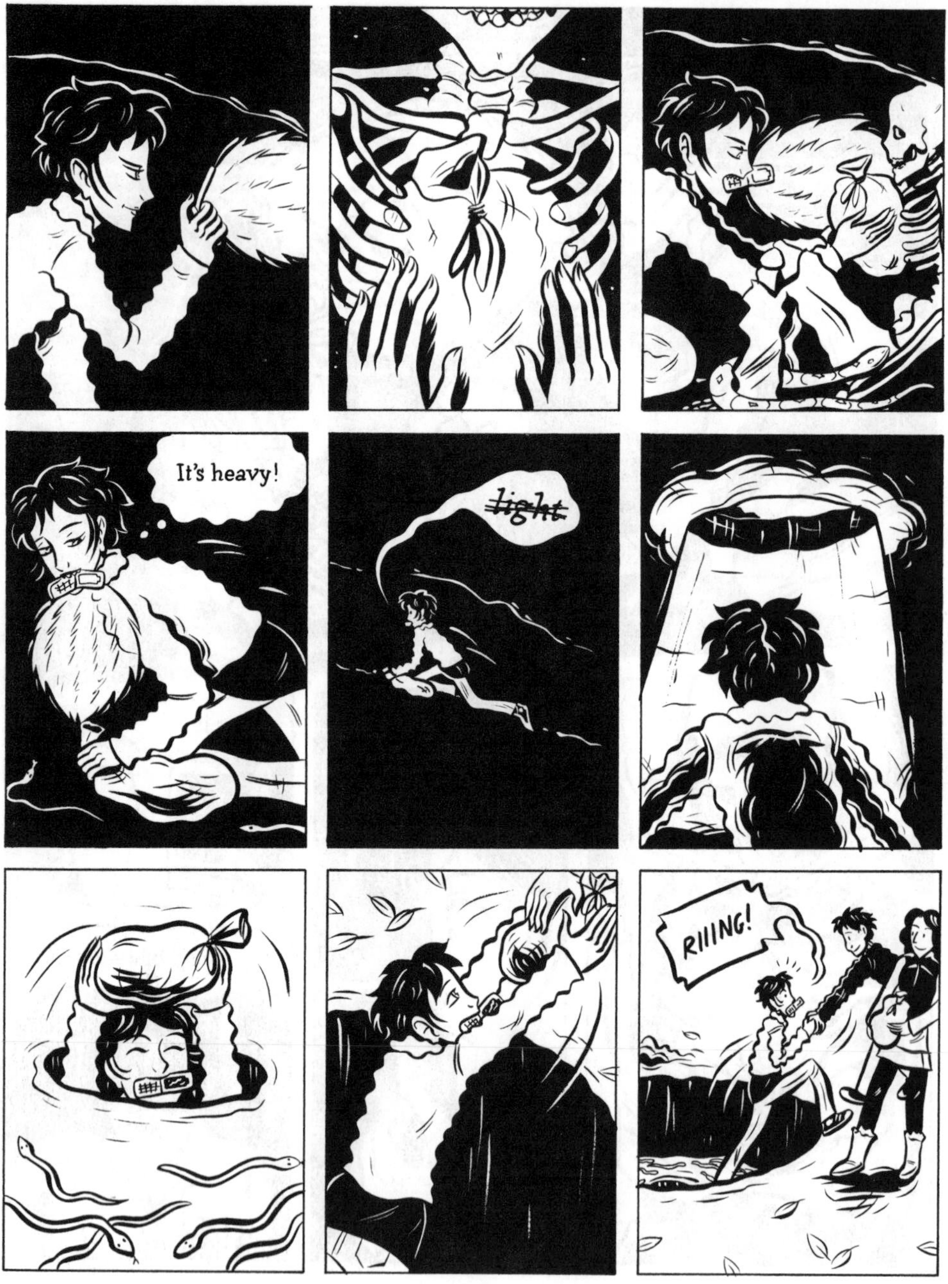
It's heavy!
light
RIIING!

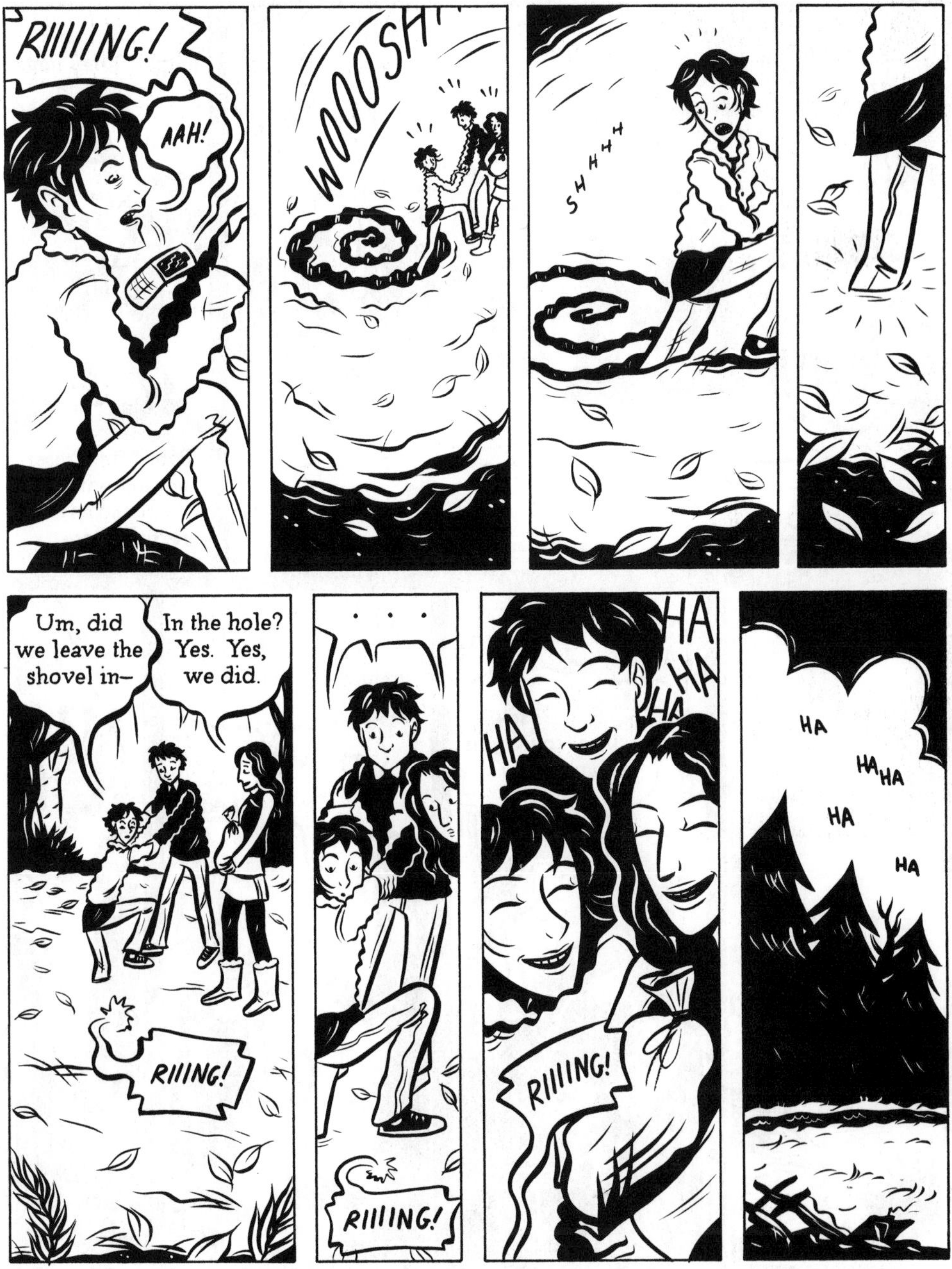
RIIIIING!
AAH!
WOOOSH
SHHHH
Um, did we leave the shovel in—
In the hole? Yes. Yes, we did.
RIIING!
. . .
RIIING!
HA HA HA HA
RIIING!
HA
HA HA
HA
HA

That coffin's empty. They never found 'im.

Poor Mrs. Fraser, not knowing her husband's final resting place . . .

sob

Shh, Josey. What could you have done?

I thought you might want this for a memento, Miss Fraser.

Thank you.

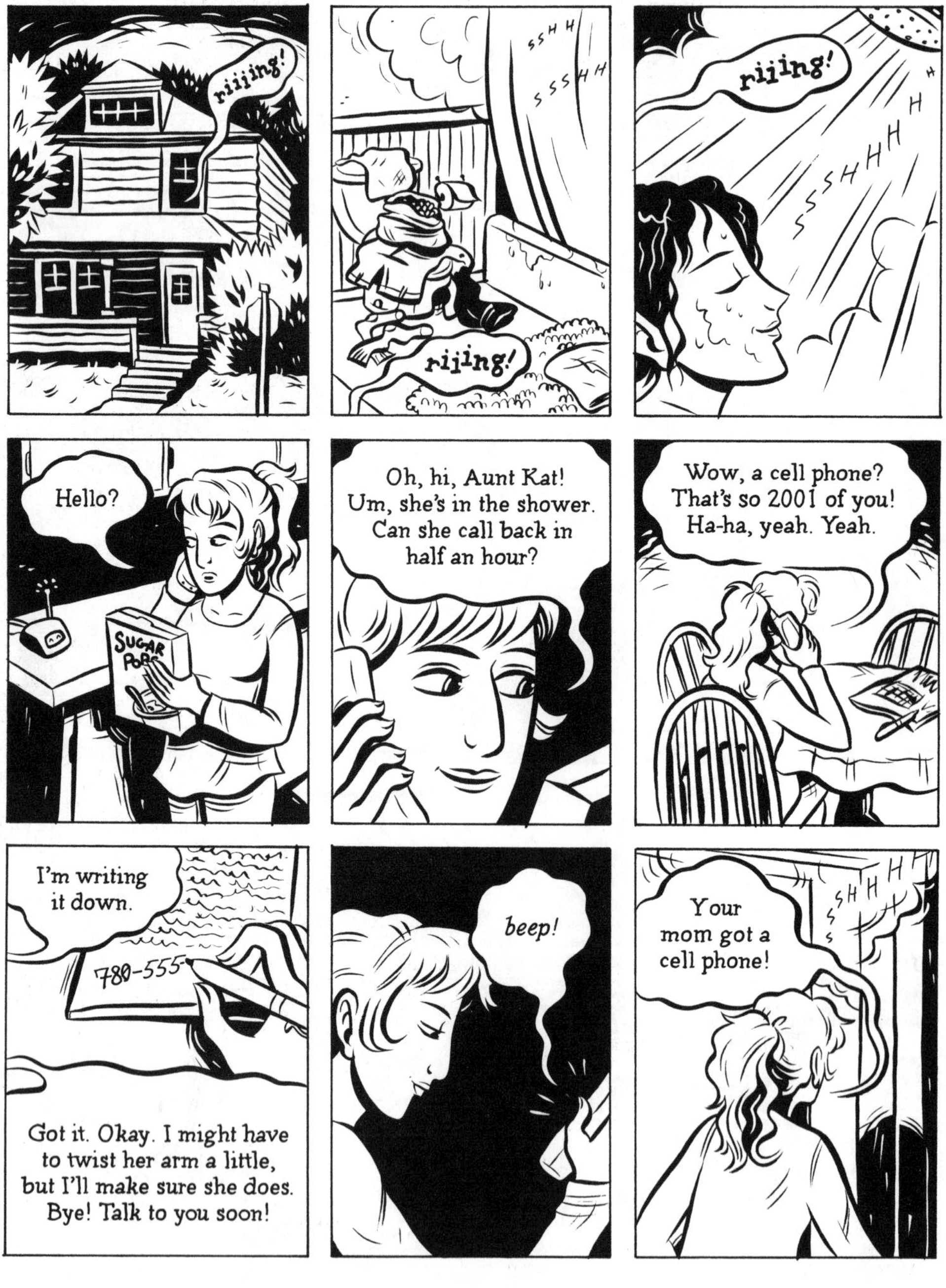
riiing!
SSHH
SSSHH
riiing!
riiing!
SSSHHHHH
Hello?
SUGAR POPS
Oh, hi, Aunt Kat! Um, she's in the shower. Can she call back in half an hour?
Wow, a cell phone? That's so 2001 of you! Ha-ha, yeah. Yeah.
I'm writing it down.
780-555
Got it. Okay. I might have to twist her arm a little, but I'll make sure she does. Bye! Talk to you soon!
beep!
SSHHH
Your mom got a cell phone!

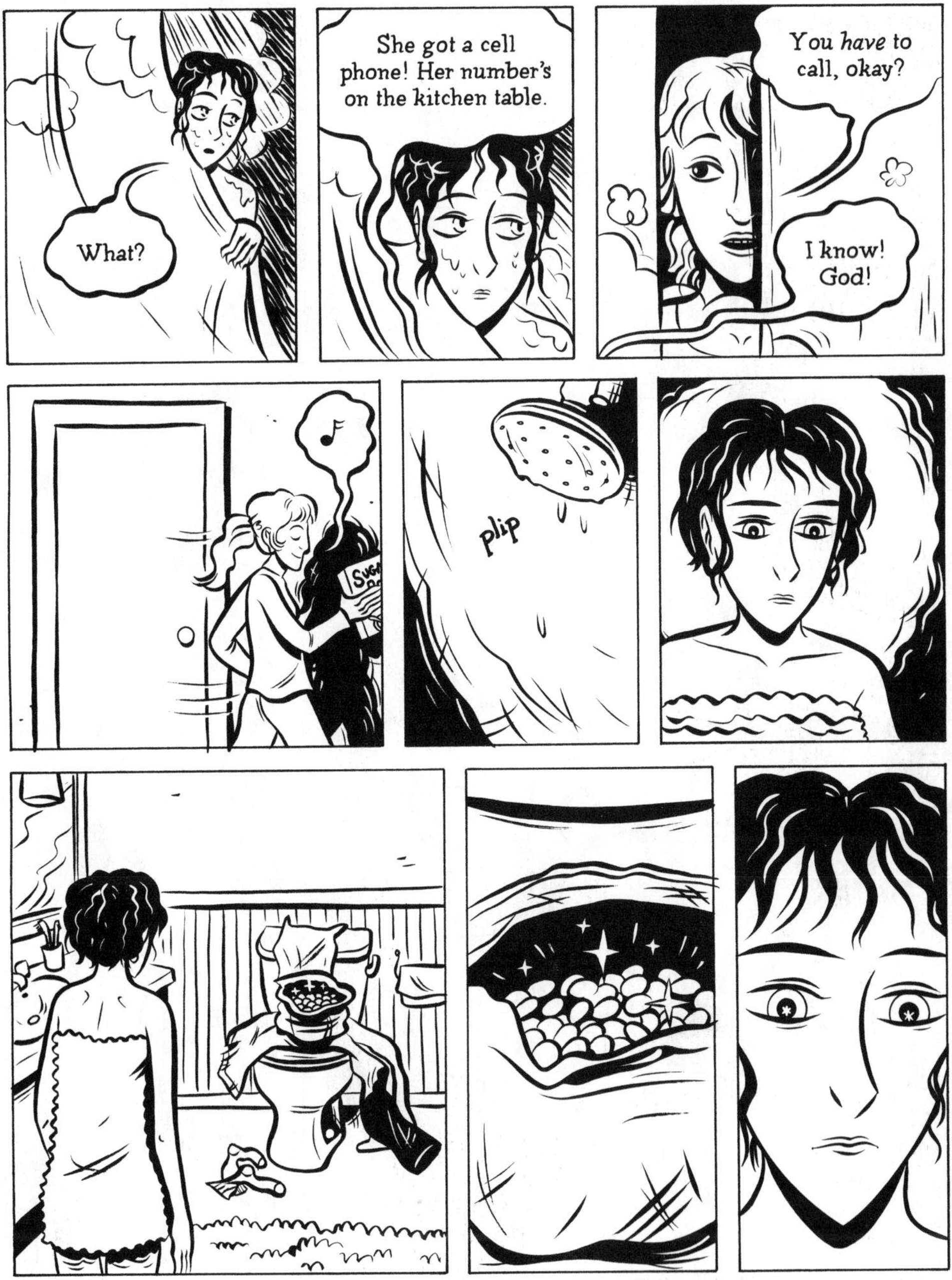
What?
She got a cell phone! Her number's on the kitchen table.
You *have* to call, okay?
I know! God!
plip

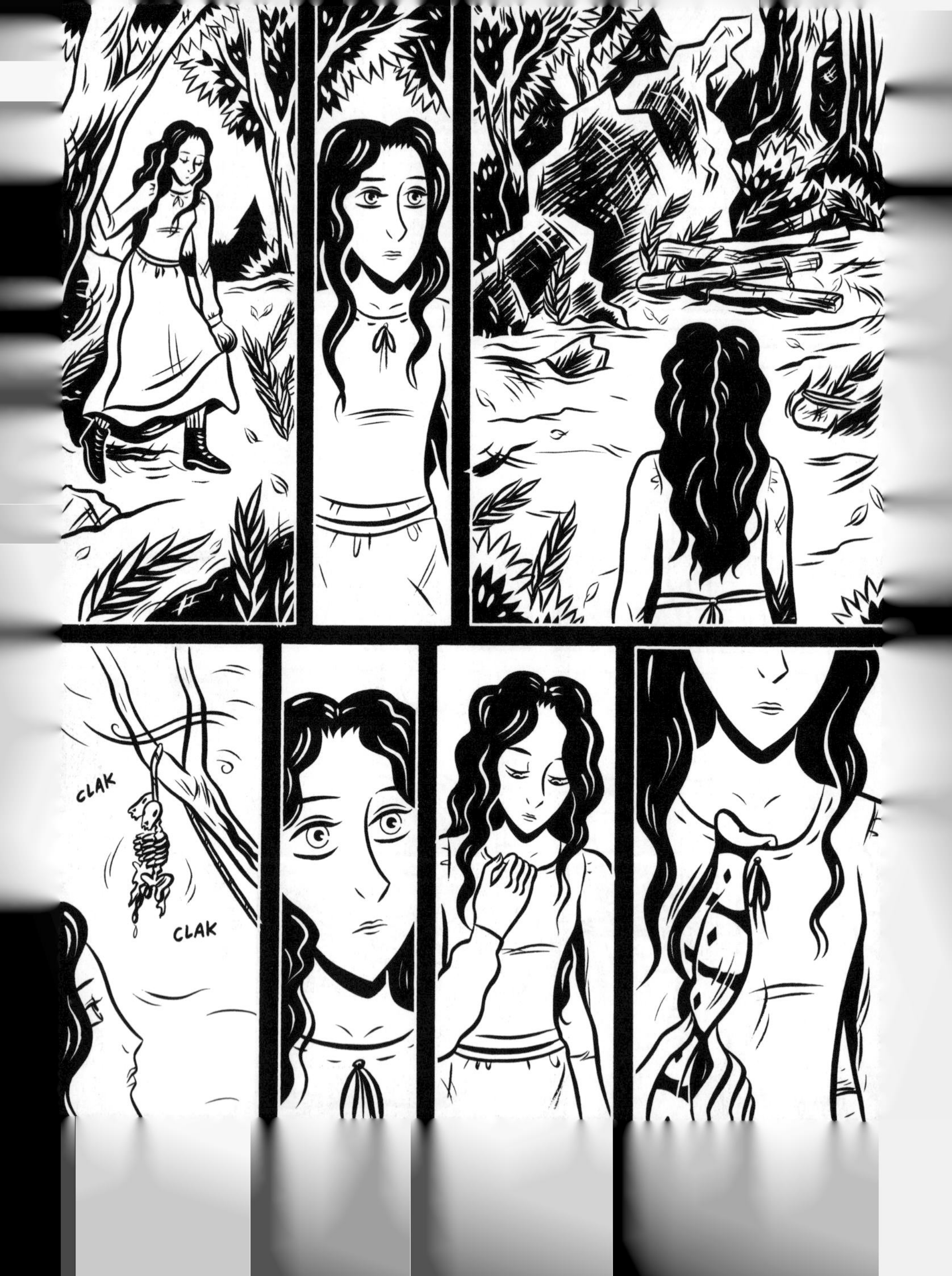
CLAK
CLAK

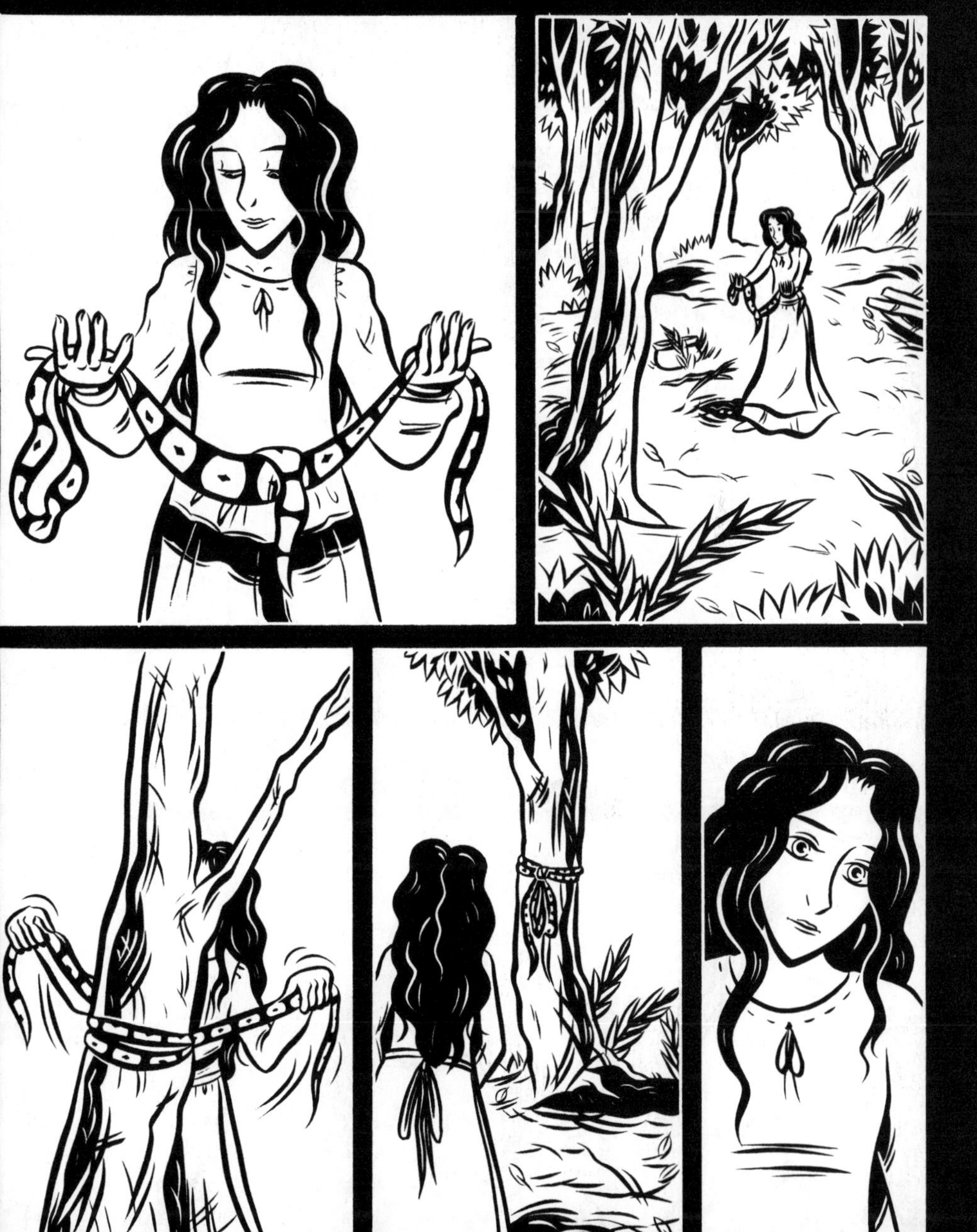

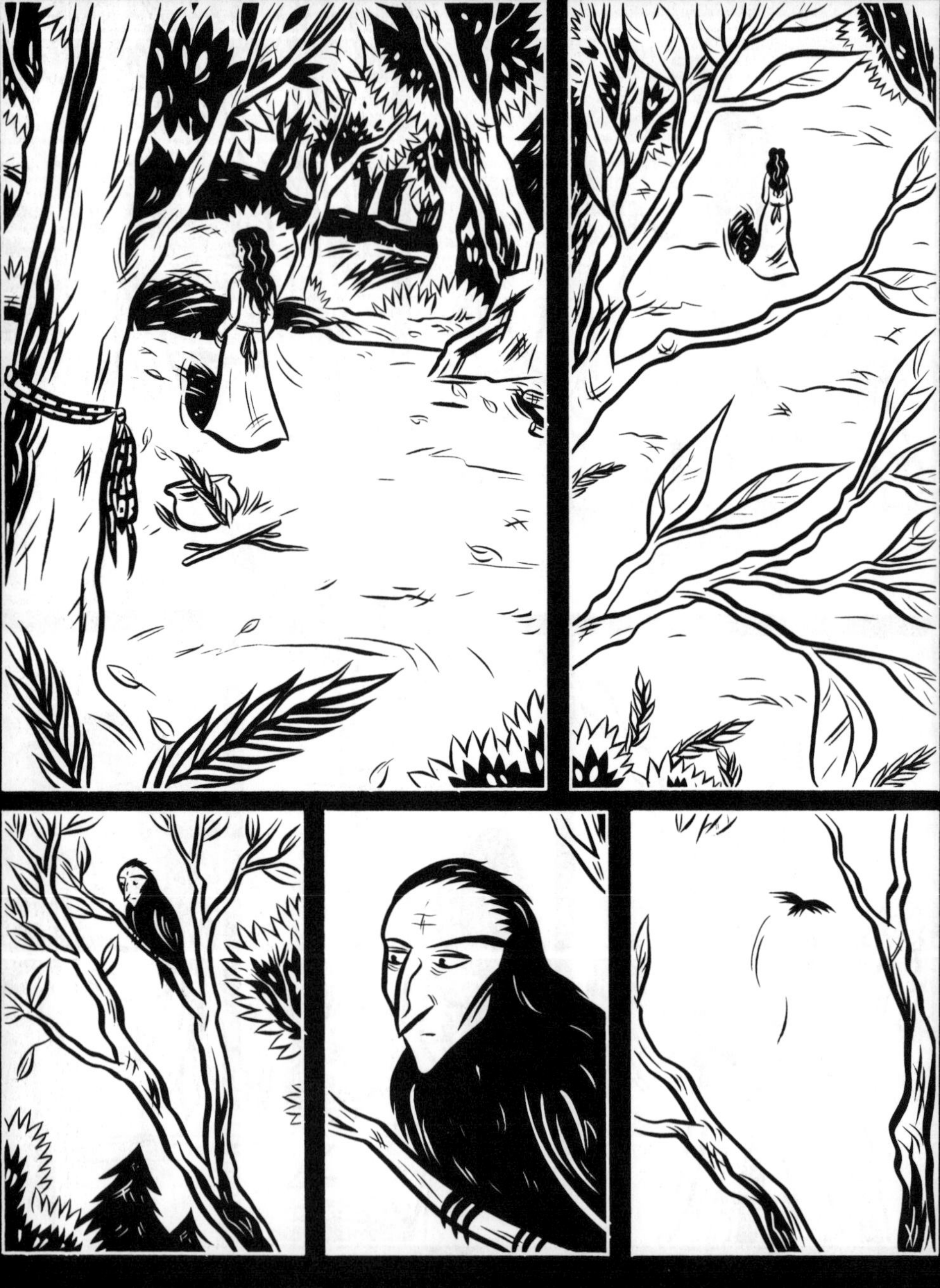

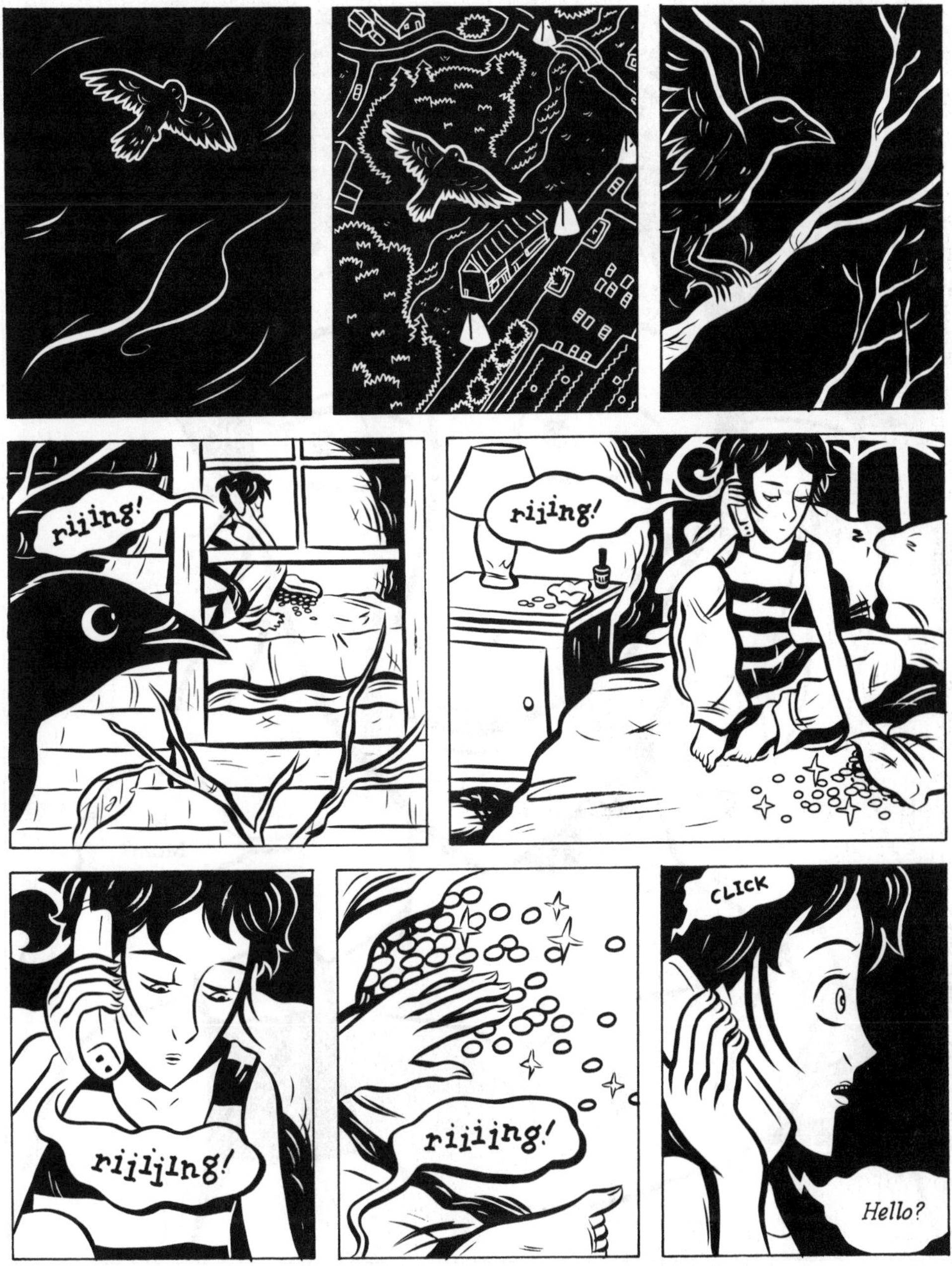
riiing!
riiing!
riiiing!
riiiing!
CLICK
Hello?

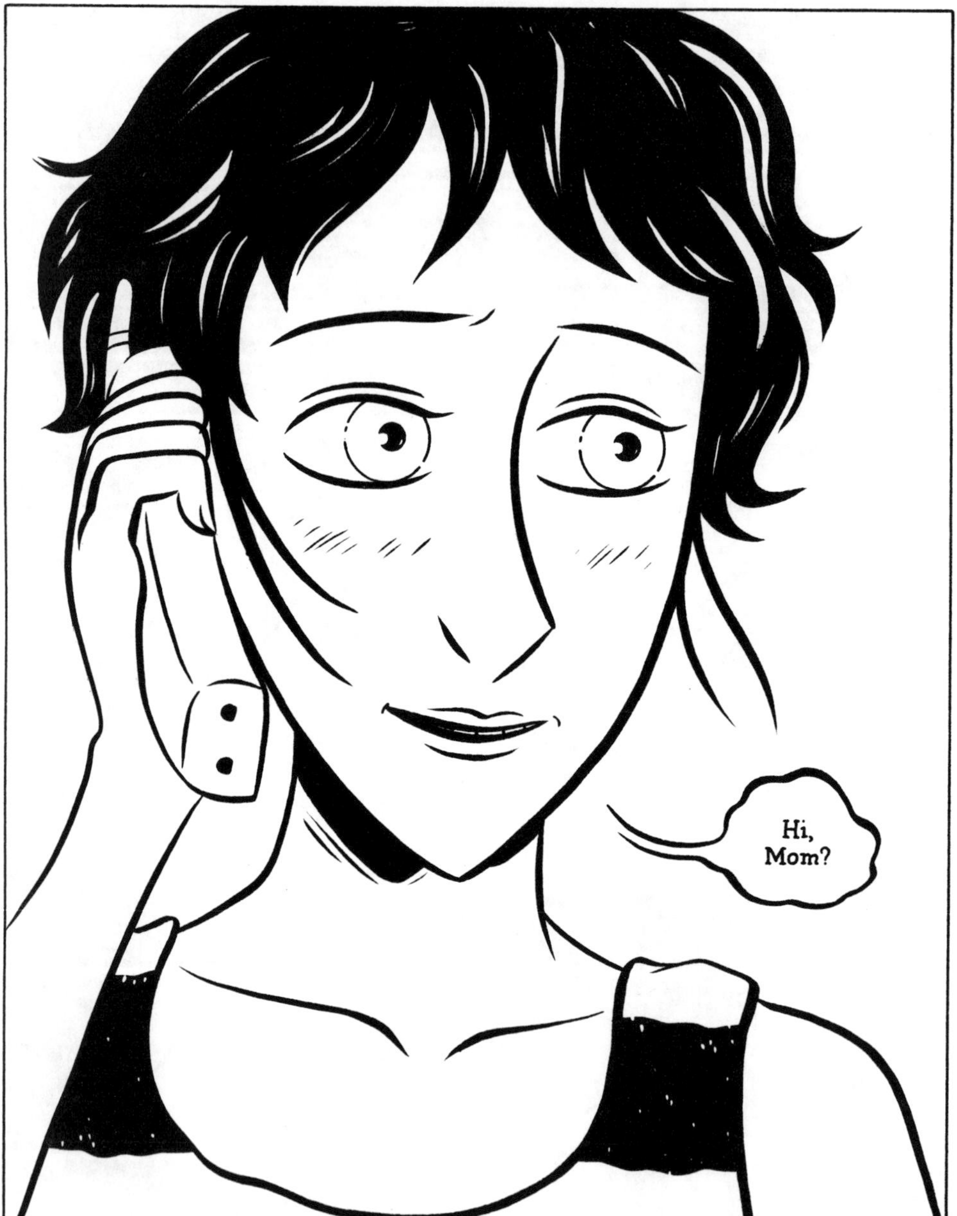
Hi, Mom?

A hug and a kiss to: my wonderful editors Ginee Seo, Jordan Brown, and Namrata Tripathi, and everyone behind the scenes at S&S, for taking such good care of me and teaching me so much; my beloved agent, Judy Hansen; Bryan Lee O'Malley, for cooking dinner most nights and letting me monopolize the drums in Rock Band; intern Evan Palmer; John Martz, for Times New Larson; Raina, Vera, Audra, Jesse, and Emily, for listening to me gripe on LJ; Tiziana and Brent, J-Dawg and G-Town, Aja, Trey, and Shige, for pizza night; Rebecca Kraatz and Joel Plaskett, who continue to inspire me as artists and people; Mom and Dad; and the cats, for keeping it real.

Note on the Illustrations

Mercury was drawn with orange and nonphoto blue Prismacolor Col-Erase pencils on smooth 11" x 14" Strathmore Bristol. It was inked with a #3 Kolinsky Raphael sable brush, Pelikan Drawing Ink A, Dr. Ph. Martin's Black Star Hicarb, Golden Fluid acrylic paint in titanium white (paired with a cheap acrylic liner brush), and good ol' Wite-out.